A PROMISE OF
STARS

DAVID GERROLD

Cover illustration and design by David Gerrold and Glenn Hauman
Interior design by ComicMix Pro Services
www.comicmix.com/pro-services

ISBN 978-1-939888-41-9 softcover

For information address
David Gerrold at his official website:
www.gerrold.com

First edition

CONTENTS

For Kjell Lindgren,
who took a tribble to space
and brought it back safely.

INTRODUCTION

Most of the stories in this collection could be considered "young adult" because most of the protagonists are in their teens. Three of them have female protagonists. Two, or maybe three, have gay characters.

This is irrelevant. In my mind, I simply see them as human beings exploring the worlds they live in—not just the solar system, but the human experience as well.

Three of these stories are short novels, 40,000 words long. One is a novella, 25,000 words. The rest are short stories, previously uncollected.

Nowhere Man was written for Baen's Online Universe and published in December of 2009. It's available as a standalone ebook on Amazon.

Turtledome was written for the 2006 Worldcon book, the theme was Space Cadets. It could have been longer, but there was a length limit. The story is also available as a standalone ebook on Amazon.

Jumping Off The Planet was written in 1998. Scott Edelman bought it for Science Fiction Age. A book-length version was published as a standalone novel by Tor books in 2000. It won the Gaylactic Spectrum Award and the Hal Clement award for best novel, and was also a Lambda award nominee. It was followed by two sequels, *Bouncing Off The Moon,* and *Leaping To The Stars.* The Science Fiction Book Club published an omnibus version called *The Far Side Of The Sky.*

Ganny Knits A Spaceship was published in August of 2009 by Baen's Online Universe.

The bonus stories appeared in various anthologies, here and there. The most notable of the bunch, *Riding Janis*, was written specifically to honor the lyrics of Janis Ian, and appeared in an anthology called *Stars: The Anthology.*

This collection is the first time that all the stories in this fictional universe have been brought together. If you don't see how *Nowhere Man* fits in, that's because Squish hasn't yet invented some of the technology that makes the later stories possible, but he will.

I had a good time exploring the solar system with all of these people. I hope you will too.

—*David Gerrold*

NOWHERE MAN

Bob Peterik thought he was funny.

Every morning, he waited just outside the door to first period, and I had to run the gauntlet—*every* morning. "That reminds me. Today is pizza day in the cafeteria!" "Watch out, duck! He's turning his head. You don't want to get hit by his nose!" "Call the fashion police, he dressed himself again!"

He was a short kid and aggressive. He played to the crowd and they encouraged him. One bully, six or seven enablers. Familiar social dynamic. I'd read about it. Now I was experiencing it first hand. I was the geek, the nerd, the kid who knew how many zeroes in a googol and what Pascal was wagering and why Zeno never caught the tortoise. I read a book a day, always had one under my arm, never one with a yellow-and-black cover. He made fun of my reading. Selfish genes. "Your nose is the most selfish set of genes. Look how big it is." Disturbed universes. "Trying to figure out where you fit in?" How to play fairy chess. Don't ask where he went with that one.

One day, I didn't plan it, it just happened. I had a hardcover copy of *The Annotated Alice*, by Lewis Carroll (pen name for mathematician Charles Dodgson), with commentary by Martin Gardner. With Tenniel's original illustrations, of course. Very big book. Very heavy. Peterik said something, I don't remember what, something stupider than usual, like "only fairies read fairy tales"—and without thinking, without conscious volition, the book came up in both my hands, came up fast, came swinging around hard and swift and slammed into his face with such impact I felt his nose go crunch, and then he went flapping backward, slamming loud into the steel lockers behind him, blood spraying, his hands flying to his face, eyes wide with surprise and shock, because this wasn't supposed to be happening, and I didn't know who was screaming, but there was a lot of noise, and I was in the center of it all, a crowd, and I was pushing Peterik up against the wall and hollering into his face, "Just shut up! Shut up! Shut up! Shut up! Just shut up already!"

And then Coach Nelson, the football coach was pulling me away. I didn't even see where he came from. He had me firmly by the arm, it hurt, I was still screaming, but he had Peterik in the grip of his other hand, and we were both being dragged across the quad toward the administration building, toward the principal's office, and Peterik was screaming too, only not the same way I was. He was screaming in pain and I was still yelling at him to shut up once and for all, just leave me alone. Only I was using a lot of words that the seventh graders would be whispering and giggling about all day long. Including a splatter of F-bombs.

Coach Nelson yanked us both to a stop just before the flagpole, where no one was around except the two kids holding the flag, waiting for the loudspeakers to play reveille so they could raise it. Nelson whirled us both around and looked at me. "Okay, you. That's enough." I had to stop cursing anyway so I could cough and catch my breath. But Coach was already turning to Peterik. "What the hell did you think was going to happen? You push the red button enough, one day something explodes." He looked back to me. "Did you hurt the book?"

I looked down. There was a little blood on the front cover. Not mine. Strange question for the gym coach to ask, the whole thing was strange. As he resumed pulling us toward the office, I realized. *He knew. So if he knew, why did he wait till now to say anything? Why didn't he stop it before? And what about the other teachers? Didn't they care either?*

The principal didn't care whose fault it was, even though he already knew. Peterik had his own permanent desk in detention. I got suspended for two days, so did Peterik, but he needed doctor time, I didn't. I came back to school carrying a copy of The Annotated Sherlock Holmes box set, two volumes. Nobody bothered me. When Peterik came back he had a steel brace taped to his nose to protect it from being broken again. The only thing he said was, "Stay away from me, you freakazoid!" Like it was my fault he was an ass. He had to have his yearbook picture taken with the bandages still on and two black eyes, a permanent record of his embarrassment and my singular triumph.

But as soon as the semester was over, I was shuffled off to the next relative in line. Aunt Patty, not my real aunt, some kind of a cousin, said that I was too rebellious and sullen and uncooperative, and she just couldn't keep up with me acting out and getting into trouble all the time, she needed her own space, and besides I'd probably be better off under the supervision of a man, but what she really meant was that she just didn't want to be bothered anymore.

So I ended up with Cousin Murray. And his cat, Schrodinger.

He wasn't even *my* cousin, but Aunt Patty's. Not surprising. I'd lost count of how many relatives I had. Great-Great-Gramma Mary had twelve children. Eight of them survived to adulthood. They averaged four children each. By the time it reached my Gramma's generation, there were over a hundred rugrats, ankle-biters, and unexpected surprises, with more on the way—not counting adoptions and foster kids, which was another family tradition—that, and divorce. I didn't know how many aunts, uncles, cousins, step-cousins, third cousins, ex-wives, foster siblings, and what-nots had fallen out of the family tree. Three of my cousins were trying to do a genealogy and somewhere I had a copy of the DVD they gave out at the last family gathering. Over a thousand people attended and that wasn't even a third of Gramma Mary's descendants.

The way all the different branches of the families overlapped and mixed and swapped, not to mention all the other families that had married in and been subsumed, it didn't seem possible to map all the relationships. There were children living with the ex-wives of the second husbands of the third stepmother. Uncle Hermie, who fancied himself a comedian, once joked that any kid still living with a blood-related parent or guardian was too clingy. Based on the evidence, my family loved children. The more the merrier. But far away please. Very far. As far as I could tell, children were trophies, to be taken out once or twice a month, paraded around family gatherings, demonstrating how pretty they were or how smart they were, or at least how well behaved they were, then the rest of the time warehoused with nannies or day-care, or shuffled through whatever boarding schools would take them in the vain hope that one day the parents wouldn't end up in front of a battery of cameras apologizing to the families of the victims. My great grand family *loved* children. They just didn't *like* them all that much.

But … Cousin Murray. He was something else. He was like something dropped in from another planet, another whole reality. As if some strange cosmic cuckoo had planted its egg in great-aunt Helen's nest. When it hatched, you didn't get another overweight insurance salesman or puffed-up lawyer. No. You got Cousin Murray. Cousin was capitalized. It was his first name. Also known as Murray the Mad Scientist. Murray the Explainer. Murray the Strange. Murray in a Strange Land. Murray in Wonderland. Weird Murray. Crazy Murray. But to me, he was just Cousin Murray, not really any stranger than the rest of the menagerie my mom had married into. Cousin Murray was the only person I'd ever met who was smarter than me. Smarter in everything. I respected that. In fact, by that time he was probably the only one in the family I respected.

If you listened to the family, Cousin Murray was scatterbrained, absent-minded, confused, confusing, and operating at a plane perpendicular to the rest of the world, but Aunt Patty was a lot more ruthless in her descriptions. She psycho-babbled, as if that would drain the rudeness from her descriptions, as if using all those clinical terms gave her some kind of power. She said Cousin Murray was obsessive-compulsive, suffered from attention-deficit-disorder, was high-level autistic, emotionally retarded, and probably had Asperger's Syndrome as well. Plus a whole bunch of other things that hadn't been defined yet, she could write a book about Cousin Murray. She was certain he would not be a good influence on me. But there was just no one else who could take me. The family would have to have a meeting about that. She'd let me know.

I was thirteen, almost fourteen. I had just completed eighth grade, and I had a genius level IQ. I wasn't supposed to know that but Gary Levine, the smarmy slimeball who worked in the office after school, peeked at everybody's scores. And then told everybody. Mine was the highest in school. 197 points. It was actually beyond measurable, but that was the number the test spit out. 64 points higher than the guy in second place, Gary Levine. That was when the bullying started. Most of it. I didn't understand. Beat up the smart kid? Where's the glory in that? What does that prove? It doesn't make you smarter or him dumber.

Being a genius is not an advantage. I know a lot of stuff, mostly because I know how to look things up. I can figure things out, mostly because I'm too obsessive-compulsive to quit. Mostly because I can't stand not knowing. So I can play three-dimensional chess and four-dimensional tic-tac-toe. I can code in CSS, Java, and HTML. BASIC is easy,

I prefer Pascal (it's cleaner), but I can work in C-Sharp if I have to. I can write a relational database in Access and a pivot-table spreadsheet in Excel. I can code Action Scripts in Flash and Photoshop, I can edit music tracks in Audacity and cut video in Pinnacle. I can write macros in Word and batch files in DOS. Big deal, anyone who can read a manual can do that. But I can go under the hood and tweak a thousand different system settings to make a system run faster and prettier. I can edit the registry without flinching. I can clean a PC that's quadruple-infected with Braviax, Virtumonde, Karina, and Vav, without losing a byte of data. I had to learn how to do that after downloading 33 gigs of cracked software.

I can jailbreak an iPhone, un-protect a Blu-Ray, and write an unbreakable encryption system based on nothing more than using irrational numbers as multiple-keys, it all depends on where you set your start point and which way you go and how many steps at a time. There are other things I can do that I don't tell people about—stuff that would earn me a visit from the FBI or the Secret Service if I admitted I knew how to do them. But I don't trust anybody enough to share that information. I've learned the hard way about trust.

But there's all the other stuff too—all the things that qualify me as a ninth-level black-belt nerd. I can program a VCR so the clock doesn't blink 12:00. I do crossword puzzles in pen. I don't do Sudoko. Too easy. I can touch the tip of my nose with my tongue. I can find Waldo. I can pronounce Spock's middle name. And I can solve a Rubik's cube in 33 moves or less, 17 is the theoretical minimum. Try me.

But guess what? Genius can be stupid too. If I'm so smart, if I know how to do all that other stuff, how come I haven't figured out how to decode the simplest of human interactions? Why do people hate other people for being right? Why is having the right answer the wrong thing to do? It doesn't make sense.

Being a genius is *lonely*.

Cousin Murray had a house in the west end of the Valley, tucked halfway into the curve of a cul-de-sac off a cul-de-sac, and no matter how many times I'd been there, which wasn't all that much, I still couldn't remember exactly where it was, which Murray said was the result of a morphological memory hole generated by the topology of the local street layout, a factor of the number of un-signaled branches and off-grid references. He showed me on the map how all the major boulevards and streets defined a specific gridwork, but inside each square of the grid the housing developments didn't always have regular layouts. Some of them were interrupted by freeways, drainage channels, high-tension routes, or train tracks. Cousin Murray's square had all four, which complicated everything. The major access streets had been laid out in three broken loops that were almost concentric except where they intersected, and all of them sprouted a lot of dead-end branches, the whole thing being designed to maximize the number of saleable lots without much regard for accessibility to those lots. There were only two signaled intersections allowing access, and one un-signaled one, to serve an area that stretched, bent, and twisted through a square mile and a half of necessary infrastructure. Cousin Murray said that's why he picked this location. Not only was it hard to find, even after you did find it, it was hard to remember how you found it. Even with a map. Even with GPS. According to the local crime statistics, Cousin Murray's housing block had never had a reported burglary. Never in the seventy years since his house had been built. Not once. Burglars couldn't find their way in. Or out.

The bad news was that neither could the fire department.

When the house behind Cousin Murray's burned to the ground, he bought the lot, fenced it off, planted a lot of leafy trees and thick hedges, and expanded his house backwards so it wrapped around a private garden with a big pool and an even bigger shade-covered koi pond. A lot of work to keep up. And Cousin Murray was probably going to want me to do it all. If he was blood-related to Aunt Patty, he would. That whole branch of the family were clean-freaks. Aunt Patty was never satisfied. She'd had me vacuuming, doing laundry, washing dishes, mowing the yard, sweeping the lawn, and a whole lot of other stuff that she said was my responsibility because everybody in a family has to earn their keep one way or another. If she saw me reading a book, she'd take it away from me until I finished my chores. If I'd already finished them, she'd make up some new ones. She didn't want a kid, she wanted a servant.

I didn't know Cousin Murray all that well, I'd been to his weird house a few times, but he was just as strange to me as he was to everyone else. He was tall, seven or eight feet at least, I couldn't tell, it was hard to estimate from my foreshortened position. He must have been gawky when he was a kid, but now he was just tall like Lurch. He towered. He loomed. I was always afraid someone would yell "timber!" and he'd come toppling onto me. But he wasn't scary. He was a friendly giant. He always called me "Squish" because, the way he told it, the first time he picked me up, my diaper went squish and that's how he always thought of me. He was the only one I ever let call me that. The only time Aunt Patty tried it, I turned around and pushed a vase off an end table. But Cousin Murray always asked what I was reading. And it wasn't just idle chatter, he was genuinely interested. And that's why I didn't mind him calling me Squish. Whatever I showed him, whether it was Carl Sagan or Richard Dawkins or Eric Berne or Jared Diamond, he'd nod and say something like, "yeah, that's a good one too." Then he'd pull out one of those little notebooks he was always carrying around, scribble down a few titles, rip out the page and hand it to me. "Try these too." Some of his suggestions were pretty good, some were way off the track. I liked *Frogs Into Princes* by Richard Bandler, all about neuro-linguistic programming, even though it was a little hard to follow at first. Strunk and White's *Elements of Style* was enlightening. I also liked *The Descent Of Woman* by Elaine Morgan, that was good and I told him so next time I saw him. I didn't know if I agreed with everything she said about semi-aquatic apes as proto-humans, but she argued her case well enough to be halfway convincing, and it was certainly something to think about. Cousin Murray applauded me for keeping an open mind, he said that was the mark of a good scientist.

Aunt Patty dropped me off at his house Sunday after the last day of school. First she had to get one more Saturday of housecleaning out of me. My penance, she called it. I called it something else, but I didn't say it aloud. Then all Saturday night I spent packing. She had a bunch of those collapsible cardboard boxes—banker's boxes they're called, because they're just the right size for holding files—and all of my clothes and books and computer gear went into the boxes as fast as she could toss them in, without any sense of order at all. She just wanted to be rid of me. Sunday morning, after an unusually generous breakfast—bacon, orange juice, waffles with whipped cream, and hot chocolate too, her way of asking penance I suppose, all topped off with a heart-to-heart (on her side anyway) about how she really did love me, but this was going to be best for both of us, I'd understand when I got older, really, and I think she really meant it, or at least she thought she did—after all that, I still had to lug all those boxes out to her car myself. It was a battered old Ford Taurus marking its territory with a permanent oil stain up and down the driveway. I had fifteen boxes, most of it books, a knapsack, and the clothes on my back. I filled the trunk, then the back seat. I had to put one box on the floor in front of the passenger seat, so I wouldn't be able to stretch out my legs for the drive. And I'd have to hold the knapsack on my lap. Plus, I'd have to listen to Aunt Patty's angry annotations about the stupidity and thoughtlessness of other drivers. It was a running conversation between her and the rest of the world. If only the rest of humanity would just follow her instructions, the world would work a lot better. Pay attention, you could learn something. I had to pay attention, she wouldn't let me wear my earphones in the car, said it was a safety hazard. If it was unsafe for the driver, it was unsafe for the passengers too. I read somewhere that adolescence is the time when you learn how to tune out old people, so I was practicing that skill. Adolescence is also that time of life when you learn how truly depressed and miserable you can make yourself, but I was already ahead of schedule on that one.

Cousin Murray's house would be the ninth place I'd lived since my mom had disappeared. Nobody knew where my dad was either, but I had no memories of him anyway. So I expected nothing. I had given up on expectations a long time ago. He was just one more off ramp on the journey. A place to eat and pee, sleep and shower, before heading on to the next place to eat and pee, sleep and shower.

Cousin Murray was already out front, waiting for us. He stopped raking leaves and waved. He wore khaki shorts and a dirty T-shirt that said, "Question *everything*." He was taller than I remembered. Was he still growing? At his age? He had hair that couldn't make up its mind if it was curly or wavy, red or gray, thinning or shaggy. It stuck out from his head like he'd been playing with Nikolai Tesla's electric balls. He was either very freckled, had a lot of age spots, or was shedding his skin for molting season. And he wore oversized glasses that made him look like a quizzical owl. The only way to tell what expression his face was showing was to look at his eyebrows, they looked like escaping caterpillars, the bushy kind. And he always had a three-day stubble. Never more, never less. How did he do *that?* How do you shave a three day length?

He waved at us again, then he pulled the big green recycling bin right into the center of his driveway, probably so Aunt Patty couldn't pull into it and drip oil stains all over his meticulous hand-laid brickwork. She grumbled loudly about his deliberate thoughtlessness as she executed a perfect seven-point turnaround at the end of the cul-de-sac, and finally screeched to an annoyed stop in front of the house. Even so, she still misjudged the arc of the turn and came in at a lopsided angle, bumping hard into the curb with the front passenger-side tire, knocking it even further out of alignment.

I popped the door and was out of the car even before she finished stomping the parking brake pedal. Cousin Murray pretended not to notice my eagerness to escape. "How're you doing, Squish?" He leaned the rake against the bin and came forward with his hand outstretched, like I was a real grownup, worthy of real manners. But I don't shake hands, Cousin Murray either forgot or he was deliberately testing me. I shoved my hands into my pockets, my way of resisting and preventing. I've never understood why people consider it friendly to perform a mutual grappling and consequent exchange of germs. Cousin Murray easily segued his gesture into a hearty slap on the shoulder instead and said, "Right. C'mon then, I'll help you unload. Your room is in the back, you know the one." He pulled open the back door of the Taurus and started pulling boxes out, shoving them into my arms. He was about to grab a couple himself when Aunt Patty came around and said, "Murray, we have to talk." Right. She was going to give him his instructions on how to handle me.

He nodded me toward the house. "Door's open. You go on. Put your stuff in the blue room."

I ended up carrying almost all the boxes in by myself. Each time I came out, Aunt Patty stopped talking and just watched me while I grabbed another box, or two if I could manage it, and staggered back into the house. Her expression was pinched, like she was annoyed not just at the interruption, but at the whole fact of my existence as well. I got the feeling Cousin Murray was just nodding his head and pretending to listen. A lot of people did that around Aunt Patty.

On what would have been my next to last trip, Cousin Murray cut her off and said, "Okay, I think I've got the idea. Thanks for everything Patty." He handed me one box, grabbed the last two himself. "Is this everything? Good. Okay, g'bye Patty. See you at Thanksgiving." He made kissy noises at her and followed me into the house.

As soon as the door shut behind us, I started. "She said I'm trouble, didn't she? I'm lazy and uncooperative, I don't do my chores and I'm a picky eater. But recently I've also developed an angry streak. I'm rebellious, anti-social, a possible sociopath, uncommunicative, sullen, disrespectful, and dangerous. She told you I attacked another boy and she's afraid to have me in the house anymore, right?"

"You were listening?"

"I'm a genius, remember."

He put his two boxes on the floor, next to all the others I'd unloaded. "It doesn't take a genius to figure out Patty." He added, "I dunno about the rest yet, but obviously she was wrong on the uncommunicative thing."

"I'm not uncommunicative," I said. "I'm passive-aggressive."

"Ah, that explains why you get beat up so much," Cousin Murray replied. "You haven't figured it out yet."

"Figured what out?"

"Passive-aggression is still aggression. Other people aren't stupid. Not as stupid as you think. They get it. Sometimes a lot quicker than you realize. That's the problem with being a genius. You underestimate everybody else."

"Um. Oh. I hadn't considered that. So what should I do instead?"

"You're the genius. You figure it out. Put that down already. C'mon, I want to show you something."

He led me around to the back of the house, into a maze of corridors and crammed-full bookshelves, through a series of rooms that had been added one at a time over a period of years, several of them at different levels, behind a sliding cabinet, into a wardrobe, and finally up a staircase to go over the koi pond, over the carport, over what used to be a guest house, past a narrow room that looked like something out of an old German expressionist film from the silent era, it had only a chair and a table and a high round window, and finally down the other side, all the way down to a large room that was actually underground, behind a locked steel door, which is where Cousin Murray did his "experiments" as he liked to call them, or "all that damned foolishness" if you listened to Aunt Patty, which I didn't.

"Here," he said, pointing. "What do you make of this?"

This was a temporary workbench. An unvarnished plank stretched across two sawhorses. A sheet of something that might have been transparent gray silk or some kind of plastic wrap or maybe a veil of fishnet, hard to tell, floated above it. And below it. Wait a minute--

I bent low to look at the material from beneath, then stood up and looked at it from above. "It goes all the way through—" I stopped, backtracked, rephrased. "It *looks like* it goes all the way through the wood."

"It looks like it because it does," he said.

"Neat trick," I admitted. "How'd you do it?"

"Take a guess."

"Umm. Polarized magnetism?"

He gave me a look. *The* look.

"Well, that's what you said you were working on last time I asked."

"That's what I always say I'm working on whenever somebody asks and I don't want to say what I'm *really* working on. Then I'd have to explain it. And most people aren't smart enough to understand the explanation. So why should I give myself the grief?"

"Um. What was that you were saying about underestimating other people?"

"Point taken. But you don't talk about your projects either, do you?" Cousin Murray's eyebrows were almost question marks.

"I don't talk about anything I don't want to."

"And that's pretty much everything, right?"

"Right."

He pointed back to the *experiment*. "So what do you think?"

"I think you found a way to pass one thing through another. I think you've got two things occupying the same place at the same time. Might be good for manufacturing. Mixing elements that don't like bonding. That kind of thing." No, I was missing something here. I touched the sheet of material. It felt ephemeral, soft, indistinct. "What is this stuff?"

"Doped graphene. Multiple sheets. Each one molecule thick. Bonded. Nano-wired. Super-conducting. Specialized wave-modulating circuitry knitted throughout—I was working on an invisibility cloak, well no, not really—but invisibility would have been a useful side-effect. Quantum-interpolation. Time-slicing. Run a current through it, the material goes out of phase with everything else. It exists in the dark spaces of nonexistence that occur between the bright moments we experience as reality. Like the frames of a film are just a lot of still pictures. Slow it down enough, you see the flicker. This stuff is like projecting another movie's frames in the flicker."

"Oh." I thought about it. "Then you get two movies at the same time. Confusing. Unless you have a way to separate them."

"Right again." Cousin Murray weaved his way around the work-tables and ducked down into a space that must have been have six or seven steps down. I heard the sound of a refrigerator door opening, some bottles clinking, then the door closed again. He came back up carrying two bottles of micro-brewed root beer. He tossed me one. I didn't open it immediately. Instead, I tapped on the side of the bottle a few times to pop the little bubbles of carbonation that would make the soda fizz out the top if I opened it right away.

"Did I ever tell you about great-Grampa Wilmer?" Cousin Murray asked. "He built one of the first movie theaters in California. The Los Angeles Palace. Oh, it's long forgotten now, but I saw my first movie there, I was five at the time. It scared the piss out of me. I'm not kidding. When Bambi's mother died, I wet my pants. I started crying. My mother had to take me home on the streetcar. It wasn't until they showed the movie on television twenty years later that I finally saw the end. But when the theater first opened, it was all silent movies. Well, not completely silent—they had an organist accompanying the movie. Have you ever seen a silent movie? In a theater? I'll take you sometime. The Silent Movie Theater on Fairfax still shows the classics. It's an adventure. Everybody should do it. It's the only way to understand the experience. You can open that bottle now, you don't have to wait. It's something else I've been working on. Non-fizzing carbonation. Try it. What do you think?"

"It's just root beer. Isn't it?" I drank, something shocked my mouth, I sprayed everywhere. "Holy crap! What is this? What did you do to it?"

"You don't like it?" He looked disappointed.

"It's…different," I admitted. I took another taste. More carefully this time. "It's very interesting. It's like…okay, how did you do it?"

"It's easy. First you have to change the natural limit of water, or any liquid for that matter, of how much CO_2 it can hold. Then—well, that's the tricky part, tailoring the fizz so it only sparkles where you want it to. I'll show you later. It's kind of funny to watch. Anyway, Grampa Wilmer invented the multiplex. Or the double-bill. Depending on how you look at it. Literally. See, the Palace was so successful that everybody copied it. Within three years there were a dozen other movie theaters within walking distance. Too much competition." He stopped, he frowned. "Do you know what an anaglyph is?"

Too easy. "It's a 3-D picture. You wear red-blue glasses, red for the left eye, blue for the right. Each color filters out the other, so each eye sees a different picture, and the brain assembles them into the illusion of depth. NASA distributes pictures of Mars that way."

"Right. Only Grampa Wilmer did it differently. He projected two movies at once. One through a red filter, one through blue. You bought a red or a blue ticket, you got red or blue glasses, and you got to see either the red or the blue movie. It almost worked. But he found out very fast that he couldn't show an action movie in red and a Keystone Kops comedy in blue. The audience laughing at Charlie Chaplin confused the audience watching the Douglas Fairbanks adventure. The audience cheering at the exploits of Zorro startled the audience watching Laurel and Hardy pushing a piano up the stairs. And the organist never knew what music to play and had to try to match both movies at once. See?" He pointed back to the strange soft cloth. "Any time you try to put two things in the same place, you get problems. Poor Grampa Wilmer. Two movies at the same time. But he forgot the law of unintended consequences." He pointed back to the bench. "Okay, now you tell me. What are the unintended consequences here?"

"Um, okay." I bent closer to the material, felt it again, rubbed it between my fingers—it felt like liquid soap in soft water, I couldn't get a grip on it. I tried to tug it, but my fingers slipped away. "It's stuck," I acknowledged. "But it shouldn't be. If it's that smooth—" I wrapped a couple of twists of it around my fingers and tugged again. "—it should pull right out." No, it was really stuck. I tugged harder. The stuff was so smooth, it slid against itself without snag and slipped right out of my grip again. It didn't even have enough friction to be tightened with a twist. Hm.

"So this stuff is bonded into the wood, right? You run a current through this, it falls through whatever stuff it's sitting on. Turn the current off halfway and it's interlinked, interwoven, interpolated, pick a word, into whatever it was falling through, right?"

Cousin Murray nodded. "Go on."

"There's more?" Yes, of course. There would be more. "It's like the ultimate solvent, right? What do you keep it in? How do you hold it? Only different. As soon as you turn the current on, there's nothing to hold it up. It slips through everything. Oh, I get it. It disconnects from the power source almost immediately. So it always ends up stuck in the workbench. Right?"

"Right."

"So this stuff isn't any good unless—waitaminnit. How the hell did you grow a sheet of graphene this big? And doping and bonding multiple sheets? They haven't even done that at M.I.T. yet—"

"Float it on oil. Never mind that now. Keep going—"

"Oh, I was going to say, you need an internal power-source. Like some kind of battery or capacitor or batacitor. But even that's no good, because as soon as you turn it on, the whole thing is going to sink through the floor anyway and head toward the center of the Earth, at least until it exhausts its power and ends up stuck in some basalt, or maybe even goes deep enough to melt. But yeah, ultimate solvent. Sort of." I finished the root beer and put the bottle down with a sense of triumph, as if I'd tackled a very difficult challenge and solved it in one.

"Yep," Cousin Murray agreed, putting his own bottle down too. "Go on."

Go on? There's more? Crap. "Um, yeah, okay. What's it good for?"

"I'm asking you. Remember the brick?"

The brick. That was a game we used to play when I was little. What's a brick? What's it good for? How many uses can you find for a brick?

Okay, number one. *Use it as an intelligence test to measure how many different ways someone can imagine how to use it.* You want more? Sure. Use it as a paperweight, use it to break a window in an emergency, wrap paper around it and use it to deliver a message through that window, use it as a chock under a tire to keep a car from rolling downhill, tie a chain around it and use it as an anchor for a rowboat, use it as a bookend, use it as a doorstop, use it for weight-lifting exercises like arm-curls and presses, practice walking with it on your head to improve your posture, put it on your back while you do push-ups, lie on your back and put it on your chest for breathing exercises to increase your lung power, use several bricks and planks to build a bookshelf, drop it from a height and measure how long it takes to hit the ground and that'll tell you how high up you are, put it in an oven and heat it up and use it as an iron, or use that same heated brick to warm a bed on a cold winter's night, put it in a fireplace and fry an egg on it, or hot dogs, or hamburgers, use it as a grill, or use a whole bunch of them as insulation, use several of them to weigh down a horse-drawn plow, use it as a surveyor's mark, use it as a mile-marker by the side of the road, use it as a flat surface underneath a page when writing notes, use it to weigh down trash bags containing body parts before you throw them into the sea, use it as a gavel, use it to crush stale bread to make breadcrumbs, use it as a nutcracker, an ice-crusher, a hammer, use it to crush glass for decorative purposes, use it as ballast, use it to balance the load on an airplane or on a space shuttle, use it as a murder weapon—a bludgeon, tie it around someone's neck to drown them, drop it on someone's head from the top of a building, throw it at Krazy Kat, use a bunch of them as the weight in a trebuchet, or hurl a bunch of them from the same trebuchet to attack the walls of a fortress, or use that same bunch of bricks as the non-explosive warhead on a smart bomb to take out a single small building with the impact alone, build a kiln or a blast furnace, tie a brick to the end of a dog's leash to keep him from wandering too far, use it to anchor the strings of helium filled balloons—or high-flying kites, paint 32 bricks red and 32 bricks black and stand them up together on end to make a checkerboard, paint twelve bricks red and twelve bricks black and play checkers with them on that same board, or play tic-tac-toe, make a giant set of dominos, use a brick as a fixed weight on one side of a balance scale, use it as a weight at the end of a very large pendulum, tie a cord to it and use it as a deadly sling, put several bricks under a vinyl-playing turntable to minimize vibrations through the floor, put another one on top of the turntable to minimize motor vibration from the turntable itself, use two bricks to raise a large computer off the floor so there's good air circulation underneath, stand it on end and use it as a sundial, use it to anchor the base of a light stand or an antenna or an IV stand so it doesn't wobble, space three of them in a triangle to anchor the legs of an unsteady tripod, make a lamp base out of it, or cover it with LEDs and use it as a lamp, use several to make a model of Stonehenge and observe the equinoxes, glue six photographs to its sides and use it as a keepsake, declare it a holy object and write prayers on it, use it as the altar in a tiny shrine, put it in the toilet tank and reduce the amount of water per flush, attach type to it and use it as a hand-held printing press, paint a whole bunch of bricks different ways and call it an art exhibit, put it in your backpack to increase your endurance, put a few in your bicycle basket to increase your leg strength, use it like a ruler to measure distance (this room is 48 brick-lengths by 36), use a lot of bricks to build a barbecue, or a wall, outline a path, or pave a walkway, a driveway, a road, a decorative crosswalk across a road, or even build a house with many bricks, you could do that too. Cousin Murray dared me to think of a hundred different uses. I stopped after 300.

Right. Remember the brick. What can you use *this* stuff for?

"Um, okay." I tried tugging the cloth again. "Without power, you could probably make some really good parachutes out of this stuff, maybe even big enough to bring a whole airplane down safely. If you could make enough of it, that's been the problem so far. Manufacturing. In addition to being super-strong it's super-soft, you could make bulletproof lingerie—though I don't know how much of a market you'd have for that. No, that wouldn't work anyway. A bullet has too much velocity. It would just push the nightgown fabric ahead of it into the hole, wouldn't it? But okay—then you could just pull on the fabric to extract the bullet, couldn't you? If you could get a grip on the material. Yeah, never mind. You could only make armor out of this if you mixed it with something that had structural strength. But hell, they're already working on using graphene for that." I stopped. I was thinking aloud. Not bad thinking, but not the right thinking—because I wasn't looking at the question Cousin Murray had actually asked. "Okay, I see the problem. What can you use *this* for?" I made a noise halfway between a sigh and a growl of frustration.

Cousin Murray grinned. "You want pizza for dinner? I'll call Guido's."

"Mushroom, onions, and tomatoes. Sausage is okay too."

"Right." He was already reaching for the phone.

We had dinner on the patio. Aunt Patty would never have served dinner on the patio, she couldn't even stand to have a window open. She would have spent the whole time fussing about ants and flies and mosquitos. She would have complained about the heat and the humidity, the glare of the sun, the unruliness of the wind, the noise of the traffic on Reseda Blvd., and the refusal of the outdoors to just calm down and behave itself.

Cousin Murray asked me what happened with Bob Peterik and I told him. He asked me if I'd planned it, I admitted I hadn't but I wished I had. He nodded and agreed. "Next time, use a biology textbook. They're the best. Heavy paper makes for a hefty book. And after you break his nose, you can look up the chapter on first aid. Try to avoid the windpipe unless you know how to do a tracheotomy with a ball point pen. But if your life is in danger, definitely go for the throat."

I asked him something I swore I'd never ask anyone, but it came blurting out anyway. "Do you know anything about my mom? What happened to her? Anything?"

He went silent for a beat, then shook his head. "I wish I did know something. I only know what everyone else knows. If there was more, I'd tell you. You deserve to know."

Eventually the conversation wandered back to the stuff in the workbench and what it might be good for.

"Nothing, right now," Cousin Murray said. "You can only use a sheet of this stuff once or twice. Then it stops working. That piece of it in the wood. If I reconnect the current, only the visible piece will work. Maybe. The part trapped in the wood is finished, stuck there forever. The stuff degrades with each use."

"And you don't know why?"

"No, I know exactly why. When it slips back into this time-slice continuum, it interpolates with whatever material already exists in the same space. It bonds with it, wood, concrete, air, whatever. That breaks up the pristine structure of the graphene sheets. It's not graphene anymore, just an embedded carbon web with a fairly regular structure."

"Oh." I must have looked disappointed.

"No, it's not that bad. I think I can fix it. I just haven't done it yet. I was thinking electrostatic repulsion, but that would only work on charged ions, it wouldn't neutralize the neutrons. But I'm positive about the positrons—"

I rolled my eyes and he stopped. Even he recognized how lame his jokes were. So lame even crutches and a wheelchair wouldn't help.

He made a wipe-the-slate-clean gesture. "You're right, it's too silly. Never mind. I can pop the field a couple times, pushing local materials aside. I just have to figure out how to encode the circuitry, that's all. Next print run, I'll try it. That should make it possible to run current through a stuck sheet and pull it out. If I can keep the current connected, but I have an idea about that too."

"So, what are you going to call this stuff?"

"Dunno. The perfect name for it is Slithereen, but something like that's been used already. I think. Slipstrene maybe. What do you think? E-E-N or E-N-E?"

I visualized the spelling. Slipstreen. Slipstrene…. "E-N-E, I think."

"Yeah. I think you're right." We ate in silence for a bit, while he turned that thought over in his mind. And I began to wonder what it was going to be like living in this very weird house. The only conversations Aunt Patty and I ever had over dinner were always about what she expected of me, my responsibilities to her, my responsibilities around the house, my failures as a person, my failures to get along at school, my sullenness and unresponsiveness at home, and whatever other inconveniences to her I might be responsible for, whenever and wherever, whatever she could extrapolate. That was not only the sum total of her imagination—it seemed to be an absolute limit, the event horizon of her personality.

Sitting here with Cousin Murray was like I'd escaped a boiler-works where they processed toxic waste into glass hammers, and fallen down a rabbit hole into a very strange, but very interesting garden. Or maybe a tornado had picked me up and carried me off somewhere. Except the Wicked Witch of the West had driven me here, and the last I had seen of her, she was still alive and cursing. But never mind that. The sense of peace, the quiet, the gentleness of spirit—it was almost overwhelming. The emotional silence. A good silence. Balanced. I kept wanting to look under the table for the trap door. There had to be a land mine, a time bomb, a three-headed dog in the basement. Or maybe just the occasional Dalek.

The thing about Cousin Murray, he was so different from everyone else in the family, it just didn't make sense. I mean, a lot of my aunts and uncles and cousins are really good people, I think. But I only see them at Thanksgiving or Christmas or big family picnics—or the occasional funeral. So I can't say for sure that they're good people, but they seem that way in small doses. But most of the family members I'd lived with, *weren't*. At least they seemed that way in *large* doses. So the question in my mind, the question that always came up for me was how could a family as normal and mundane and boring as Great-Great-Gramma Mary's offspring produce someone like Cousin Murray? Where exactly did *he* come from? Even the cousins who were working on the Great-Great-Family Genealogy hadn't figured that part out. On the other hand, they did find an uncle who'd run for vice-president with Norman Thomas on the Socialist ticket, and another uncle who'd been hung as a horse thief (which I thought was pretty impressive even though nobody else did), and if you went far enough back, you not only found Hungarian royalty, but even a possible link to Vlad the Impaler which would have been the most impressive part of the bloodline if it weren't for Cousin Murray.

Cousin Murray's brain doesn't work in any way that anyone can really follow. I certainly can't. Well, maybe sometimes, but most of the time no. It's like he's from another dimension entirely, an alternate reality where rationality isn't defined by how well you follow the rules or how well you get along with other people, but by some other criteria altogether. Or maybe it has nothing to do with rationality at all because it's not derived from the same logic that ordinary human beings use. I wanted to see the world the way Cousin Murray did—even a little bit, if only so I could understand him. But if I could see the world his way, then would I ever be able to see it my way again? Would I want to?

It's like that thing Voltaire said about learning Russian. Would it be valuable to learn to read and write and speak in Russian? The only way to find out if it's useful or valuable is to do it. But after you learn Russian, would that change your perspective so much that you would be convinced it *was* valuable?

On the other hand, if Peterik and his stupid friends were the best that ordinary had to offer, then ordinary wasn't anything I wanted anyway. And besides, every once in a while, Cousin Murray invented stuff like slitherene. How could ordinary compete with that?

It wasn't that I was worried that I wouldn't fit in at Cousin Murray's. I knew how to not fit in, I'd been doing it all my life. It was the very real possibility that I *would* fit in here that worried me. I didn't know how to do that. And if I did fit in, then what? I'd let my guard down, I'd start settling in, I'd relax, I'd feel safe—and then I'd be all the more vulnerable to hurt and betrayal as soon as Aunt Patty or anyone else in the family had another idea about what would be best for me. I couldn't imagine Cousin Murray sending me away. He liked me. He said so.

Crap. I hated this. At least, at Aunt Patty's I knew what to protect myself against. Aunt Patty.

So I did what I always did when things got tricky. I changed the subject.

"Maybe slitherene would be useful as shielding if you could wrap stuff up in it. Or maybe you could make some kind of a box or a bag out of it. But you couldn't put anything in it, because as soon as you turned the power on, it'd fall right through whatever was inside it. Or the other way around—if you had some way to pick it up, whatever was inside would just fall through the bottom. And if you did make a bag, how would you carry it? But if you could figure out a way for the interpolation field to include everything inside the bag, that might be useful. You could push stuff through walls, like that big fat guy who was so huge, like 350 kilos, they had to cut a hole in the wall to get his body out of the house, that would be useful. Or delivering pianos, like Laurel and Hardy? You won't need doors anymore, just walls. Hey, there's an idea. You could make electric doors out of this stuff. Only when the door is turned on can you pass through. What if every passenger on an airplane had an electric emergency door? They could all get out of a crashed plane at the same time. Or maybe dirt-proof clothes. You turn on the field and the dirt falls away. And you could get undressed in an instant, just by flicking a switch and letting your clothes fall right through you to the floor, no that's no good, they'd fall *through* the floor. You gotta do something about that gravity problem. But see, there's the thing. If you could find a way to put stuff in it and not have it fall through, then you might have something. Ohell, even if you could just make the field inclusionary, you could use it for toxic waste disposal. Put the plutonium or whatever in a canister, put the canister inside a bag or a box of slippy-slidy, turn it on, and send the hazmat straight to the center of the Earth. Or at least as far as Pellucidar."

Cousin Murray listened to me prattle, amused at first, but then about the time I started talking about self-powering the stuff, he got a thoughtful expression on his face. He put his last slice of pizza down, only half-eaten. He did that funny thinking-and-agreeing gesture he always did, poking the air with both forefingers at once. "You might have something there. You just might have something. See, there's been some work with nanowires—using them as batacitors. Fairly simple really, because they haven't solved the manufacturing problem yet. No, I'm not going to tell them. I don't need all that attention. But see, we could also use nanotube arrays as solar-energy collectors, tuned for the entire spectrum, not just visible light. Infra-red alone will push it up past 50% efficiency. I've got test panels on the roof, but not too many, I don't want the Department of Water and Power to start asking questions why I'm uploading so much electricity. Never mind. But infra-red collectors could keep the batacitors permanently charged. See, that's what this stuff needs. It has to be its own permanent power source. I could interpolate a nanopower array into the graphene, growing it simultaneously, a power fabric, all knitted and interwoven. So the interpolation fields can function indefinitely. I mean, unless you switch them off. It's no big deal. The circuitry has logic gates. I can knit a whole computer system into it if I have to." He picked up his pizza again, cold by now, but didn't take a bite. He kept on extrapolating the hows and the whats. He lost me a couple times, but I kept up with most of it. He could have had three Nobel prizes before he got to his next slice.

"So, what do you think, Squish?"

The look on his face was as eager and enthusiastic as a dog discovering a juicy spare rib. I hated to disagree. But… "Okay, yeah—I trust you know how to do all that, but that doesn't solve the *other* problem. Once you turn it on, it's gone. It slips away and falls straight down into the Earth."

"No, that's not a problem at all—"

"Huh?"

"You gotta pay closer attention, grasshopper. Remember I said I can knit the graphene any way I want? I can program the interpolation circuits individually or in any combination, to do anything I want. I can program a gradient. I can shade it from full on to full off across a single sheet, or multiple sheets. That'll give me an electric tendon. There's the handle. I can put an on-off switch anywhere I want. I can program the circuitry to do whatever I need."

"So you could make a carry-bag or a container of this stuff?"

"I think so. I'm pretty sure it'll work."

"And whatever it holds, it won't fall out?"

"I think it's doable. I think. If I can create overlapping fields without wave interference creating cancellation effects, I should be able to expand the interpolation series to include interior spaces. It's a question of programming. The tricky part will be focusing the expansion inward while limiting the event horizon to the surface of the outer side. Hmm." He picked up his pizza and took a large bite. "Yeah, I think so." He leaned back in his chair, chewing thoughtfully. "It's gonna be a late night for me. I've got a lot of coding to do."

"Can I help?"

He frowned, considering. "I wrote my own programming language, I never got around to writing any documentation for it. I don't know if you could—"

"Lemme have a look—"

"It might take longer to teach you than to just write the code myself."

"I'm a genius, remember?"

He shrugged. "Okay, let's clean up these plates—"

"Hey, Cuz?"

He stopped. "Yes?"

"Something just occurred to me. Do you think you could make a suit of this stuff?"

"Sure why?"

"So a human being could go invisible and walk through walls?"

"Like a super-hero? Like—I dunno, is there a super-hero with that power?"

"I haven't kept up," I admitted. "Mostly it's speed or strength or the ability to fly. Adolescent fantasies."

"Hey, don't put down adolescence. That's where you invent the adult you're going to be." He scratched his stubbly chin. "Super-hero, huh?"

"No, I was thinking about how doctors could use this, you could vaccinate people without needles. Or do operations without having to cut the skin. Firemen could wear slitherene suits to rescue people from burning buildings. Or cops could rescue hostages. Maybe the army could use it too, to move troops undetected through forests or cities. Or—hey! If you really could make the effect include whatever was inside, this would be the perfect armor for soldiers. Bullets and grenades and everything would go right through them without stopping, without making holes or blowing them to bits. And it'd be great for spies to sneak into enemy bases undetected. Or assassins. You could have a handful of…I dunno, salt or dirt or even poop. You reach inside someone, you let go, you pull your hand out. They're poisoned or infected. Ohell, even a balloon. All that air inside the body, inside the blood vessels—" I stopped myself. I could think of more ways to abuse slitherene than use it. And if I could think of all these things, then so could a lot of other people. People we wouldn't want to trust with this kind of power. I looked across the table to Cousin Murray. His expression mirrored mine. Horror. "You gotta destroy this stuff. It's too dangerous."

"Yeah, I know." And then he added, "But it's just so *interesting*. All the possibilities."

"Cousin?"

"Yeah?"

"You can't trust other people to use this stuff wisely. I mean, you just can't. This country—the people, the society, the government, the thinking—everybody is…" I held up my hands in frustration. "…the only word I can think of is *sick*. Everything is about revenge. Getting even. Hurting back. I mean, look at all the movies. It's almost every movie made. Somebody does something bad to you—so that justifies you doing something even worse. And the books and the TV shows aren't any better. And the video games—same thing. Shoot the bad guys. Why is it all right to shoot them? Because they're bad guys or zombies or mutants. They're not human. As soon as you decide someone isn't human, it's all right to shoot them. Or bomb them. Or march them into gas chambers. That's what's wrong with human beings. We keep looking for reasons to justify hurting each other. It's like the only thing holding us back is that we don't have a good reason. So we make something up. And as soon as we can make it up that the other guy is a jerk, then it's all right to get all stupid and ugly and cut them off in traffic or call them names or...." I ran out of breath and words at the same time.

"Or hit them in the face with a book, right? Like you and whatsisname?"

"Yeah, like me and Bob Peterik. You think I'm proud of that? Breaking his nose? Yeah, at the time, and maybe for a couple days after. Except not really, because if you think about it, I went down to his level. Just because he acted like a jerk doesn't make it all right for me to act like one too. You want to know the truth? I'm ashamed. Embarrassed. Because I broke my own rules. I don't fight. Not because I'm afraid—but because it's stupid. Fighting is an admission of failure. We're supposed to be rational intelligent beings, able to disagree without putting our hands on each other. That's what we all pretend to be. That's what we keep saying we are. But the news is full of evidence that we're anything but."

Cousin Murray nodded. "You could be right. It sure looks that way. But...let's try a thought experiment. Do you think anyone could be trusted with slipstrene? Do you think *you* could be trusted with slipstrene?"

"Probably not."

"You're absolutely sure about that?"

I shrugged. "I hit him real hard with that book. And I have to admit, it was satisfying when I did it. But I can't guarantee I'll never lose my temper again. What if someone hurt you? I'd want to hurt him back."

"Mm."

"Cousin, we're 99% chimpanzee. The one percent that isn't chimpanzee just isn't enough. Not yet. You get out in the world, you'll see. People are fat and lazy and selfish and ugly and they all do stupid and self-destructive things. They don't eat rationally, that's why there are so many fat people. They don't raise their children rationally, that's why there are so many gangsters. They don't vote rationally, that's why the government is screwed up the way it is. Nobody is rational. Maybe you and me, maybe, but I'm not so sure about me. Or you. I mean, how could we tell? We could be just as crazy. Or crazier. Because we know better and we're not doing anything about it. We're just two more people eating and pooping and using up the planet, complaining about all the others who are doing the same thing."

"Yup. You're quite the little cynic, aren't you?"

"No, I'm not." I had a very strange feeling inside, almost like I wanted to cry. "Cousin, this is what you don't get, what nobody gets about me. I'm a hopeless romantic. Really. I still believe it's possible for human beings to do better, I really do. But we're just not there yet. We're not even close. There's still too much work to do. Too much superstition and anger and stupidity and selfishness. And all of our best tools—especially language—are being put at service of all the wrong things. All our darker, most selfish impulses. At best…right now, human beings are the missing link between apes and civilized beings."

Cousin Murray wasn't usually at a loss for words, but now he studied what was left of his pizza as if it had become the most important thing in the world. "I dunno," he said. "You're a lot more than I expected. I knew you were smart. I didn't know you were a philosopher."

"That's not philosophy. That's just me ranting."

"No. Trust me. That's philosophy. And a damn good philosophy, if I'm any judge."

"Oh."

We both fell silent again, concentrated on the last few slices of pizza.

Until—one of the time-bombs he'd shoved down my throat finally went off. "You said something before. About inventing an identity. Like a super-hero. Do you really think I could be a super-hero?"

"Sure," he said. "Why not?"

"No, be serious."

"I am being serious. What's the essential qualification for a super-hero? A super power?"

I shook my head. "Batman doesn't have any super powers, just good physical training. C'mon, Cuz, give me a hard question. What makes anyone a hero is a commitment to justice. Otherwise, you're just like everyone else." I added quietly, "And I don't want to be like everyone else!"

"Okay, good. Very good. That's why you're qualified. You can tell the difference. And you know what's wanted and needed. Now, here's the part they don't tell you in the comic books. It's a choice. It's always a choice, all day long, every minute of the day, you are always choosing. Given the choice—and you always have the choice—what are you going to choose?"

"Hmm. Yeah, I guess. I mean, it looks like an easy question, the answer is obvious, right? But I keep thinking about all that money in the bank vault. I mean, that's really tempting. Just go in and help yourself, no one will ever know."

"Can you resist helping yourself?"

"Yeah. I think so. Because, if I took it, I'd be hurting the people responsible for it. They'd be suspects. At the very least, they'd lose their jobs."

"See, that's why you could be a super-hero. The one percent of you that isn't chimpanzee is smart enough to consider the consequences."

"Is that it? Is that all it takes? Just one percent?"

"What do you think?"

I thought. One percent can be enough—it can push this way, it can push that. Which way did I want to push?

Cousin Murray studied me, waiting for an answer.

"I think I'll need an exciting name. And a secret identity. If you can make the slipstrene work, then all I need is a costume."

"And a name. Can't be a super-hero without a super name."

"That shouldn't be too hard—"

Actually it was.

It's not easy to name a super-hero. The name has to evoke the superpower. Like Hulk or Plastic Man or Flash. But it also has to have a certain vigorous snap to it. We talked about names almost every day. Breakfast, lunch, dinner. While we worked on everything else. We made lists of names. We crossed off most of them. I couldn't be The Shadow. Lamont Cranston was already The Shadow. I couldn't be The Ninja, there were already too many uncapitalized ninjas. And the capitalized ones were turtles. And besides I didn't have any real martial arts skills— at least nothing that didn't require a hardcover copy of The Annotated Alice. Nemesis was already taken, though not an A-lister. Shade was a golden age Flash villain. I hated the name Slipstream. Slider wasn't any better, Sliderman was worse. Shadowman was sort of okay. I kinda favored Dark or Darkness, but definitely not Darkman. I could have been The Ghost, but that just didn't feel right, it had deathly connotations.

Cousin Murray remembered an old Mickey Mouse comic book from the forties, in which Mickey chased a mysterious thief in a black robe. He was called The Blot. When they finally caught him and took his hood off, The Blot looked just like Walt Disney. That was the cartoonist's in-joke. We laughed about that, but never considered the name seriously. We had no idea what a finished slipstrene suit would look like when it was working—and I didn't want to be a blot.

Choosing the right name wasn't the hard part, except it was. We worried at it almost every day without ever coming to a decision. The right answer wasn't an objective reality, but a subjective experience. It was embarrassing to admit, but neither Cousin Murray nor myself had a lot of personal experience with personal experience. Every other part of the puzzle was meticulous. The various questions defined their solutions with precise physical limits. The technical challenges were the best kind, because the trickier the problem, the more fun it was to outthink it. It was focused math and quantum physics, circuit design, programming, and micro-engineering. I was in heaven. This was going to be the best summer vacation ever.

Everything had to be tested. We discovered very quickly that you couldn't stitch panels together to make a bag or a suit. As soon as you turned the power on, all the panels separated from the threads. So Cousin Murray had to figure out a way to grow graphene sheets on a mocked-up shape of the final form. Bags were easy. We made several different size knapsacks and utility belts and capes and moccasins. But the test mannequin was a lot trickier, especially around the crotch and the armpits and the head. But the hood wouldn't need eye-slots, Cousin Murray fiddled with the circuitry to make the area around the eyes one-way transparent so I would be able to see out.

Programming the suit was the hardest part, not because we didn't know how, but because there were so many different complexities to include. For instance, to keep me from sinking into the Earth, the interpolation fields in the soles of the moccasins would be turned off whenever my weight was on them. But if I lifted my foot off the floor, the fields came on, and I could step through the wall. As soon as my foot came down on the other side—and this was the tricky part, recognizing the floor, we had to put radar sensors in the soles—the fields switched off again and I could put my weight down. And we had to program failsafes too—if my foot went down too far, down into the floor, the sole wouldn't solidify until after I lifted it out again, that required another set of sensory circuits. But what if both soles went wonky and I started slipping down into the Earth, then what? We hadn't figured that part out yet. They don't tell you about these things in the comic books. But I was terrified of sinking down into the Earth with no way back.

But even before we could start growing the first prototype suit, I had to learn how to control it. Our first idea was to put multiple control surfaces all over the suit, one at belt-buckle height right in front of my navel, one on my right wrist, one on my left, two more on the sides of my ankles, another on the back of my neck, another on my forehead. All I would have to do was tap the right pattern of commands—but as soon as we realized we could program the entire suit to recognize any pattern of taps applied anywhere on its surface, we didn't need control surfaces. I learned Morse code and practiced tapping commands until it became a reflex. Like typing.

Oh, and then there was that other thing. Air. Breathing. Once the suit was turned on, I wouldn't be able to breathe. I'd slip right through the air. So I'd be limited to very short excursions, unless I carried an oxygen supply with me. Or maybe we could diddle the fabric to grab atmosphere in its immediate vicinity so I was always functioning in an envelope of fresh air? Hmm, that would work, but it would require some tricky reprogramming. The problem with that was that I would sacrifice a little bit of invisibility, I'd leave ripples in the air, vibrations that could be picked up by motion detectors. So I'd have to be able to turn the oxygen refreshing circuitry off for situations like that, and--oh, crap. This wasn't going to work.

"Cousin Murray?"

He looked up from the fabber he was filling with oil.

"We've got a problem."

He stopped what he was doing.

"Well, half a problem, really. See, when you turn the slipstrene on, you leave a vacuum. It's not there anymore, not in this time-slice. So it's like it's vanished and the air rushes in to fill the space where it was. That's not the problem. Coming back is the problem. It'll pop back into a space where something already exists. Air. It'll be like the stuff that got stuck in the bench. It'll bond. It'll degrade. And if there's a living thing inside the suit…he'll die. I'll die."

"Yeah," Cousin Murray nodded. "That could ruin your whole day." He resume pouring oil.

"It's not going to work."

"Hm," he said. "I guess not."

"You're quitting?"

"Does it look like I'm quitting?"

"But—but—" I stopped. "Okay, what am I missing?"

"Nothing that I can see."

"You're taking this awfully calmly. Oh, I get it. You knew about this. You were waiting to see if I would spot it. You already have a fix. Right?"

"Nope." He put down the empty can of oil. "I haven't been thinking about that part of the challenge at all. Oh, I would have seen it, sooner or later, when we got to that point. I just wasn't thinking about it now. But you saw it first. And yes, it will be a problem. And no, I don't know if it's fixable. Not yet. Maybe I'll have to sleep on it." He closed the cover on the fabrication tank, pulled off his plastic gloves, and tossed them in the trash bin. "Want a root beer?"

"No. Yes. But—why aren't you upset?"

"No point in it. Will getting upset help me solve the problem faster? Or will it use up time better spent figuring out what to do about it? Here's a clue, Squish. The single stupidest response to a problem is the emotional one."

"Oh."

He handed me a bottle of root beer and sat down on a stool. I sat down on the stool opposite, expecting another one of those deep discussions that had a lesson buried at the bottom. But Cousin Murray didn't say anything at all. He just stared off into space. "Yeah. I guess it seemed like a good idea at the time. But maybe the world doesn't need another super-hero. Or any super-heroes at all. Did you ever realize the inherent problem of super-heroes?"

"Huh?"

"Super-heroes attract super-villains. Batman gets the Joker, Spiderman gets the Green Goblin, Bugs Bunny gets Elmer Fudd...."

"Bugs Bunny isn't a super-hero."

"It's all a matter of perspective. Where does he get all those props and costumes so fast? You also want to notice that the villains always have powers and abilities in direct proportion to those of the hero. When you create a position, you automatically create its *opposition*. Maybe we're lucky we can't make you a super-suit. What kind of super-villains will you run into?"

"I hadn't thought about that. You think so?"

He shrugged. "It's the law of opposites. God has the devil. Jesus has the antichrist. Angels have demons. Cherubs have imps. Santa Claus has Satan Claus—"

"Okay, now you're just being silly."

"It's time for silliness. Whenever you hit a brick wall, you should always shout *'Boinnnnngggg!'* and stagger around for a bit with a stupid expression in your face." He checked my skeptical expression. "Or maybe not. The point is, you shouldn't take yourself too seriously. Life ain't permanent, nohow."

"And the bad news is…?"

"The bad news is, you're not taking advantage of the opportunity."

"I'm sorry. I'm missing something. What opportunity?"

"The opportunity to sit and have a root beer, of course." He waved his bottle at me. "Drink up."

"Cousin, I came here with a problem. You keep making jokes. Bad ones."

"The good ones cost more. Okay, here. Consider this problem instead. Suppose everything works the way we intend it to and we finally do have a working slipstrene suit that you can put on and go anywhere you want, walking through walls with impunity. Then what? What are you going to use it for?"

"The usual, of course." His question annoyed me. "Truth, justice, and the American way."

"Okay, that's good. Now, putting aside the inevitable discussion of definitions, because that's a dead-end conversation, let's talk about the how. The specifics. We know who you're going to be, what are you going to *do?*"

"Like you said, I'm going to walk through walls."

"Which walls? Where? And after you go through them, then what?"

"Well, uh. Okay. I'll—I mean, there are…. Um. I could—"

He raised one bushy eyebrow. It looked like a caterpillar attempting a split. Impressive. A conversation stopper even. "Squish?" He called me back to attention. "You gotta think beyond the girls' locker room."

I sort of blushed. It was a stupid joke, but it landed home anyway. I shrugged and did that arrogant know-it-all genius thing that really only pretends humility. "I can fantasize, can't I? It's part of the natural curios-ity of adolescence. I expect to start puberty any day now." A prospect I was not particularly excited about. Even though my physical develop-ment wasn't the only part of my life where I was behind my peers—my social integration was the bigger failure to launch—I didn't see where attempting to join the human mating pool was going to get me anything but more ridicule, rejection, and humiliation. Given the 99% congru-ence of human and chimpanzee DNA, it didn't seem all that desirable anyway. And there weren't any other alternatives. I must have been a genetic mutation of some kind.

Cousin Murray was still talking. "I didn't say you shouldn't think about it. I said you need to think *beyond* it. Under what circumstances is it useful to walk through walls invisibly?"

"Um, okay." I came back to the subject at hand. "Um. So let's say you know where there's a crack house. You go in, invisibly, you take the drugs and the money out. Invisibly. You drop the drugs on the floor of the police evidence room. You…um…give the money to charity. Um. Minus ten percent for expenses?"

"And then what happens? At the crack house, when they discover that the drugs and the money have disappeared, what happens next? Somebody gets shot, right? Maybe a whole bunch of people."

"Yeah, but—" I was going to say, "they're only drug dealers," but I already knew how Cousin Murray would respond. "They're human be-ings. Even the worst human being is still a human being."

He must have seen the crestfallen expression on my face. The uh-oh look. The realization. There are rules, you have to behave them. Otherwise, you're not the hero after all. You're…something else. And not a good something else.

"Yeah, you might want to think about this, Squish."

Crap. And double-crap.

I came to Cousin Murray thinking we only had one problem—now we had two. Not just being a super-hero, but *thinking* like one. I mum-bled some of the words that would have gotten me a lecture from Aunt Patty. Cousin Murray ignored them. Crap. This super-hero business was a lot more complicated than I thought. We sat on our separate stools, opposite each other, and stared sourly at each other.

"Okay," I said finally. "What *can* we do?"

Cousin Murray shrugged. "Dunno."

"Um. Hello? Help me out here?"

"Can't."

"Why not?"

"It's your plan, not mine."

"It's not any plan at all. Yet."

"Maybe that's the problem."

We sat in silence a while longer. Something else. "Remember what you said the other day?"

"What?"

"About this being the best cat-burglar suit ever?"

"Yeah?"

"And I said I'm not going to be a cat-burglar."

"Yeah?"

"And you said that's all this thing is really going to good for. Breaking and entering. And spying."

"Yep, I did say that."

"That's what you're talking about, isn't it?"

He half-nodded, waiting.

"So…if I'm committed to upholding the law, then I can't do it by breaking the law, can I?"

"Probably not."

"So…is there any situation at all that would justify using the suit? I mean, if we could actually make one that works."

"You tell me."

"Um. How about saving a life? How about some situation where the good outweighs the bad? Like saving a baby from a kidnapper."

"You're still *technically* in violation of the law. Only the police have the authority, not ordinary citizens."

"So you're saying Batman and Superman and Spiderman—"

"Uh-huh. They're operating outside the law too. Batman is trespassing when he stands on the roof of any building he doesn't own. He's violating all kinds of public safety laws when he goes swinging around buildings. Same with Spiderman. And Superman is an illegal alien, of course. He's never been naturalized. Are you starting to get it, kiddo? Super-heroes are all vigilantes. That's why there aren't any in real life."

He scratched his head and added, I don't think they'd book you for saving a life, but…if I understand you correctly, you want to be a secret super-hero. Which is marginally better, but you're likely to leave a trail of very confusing unanswerable questions."

And that's pretty much where that conversation ended. And probably the slipstrene project as well. Cousin Murray had this thing about rules. Ethics. What's your relationship with the rules? If you think that rules are for other people, then your behavior is going to reflect that, you'll ignore them. If you think that rules are something that someone else is imposing on you, you'll break them, you'll rebel. But if you invent a set of rules for yourself and they're your rules to live by because you say so, then that's your ground of being, the foundation on which you build your identity. Your relationship with the rules determines who you are. At least, that's what Cousin Murray said. I mean, logically it made sense—but from my perspective, rules could be a damn nuisance. Like the rule about not smashing Peterik in the face with a hardcover copy of The Annotated Alice. That wasn't a rule I made up, but it was a rule I lived by, and every day Peterik did his best to make my morning miserable. Until the day I broke the rule. After that he left me alone. So was I right or wrong? Or was there another way to make him stop and I'd missed it?

This whole thing pissed me off. Frustrated me. Made me crazy. It was like that business of choosing a name, only worse. Math puzzles, engineering challenges, programming tasks, physical goals, all those things were tangible and specific and finite. Ultimately there was a clear solution. You could define the problem precisely. You could find an answer that fit the sweet-spot of all the overlapping conditions. You could *win*. And the victory over the physical universe would be satisfyingly sweet.

But the subjective domain, all that stuff that occurs in the messy fuzzy world of human relationships—*argh*. Or sometimes *aaauuurrrggghhh*. No easy answers, no satisfying solutions, no way to resolve the situation in a way that felt physically right. It was all *whatever you choose*. So how is anyone supposed to know how to choose correctly? Rationally? If everyone has their own opinions and if all opinions are equal—? No. All opinions are *not* equal. Some opinions are stupid opinions and some opinions are *informed* and *expert* opinions. But in the world where human lives collide with each other like bumper cars at the county fair, everybody has to treat everybody else as if their stupid opinions are just as credible as the most informed and intelligent and thoughtful insights. That's crap. And a few stronger words too.

So how am I—a nearly-pubescent adolescent super-genius—supposed to sort out an ethical dilemma that a hundred generations of humanity have not only failed to resolve, but muddied up so well that I could probably find a whole library of arguments to justify any answer I wanted to choose? I mean, okay, I'm not embarrassed about the super-genius part, but there have to have been a lot of folks just as smart as me in the last two thousand years, or maybe even smarter, who must have given this some thought. And the best that any of them have come up yet with is "treat everybody else the way you want to be treated yourself." Yeah, that works fine—if everybody does it. But it stops working the day even one person says, "Screw this." It stopped working a long time ago.

Never mind. The only person I know who's interested in this kind of question is Cousin Murray. Everyone else just makes noises about having to give the goldfish a bath and could we continue this conversation some other time? Oh, except Aunt Patty. She always had an answer. "If you'd just listen to me, young man—" Uh-huh, yeah, thanks. I've gotta go give the goldfish a bath. So, yeah, I know how that works from both sides.

So that—plus my frustration about maybe not being able to build a slipstrene suit after all—put me in a pretty bleak mood. When I start feeling like that, I get on my bicycle and go somewhere. The bicycle alone qualifies me as a major geek. Other kids use skateboards. I ride a bike. With a helmet.

Because I once saw what happened to a kid who wasn't wearing his helmet. He didn't do much afterward. Except he twitched a lot. And he didn't talk very well, and even when he did get a few words out, it was hard to tell what he meant, and even if you could figure out what he meant, it just wasn't very compelling dialog. "I like you," isn't much of a conversation the first time, and it doesn't get any better the twelfth or twentieth time either. Even with a perpetually vacant smile. Oh, and he drooled too. It wasn't pretty. It made me uncomfortable. Because before the accident he had been one of the few people who could force me into a stalemate in chess. So I wore the brain-bucket and pretended it didn't look as silly as it did. And every so often, out of a sense of something that looked like but wasn't really *duty*, I'd hop on my bike and ride over and sit with him for a while. Because as horrible as it made me feel to see him like this, it also made me feel a little bit superior. Because no matter how bad the rest of my life was, at least it wasn't this bad.

Except that he had someone to take care of him, everywhere. Feed him, change his diaper, wheel him around, even change the channel for him. He didn't have anything to worry about, not even keeping up his end of the conversation. "I like you," and a smile seemed to be sufficient enough to make his mom and his nurse happy. And if anybody anywhere said anything rude or stupid to him or about him, he wasn't capable now of feeling any real hurt. Even Peterik couldn't touch him. There's no fun in bullying someone who just laughs and giggles no matter what you say. Even making him pee in his diaper is only funny the first nine or twelve times. After that, there's no point. Nothing's going to be different.

I think it made his mom uncomfortable to have me around, so I didn't go over there a lot. Maybe I reminded her of the way her son used to be. Maybe every time she saw me, she couldn't help but think about the accident. Maybe she even blamed me for the accident. I didn't know. Like a lot of grownups, she never really said what she was thinking. She said what she was supposed to say, even as the lines around her mouth and eyes grew tighter and more strained.

And maybe the accident *was* my fault. We were riding as hard as we could, trying to get away from Peterik and his older brother and their buddies, following us in that ugly jacked-up Land Rover with four 18-inch subwoofers pounding out a ferocious beat, like a street shark thundering after us. They were laughing, wanting to run us off the street again, because there's nothing funnier than seeing dorks fall down. And probably it *was* my fault, because I didn't look where I was going and he followed me as we cut across the T-shaped intersection just as the crazy woman in the silver SUV decided to occupy the same space, because beating the light and yammering on her cell phone were more important than paying attention to the real world. She swerved to miss me and slammed into my friend—my *only* friend—and crunched him and his bicycle into the decorative brick wall across the bar of the T.

So I ended up sitting on what used to be grass, under what was supposed to be a tree, in a place that pretended to be a park, practicing feeling sorry for myself, because like everything else around me, I wasn't very good at being anything at all.

Someone screaming somewhere, a shrill piercing voice. Across the lawn, a little kid screaming. Running and pointing. Johnny hit me back first. There, that explains everything you need to know about human beings. It's all about hurting back before you get hurt, instead of getting hurt. And if you do get hurt, then hurt back bigger.

Being smarter than all the other chimpanzees wasn't an advantage. Not if they were bigger. They defined the game. I'm bigger, I win. If you're not a chimpanzee, you can't win. That's how it felt. That I'm not one of *them*. I'm something that fell out of the sky, I'm being raised by apes. The best I can ever be is a feral whatever I should have been.

That's one way to be insane.

Or, the more rational way. I am a chimpanzee too. I'm a smarter chimpanzee. I can't stop being a chimpanzee, the best I can do is use my smarts to win at the chimpanzee game. (Or change the game so the other chimps couldn't win at all. Except I'm not in a position to do that yet. So....)

But the nasty truth was this. I *am* a chimpanzee and I *do* want revenge. Lots of it. Ugly painful brutal revenge. Revenge that hurts, not just for a little while, but forever. Revenge that burns like excruciating acid all the way down to the bottom of their filthy black souls. Revenge on the stupid woman driving that damned SUV. Revenge on Peterik for being such a jerk. Revenge on his big stupid brother who encouraged him to be the jerk he was. Revenge on all the stupid people in the world. And that pretty much meant almost everybody except me and Cousin Murray, and sometimes I wasn't even all that sure about Cousin Murray.

Vigilante.

That was the word that popped up.

Super-heroes are all vigilantes. They all operate outside the law. They all make their own rules. And they all choose their own targets—no, not really. In the comic books, the targets choose the heroes, dropping in one at a time, one a month, to bedevil the hero for a precise number of pages, until beaten back or immobilized or even defeated one more time. But never killed. Not because super-heroes don't kill, but because if they kill the bad guy, he can't come back in six months to try again.

But vigilantes. Yes.

Maybe that's part of the appeal of being a super-hero. Not just the super-powers, but living outside the boundaries—knowing that the rules are for ordinary people, that your powers not only grant you the ability but the license to use them, however you choose. You choose.

Be a super-hero or be a super-villain.

Do good or do evil.

Yeah, there's the question. Why do I want to do good for anyone at all? All those chimpanzees pretending to sentience? Selfish, arrogant, thoughtless? Why would I want to help any of them? Why should I?

Because it's the right thing to do?

Right.

But what's in it for me? What do I get out of it?

Nothing. Not a thing, really. The satisfaction of a job well done? Sure. That's another one of those polite little fictions that chimpanzees invent to mitigate the pain.

So why do it?

Because it's the right thing to do anyway.

Because—if I don't do it, then I'm just as bad as they are. If I don't do the right thing, then I'm just another selfish, arrogant, thoughtless monkey. That's why.

Okay. I can live with that.

It's still an arrogant answer. I'll do it because I'm better than they are. It's as arrogant as an evil overlord, or even a benevolent overlord. But I can live with it, because it's the right kind of arrogance. Maybe that's how Superman feels. I'm not Superman, but—never mind. I can still be a vigilante.

Because. It's the right thing to do.

Behind me, two moms were screaming at each other, each blaming the other for not controlling her ill-behaved accident of genetic recombinance before turning it loose on an unsuspecting populace. It was an argument neither could win. Both would go home feeling self-righteous, angry, and unfulfilled. It was ironic because while the two parents were screeching at each other like petulant toddlers, the toddlers were running around the sandbox, laughing. Until their mommies saw them playing together, until their mommies yanked them apart, until their mommies insisted that they hate each other because their mommies said they should. That's how it starts. Everything. We learn it from each other.

I didn't have to have the whole answer. Not yet. But I had a better sense now of what it would look like when I did have it. I might be a chimpanzee. Or maybe not. But I didn't have to behave like one. What was it Captain Kirk said? "Yes, I'm descended from killer apes. But today I choose not to kill." Something like that.

Oh—also on the ride back, I figured out how to solve the *other* problem. The one about internal molecular contamination upon reintegration to the operative time-slice. See, all you had to do was time-slice *out* all of the stuff that would be in your way when you time-slice *in*. If I understood the physics correctly, if we could program an autonomic control system, we could extrapolate the area of intersection, create a virtual object where the real object is going to reenter the continuum and swap out one for the other, leaving the other existing in an alternate time-slice until—um, okay we could work on that part. Maybe we could somehow store it so that when the person wearing the slipstrene suit slipped out, the stored air would replace him, there wouldn't even be a pop in the air. I was pretty sure that Cousin Murray would—

I felt the booming before I heard it. Stopped anapestic beat. Two short beats, a long beat, then a pause. Interferes with brain patterns. Also bad for the heart, because it disrupts the natural rhythm. Makes all the muscles in the body go weak. An old Stones song. *Gimme Shelter.* That's how I knew it was them. Even before I knew which song. I didn't even look back, just steered over to the side, hopped my bike up onto the curb, across the grass, stopped, turned and waited for them to pass. Only they didn't.

The Land Rover screeched to a halt opposite me. All four of them gave me the mad dog stare. Big and Little, and their two worst friends. I took my helmet off, giving it a half-twirl to loop the chin strap around my wrist. I hooked my fist around the interior bar so I was gripping it like a shield. Or a weapon.

See, the thing about my helmet, it really *is* dorky. The accident scared me. Polystyrene is a pretty good shock absorber for falling down, but it doesn't really stop your head from getting crunched between the grillwork of an SUV and a decorative wall. So Cousin Murray built a new helmet for me, a padded framework of steel bars, one around the circumference, three crossing laterally, and two going front to back with dinosaur ridges for style. The whole thing weighed as much as a good sized saucepan and for the first few days, my neck muscles were sore. But with a USB receiver mounted in the center of the netting it was a pretty good directional antenna for wi-fi.

The helmet also had multiple mounts for cameras and microphones. With two big parabolic reflectors that made me look like a cybernetic Mickey Mouse, I could clearly tune into conversations half a kilometer away. I could apply noise-processing to the stereo feeds to clarify the signal even more, giving me another couple hundred meters of eavesdropping. With binocular mini-cams attached to the sides, I could have telescopic stereo night-vision. There's another super-hero identity Cyborg MouseMan. But today, it was just a helmet.

The four of them got out of the Land Rover. I could have gotten on my bike, but I doubted I could get up to speed fast enough to outrun them, and even if I could, they'd come after me in the car. I was trapped. I said, "I don't think this is a good idea."

Peterik, still wearing the brace across his nose, said, "I do."

"This isn't going to prove anything."

"I have to get even," he said.

"This isn't getting even. This is four against one." I really wished I had a slipstrene suit right then.

Peterik feinted, I flinched. I'm not a fighter. I'm not a lover either. I'm not anything. Except a target. Big Bother and the other two spread out in a half circle around me. Not good.

"Um. I really think you should get back in your car and drive off. Really."

"Yeah, right." He spat at me.

"This is your last chance," I said. It sounded silly, even to me. But—I meant it. I took a deep breath, tightening my grip on my helmet—

Big Bother lunged and I swung the helmet at him, he jumped back. Then he jumped forward, grabbing at the helmet, yanking it hard to snatch it away from me. The chin strap tightened around my arm and he almost pulled me off balance, but I pressed the little button next to my thumb and the homemade taser circuit kicked in—you can make one real easy, I found the instructions on the Internet—only I used a 9-volt battery instead. He didn't even have time to scream, he just went rigid for an instant, then jerked away, horrified and hollering, words even I didn't know, eyes wide with fear and rage and confusion.

I swung the helmet again, a few more times, and they all backed away. But now Big and Little were mad with rage. Even more determined to have revenge, the bloodier the better. Little Peterik ran back to the Land Rover, scrambled around in the back, and came up with an aluminum baseball bat. He came running at me, swearing and swinging wildly. My turn to jump back. I swung the helmet at him, missing him narrowly, except this time I pushed the *other* little button and the connected canister of high-pressure homemade pepper spray went *Ffft!*— stinging and stinking and staining him with indelible red dye that looked like blood and smelled like the back end of a cabbage-filled warthog. He'd be a week getting the stink off. He shrieked and clawed at his eyes. Then Big came after me again and this time when I swung the helmet, I connected—even though it was more by accident than intention—the helmet only grazed the side of his head, but it was enough, because he staggered back, just a little, and I stepped in and swung again and this time I slammed him sideways, hard, and the dinosaur spikes must have gone into his cheek because he grunted and went down and I came down on top of him hammering at him like a wild man, not for me, but for a promising life ended in a goddamn wheelchair. For chasing me in his car, for teaching his brother to be a bully, but mostly for taking away the only real friend I'd ever known. I pounded him hard, again and again, even after he put his arms up to cover his face, screaming at me to stop, please, stop already. Blood splashed from his face and I leapt back, horrified at my own anger, but still enjoying it way too much. I was the monster they wanted me to be. I whirled to look at little friend and big friend. "You want some of this too?"

They backed away, holding up their hands defensively. "We got no fight with you."

"Any of you ever come near me again, *ever*, I'll kill you. I mean *kill*. As in dead. Stinking, decomposing, decaying, buried in the ground forever dead. I mean it. If you even chase a bicyclist again, any bicyclist ever, I'll torch your car." And just to prove I meant it, I walked over to the Land Rover and jammed my pocket knife into the right front tire, deflating it almost instantly. Then I picked up my bike and rode home. Terrified.

I expected that the police would be waiting for me when I got there, but no. Maybe Peterik's brother was too embarrassed to admit he'd been beaten up by a guy half his weight. Or maybe he was still getting his face stitched up. He must have known I could identify him as a guy who liked to run bicyclists off the road. The cops in this end of the valley weren't too fond of that trick since the accident. And maybe that's why the Peteriks had singled me out for all the special attention—to keep me terrified, to keep me from talking. And that's why I'd asked Cousin Murray to fix my helmet. He didn't know about the taser or the canister of spray, that was my doing. And yeah, I knew it was illegal, but it was still preferable than getting crunched into a wall.

I put my bike in the garage, walked into the kitchen, washed my hands, washed my face, drank a glass of ice-water, and stood over the sink shaking for a long time. Finally, after a century or two, my heartbeat returned to normal. Finally I caught my breath. Finally I sat down and just sat. And breathed. And tried not to think about what had just happened and what could have happened instead.

Until Schrodinger walked in, bumped my knee with his head, made a dark prowly sound, rubbed his fat hairy body against my shin, and meowed in no uncertain terms that no one had fed the cat today. So I got up, filled his water dish, poured some dry food into one bowl, opened a little plastic pouch of wet food into the other, and got out of the way while he began the marvelous process of transforming all that tuna-smelling protein into disgusting little clumps of litter-covered cat turds.

Watching a cat eat is only interesting for about four seconds. But it reminded me I still had other responsibilities. I rummaged in the bottom drawer next to the sink and pulled out an apron, the last clean one was frilly and yellow, probably the detritus of a visit from Aunt Patty, it didn't matter, when you work with chemicals you get in the habit of wearing an apron all the time and you don't care what it looks like. I pulled it on without thinking and started prepping dinner. It was something to do that didn't require a lot of thinking. Because the thinking part of my brain was working on something else. A simple salad, some English muffins, a couple of Polish sausages, maybe some baked beans, a bottle of Cousin Murray's latest cola formula, that should do it—

He came into the kitchen just as I finished setting the table. He had one of those looks on his face. Or maybe he just seemed more detached than usual because he was concentrating on cleaning his glasses, wiping them gently with a slipstrene cloth. Before I could say anything, the phone rang. Perfect timing. I was closest, so I picked it up.

It was Aunt Patty. She did not sound happy. "Let me speak to Murray," she snapped. I handed him the phone. He put his glasses back on and listened. He motioned me to be quiet. His side of the conversation was mostly, "Uh-huh...uh-huh...uh-huh...really? That doesn't sound like Squish. Well, okay...send them over here. We'll talk to them." He hung up thoughtfully.

He blinked, looking around as if he'd never seen a kitchen before, then sat down at the table, folded his hands in front of his chin, and stared at me. Not judging. Just curious. "What happened?"

"What'd she tell you?"

"Not much. She said the police showed up at her place looking for you. Apparently they didn't know you'd moved. She gave them this address."

"Good old Aunt Patty—"

"What'd you expect her to do?"

I didn't answer.

"So what's this all about, Squish? The police didn't say."

"It's a long story—"

"We have time. At least twenty or thirty minutes before they get here."

I put one plate in front of him, another at my place. Sat down. Thought about speaking. Drank some cola instead. Thought about what to say. Started eating instead. Heart wasn't in it. Didn't look at him. It wasn't that I didn't want to talk. I just didn't know how to say it yet. There was too much, all of it interconnected. I didn't know where to start. All the different fragments whirled around inside of me, bumping and jostling and squirming uncomfortably. Tell Robby the Robot to shoot Captain J.J. Adams and he goes into brain freeze. This was worse. Robby didn't have to explain himself to Cousin Murray.

After three bites, I put my fork down. "Okay," I said.

He waited for me to go on.

"I'm not a very good person."

Eyebrow.

"I have…a temper. An anger-management problem."

The eyebrow came down. "That's not news."

"I got into a fight with the Peterik brothers today."

"Mm." He squinted across the table. "I don't see any bruises or blood. What happened?"

"Um. I sorta lost control. I almost killed Jeff. The big one. I hit him with my helmet. More than once. The new helmet. I cut him up pretty good. I might have broke his nose. I dunno."

"Did you shpritz him with your special stink-oil spray?"

"No, I used that on Bob. Hey, how did you know about the spray?"

"I know more than you think. Did you use the taser too?"

"Uh—yeah. I did. On Jeff. It worked really good."

"I'm sure."

"You should have seen him go down. You would have been impressed."

"You know," Cousin Murray said slowly, thoughtfully, "What you did—it *is* illegal."

"Yeah, I know. Um…what're you going to say to the police?"

"Haven't decided."

"I'm in trouble, aren't I?"

"Yeah," he agreed. "But you knew what you were doing when you modified the helmet. And you did it anyway."

"I had to."

"Uh-huh. That's your story and you're sticking to it."

"You disapprove."

"You made a choice, Squish. Everything is a choice. The question isn't what you're going to choose. The question is whether you're willing to accept the consequences of your choice."

I didn't reply to that. I turned it over in my head for a while.

"And it's okay with you if I make a wrong or a stupid choice? Aren't you supposed to teach me better?"

He steepled his fingers in front of him and looked across at me. "You wouldn't have added those things to your helmet unless you felt you needed them. And… you wouldn't have used them unless you felt it was absolutely necessary."

My hands were trembling. I put them in my lap, between my legs. I lowered my eyes. "Yeah. It was. I think they wanted to—well, maybe not kill me, but hurt me real bad. I didn't think I had a choice."

"You always have a choice. In this case, you chose to be prepared. Based on the evidence, you chose right. I'm glad you defended yourself, Squish. That's nothing to be embarrassed about." He returned to his dinner. "Besides, if you had gotten killed, it would have ruined my whole day."

"There's something else," I said. Besides, his joke wasn't funny.

"Yes?" He put his fork back down and waited.

I took a breath. "I think I'm beginning to get it. I mean, the whole thing about heroes—especially super-heroes. They just do what's right because it's right. The whole vigilante thing, that really doesn't matter, does it? Because heroes live by a higher code of justice, the *highest* code."

"And that code is?"

"Doing right."

"Yeah, and how do you define that?"

"Um." I stopped. Considered. Admitted, "I don't know—I mean, I don't know the specifics. I don't know how to say it. I just know that sometimes the rules aren't enough. Sometimes the rules don't work. Sometimes an injustice is just so great, it's like the whole universe is screaming in outrage. And what's right is what's right, no matter what the rules might say. But see—this is the part I'm having the most trouble with. Knowing how to tell what's right. I mean, once in a while, yeah, it's obvious. But how do you know what's right all the time?"

"When you figure it out, let me know. The King of Sweden will hang a medal around your neck."

"Huh?" First I had to decode his sentence. Then I had to decode it a second time. Finally I got it. Nobody knows the answer. Crap.

"Okay," I said. "That's what I was afraid of. Super-heroes have to figure it out for themselves what the right thing is, don't they? There's nobody to tell them. Once they assume the responsibility of doing, they also assume the responsibility of deciding."

"Sounds about right to me. Why is that bad news?"

"Because it means that even super-heroes can be wrong. Super-heroes can make mistakes, just like anybody else. It means that even if we could make a slipstrene suit, and I could slip in and out of walls, I might still miscalculate somewhere and do something that hurts good people."

"Yes, that's always a possibility. Even if you're not a super-hero."

"So…if I understand this right, it's not about not making mistakes—it's about…using mistakes as a chance to do better. It's like when we're programming something or engineering something, if we make a mistake, we recognize it, we analyze what we did wrong, we fix it, we test it, and we remember it so we don't do it again." I felt myself frowning as I took the next procedural step. "Does the same thing work with people?"

Cousin Murray grinned. "Only the logical ones."

"So, not very many."

"Right. Not very many."

I stood up and started cleaning the table. Stopped myself. "Oh, something else. I figured out how to make the slipstrene suit work."

He took out his pocket watch and looked at it. "Hm. Six and a half hours."

"No. I figured it out on the ride home. Before the Peteriks. So that would be…um, three hours. Approximately."

"Point taken—"

The doorbell rang.

He pointed at me. "You. Sit down. Stay seated. Don't speak unless I tell you to. Answer questions honestly. But don't volunteer anything."

I sat.

Cousin Murray went to the front door. Some indistinct mumbling for a while. I heard Cousin Murray say, "Yes, I'm his legal guardian," and then he came back into the kitchen followed by two police officers in black uniforms. A black man, a white woman. Didn't look friendly. Wouldn't want to get into a fight with either of them. "These officers have some questions for you."

I swallowed hard.

The woman officer stepped forward. "The Peterik brothers said you attacked them."

I didn't say anything.

The black cop leaned in. "Son, you could be in a lot of trouble. Jeff Peterik needed thirteen stitches up the side of his face. He said you hit him with your bicycle helmet. Repeatedly."

Cousin Murray put his hand on my shoulder. "Don't answer." To the officers, he said. "If you're accusing this boy of anything, then I'll want a lawyer present."

"We just want to ask him some questions."

"No. I don't think so. You're talking about felonious assault."

The woman cop started to explain that it would be a lot better all around if—

Cousin Murray cut her off. "Wait a minute, wait a minute—you're saying he beat up Jeff Peterik with a bicycle helmet?" He stepped into the service porch and rummaged around for a bit, came back with the old plastic helmet I used to wear—before the accident scared me so bad. "Like this?"

He handed it to the female officer, she hefted it to test its weight, it was very light, she handed it to the man. He hefted it as well. "Son, is this your helmet?"

"You can answer that, Squish."

I nodded.

"Not much of a weapon, is it?" said Cousin Murray. "How big did you say this Peterik boy is?"

"Eighteen. Twelfth grade. Big for his age. Two hundred pounds, maybe two-twenty. He's on the football team."

"Mm." Cousin Murray nodded. "Squish, stand up."

I stood. I realized I was still wearing the apron. The frilly yellow one. Both the cops looked at me oddly.

Cousin Murray put his hand on my shoulder. "How much do you weigh, Squish?"

"Forty-four."

The black cop looked confused. "Pounds?"

"No, kilos. Ninety-seven pounds."

"How tall are you?"

"One point six three. Meters. Five foot four."

"Uh-huh," Cousin Murray said with finality. He faced both cops directly. "So you're saying that this boy, all ninety-seven pounds of him beat up a two hundred and twenty pound football player—over six feet tall, right?—with nothing more than a plastic bicycle helmet? Am I missing something here? I mean, I'm not a detective, but this is a little hard to believe." He diddled one of the frilly yellow straps of the apron with his fingers, as if it was the most natural thing in the world for me to be wearing it.

The black cop was frowning. The woman cop eased her posture, even conceded a grudging smile. "It is a stretch."

"I mean—" Cousin Murray turned and looked at me. "No offense, Squish, but you're not exactly Sasquatch." Back to the cops. "Why would the Peterik boy even say such a thing—that he'd been beaten up by someone half his size?" He shook his head. "Y'know, you might want to check the family background there. From everything Squish tells me, I think the dad beats those kids, maybe that's what happened—"

The female cop stopped him. "The family has a history of domestic violence. And both the boys have been in trouble before as well. From the look of their injuries, we think they got jumped by a gang. What we can't figure out is why they would want to blame your nephew."

"Cousin," Murray corrected.

"Cousin."

"There was some trouble at school last semester. Bullying. The little Peterik. Bob. I don't know all the details."

"Ah," she nodded. "Okay, that makes sense." She looked at me again. "Cute apron." To Cousin Murray she said, "All right, thanks for your time. We had to check it out."

But Cousin Murray wasn't through. "Are we going to have any more trouble with those boys? Should we get a restraining order?"

The black cop said,. "If they bother you again, it might be a good idea. We told them to stay away, that's the best way to prevent any future incidents, but your nephew—cousin—should stay out of their neighborhood."

"Count on it," I mumbled. Cousin Murray's hand tightened on my shoulder.

The female officer added, "I don't think Jeff Peterik is going to tell too many people that an eighth-grader beat him up. It could cost him his chance at a football scholarship." They started for the door. At the last moment, the woman stopped and looked at me like we both shared a secret. "But next time—don't have a next time, okay?"

"Uh. Okay."

After they left, Cousin Murray and I looked at each other. I didn't know whether to laugh or cry. Really.

"*Next* time?"

"Better not be."

"*You* were lucky."

"You were *brilliant*."

"Yes, I know. But you were lucky. The picture of skinny little you beating up a great big football player with a plastic helmet? They couldn't sell that case to a prosecutor. And a prosecutor wouldn't take it before a judge. And if it ever did come to a trial, you wouldn't even have to testify. Four big thugs against one skinny little geek? Don't be silly. We might even have you wear the apron. No, it'll never get that far, but if it did you could easily claim self-defense, imminent threat of bodily harm, all of that. We wouldn't have too much trouble winning over a jury."

"You really think--?"

"I really think it's not gonna happen. And you have more important things to worry about. Like do you still want to be a super-hero?"

"Um. I think...I still have a lot to learn."

"Is that a yes or a no?"

"It's a yes, I want to learn."

"Good answer."

I stayed close to home after that. Not just because it was a good idea, but because we had a lot of work to do. It doesn't matter how good the plan is, what matters is the execution. Programming has to be zero-tolerance. You can't afford to have the system hang up on a divide/zero error, so every function, every procedure, every process, every object, every module, every agent, every black-box has to be self-testing, self-correcting, practically self-aware. Likewise, all the engineering has to be zero-defects. Especially if you're inside and the alternative is instantaneous integration with whatever you're passing through. Everything had to be accurate to the nanometer. So we did a lot of experimenting, a lot of testing, a lot of triple-channel construction, and most of all, a lot of monitoring. Half of what we had to do involved building the tools to build the tools we'd need to monitor everything else we were building.

Bit by bit, step by step, day by day, we progressed. I learned how to lay a micro-pure oil bath, learned how to maintain a clean room, learned how to program a nano-printer, learned how to layer sheets of graphene with nano-circuits, even learned how to swear in Pascal. ("Goto Hell;") But even that wasn't enough. Even after we'd learned how to manufacture sheets of what Murray called perma-strene, slipstrene that didn't degrade every time you used it, we were still a long way from building a suit. You can't sew slipstrene, when you turn it on, the threads just fall away. In theory, we could have woven slipstrene threads, it wasn't technically impossible, but it would have been an engineering nightmare. Integrating it with the rest of the circuitry would have magnified the programming problem tenfold, at least.

No, the smartest way would be to weave the slipstrene directly in its final form as one big piece. And that really complicated the problem because that meant three-dimensional fabbing. That meant we couldn't just generate a flat repeating pattern and overlay circuitry. No, we'd have to generate a complete three-dimensional model of each layer of graphene and all the layers of embedded control circuits between them. And after we did that, we'd have to program the fabricator to produce the whole thing without a single glitch or error from top to bottom.

Considering that we were barely down to one error per billion and the final slipstrene suit needed several umpty-gazillion nano-nodes, we were mathematically screwed. Even with our best engineering, we'd still have at least a billion errors. Which was a billion too many for my comfort zone. Cousin Murray put it best. "Integrity isn't just a word for politicians to abuse every election season, engineers use it too—to describe how well something holds gas or liquid. Like a balloon. It doesn't matter how good the rest of the rubber is, the air still goes out the hole. So how many holes do you want in your balloon? Or the hull of your submarine? Or your perma-strene suit?" Considering that I was going to be *inside* the suit, my answer was *none*.

After fifteen minutes of total funk, the absolute maximum amount of time that Cousin Murray would allocate for any size funk, any color (this one was black), Cousin Murray declared a mental health day, scooped me up under one arm, carried me screaming out to the garage, dropped me into the passenger seat of his old green '67 Mustang convertible, and backed out of the driveway, not answering the question of where we were going, not even speaking at all.

Actually, it didn't matter where we went. We just had to get out of the house for a while. We had been working so hard on this thing, we were almost as pale as Edmond Dantes after eight years in the *Château d'If*. (Look it up, it's a plot point, that's how the smugglers knew he was a convict.) I figured, okay, we'll go scarf down some pizza, or maybe we'll go sit in a dark theater and watch over-priced actors pretend to know what they're talking about while they pretend they're fighting impending doom from aliens, asteroids, virii, or even Regulan bloodworms. I dunno. I doubt I could care less. But the special effects are fun. Sometimes.

But no. We ended up at Aunt Patty's. I figured it out half a mile before we got there and it gave me an uneasy feeling in my gut. What was going on? When we pulled up in front of her house, I didn't know if I was confused or angry or just feeling betrayed. The best I could manage was a puzzled, "Huh? "Are we taking her with us?"

"Nope. We're here." He pulled the parking break, a ratchet sound.

"But I thought this was supposed to be a mental health day?"

"It is."

"How can it be mental health if we're visiting Aunt Patty?"

He turned to face me. "The reason you are unhappy—any time you are unhappy, *every* time you are unhappy, frustrated, angry, sad, depressed, whatever—the reason is because you are too focused on yourself. If you want to stop being upset, you have to do something for someone else. Focus out instead of in." He undid his seat belt, opened his car door and got out. "Are you coming?"

I made a noise halfway between a grunt and a groan, then started to climb out of the car. That's when I saw it. Somebody had scrawled ugly red and black graffiti all over the front of the house. "A faggot lives here."

And a lot of other words I had been taught not to say wherever someone else might overhear them. "Uh—?"

"Yeah," he said.

"They think I still live here?"

"Looks like it."

"Idiots."

Cousin Murray was already opening the trunk of the car, pulling out cans of paint and heavy tarps. Without him even asking, I began helping. "When did they do this?"

"Last night."

"Why didn't you tell me?"

"I wanted you to see it for yourself." He handed me a stack of paint trays, clean rags, and several new rollers of different sizes. "Consequences," he said. "There are always consequences. Come on, let's go to work."

"Shouldn't we say hello to Aunt Patty first?" I followed him up the walk.

He shook his head. "She's still pretty upset. This frightened her very badly." He laid out one of the tarps across the lawn and began opening the first can of paint. "It'll probably need two coats. We'll do three. I'll sand down the trim, you'll start on the stucco, when that's done we'll both work on the doors and molding. That's going to take some precision." He handed me an old oversized T-shirt that hung down to my knees. "Put this on, you don't want to ruin your jeans. And stop making that noise."

"What noise?"

"That one. That growly noise. And the other one too. The bitter sigh of frustration."

Cousin Murray having just denied me half my vocabulary, I worked in silence. It wasn't hard. It was just time-consuming. I pushed and pulled the roller back and forth through the bright pink paint, then pushed it up and down, rolling over the ugly graffiti, covering it again and again, watching it disappear a little more under each succeeding stroke. The paint was thick, but Cousin Murray was right. It would need three coats. And we'd have to do the whole front of the house. It was the same color paint, but the old paint had faded so much, the new layers didn't match.

While I was painting around one of the front windows, the curtain parted just a little and Aunt Patty peeked out at me. Her expression was frightened. And hurt. I knew she blamed me. The curtain closed again and I felt worse than ever. I started working faster. I wanted to finish this job and get away from here as quickly as I could.

But a few minutes later, she came out the front door. She was carrying a tray with two glasses and a pitcher of that godawful pink lemonade she always served to guests. But she looked like she'd been crying. Her eyes were red, her face was puffy. She put the tray down on the front porch, looked like she wanted to say something, then turned and went back into the house. I turned to Cousin Murray. "Y'know, this isn't fair! The Peteriks should be doing this, not us! They're the ones who tagged the house."

"Yep," Cousin Murray agreed. "Do you think you can convince them to do it?"

"Can't we report them to the police?"

"We could. Do you really want to open that can of worms?"

"Uh...." I thought about it. "No, I guess not."

"I didn't think so." He stepped back to study his work on the double front doors and wide molding around them. He grunted and put the hand-sander down. "All right. Take a break, Squish. Let's have some lemonade while it's still cold." He filled both glasses. It was sharp and sweet at the same time. Better than I remembered.

Another hour of work and we had finished the second coat of pink. Except for a few hash marks left on the molding, the ugly graffiti was gone. We both stepped back to the sidewalk and studied the front of the house. "What do you think?" I asked.

"Might could get away with it." He scratched his ear. "But if you look closely, you can still see the faintest hints of it."

"Yeah," I admitted. "We should do the third coat." We walked back toward the house.

Aunt Patty came out to greet us. She had changed clothes, something bright, almost a party dress, and she had put on fresh makeup. "Thank you, boys," she said in a voice unnaturally soft. She came up to me, her eyes almost moist. "You're a good boy. Thank you for doing this." Then she patted my head, startling me speechless. She'd never touched me before. "Murray said you'd want to rush over here and make this right as soon as you heard. I didn't believe him, but here you are—what a good boy." To Murray, she said, "Do you want to stay for dinner?"

Cousin Murray looked to me. "I think Squish had plans for tonight—"

"No," I interrupted. "Dinner sounds good. We can do that." I didn't know why I said it, but it felt like the right thing to say.

The last coat didn't take long. Mostly we focused on the places where we imagined we could still see hints of the taggers' work. Aunt Patty came out again while we were working on the trim. It was a painstaking process, we had to use the little brushes and apply the paint smoothly and evenly without letting it drip or build up. She held up two bottles of salad dressing, a silent question, but neither Cousin Murray nor I turned around. Finally, in frustration, she said. "It doesn't have to be perfect, you know. It wasn't perfect to begin with."

Something about the way she said it, both Cousin Murray and I stopped and turned around to look at her.

"For God's sake, Murray! You're a physicist—and an engineer! You should know that perfection is impossible in the physical universe. The best you're ever going to get is excellence. Be satisfied with that. Striving for perfection will just drive you crazy. In your case, *crazier*. I think we'll go with the Italian dressing." And then she went back into the house.

Cousin Murray and I looked at each other, astonished.

I spoke first. "Who was that woman and what did she do with the real Aunt Patty?"

"That *was* the real Aunt Patty. You didn't know she had a doctorate, did you?"

"You're kidding."

"Am I famous for my jokes?"

"You mean it?"

"Uh-huh."

Abruptly, he threw down his paint brush. "Son of a bitch!"

"*What?!* What happened—?!"

He picked up the paint brush, wiped the grass off it with a rag. "She just told us how to make the perma-strene work."

"Huh?"

"It doesn't *have* to be perfect. Just *excellent.*"

"Um, excuse me? What about integrity? Holes in the balloon and all that?"

"How big are the holes? How many different layers of slipstrene are we using? We're putting on three coats. They overlap! They cover up each other's holes! We don't have to be perfect, just excellent! We're back in business!"

Dinner was Aunt Patty's specialty, chicken and dumplings, baked with peaches and cinnamon and honey. Mostly, she made it only on holidays or special occasions. Of all the things she cooked, this was one of my favorites. And I told her so. She smiled, surprised at the courtesy. "Thank you."

"How come you never told me you had a Ph.D.?"

"You never asked. You never asked me anything."

"I wish I'd known. What did you get your degree in?"

"Philosophy."

I stared at her, dumbfounded. "Really?"

She nodded. "Do you want some more mashed potatoes? Peas?" Her serving spoon dipped.

"Real philosophy? Like *Zen and the Art of Motorcycle Maintenance?* Like Bertrand Russell? Like Heidegger and Kant and Sartre?"

"And Spinoza and Leibniz and Nietzsche and Descartes." Her spoon hovered over my plate, like a steam-shovel waiting to drop its load.

"Yes, I would like some more, please." Plop, plop. "So, um, maybe I should ask you? Is there an absolute right? Or an absolute wrong?"

She frowned. "It depends on the school of philosophy you subscribe to. If you're an absolutist, yes. If you're not, no. The fact that there are at least two separate schools of thought on the subject is a pretty good argument in favor of the relativistic view. It depends on where you're standing." She scooped some more peas onto my plate.

I looked at Cousin Murray for reaction. He spread his hands, palms up, as if to say, "I had nothing to do with this." We both must have looked quizzical, because Aunt Patty added, "If I understand your question, correctly, ultimately it's a matter of individual perspective."

"Personal responsibility?"

"Yes, that would be another way of saying it."

Cousin Murray looked amused. I couldn't tell what expression I wore, not from this side of my face, but I knew I felt peculiar, like I was standing on the edge of a very high dive. It's a long way down, but sooner or later, you gotta jump. You won't know if it hurts till you hit bottom. It might hurt. It probably *will* hurt. But you're already here, aren't you, what are you waiting for? Ick.

I did the dishes for Aunt Patty, surprising her even more. I guess everything pointed to the same answer. A great big uncomfortable *yes, you are going to have a perma-strene suit, what are you going to do with it?*

Every time I thought I'd found some really good reason why we couldn't continue, I also discovered an even better reason why we could. And should. It was like the whole universe was pushing me forward, no matter how I felt about it.

On the drive home, I said, "I think I solved another problem too."

"Oh?"

"Well, you know how we were worried that the suit could run out of power and I might reintegrate inside of something?"

"Yeah?"

"Well, what if we attached a long long long perma-strene umbilical attached to a generator? That would keep it powered and if the generator failed, the suit would still have full power in its batteries, more than enough for me to get to safety."

"That would work."

"Even more important, if I tripped and fell and started slipping down into the ground, you could use the umbilical to pull me back up."

"Mm, I like the idea. We could do the suit and the cord as two separate items and have them integrate through multiple overlapping handshake protocols. It shouldn't be too hard a programming process, a lot easier than the suit. Oh, that reminds me, I had an idea too, for a primary control system. We'll keep the taps, you'll never know when you might need them, but we can also program the suit to listen for subvocalizations, so you could subverbalize, "Suit on" to activate it or "Suit off" to stop.

A couple days later we went shopping for tights and a leotard. I specified black as being the least embarrassing, but Cousin Murray bought several different kinds so he could test the materials for "breathing" and how well they wicked away moisture. The sales lady looked at us weird, but I figured it wasn't worth the time or the trouble to explain how Cousin Murray needed to scan me with lasers so he could build a three-dimensional model of my body in the computer so we could fabricate a form-fitting suit so I could play super-hero—what would that do to her expression?

Cousin Murray planned a series of tests, mockups of everything, to see how well the suit would fit, if I needed more space up here or down there or even back here, whether it would ride up or down or get caught in the various nooks and crannies and cracks and crevices of the human body. No sense in making a suit that administered its own wedgies. It wouldn't be any good if I couldn't move in it, but it would be even worse if I was so uncomfortable I couldn't wear it for any length of time.

Which was sort of related to the *other* question we had to resolve. Could a human being even *survive* in a slipstrene suit? Would the material breathe? Would moisture evaporate or get trapped inside? If I started sweating would I cook myself in the high-tech equivalent of plastic wrap? And how would I breathe once I was time-sliced out of the continuum? Where was I going to get oxygen? How would I inhale? Exhale?

All of this meant more circuitry and more programming and more testing. Molecules of oxygen within a one-millimeter radius of the suit would be time-sliced in. Molecules of carbon monoxide would be time-sliced out, returned to real-time. Moisture—sweat—would be wicked out the same way. Depending on the environment, I might leave barely perceptible ripples in the air and possibly a slight scent trail. Both of these functions could be turned off for short periods of time, because there are places in the world where motion detectors and scent detectors really *are* that sensitive, but the internal sensors would automatically turn them back on if my ability to function became impaired. Survival was more important than avoiding detection.

We also talked about some kind of automatic waste removal, in case I had to pee or poop, but Cousin Murray said that wasn't something we needed to work on right now. Maybe for the second-generation suit. Or third. Whatever.

And then, finally, we had to solve some basic mechanical problems. We were going to have to fabricate a mannequin based on the laser-scanned computer model of my body. Then we were going to print the suit layer by layer on the mannequin. What would be best? Fabbing it horizontally or vertically? Vertically, we'd need a tall narrow tank; horizontally, a broad flat one. It would be a lot easier if we could just fab the suit all folded up neatly or even laid out all spread-eagled like Da Vinci's *Vitruvian Man,* but layering it onto a mannequin was the only way to keep all the parts separate during printing. We could fab the mannequin inside the suit at the same time, printing both up layer by layer simultaneously. After we finish, we connect the suit, turn it on, and it falls right off the mannequin.

If we printed vertically we could use the fabrication tank that Cousin Murray had already built. If we wanted to do it horizontally, we'd need to build a unit four times as long, but fabrication would be four times faster.

But it would mean emptying out one of the back bedrooms and turning it into a whole production facility.

We finally decided we'd need a bigger fabrication tank sooner or later anyway, so decided to just get it over with now. We spent one weekend boxing up Cousin's collection of books and records and tapes and laserdiscs and CDs and DVDs and everything else he'd stashed in there, including several ancient computers and several shelves of legendary software. There was a Northstar Horizon and an Apple //c and a TRS-80, something called an Amiga, a Kaypro 10, a PC-clone running an 8086 at 4mhz, and one of the first laptops ever built, a Kaypro clamshell that ran MS-DOS on a black-and-white screen. Heavy, ugly, impressive as hell. On the shelves I found CP/M, Bazic Compiler, Visicalc, Lotus 1-2-3, WordStar, NewStar, dBase II, Quattro Pro, Turbo Pascal (all the way from 1.0 to Object Pascal 5.5), Visual Basic, Sprint, Tornado Notes, TapCIS, Colossal Cave Adventure, Chessmaster, Zork, Flight Simulator 3.0, Wolfenstein 3D, Doom—it was like an antique shop for cybernauts. "You actually used all this stuff?"

"No, I just bought it to stash it away in here in case I ever had a sarcastic relative."

"Oh, okay." I added, "So now you can get rid of it, right?"

"Wrong. If the 80's ever come back, I'll be ready for them ahead of time."

"Good thinking. I guess."

Building a fabber is easy. You need a tank to hold the oil, that's the fabrication bed. Then you need a loom, a big frame mounted just above the oil—that's to hold the shuttle, a set of rods that move back and forth across the frame. The shuttle holds tanks and tubes and wires feeding an array of precision inkjet printheads that spit out a precisely-controlled pattern of whatever stuff you're using to fabricate your object—it's a printer, just like the kind that spits out a precisely-controlled pattern of colored dots across a piece of paper to print a detailed photograph, the more dots the more detail—only a fabber does it more than once, the shuttle goes back and forth, back and forth, one layer at a time, building up a whole three-dimensional object. It'll work with whatever you can spray out of the jets: metal, plastic, polymer, silicon, N and P semiconductor materials to print a circuit, whatever you can shoot through a jet—even carbon particles that want to assemble themselves into nano-tubes. That's a little tricky, but Cousin Murray figured it out while playing around with liquid helium, super-fluids, super-conductors, and what he liked to call polarized magnetism—his euphemism for stuff that would take too long to explain to anyone who wouldn't understand anyway. But that was the whole basis for perma-strene. Cousin Murray also had an idea that he could print organic materials on a collagen web, seeding the matrices with appropriate DNA and grow steaks and chops and organ replacements, but that was a project for next summer.

The bad news is that it all has to be done inside a clean room inside a clean room inside a clean room. Unidirectional. Class 1,000,000. That means less than one particle of schmutz per gazillion. Actually that means less than one particle of *detectable* schmutz.

That meant we had to refinish the room, paint it with special non-abrading paint, put in air-filters and air-scrubbers, and hang strips of laminated plastic, and lay down panels of special decking laminated with semi-perma-strene weave to help pass dirt down and away from the fab-bing tank. Then after we cleaned and cleaned and cleaned the room, we had to build and clean and clean and clean the tank itself. Then we installed tanks of pure nitrogen and oxygen so we could create a positive air pressure within the room so dust particles would go out, not in.

And then after everything was built, we had to test it and clean it and scrub it and test it and clean it and scrub it repeatedly until we had our error rate down to one part per schmillion. Even though our math said we could allow one error per hundred million nodes, we weren't willing to settle for that. We spent weeks on that room. Meanwhile we contin-ued to fab different circuitry formulations in the little tank. We tested everything. Because a human body isn't a simple mathematical solid, we practiced making miniature suits of all sizes. We used action figures as the mannequins. We got pretty good at sending Captain Kirk to the center of the Earth—where no action figure had gone before—except we always attached a perma-strene umbilical so we could yank him back.

It was beginning of August before we had the big tank operational, but the first few times we tried to fabricate a whole suit, we ran into all kinds of stupid mechanical glitches. The physical universe was casting its vote. So even though we'd proven that a miniature perma-strene suit was theoretically possible, in actual practice a full-size suit might not be do-able. It was never this hard in the movies or the comic books. The hero just turned to his trusty side-kick and said, "I need a left-handed moebius wrench with a sub-thermal transfusor attachment" and in the next scene or the next panel, he had one. Trusty sidekicks—or hunchbacks named Igor—never had a problem. "Scotty, make me a perma-strene suit."

"Aye, Cap'n. Not a problem. I'll cross-polarize the plastron-synthibulators and have it for you in twenty minutes. Three sizes to allow for dynamic fluxion in the circumference of your equator." See how easy it is if you don't have to do it yourself?

The first time we actually got a pair of slipstrene tights that didn't shred when we pulled them off the mannequin, I was thrilled and terrified—thrilled that we'd completed a piece and terrified that they'd rip if I touched them. And these were just a mockup, not actual functioning perma-strene. After they'd spent an hour or so rotating on the drying drum, Cousin Murray asked me to try them on.

I held them out in front of me and looked at them skeptically. They shimmered, they glistened. They looked like something I wouldn't wear on a dare. And they felt like somebody's lingerie. Too soft, too silky, too light. And almost transparent. Very embarrassing.

"These are just a test," Cousin Murray said. "When we get to an actual production suit, the material will be a lot darker. But let's see if these fit. Can you move in them okay?"

They fit. And I could move. The material felt cool as I pulled the tights up over my legs, but it began to warm up almost immediately, just from the heat of my body. I ran my hands up and down my legs, I felt as smooth as a plastic mannequin. Unreal. I turned around to face the full-length mirror and blushed. I looked like I was ready to play Puck in a high school production of A Midsummer Night's Dream. Only the slipstrene tights had fitted so perfectly to my body that they outlined parts of me in embarrassing detail. Maybe Puck wouldn't mind the display, but I did. "Lord, what fools these mortals be!"

I twisted back and forth and the slipstrene followed my every move, but when I bent over and stretched to touch my toes, the material split up the back with a soft whoofling sound. I felt suddenly cold and breezy. Neither Cousin Murray nor I said anything for a moment. I twisted around to look at my backside in the mirror. Um, not good. "Perhaps we should rethink the outfit. Does it really have to be tights?"

"That was only one layer thick, Squish. Multiple layers wouldn't do that."

"Yeah, that's all I need. To be invisible, except for my disembodied ass floating down the street."

Cousin Murray smiled. It was a funny idea. As I began to pull the tights off, he said, "This was a productive test, Squish. Fundamental. Revealing."

I pulled on my robe. "You're right," I agreed. "You're *not* famous for your jokes."

But over the next few days, we began considering alternatives. Slipstrene pajamas—a fairly loose garment instead of a tight bodysuit. Or perhaps a great enveloping robe—like Mickey Mouse's mysterious Blot who turned out to look like Walt Disney when they pulled off the robe. There were advantages and disadvantages to all three. A slipstrene body-suit could be worn under regular clothing. Maybe pajamas could too. But if I turned the suit on, my clothes would fall off of me and I'd be nowhere in an instant. Or a loose balloon suit that I could wear *over* my clothes, programmed to be invisible. But a big hooded robe could be worn over everything and could be easily pulled on or off. And it could be packed away in a very small space. Slipstrene was extremely soft and light. A slipstrene robe or cape could probably be stuffed into a back pocket, making no more of a bulge than a wallet. I wouldn't have to worry about leaving my clothes behind, I'd have shoes, pockets, backpack, whatever the hooded robe could cover. Hmm.

Finally, we decided to build and test prototypes of all three. That would be the best way to find out which was the most practical applica-tion of a perma-strene suit.

We did the skintight suit first, we made it in three pieces. The bot-tom piece was a pair of tights that came all the way up to my nipples. The material was strong enough, we didn't need soles at the bottom of the foot-pieces, but we put soles in anyway, for comfort. The middle piece was a crew-neck shirt with long-sleeves ending in gloves. It went almost all the way down to my crotch, so my torso and groin area were double-covered. The hood fit tight around my head and neck, it had overlaps for my shoulders, chest and back. The mockup had holes for my eyes and nose and mouth, the final suit wouldn't need it; we'd pro-grammed one-way transparency for the eyes and oxygen pass-through for the nose and mouth. Only oxygen, I would be immune to anything toxic in the air. We'd talked about vulnerabilities. What defenses could someone have against a perma-strene ninja? Make the room air-tight and fill it with nerve gas. So we made the suit impermeable to anything but oxygen. Built-in sensors would report any anomalies in the atmosphere.

As a bonus, this also meant I could probably stay underwater indefinitely as the suit could extract oxygen from the surrounding liquid. It should be enough for me to breathe. Maybe. We'd have to test it.

There was also a harness for the perma-strene umbilical we'd talked about. Once we had a working suit, we'd only test it with the umbilical attached. There would be no going solo. Not yet. Not for a long time. Because the suit was in three pieces and the umbilical was a fourth, we had to program all the pieces to network together and operate in unison. Astonishingly, the first tests of the proximity network went off without a glitch. We actually hit the theoretical sweet spot. The results were so positive that both Cousin Murray and I refused to accept them and did a line-by-line recheck of the code to see where we'd screwed up. We found six procedural bugs, none of which had gone off or would have gone off in any conceivable operational situation. So we switched places and kept looking.

The second prototype was the one we called the pajama suit. It was pretty much like the skintight, only fat, so it would be baggy everywhere except the hands and feet. If the skintight was like wearing somebody's panties, the pajama suit was even more so. I felt like a captured harem boy. But the baggy suit was a lot more comfortable and a lot easier to move in. It was kinda like being naked, only not.

The third prototype was a large voluminous hooded robe. It draped over me and even dragged a little bit on the floor. In the mirror, I looked like death, all pale and ghostly. All I needed was a scythe. We even thought about putting a hint of a ghostly skull and glowing red eyes in the hood. Except I was a little too short to be death. Let alone an Imperial Stormtrooper.

We were so busy, sometimes working 18-hour days, that I didn't have time to think about what the Peteriks had done to Aunt Patty's house. I was still angry at them, and somewhere in the back of my mind, the idea of revenge was still simmering, but whenever the subject came up, Cousin Murray would say something like, "We have more important things to do," or, "Why are you giving them a room rent-free in your head?" But the thing he said that had the most effect was, "Just because they want to roll around in the gutter doesn't mean you're obligated to get down there too and roll around with them." Good point.

Cousin Murray's original fabber had only one print-head on a single arm. Second generation, he had six print-heads. But for the big fabber, he put a whole row of 128 print-heads on the arm so it didn't have to move back and forth, only across. Then he added another 24 arms, so that instead of a single print-head, he had an array of 3200 print-heads working simultaneously. Each time the array moved across the print-bed, it laid down 25 layers. 4 passes a second, 6000 layers a minute, 360,000 layers an hour, 8,640,000 layers a day. Too slow. If we had to build the suit one layer of nano-tubes at a time, we'd finish the first one just in time for me to be buried in it. But this was the other part of Cousin Murray's genius, he'd figured out a way to have the whole thing be self-assembling. He only printed the necessary cues and the perma-strene would automatically assemble itself to fit. The molecules needed to share electrons, so they *had* to attach, and they could only attach a certain way. They grew like perfect crystals. The first few times it took a while to get it working, but eventually we figured out how to structure the matrices, optimally aligning all the internal patterns. We could compile a complete prototype suit perfectly fitted overnight, perfectly fitted around a lightweight mannequin shell that we fabbed inside it to hold its shape. We'd peel it off in the morning, air-dry it, scan it for defects, test whatever else we needed to test, make whatever corrections necessary, and start another prototype compiling before we went to bed.

There were a lot of things to test, more than I would have thought when we started.

We had to test that the moccasin-soles would work consistently, switching on and off when they were supposed to. We did that by fabbing a whole bunch of "shoes" and putting them on a rotating wheel, with monitors to test when they switched on, when they switched off, and if they missed or failed. We tested several different algorithms and a lot of different timings.

We had to test the oxygen pass-through, whether or not the wearer of the suit—that's me—would be able to inhale enough fresh air to keep functioning. That required a lot more tweaking than I expected. We had to extend the suit's capture-aura, sometimes out to a hundred centimeters. That meant proximity filters and atmospheric sensors to automatically shut down the oxygen capture whenever I might pass too close to another object, especially another living thing.

And then, finally, after we could consistently manufacture a working perma-strene fabric, we had to make sure it wouldn't atomize whatever was inside when the field was on. We made mockups of several different size perma-strene cages, to make sure that they would fab without glitches, then we made one for real. It was just large enough to hold a cat, or a small dog. We put it on the lab table and carefully packed it with all kinds of sensors and monitors, a camcorder, Cousin Murray's watch—synchronized to the atomic clock in Boulder, Colorado, and even a plastic-bag full of water with a thermometer in it, to represent a human being. We sacrificed a McDonald's cheezburger to the ceiling cat, put it in the box too, closed the lid, and looked at each other. We'd made the cage battery-powered with a gradient handle. We looped a strap around the handle, just in case, then Cousin Murray reached for the remote control and powered up the perma-strene. The cage disappeared, the handle fell to the table, but not through it.

That was it? Cousin Murray stepped forward. He didn't touch the handle, he poked it with a wooden broomstick. He grabbed the strap that was looped around the handle and pulled. The handle moved.

He lifted and the handle came up, hanging as if it were connected to nothing at all. It just faded away at the bottom. Finally, Cousin Murray grabbed the handle. He swung it around, slowly at first, then faster. He waved it through the air, passing the invisible cage first through the table, then through a wall, through the floor, and finally, even through one of the old computers that we used for googling and not much else.

Apparently, it worked.

Still holding the handle, he pressed the remote control again, and the cage reappeared. His hand jerked slightly with the sudden weight.

He put the cage on the table gingerly. We opened it. We stared in. Everything looked fine. One by one, we pulled the contents out and examined them. All of the electronics were still running. The bag of water was still the same temperature, maybe a degree or two higher, but that could have been from the proximity of the electronics.

There was just *one little anomaly.* The cheeseburger was cold and hard and dried out. The camcorder had filled its entire two-hour memory card. And Cousin Murray's watch was now six hours ahead. All of the other sensors and monitors had recorded at least four or five hours of data before their batteries ran out.

"Hm," said Cousin Murray. "I thought I'd allowed for that."

Right. The size of the individual time-slices.

If the real-world was running at 60 frames per second (actually a lot more than that, but this is just for example) and I'm running at 60 fps, then we should match perfectly. But if my time-slices are just a little bit longer than the real world then I'm actually experiencing more actual linear time. If we're talking about 60 gazillion frames per second, then even the slightest smidge of difference is a lot. It's 60 gazillion smidges. It adds up.

We confirmed this by looking at the videos. On screen, the second hand of the watch moved at a normal rate, but everything outside the perma-strene cage was colored a dim red and moved in very slow motion. It also looked shimmery, but that might have been an effect of shooting through the perma-strene. Cousin Murray had pointed the camera at me, at himself, at Schrodinger the cat. We looked like statues. Shrodinger hung in the air, suspended in mid-leap from table to floor.

It was a switching problem. On. Off. On. Off. There's a tiny little gap when something is neither on nor off. It takes time to send the signal and coordinate all the different bits and pieces. Because the switches had an inherent physicality, they couldn't have the instantaneous response of the universe they existed in. So that little bit of time when the fields were neither on nor off—there's where we were picking up all the extra smidges that added up and effectively accelerated the wearer of the suit by a factor of twelve.

That wasn't necessarily a bad thing—it would mean I'd be like the Flash, zipping in and out so fast, I'd be an invisible blur. But Cousin Murray saw it as a potential drawback. I could end up with my bio-rhythms all screwed up in a case of permanent jet-lag. We couldn't accelerate the switching, and that meant we couldn't shorten or remove those 60 gazillion smidges; but we *could* adjust the number of frames per second that I would exist out of phase with the rest of the universe. If an object existed for fewer frames, then that would make up for all the extra smidges and the object inside the perma-strene cage—or the wearer of a perma-strene suit—could be brought back into chronological congruence.

But it was even better than that. Because if the frame rate was adjustable *and controllable*, then the wearer of the suit could speed up or slow down his relationship with real-time. Cousin Murray and I both realized that at the same time. He said, "Oof." I said, "Wow."

The programming and testing and more programming and more testing took us right up to Labor Day and the beginning of the new school semester. While everybody else was taking the weekend off, having barbecues or going off to big science fiction conventions, we were testing perma-strene cages on living things. We passed an empty cage through some white mice, they didn't even notice. Neither did Schrodinger. Then we put one of the mice in the cage and did it again. Neither Schrodinger nor the mouse were affected in any way we could tell, although the mouse might not have appreciated being passed through the insides of a cat.

We put Schrodinger in the cage and passed him through walls, metal, computers, and finally even through Cousin Murray and myself. Neither of us felt anything. We had an LED flashlight and a camera inside the cage with the animals. The first videos revealed that the mouse jumped slowly around. The later videos showed Schrodinger clutching the bottom of the cage and hissing. He was clearly unhappy about being cooped up and swung around. He came out of the cage meowing his extreme feline annoyance, but that was normal for Schrodinger. It might have been discomfort, or even actual physical pain. Or it might have been simple annoyance at being put into a cage. But it could have just as easily been panic at being passed through walls and tables, working computers and Cousin Murray's torso. Or maybe it was just his usual demands for tuna.

The one thing we weren't sure of was the one thing we couldn't test. What would it *feel* like to be time-sliced? Somebody would actually have to sit inside a perma-strene cage or put on a perma-strene suit and power it up. It would be like Yuri Gagarin, the first guy to ride a rocket into space and orbit the Earth. It would be like Faust Vrančić, a fellow from Croatia who invented the first parachute and tested it by leaping off a Venetian tower—in the year 1617! Can you imagine jumping off the top of a building with nothing but a silk shroud tied to your back? It would be like the man (or maybe a woman) who ate the first oyster, but nobody knows who that was. You're stepping into the unknown and you have no guarantee you're going to get back.

Cousin Murray and I got into a ferocious day-long argument about which one of us would wear the hooded robe first. We'd played the hi-def videos of Schrodinger in the cage over and over, looking for any visible signs of physical stress discomfort. We couldn't see any. We did an extended test, putting six white mice in a perma-strene cage overnight. They were still alive the next morning when we turned off the power and reintegrated them to the local chronocity. The videos did show them bouncing around the cage oddly, climbing on the walls and lid as if there were no gravity inside. Did gravity work in alternate time? We didn't know. We could argue it either way.

Cousin Murray insisted that he had to be the test subject in case anything went wrong. I argued that was the reason why it was better for me to wear the suit. If something went wrong, he'd be in a position to fix it. I wouldn't know what to do if he got into trouble. That argument finally convinced him. Besides, I could fit inside the large cage we'd used for Schrodinger and he couldn't.

We hung the cage from the ceiling, leaving only an inch of space between it and the floor. I climbed in, curled up with my knees to my chest, my arms around my legs. The cage wobbled and swung a little. Cousin Murray steadied it and secured two extra straps to the handle, just to be sure, and closed the lid. He had an uncertain expression on his face. The perma-strene was thin enough that I could see everything outside as if I was looking through a veil.

The first test was supposed to be for one second. The outside world went shimmery for three seconds, then returned to normal. Cousin Murray opened the lid and looked in at me. "Well?"

"I felt like I was falling. But slowly."

"Mm. Okay. We'll test that next. Anything else?"

"Yeah. We still need to adjust the timing."

"I know. I'm still calibrating the control-programming. Another week, I should be able to fine-tune it down to the millisecond. There's the irony, Squish. The more accuracy we want, the longer it takes to calibrate, because we have to compile enough little smidges to measure. Okay. Anything else?"

"Everything looked shimmery, kinda reddish. Just like the video. Only more shimmery and more red than the camera showed."

"Okay, we expected that. Obviously, the light waves are slowing down, red-shifting. Anything else?"

I couldn't think of anything. I shook my head.

"Ready for the ten second test?"

I nodded, he closed the lid. Everything went shimmery again. It was like Fantasyland at night, lots of pretty lights. This time the feeling of falling was more pronounced. It wasn't like suddenly switching it off—instead, it just faded away, like an elevator going down and down. I held up the camera, pointed it at the world, pointed it at my face, made a couple of inane observations. Meanwhile Cousin Murray slowly grabbed the handle of the cage and gave it a slight push. I swung back and forth more than I would have normally. Thirty seconds later, Cousin Murray stopped the cage from swinging, opened the lid, and looked in at me. I was still sitting in the same position, knees to chest, arms around my knees.

I reported my observations about the gravity. I could see his mind working already. Mine too. Would we have to make corrections in the programming? Or would the weight of the soles be enough? Would I be able to leap higher? Maybe not tall buildings in a single bound, but two or three meters? Interesting thoughts. We both came back to the present at the same time.

"Thirty seconds?" he asked.

"Thirty seconds," I confirmed. Ninety seconds inside.

Gravity dropped away. This time, while I watched, a ghostly Cousin Murray slowly grabbed the handle of the cage and gave it a hard push. The cage swung all the way from one side of the room to the other. We had noticed that before, when we were swinging Schrodinger around. The mass effectively disappeared. The result was the cancelization of inertia. Hmm, this would be a lot of fun at amusement parks. A free fall experience. Ohell, this was more important than that. We could build an inertia-less drive! Wouldn't that be something? You could carry all your groceries home in a weightless bag. Or you could go to the moon and Mars on almost no fuel. We could adjust the internal time so the passengers would only experience an hour or two inside. Hell, we could go to the stars. We could damn near approach light-speed. And we wouldn't need to hibernate the crew! And if we wrapped our spaceship in perma-strene, they'd be immune to all forms of cosmic radiation, especially the really nasty gamma rays. Maybe we could even send a ship through a black hole and see what's on the inside? Theoretically, we should be able to. If the perma-strene field is an exception to gravity, we should. Here on Earth—we could rescue trapped miners, we could build crash-proof airplanes. Maybe automobiles too. We could make trains that wouldn't crush cars and trucks and guys walking on the tracks with their headphones too loud. Whew.

When Cousin Murray opened the lid, I was so full of ideas, I must have been babbling. He ignored me. Instead he pulled out the medical tricorder he'd attached to me and looked at my EKG, my EEG, my temperature, my blood oxygen, my adrenaline levels, everything. "You got a little excited in there."

"Yeah, I did. Wait'll you play the tape. You'll see, you'll hear. I figured it out. This is the most important invention in human history! Adjustable time-slicing is going to change everything. Let's say you need to pull an all-nighter. You can still get eight hours sleep before you have to get up and go to school or work. Or you could make a big perma-strene greenhouse, adjust the internal time, and grow crops overnight. Nobody will ever have to starve again. You could big build complex machines as fast as you needed them. You could put an ordinary computer inside a box and speed it up so fast you could run thousand-year programs in a few minutes. Instant super-computer. No more unsolvable problems! Instant code-breaking.

"Or you could run time the other way too, slowing it down! You wouldn't have to hibernate a spaceship crew, just put them in slow-time. And really sick people too. They could go into stop-time until a cure was found. Or you could use the perma-cage in the kitchen. Cook a whole turkey in a minute, then put it in stop-time and take each meal out whenever you get hungry, still hot and fresh and ready to eat. Cousin Murray, you've invented a stasis box and an inertia-less drive and probably even the stuff that beanstalks are made of—a beanstalk that can't be destroyed by an airplane flying into it. Buildings too! Put a perma-strene wrapper around something with a stop-time field inside and the force of anything that hits it or explodes against it is slowed down so much the kinetic energy takes years to get through. More than enough time to peel off the wrapper and move it to a safe place. Here's another! You could push a perma-strene tunnel through a mountain instantaneously. I'll bet we haven't even begun to realize all the things we're going to be able to invent. We should buy plane tickets to Sweden right now. You're going to win the Nobel Price. We're going to be rich!"

Cousin Murray ignored most of what I said, or if he heard any of it, he gave no immediate sign. He just continued to study the bio-monitors, looking for evidence of something, anything. When I finally calmed down, we put everything aside and went out for pizza to celebrate. The folks at Guido's were happy to see us, we hadn't been in for a while, and they'd missed us.

As excited as I still was about the possibilities of perma-strene, Cousin Murray was still preoccupied with the engineering. "It's the fact that you can still see things inside the cage that puzzles me. If you were totally time-sliced out, you shouldn't be able to perceive any light at all. And the fact that gravity falls away gently instead of just switching off. That suggests that that certain electromagnetic wave effects transcend or include or move across all the possible time-interpolations. Or maybe they just resonate through the material like it's an antenna. If that's so, then you and I can communicate when the field is on. Digital walkie-talkies should do it. I'll have to build a frequency-slider to adjust for any time-differential, it'll need to recognize the handshake protocol even when it's red- or blue-shifted, and then adjust and compensate appropriately, but it shouldn't be too hard to program, and then I expect we'll be able to communicate with each other when you're inside. That should be the last piece of the puzzle. Give me a couple days, maybe a week, to do the programming, and we'll want to do a few more tests with the cage to calibrate the timing...but I think we're just about ready to try for a working suit." He looked over at me. "What?"

"Remember what I said about light speed?"

"Yes?"

"Um, I was just wondering. What if you had a perma-strene cable from here to oh, say Mars. And you sped up the time inside it super-fast and shot a laser beam down its length. The message would get there almost instantaneously, wouldn't it? You'd be transmitting data faster than light, wouldn't you?"

He stopped, half a slice of pizza in his mouth.

"Or what would happen if you put one perma-strene cage inside another? What if the outer cage was set to go super-fast so the rest of the universe was going super-slow outside? What if the inner cage was set to go super-slow by the same factor? Wouldn't you have a mechanism for traveling faster than light?"

Very slowly, he put the rest of the pizza slice back on his plate. He pushed it around with his finger for a moment. "Mm," he said. "Those are good questions, Squish." He frowned as he continued to consider the implications of what I'd said. "You might be onto something."

"To hell with being a super-hero," I said. "I wanna go to Mars. Don't you?"

"Hmmm," he said. This time, much more thoughtfully. "One thing at a time. I think...we'd better focus on solving this week's challenges before we start worrying about next year's goals. But, yeah. Mars. The moon first, then Mars."

And then the next day, I started ninth grade.

Which is nowhere near as much fun as other people would have you believe. Mostly, it's boring. And if you're a super-genius, which I think I can justifiably claim to be, then it's exquisitely excruciatingly terminally boring. With a capital Dull. I mean, I could understand why I thought it was a waste of time, this side-angle-side stuff wasn't just primitive, it was *obvious*—I could be much more productive at home helping Cousin Murray fab a working prototype. But all the *other* kids, they were just doing bored as an attitude, as a way to pretend currency in the contemporary. They were bored because they were too stupid to figure out that discovering things is an adventure. This is why I'm a cynic. I don't think anybody is dumb, I think it's a habit you get into. And once you're comfortable being dumb, doing anything else is *un*comfortable. It's bad enough seeing other kids do it. It's even worse seeing teachers doing it, because they're not doing anything to break the cycle.

Maybe that's why everybody runs around creating all this drama about who likes who and who doesn't anymore and who's getting tits and who isn't and all the other little ways of psychological bullying and intimidation. Because it's better than being bored. Maybe that was the problem with the Peteriks. Or not. As many books as I'd read about adolescence and bullying and psychological development, most of my experience was still on the receiving end. Which gave me a somewhat less-than-enthusiastic view of the entire process. I just wanted to be left alone to do my own stuff.

Mostly, the other kids at school did leave me alone. I made them uncomfortable. Every so often, someone would say something to me or ask me a question and my response would be so perpendicular to whatever space-time continuum they were existing in that one of us would end up staring at the other with a confused expression. My interactions with others were generally surreal. From both sides.

The good news, I didn't see Peterik for the first week and a half. Maybe his schedule was so different than mine our paths would never cross. Maybe he wasn't even attending school here. Maybe he'd moved. Maybe he'd fallen under a bus. And maybe when pigs start flying, I'll get frequent-flyer miles with a bacon-lettuce-and-tomato sandwich. And then, one lunch period, just when I was beginning to think this semester might not be so bad after all—

I was halfway through a peanut butter and jelly sandwich and a third of the way through *The Farthest Reaches Of Human Nature* by Abraham Harold Maslow when somebody stepped in front of me, blocking my light. I looked up. Peterik. And two henchmen. His nose was still misshapen, apparently it hadn't been properly reset after it's unfortunate encounter with Lewis Carroll. But that was as far as I got in my assessment. Peterik grabbed my sandwich, peeled it apart, and slapped the two pieces of bread face down onto the pages of the book. Then slapped the book shut. "Welcome to high school," he said, and walked away, laughing with his buddies. Uh-huh.

"Of course, you realize…" I said softly in my best Mel Blanc imitation, "…this means war." He didn't hear me. But that was okay. I did. And I knew I meant it. It wasn't the insult to me that hurt—it was the damage to the book. Books are sacred. Books are what separate us from chimpanzees. Not respecting what a book represents—the opportunity to learn better—that's the real failure. That's a commitment to stay stupid. Of all the things Bob Peterik ever did, this one was the worst. No, the second worst. But bad enough to start me thinking about revenge again.

I opened the book, extracted the bread, and started cleaning the mess off the pages as best as I could. There really isn't a good way to remove either peanut butter or strawberry jelly from a book page and while Abraham Maslow's last book wasn't exactly ruined, it was going to carry the wounds of this encounter forever, an ironic testimony to the *nearest* reaches of human nature. I had an electronic edition of the book on my laptop, I'd be able to read the obscured pages later, but I don't like reading off a screen, it's like staring into a light bulb. Besides, a real book smells better. Most of them anyway. The ones that *don't* smell like peanut butter.

There are a lot of ways to stop a bully, but most of them require the cooperation of the community in which the bully operates. Bullies require an audience. They're attention-whores. There's not a lot of payoff in picking on a kid when there's no one around to see. When you play for the crowd you build up a reputation as someone to be feared. If you can train the crowd to say, "Stop it," you take away the payoff. That did not seem to be an option available to someone like me, already a loner.

Another way is to give the bully a responsibility—tell him he's in charge of protecting the smaller kids so nobody picks on them. Shift his behavior from a negative set of transactions to a positive set. Yeah, I couldn't see that one working for me either.

The third way is to destroy the bully's power. Humiliate him. In public. So badly that he'll never again be able to function as a threat. Hmm. Double-hmm. I thought about it for the rest of the day.

That afternoon, we pulled the first working prototype suit out of the tank. A skintight. As we pulled the separate pieces off the mannequin-forms, I told Cousin Murray what had happened at school. "The thing is, I had pretty much decided I didn't need any more revenge on him. We've got so much better stuff to work on, I wasn't thinking about him at all. But now—if I don't do something, he's not going to leave me alone. The next nine months will be hell."

"You do have a point there."

"And it's not just me. He picks on everyone now. It's like he's turned into Darth Nasty or something."

"So what do you want to do?"

"I'm thinking...Bugs Bunny."

"Eh?"

I explained. "Nobody ever beats the rabbit. Never. Not because he's stronger. But because he's smarter. And funnier. His only weapon is ridicule. He embarrasses Yosemite Sam until he implodes."

"You think that will work?"

"It should. Peterik takes himself too seriously. He won't know how to respond."

"Just what do you have in mind?"

I explained.

Cousin Murray never laughs out loud. He didn't laugh out loud this time either. But as he visualized the image, the corners of his mouth crinkled up into a smile. And he actually let out a small chuckle. "You know, officially, I'm supposed to disapprove. As your guardian, I'm supposed to advise a rational and adult solution to the problem. But...considering the nature of the situation, you might be right. Are you willing to accept the consequences?"

I nodded. I didn't see any possible consequences. Peterik would never know what hit him.

"Well, it might be a good operational field test. Here, help me hang this up. We'll run the integrity suite and if everything is still coming up green after dinner, we might try a test run. If you want."

If I want. Do ursines defecate in arboreal eco-systems? If I want. Right.

I never ate dinner so fast in my life. I never loaded the dishwasher so fast either. I don't even remember what we ate. I think some of it was white. Maybe some of it was green. Something red too. I might have chewed some of it before swallowing. "Okay, I'm ready. Let's go see if the suit passed its integrity tests!" I practically ran to the lab, then I had to wait until Cousin Murray *walked* in behind me. Didn't he have any sense how important this was?

He walked over to his computer, studied the big monitor, clicked on this, clicked on that, squinted at some graphs, peered at some numbers, frowned at nothing in particular, scratched his head, cleaned his glasses, wiped his nose, cleared his throat, adjusted his belt, wiggled his finger in his ear, ran his fingers through his hair, rubbed his chin, cleared his throat again, and finally said, "Okay, it's good." He walked over to the test rack and carefully unhooked the suit from the perma-strene clips we used to hang it up. He held it up to the light, turned it this way and that, peered at it, squinted through it, sniffed it, did everything but lick it to see what it tasted like.

Finally, after several impatient Christmas mornings, he handed me the suit. "All right, Squish. Try it on, let's see if it works."

By now I'd tried on so many test-weaves and non-working proto-types, pulling on the tights, the T-shirt, the hood, adjusting them for comfort—it was a familiar process. Cousin Murray had been tweaking the perma-strene for weeks now, making it so light and airy, it almost wasn't there. I felt naked. He said that was a side-effect of the residual energy in the system. After a week or so of trying to discharge it and not getting anywhere, we decided to stop trying. It wasn't a quirk, it was a feature. I still felt naked.

I usually stripped naked before pulling on the suit anyway. I didn't like the way it bunched up my shorts. The one time I tried wearing briefs it made a line across my butt. Not that anybody would ever see, but super-heroes aren't supposed to have underwear lines. I felt self-conscious. As if everything was showing. Everything.

Cousin Murray attached the umbilical to me and we waited until all three pieces of the suit showed up on the network. While he ran a whole bunch of readiness checks, I practiced stretching and moving. Did I mention that I felt naked and embarrassed and self-conscious?

Finally, we were both ready. This was it. Cousin Murray looked at me, I looked at him. Neither of us knew what to say. This might be a legendary moment. It should be. I didn't want to spoil it by saying something stupid, but I sure as hell didn't want to say anything as dumb as "one small step blah blah blah." I mean, couldn't Neil Armstrong have been just a little bit more…I dunno, *real?*

"Okay," Cousin Murray adjusted his headset, rearranged the video camera pointed at me. "First test. Three seconds. I'll initiate, I'll bring you back. Ready?"

"Ready."

"Good luck."

"If you did your job right, I won't need any good luck."

That might have been the wrong thing to say. His finger hesitated over the button.

"Come on, Cuz. Let's make history."

His finger stabbed.

The world glowed. And I felt naked. Even more naked than before. And light—lighter than air. The only thing holding me down were the weights in the gradient soles of my tights. I had just enough time for half a test bounce when the suit chimed and I popped back into real-space. I mis-timed my bounce and landed hard, but caught myself and laughed. I padded over to Cousin Murray and he checked the suit's internal clock against the time signal from Boulder. He grinned. Synchronized to the millisecond.

"All right, Squish. Your turn. This time, ten seconds. You initiate, I bring you back. Ready?"

I waved and said, "Suit on!" Everything went shimmery. Kewl.

"Can you hear me?"

"Five by five."

"Copy that. Same here."

"I'm going to try a jump now."

"Go for it."

I crouched, I jumped. Higher than I expected. I went right through the ceiling, got a quick glimpse of the insulation in the attic, then came back down just as quickly, not like a balloon at all, hard enough to hurt. Of course—I was still accelerating at 9.8 meters per second per second. Simple calculus. I reached over to the table and passed my hand through the wooden blocks we'd stacked there. The suit chimed and I popped back.

"We need to sound the warning chime earlier," I said. "I nearly got caught with my hand in a wooden block."

He nodded and scribbled the note on his clipboard. Looking up, he said, "The proximity sensors won't let you reintegrate unless you're clear, but you're right. You do need more time. Okay, thirty seconds. This time, you give the command to come back. If you're not back in forty, I bring you back. Ready?"

"Ready. Suit on."

Shimmery again. "Can you hear me?"

"Five by five."

"Copy that."

"Hey, Cuz?"

"Yeah, Squish?"

"I wonder. Is there something we could do, some kind of night goggles or something to reduce the shimmery look. Maybe if we had a little more visual persistence, we could make things look ghostly instead of wavery. It'd be a lot easier to see things."

"Good point. Let me think about it."

"Okay, let's try the gloves now. Hands on," I said. Just as we'd created gradient fields to the soles of my tights, we'd also created gradient fields for my gloves, so I could pick things up and manipulate them while in the suit. We tested that by having me knock over stacks of blocks, pick up weights, pour a glass of water over myself. The blocks fell down, the weights weren't heavy, but they still had inertia in their own time-slice, so that was something else I needed to be aware of. The water poured right through me and splashed on the floor.

"How was that?"

"Very impressive. Claude Rains couldn't have done any better."

"Or Kevin Bacon."

"Right."

"Okay, I'm coming back now. Suit off."

Nothing happened. Everything stayed shimmery.

"Suit off," I repeated.

Nope. Still nothing. Still shimmery.

This could get scary.

Was it me? Was it the suit? Had we miscalculated something? Would I have to wait for the suit to run out of power before I came back? That wouldn't be too long, we were only giving it fifteen minutes of internal power right now. Later on, if there *was* a later on--

"Suit off. Suit off. Suit off. Um, Cuz?"

"Yeah, I hear you."

"It's not working."

"Yeah, I can see that. Okay, I'll bring you back."

And then, just as smoothly as if nothing weird had happened at all, the world came back to normal. I peeled back the hood, pulled it off my head. We looked at each other, both breathing hard, both terrified at what had almost happened. "Okay, it wasn't me, and it wasn't the suit. It was something in the command programming."

"That's where we're going to look first." Cousin Murray put his hand on my shoulder. "If anything had happened to you, Squish—"

"Yeah, I know, it would have ruined your whole day."

"—I would have never forgiven myself." He sat down on his stool and stared at me, eyes wide. Shining with incongruous moisture. "When you first moved in, I had…doubts. Concerns. But…the truth is, I'm glad you're here. I can't remember a time when I've had so much fun with anybody—" He stopped to wipe his eyes quickly with his thumb and forefinger. "I mean…." He didn't know how to say it. Neither did I. So I just went over and hugged him, holding him as hard as I could. After a brief hesitation, he wrapped his huge arms around me and held me just as tight, his huge hand pressed right into the small of my back like a great protecting bear paw. I felt…very strange. Almost like I wanted to cry. I hadn't hugged another person since…since…. I didn't remember ever hugging another human being. And then I did choke back something that might have been a sob, it felt hard in the back of my throat.

And then, after a bit, we both broke apart embarrassed. Happy, but still embarrassed. And of course, we both covered our reactions badly, because that's how geek families have moments. Cousin Murray turned abruptly to the computer and I turned my back for modesty as I started pulling off the suit and we both made noises about running more tests and checking the internal sensors and microphones and walking through the command-program line by line and stuff like that.

There's a story, maybe apocryphal, or maybe I just don't remember when or where I heard it, about an airport failure. They were worried about a power failure shutting down the control tower and the runway lights, so they built a very expensive emergency power system that would switch on automatically if there was any kind of a power failure. They tested it rigorously and it worked perfectly in every test. A few months later, there was a terrible storm and the power was knocked out all over the city. But at the airport—the emergency power system didn't switch on either. Why? It took them awhile to figure it out. The emergency power controls were on the primary circuits. When the main power went off, so did they. There was no way to tell the emergency power system to start up.

So yes, everything worked. Exactly as designed. Except they just didn't get the result they intended.

That was the first thought that popped into my mind when we began debugging.

Everything worked. We knew it worked. We'd tested every piece rigorously. We just hadn't tested the system *as a whole*. Somewhere, we'd assumed that the voice-operated controls were still connected when the suit was on. Oops. And double-oops. We went straight to the debugger. We found it as soon as we started stepping through the code. Right. There it was. Out of the loop. We were still controlling the suit externally. As soon as I said "Suit on," the voice controls were time-sliced and isolated and totally out of the circuit. Du-uh. Cousin Murray and I looked at each other embarrassed. Sometimes you can be so smart you're stupid.

It was a simple programming fix, but we didn't approach it casually. Because what we were doing was making the suit totally independent, free of all external controls—isolated from everything. Including all possibility of help or rescue. So Cousin Murray wrote his solution to the problem, I wrote mine—then we looked at each other's code. We were both over-thorough. Good. We implemented all the best features of both solutions, then ran the new code through a simulator for an hour. Ten thousand iterations. Then we ported the code over to the suit and set up a test suite. The suit would turn itself on and off every three seconds. All night long. And all day long. For at least three days. Long enough to build and test a second prototype.

It was a long evening, longer than we expected, but worthwhile. Cousin Murray announced he was so frustrated with all the delays that he was going to start fabbing the biggest perma-strene panels he could—so he could line the clean room with them and turn it into a giant perma-strene cage. Running the cage in fast-time he'd be able to fabricate whatever he wanted in a matter of minutes. I liked the idea because it meant I could stay up late, then go into the fabrication room, sleep as long as I want, wake up when I felt like it, and walk out again with hours to spare. I could take a leisurely shower, have an ample breakfast, do my homework, and still get to school early.

By the end of the week, we had two more working skintight suits and we were ready to start fabbing balloon suits next. Meanwhile, I'd collected everything I needed for Operation Blue Ball. In the privacy of my room, I rehearsed each step. I knew what I'd need, when I'd need it, and I had a pretty good idea how long each procedure would take. We'd tested all three of the suits and I had racked up six hours of suit time, including an hour of stop-time and another hour of fast-time. Cousin Murray was halfway through turning the fabrication room into a perma-strene cage, but he took the time to fab a perma-strene knapsack for me and link it to the suits.

On Friday, I was ready. Well, the plan was ready. I was still dithering, having one of those semi-existential internal monologues about the morality of revenge. The mechanics of it—the what and the how—were fairly direct. The justification for doing it, that was another question altogether.

The why of it should have been simple too. He *deserved* it.

But that wasn't good enough for me. Or for Cousin Murray. Maybe Peterik deserved everything he got *and more*. But who appointed me to be the delivery boy? Why was it my responsibility—privilege?—obligation?—to inflict harm and humiliation on him? Or anyone?

Just saying that I accept the job of vigilante isn't answer enough. It's too convenient. It's a too-easy justification for being a different kind of bully.

Cousin Murray saw me walking restlessly back and forth in the mental cage I'd constructed, saw me pacing through the house, picking things up, putting them down, rearranging stuff for no apparent reason, fussing over the details of this and that and the other thing—but didn't say anything at all until I went to him and said, "Okay, it's been great fun planning this out. I could do it. I've rehearsed it in my head enough times, I've practiced each and every step. The doing-ness is handled. And

I could stop now and be satisfied that I know I could do it if I had to. It's whether or not I should do it that's bothering me. I need a *good* reason."

"Mm," said Cousin Murray. "A good reason." He scratched the back of his neck while he considered the question. "Well, you might want to take a step back from your question. What's a good reason for doing anything?"

"Because it's the right thing to do?"

"Are you asking me or telling me? I noticed a question mark on the end of that sentence."

"I'm telling you."

"Yeah, and that brings us back to the fundamental existential dilemma that you've been struggling with all your life. How do you know what's right and what's wrong?"

"Uh, can I buy a vowel?"

"You can buy a whole clue, if you want."

"Okay, I'll do the dishes tonight."

"You'll do them anyway, it's your turn."

"Tomorrow night then."

"Fair enough. Okay, here's your clue. Maybe it's the way you're asking the question. You're casting it in terms of good and bad. What would happen to your question if you recast it?"

"It'd be a different question."

"And maybe it would be a more accurate question."

"Okay, instead of good and bad--?"

"Past and future."

I shook my head, confused. "I don't—"

"Of course not. If you did, you wouldn't have asked. Try it this way. Good reasons are always focused on the future—on what's next. Bad reasons are always focused on the past—usually on what you're still feeling angry about."

"Oh," I said.

I didn't say anything else for a bit. I had to sort this out. Revenge—that was about getting even for something that happened in the past. So...okay, revenge is a bad reason. So what would the opposite be? What's a future reason as opposed to a past reason? Oh. Wait. I got it.

"A good reason," I began slowly and carefully, "...would be that this will prevent something bad from happening in the future. It will stop him from hurting me again. No, not just that. It will stop him from hurting anyone else ever again."

"That's a little ambitious, but yes, you're on the right track." I must have looked puzzled, because he said, "It was a trick question, Squish. It's not about the reasons. It's never about the reasons—it's always about the results. Reasons aren't good or bad, they just are—they're the story you tell yourself to justify what you're going to do anyway. So the question here is really *what result do you want to produce?* And if you're still not clear about the answer, take the question a step larger. What's going to produce the best result for the most people?"

"Oh," I said again. "Keeping him from hurting anyone—everyone."

"Right," said Cousin Murray. "So it's not just about stopping Peterik, it's about *changing* him. In this case…well, you want to create an experience of such enormous confusion and doubt and uncertainty that it shatters his arrogance—*traumatically.* That requires an enormous psychological sledgehammer. Whether or not it's personally satisfying to you is irrelevant in the face of the larger question, will it accomplish a greater good?"

"Yeah," I said. "You're right. Let me walk this around the block for a day or two."

Actually, it didn't take that long. I just wanted to be sure in my own head. So I did one of those things that Aunt Patty always nagged me to do, and which I'd always ignored because it sounded like just another spoonful of psychobabble think-ology from Professor Marvel. Try to look at things from the other person's point of view and see what it feels like for them. Because Aunt Patty always meant she wanted me to look at it from *her* point of view and agree with her. But this time, I needed to think about what Peterik would feel, what his buddies would see, what everybody else would see, and how ultimately in the end, how everybody he picked on would think and feel about him.

Yeah, okay. It worked.

I wasn't exactly absolved. More like, I was *re*solved.

And that clarified my *real* reluctance.

I couldn't just sit around and wait for Peterik to do something. I was going to have to *incite* him. My usual way of being was to go invisible in the hopes that he'd find something more interesting to do than verbally assault me. But some days, without warning, he'd just be there. He'd seek me out. My best guess was that he did it when he was bored or angry or frustrated or feeling just plain nasty—and needed to show off to the guys he hung out with. No, I needed to control the situation more than that. To make this work, I was going to have to call attention to myself. No, not just that. I was going to have to piss him off so bad that he'd deliberately seek me out.

See, that's the thing about being a genius with mild obsessive-compulsive disorder. Anyone else would have just done it. I had to *plan* it down to the last little detail.

Peterik always rode to school with his Big Bother. Ever since Big Bother got his driver's license, the two of them were a stopped anapestic nuisance all over the west end of the valley. You always knew when they arrived at school, you could hear the subwoofers booming as they circled the campus a few times before pulling into the parking lot, shouting at friends and hurling epithets and trash at anyone they disliked.

Monday morning, I parked myself at the west side entrance, the closest one to the parking lot. I sat cross-legged on one of the low brick walls that lined the steps up to the wide double-doors. My position was carefully chosen, within easy eyesight of Coach Nelson who always took Monday monitor duty—and who always gave Big Bother a useless warning to turn down the boomers. Big Bother always replied that Coach Nelson had no authority over anything that happened off the campus and that included the streets.

I heard the beat even before the Land Rover came around roaring and screeching around the corner. *Sympathy For The Devil.*. Peterik hopped out of Big Bother's testosterone-substitute and came bouncing up the three easy steps to the door. His eyes narrowed as he saw me. "Good morning, faggot," he called.

"I know what your problem is," I said quietly. He slowed down, in spite of himself. "You're afraid that everyone will find out you have a tiny penis."

"And you'd just love to get your mouth around it, wouldn't you?"

"No, thanks." And then, startling even myself, I added, "I want a meal, not a snack." Wow, where did that come from?

Having exhausted the limits of his vocabulary, Peterik had no further verbal response. He feinted a punch toward me.

"Proves my point." I held up my pinky finger and smiled knowingly. "Tiny penis."

I repeated the gesture when he passed me in the hallway between second and third periods. He asked me what that was, a sissy way of giving someone the finger—I said no. Just reminding him that my little finger was still bigger than his dick with a hard-on. Behind me, two girls giggled. By lunch that remark would be all over ninth grade. He'd have to kill me to regain his honor. In his mind, anyway.

I usually ate lunch in the dark quiet corner of the quad where the multi-purpose room butted up against the row of cafeteria serving windows. I always sat facing outward. I liked keeping my back to the wall, something Wild Bill Hickock should have remembered before he sat down to play poker. Behind me was a row of lockers, nothing else. One of the lockers was mine, so it was convenient. In front of me was a thick pole, so I was mostly out of sight of the other kids. There were doors to the boys and girls lavatories off in the corner so there was some occasional traffic past my table, but not a lot of other company. This was the ultra-nerd section. Which meant this table was so tainted by my presence that not even the real nerds would sit anywhere near here. The bad news was that Peterik always knew exactly where to find me. But that was what I was counting on. I had my perma-strene knapsack across one shoulder. I wore the skintight suit under my clothes. This tight, it was practically invisible unless you looked very closely, and nobody ever came near enough to me or stayed long enough to look that closely. I make people uncomfortable, I know that. I sat down at the table and waited. I had eaten a big breakfast so I wasn't hungry now. I had left my books in my locker. I had nothing in front of me at all. I sat quietly with my hands in my lap.

Nothing happened.

Peterik never showed up.

After twenty minutes, I got up and carefully circled the quad. He wasn't anywhere to be found. Not anywhere he might have been hanging out. Not anywhere at all.

Just before fifth period, a girl I barely knew stopped me in the hall. "Hey, weird kid. You better watch out. Peterik is really pissed at you."

"Did he say what he's gonna do?"

"Uh-uh. If I was you, I'd stay home for a few days. Like the rest of my life."

"Yeah, I'll do that. Hey?"

"What?"

"Thanks."

"Don't tell anybody I told you."

And then she was gone, before I could say, "I couldn't anyway. I don't know your name."

Tuesday morning, during first break, I went to my locker to drop off my books. I knew something was wrong even before I opened it. The lock was sticky with some kind of goo—vaseline?—it didn't bother me, I was wearing the skintight suit again. Half a second in alternate-time and it would all just fall away. I'd be dirt-free. Cleaner than even an industrial detox facility could manage.

Inside the locker—whew! The stench was horrible. Somebody had crapped in my locker. Well, no. there was a pile of old clothes or rags or something, soaked in stale piss and shit and vomit and stuff that smelled like rotten eggs and worse. Big Bother must have helped with this. They must have filled a bucket—I could imagine it now, both of them, maybe a whole bunch of them, drinking beer and eating chili-burgers and laughing, and one at a time each one of them adding his own abominable abdominal contributions to the bucket, then sneaking onto campus sometime late last night or early this morning, cracking the combination to my locker—not that hard, the damn things clicked loud enough to be embarrassingly audible—and dumping the whole mess in. Ha ha ha. Very clever.

I wasn't angry. Okay, a little bit annoyed at the inconvenience. But I was already thinking. This wasn't Peterik's revenge. This was a warmup. Something to throw me off balance. Uh-huh.

I already knew what Cousin Murray would say. "There's no such thing as a problem. There are only opportunities." And this was another opportunity. A small stinking opportunity. A very nice one. I knew exactly what to do with it. In fact, I could think of three different things to do.

I closed my locker.

Looked around to see if anyone was watching. If they were, I didn't see them.

Lunchtime. As before, I had my perma-strene knapsack across one shoulder. I wore the skintight suit under my clothes. I sat at the table and waited.

I didn't have to wait long.

Peterik came striding through the lunchroom tables like a man on a mission from God, followed by several acolytes, disciples, and apprentice thugs.

I put on the night-vision goggles Cousin Murray had bought off eBay. I pulled the hood over my head. The skintight was already set for invisibility so except for the abnormal flatness of my hair, I probably looked like a perfectly normal geek wearing very weird glasses.

"Hey! Jerkwad!" He shouted. People turned around to look. "Open your locker. I got a surprise for you."

Yeah. Right. He was going to shove my face into that mess.

"Turn blue," I said.

"Didn't you hear me, faggot?! I gave you an order!"

I gave him the familiar pinky salute. "Turn blue!"

That was enough. His face reddened, his features tightened into an ugly grimace. He started to lunge—

"Suit on. Stop-time. Hands on."

Peterik froze. The whole world shimmered and froze. Everything became slightly transparent.

It worked.

Peterik and his henchmen were statues. Everybody in the quad—motionless. An airplane overhead hung in the sky. My clothes were frozen into position around me.

It was an illusion. Everything was still moving, just too slowly for me to perceive. Stop-time was a ratio of 115,200 to 1. While everyone else experienced only a 32nd of a second, I would live through a whole hour.

I stood up, leaving my clothes standing in place at the table like a hollow wrapper. They would fall imperceptibly while I was working, I'd come back and pick them up when I was done. I'd go into the boys' lavatory before returning to real-time. I'd go into a locked stall and redress in privacy. If not there, I had three other locations picked out.

I knew I had a lot to do, but for the first few moments I just enjoyed the feeling of freedom, of liberation, of nakedness, of absolute silliness. I danced up and down the rows between the tables, singing out loud. "He's a real nowhere man! Sitting in his nowhere land!" I felt *free*—free at last. If anyone could have seen me, I would have looked like a shimmering naked elf. But I was not only invisible to the world, I was also moving too fast for anyone to see. It was so tempting. I could have done all sorts of nasty practical jokes to everyone in the quad—like tilt the smug girl's can of Pepsi up just a little bit so it would dribble out all over her chin when time resumed.

But no. She'd never treated me badly. Just ignored me. It wouldn't be fair. Besides, I'd promised to limit myself to the one single target who deserved it. But even so, the feeling of power was exhilarating.

The first Step in Operation Blue Ball was to take a smoke bomb out of my knapsack, put it between Peterik's feet and set it off. I backed far enough away that I was out of everyone's view. "Suit off." In less than half a second, the smoke cloud exploded chest-high around him. "Suit on. Hands on." Perfect timing. I was glad I'd practiced in the back yard. Now Peterik was frozen in a cloud of white smoke. I'd mixed the smoke myself.

Second step was to strip him naked. And I wasn't going to be polite about it. I pulled out my tin snips and began cutting his clothes off of him. All of his clothes. I did spare the expensive belt he liked to brag about, but I made sure to shred everything else. It didn't take long. Hm. I was right. He did have a small penis. Almost hairless. That explained a lot. I almost felt sorry for him. But, no—not that sorry.

I took all the pieces and spread them out across the stone tiles of the cafeteria as if his clothes had exploded off of him. I left him his shoes. Mostly because I wasn't sure it would be safe to lift his feet to remove them. Given the sudden jerking back and forth that he would experience, I might risk breaking his legs. And I didn't want to hurt him, only humiliate him.

I did consider stripping the clothes off the goons he'd brought along as his audience. After all, they were the enablers. But that would only have diluted the humiliation across all of them. I needed Peterik to understand that he was the only target. If I understood the transactional dynamics correctly, having him be the only one to suddenly turn blue and naked would make him the *specific* object of ridicule. As the focus of the embarrassment, he would immediately lose whatever authority he had to steer this group of thugs and chimpanzees. It was this simple—the butt of the joke can't also be the Alpha. The Alpha has to be sacred. Untouchable. Once it's demonstrated that the Alpha has lost control of events, the betas stop laughing with him and start laughing *at* him. And that was my goal—taking away Peterik's power to hurt. So as tempting as it was, everybody else was strictly off-limits.

The third step in Operation Blue Ball was to paint Peterik bright blue. I'd experimented with different kinds of spray paint, marking pens, ink, etc. Which was fastest? Which looked brightest? I finally settled on a jar of thick makeup I'd picked up at a costume shop. It would take a lot of personal attention, but the effect had to be just right. I'd perfumed the makeup with vanilla and baby powder and a few other embarrassingly sweet and feminine fragrances. Little Bobby Peterik was going to smell really pretty in a few seconds. I used a wide sponge to wipe on thick generous layers. It would glisten wetly for twenty or thirty seconds before drying. That would be just fine. It would add to the effect.

After I finished, Peterik was completely blue from head to ankle. I expected the next step would be the trickiest part—but it turned out a lot easier than I expected because things would hang in the air as soon as I let go of them. Once they were out of my personal time-field they were frozen. I put a big white diaper on Peterik. And then a bright white stocking cap, oversized. The effect was pretty good. The fact that Peterik was just a little bit swayback, had a big ass and a cute pudgy little belly added to the effect.

Finally, I stuffed everything into the knapsack, scissors, smoke bomb, blue makeup, sponge, and even my own clothes—which were by now half-slumped to the bench where I'd been sitting. I replaced the smoke bomb underneath him, stepped well away and said, "Suit off. Suit on." Just enough for the smoke bomb to surround him with even more smoke. I walked back, picked up the frozen smoke bomb, put it inside a plastic bag, and into my knapsack. I'd get rid of it before I reentered normal-time. In the empty lot behind the football field, behind the bleachers, a construction crew had dumped a large hill of dirt. I could walk right through the chain link fence, through the bleachers, across the football field, through the opposite bleachers, through the next chain link fence, through a low stone wall, up to the pile of dirt, and shove the smoke bomb into it. I hated the idea of leaving even this much evidence but I assumed that by the time the empty canister was discovered so much time would have passed that maybe no one would make the connection.

But first—that mess in my locker. I was going to dump some of it into Peterik's diaper and some of it between his legs. And maybe just a smidge under his stocking cap. And maybe a little dirty sanchez on his upper lip. And possibly a goatee.

As obnoxious as the stuff in my locker was, in stop-time I wouldn't be able to smell it. The suit only passed oxygen and nitrogen, nothing else. And touching the crap was a non-issue. The perma-strene suit was safer than a latex body-condom. "Hands on," I could carry it. "Hands off," and any residual goo would fall away. "Arms on," and I could scoop up the whole mess.

—but as I lifted it, something flashed—a bright white point of light in the center of the rags. And it was *hot!* Even inside the perma-strene I could feel it. And whatever it was, it was searingly bright, even through the glasses. And it was growing, getting brighter. And hotter. Expanding to the size of a marble.

Oh, crap.

I was looking at an explosion.

In slow motion. *Very* slow motion.

Those bastards.

Some kind of a booby-trap—

This was so far beyond bullying—

Psychopaths. Absolute psychopaths—

I whirled around in alarm. I was surrounded by statues of students, frozen in the position of eating, chatting, joking, laughing, studying. Many of them looking over at Peterik in anticipation of what he was about to do to that weird super-geek who always sat in the corner. Oh crap crap crap crap crap. I needed to talk to Cousin Murray—except he was frozen in time too. I was on my own. I had to figure this out myself. Okay, no problem. I could—no, that wouldn't work. How fast did an explosion happen anyway? There must be four hundred kids in here. How big a boom was happening here?

Okay, wait. Think this through, Squish. You have time, a little bit—

I emptied the knapsack, dumping all of my stuff to the ground. Then I shoved the entire contents of my locker, the sodden rags, the expanding marble of light, into it instead—I'd practiced loading it before, but never with a bomb—but if I was right, field integrity would enclose the boom. If I was wrong, the explosion would pass right through the bag.

Even as I pulled it shut, I was already running. I slung the knapsack over my shoulder. Hands off. Arms off. No, not that way—this way! I ran straight through the buildings! To the parking lot! Big Bother always parked his Land Rover in the same spot—it was his spot, nobody else dared to park there, unless they wanted their car vandalized. Nobody even parked close to it.

There it was. Locked up. No problem. I stepped inside it. The whole back seat had been replaced by a rank of gigantic subwoofers. I upended the knapsack, dumping out most of the stinking rags, dumping out the explosion. A cherry bomb? A dynamite cap? Something bigger? Something homemade? Big Bother had an ugly reputation. The brightness was the size of a golf ball, a tennis ball, a basketball—it hung in the air, falling too slowly to see.

I leapt backward out of the car. This was going to be ugly.

Out of breath, I hurried back to the cafeteria. There was no need to hurry, but I hurried anyway. I was angry now. Very angry. I still had three of the dirty rags in the knapsack. I used one to rub a little stinky spot on the back of Peterik's diaper. I used another to smear the whole area around his mouth. I wasn't neat about it. I finished by shoving all three into the back of his diaper, so he was carrying a very nasty load.

Then I stopped and caught my breath.

Had I forgotten anything? Had I missed anything?

"Bag on." I waved it around. "Bag off." I shook it. "Bag on." I waved it around some more. I did this a few times until I was sure the knapsack was free of any residue and stink. Just the same, I felt like I should toss it into the wash machine when I got home—a gut-level feeling about cleanliness.

All that was left to do was pick up my clothes, find a place to change, and reenter normal time. I headed off toward the farthest corner of the campus—went *around* the people instead of through them, not courtesy, it was just kind of unnerving—all the way to the administration building, to the boys lavatory next to the teacher's lounge where no one ever went because that was the restroom the boys' vice principal inspected most frequently. I went into the last stall on the end, the large one for the disabled students, locked myself in, turned the suit off, pulled the hood off, tossed the goggles into the knapsack, put my regular glasses on, and dressed as quickly as I could. I was tempted to take the suit off before dressing, but no—I might need it again.

I splashed water on my face, took a whole bunch of deep breaths, dried my face with a couple of paper towels, and walked back out into the world. There was some commotion over at the cafeteria. A lot of noise, some laughter, some indistinct screaming. Coach Nelson was dragging a frenzied, stinking, five-foot smurf toward the administration building. A few students were following, photographing the whole thing with their phones. This was going to be on YouTube before sixth period.

In the lunchroom itself, there was more consternation, clusters of kids excitedly comparing their stories, trying to figure out what they'd seen. Especially the ones who'd been standing around Peterik. They were the most confused, trying to explain what happened to a couple of stern-looking teachers. "I'm not making this up. I'm telling you what I saw. I was standing right here. Super-dork did something to Peterik. He said, 'Turn blue!' He said it twice. And then there was a big bang! The super-dork disintegrated from the force of the blast! First him, then his clothes! And there was a big puff of white smoke—all around Peterik. And then when the smoke cleared, Peterik was a smurf! All blue and stinking. The dork did it. He smurf-bombed him! Some kind of chemical landmine he made up in his secret laboratory or something. How should I know how he did it?"

"Do you realize how stupid that story sounds," I said, walking past. They all turned to look at me. Amazed. I shrugged and gave them the kind of skeptical look that suggested they were being bigger idiots than usual.

One of the teachers held out a hand to stop me. Mr. Crowther from the computing lab. "You know anything about this?"

"I was nowhere near here. I just came from—" I pointed back over my shoulder. "You saw me. Who was the big blue smurf? Was that Peterik?" To his buddies, I said, "It's a good look for him." I patted the sides of my belly to emphasize my point. "He's got the right shape for it." To the teachers, I added, "What happened? Are we having some kind of a—what? Silly hat day? Halloween is in October, isn't it? Or did they change it? Stupid holiday anyway. Dressing up in silly clothes to go begging for bad candy."

"You—" The teacher jerked his thumb. "Out of here."

And then we were all distracted by the sounds of fire engines howling into the parking lot.

Apparently, something had exploded and caught fire inside Big Bother's Land Rover. Totaled his seats, his stereo, and his subwoofers. Also scorched the gleaming paint of the body, leaving it all blistered and peeling. What a mess. Not quite enough to wreck the car, but Big Bother wouldn't be driving it for awhile. I heard cheering and applause and laughter from the gathering crowd of students—made all the sweet-er by the sudden harmonic counterpoint of Jeff Peterik's outrage and obscenities.

Cousin Murray was waiting for me in the kitchen when I walked in. "So? How'd it go?"

"It went," I said. I tossed the knapsack on the table. "But this super-hero stuff is hard work. More work than it's worth. If I'm going to punk somebody, I want to do it on a much bigger scale. Let's go to Mars instead."

"Okay. But the moon first, remember?"

"Okay."

And that's why there's a big black monolith in Clavius crater. Waiting.

TIME CAPSULE 2120: ACTUAL COMMENTS FROM LUNAR TOURISTS

Why does the water come out of the shower so slow? Can you turn up the gravity?

Why do I have to wear a spacesuit to go outside? Can't you fill up the outside with air too?

You should lower prices so more people can visit the moon.

Can you do something about the long days and nights? It's hard to know when I'm supposed to sleep and when I'm supposed to be awake.

Can you turn down the temperature in the summer domes? It's too hot.

Can you raise the temperature in the winter domes? It's too cold to play in the snow.

Need more signs in the domes to keep the area pristine.

My wife got stung by a bee while visiting a farm dome. Please eradicate these annoying creatures.

Too many rocks in the Lunar hills. Not enough scenery.

No marked hiking trails in the Lunar wilderness.

Guide wouldn't let us fit our feet into Armstrong's footprints.

Please pave hiking trails to make Lunar hiking easier.

Chairlifts need to be in some places so that we can get to wonderful views without having to hike to them.

Reflectors need to be placed on rocks every 10 meters so people can hike at night with flashlights.

A McDonald's would be nice.

My room is very hot. How do I open a window?

Where do we go to see the vacuum? We looked out the window but there was nothing there.

My husband said he saw the vacuum and it was nothing. Can you make it more interesting?

Why are there so many rocks out there? Don't they ever clean up the landscape?

The daylight is too bright. Can you turn it down?

We went to one of the moon's oceans today and I couldn't even find a seashell. How come?

TURTLEDOME

We came up the Ecuador beanstalk, only twelve of us, not the twins; Mik and Max couldn't boost because they were still in transition and three days of free fall would screw up their integration, bad planning on their part; but that meant we'd be short-handed, so we spent most of the ride up juggling the mission schedule. We felt bad about it, but not bad enough to step aside and let the backup troop take our slot. This was Lunar Quest 24 and we'd been waiting for this day too long.

At the top of the beanstalk, we crammed into two cargo pods, six bods to a pod; sausage-shaped capsules filled with minimal life-support, maximum supplies, and us—and not a lot more. There wasn't room. We separated from the line and fell up toward Luna. We fell for three days, finally looping deep into the Lunar well, where we circled the drain for eight and a half hours.

The pods were as big as buses, bigger even, but after three and a half days of us breathing each other's farts, they started to feel cramped. We had work to do, of course, but most of the time, we were just hot bods in transport.

We were all excited about the opportunity, of course, but it wasn't just the Quest—there was a much larger possibility behind it.

If we were good enough, if we could prove ourselves—

No. If *I* was good enough, if *I* could prove to them and to myself that I could be a real asset on Luna—then maybe I could earn a permanent berth. Nearly a quarter of all Lunar Quest participants were invited, so the odds weren't impossible. I just had to demonstrate the kind of commitment and ability that consistently produces success. I didn't know if I had that—I wouldn't know until I was tested, but I'd spent two years studying everything there was to know about Luna. All that preparation had to count for something.

But was I willing to leave Earth behind *forever*? Because that's what it really meant. After a few years on Luna, you lose half your bone and muscle mass. You can't go back to Terra unless you wear an exo-skeleton, or unless you spend a year in a centrifuge, building yourself back up. So that meant never again seeing family and friends and favorite places.

I didn't have a family, not any more. And that's something I don't discuss with anyone. As for friends, well even my best friends know I don't have any best friends. But that's okay too. Luna is the land of solitude. You have to be able to stand desolation and silence and barren emptiness, from here to forever. And then you have to be able to shift gears instantly and deal with people both in your face and far away. I can do that, I think. I keep to myself when I have things to do. I get along with people when I have to. My personality profile says I can work well with others, I'm just not expressive. But I think that's an asset.

See, here's the thing. Luna is the new frontier, but it isn't a frontier with fresh air and clean water unless you make it yourself. And it isn't a frontier where you can get rich, because it costs as much to survive as you can earn; but even if you did get rich, there isn't a lot to buy on Luna, except another lot on Luna. Big deal.

So what's the big appeal? Why did I want to be here so badly? Good question, and one I still hadn't answered with certainty. I just wanted it. Why does anyone want anything? And why does anyone want to emigrate to Luna where life is hard and lonely and dangerous, where emigration isn't an adventure as much as it's a life sentence?

So, why?

Because—and this is only true for me, I don't know if it's true for anyone else—it's one step closer to the stars. It's part of the grand leap outward. And, even though I only know this from the simulations, I know that this is the part that chews me up inside, fills me with emotion, I want to look up into the star-spread darkness and see the Earth *overhead*. I want to see the Big Blue Marble from a magnificent distance and know that I'm not there. I'm *here*.

But maybe that's *not* the reason. Maybe, that's the nice face I just put on, because the part I don't tell anyone, is that I'm so disgusted with most of humanity, the way people beat each other up and beat each other down—all the liars and takers and gimme pigs—I don't want to be a part of them anymore. It isn't that I want to be alone; I just want to be as far away from people as possible.

I think that's it. I'm not sure. And maybe nobody else knows either. Maybe nobody knows until they're actually *here*.

So we rode the pods, pretending that we had time to waste. We invented a few more variations on Guess-Again—an old logic game of yes-or-no questions. Each player makes up his own rule about how to answer a question and all the other players have to guess it. The winner is the last one whose rule remains unguessed. We had one round that lasted the better part of a shift because Libby's rule had him answering the question put to the previous person. That one took awhile to figure out. Libby's nickname was Slipstick, partly because of something we found in an old story, but more because of something he used to keep in his panties, even when he was a girl. And that was because of that other thing he used to say, "Put on your big girl panties and deal with it," which started a long-smoldering argument with Jasmine who was sort of a traditionalist, insisting that boys should wear boys' underwear and girls should wear girls' underwear, and not mix things up because the gender-map was confused enough already, and Libby replied that he was going to wear whatever he wanted whenever he wanted, underwear doesn't have any gender, only fit and comfort, and anyone who doesn't wear comfortable underwear is an idiot, and this argument went on for a week or two until Libby finally said, "if you're such a traditionalist, *Jasmine*, then why do you still have a girl's name?"

"Jasmine is only a female name when it's on a girl. And it's a male name when it's on a boy."

"Right. Just like underwear."

"No, it's *not* the same—" But the argument was clearly over. Jasmine sputtered, made a face of frustration, and stormed out of the room.

The disagreement between them had only been a symptom of a much deeper enmity. Whatever the underlying cause, the two of them were now entangled in a perpetually simmering stalemate, a smoldering anger that regularly erupted whenever a suitably minor provocation could be found. The rest of us dealt with it by keeping them in different pods whenever we could manage. But we couldn't always, so it made troop management a lot more … um, interesting.

After that, we argued about a lot of other stuff. Stuff that Libby and Jasmine weren't likely to have serious opinions on. Like the physiognomy of famous factresses and if you could have sex with any person in the solar system who would you choose as your first choice? And which of you would be the girl? Or would you prefer girl-on-girl or boy-on-boy? And why? And why the pod had such a strange smell, not unpleasant, just strange.

Then we speculated on whether the stockholder system was inherently more fair than equal representation and why the lifespan of a democracy was approximately ten generations, and after that it was all momentum and borrowed time. We argued whether memetic monocultures were inherently stronger or weaker than hybrids. And if the mociology of info-torrents was the chicken or the egg in relationship to transitory memes—and which was more important, short-term or long-term memes.

Then we talked about sex again, because even though nothing was likely to happen below the belt, not for a while anyway, we could still talk about it and live in hope. Except conversations about sex always unnerve me. What are you supposed to say? Or not say? And even if you don't say anything, one of the trips, Jason or Jonah or Jorge, will notice that and say that proves something too. (Personally, I think the only thing they know about boobs comes from playing with their own, but I wouldn't say that aloud.)

Finally, after five or six times around the moon, we'd spiraled in close enough to splat. We strapped in and bubbled up the pods, inside and out. The autopilot made some attitude adjustments, fired its main tubes for a few seconds, and eventually bounced us down into the Sea of Screams, that big empty space northeast of Shanghai Station where most of the pods (and most of the private ships too) come down.

Shanghai Station isn't much to look at— from above it's just a scattering of gray lumps and spindly light-poles. We only got a quick look at it as we passed over, but we'd had to study its layout as part of our training, in case we had to divert. The truth is, if it weren't for the big red arrows—two klicks each—laid across the gritty gray sawdust, it'd be too easy to miss. There were no other visual cues.

The gray lumps were Lunar-crete domes. You lay down a big plastic bag, you mix up some fresh Lunar-crete and pour it over the bag. Then you inflate the bag. It takes about an hour. The Lunar-crete hardens, you spray it with sealant. You wait an hour, then attach an airlock, go into the lock and cut a door into the dome. The limit to the size dome you can inflate is how big a bag you have, how much Lunar-crete you can mix, and how much air you can put into the bag.

It's faster and easier than sandbag igloos—but sandbag igloos are good too, if you don't have a big plastic bag, if you don't have any Lunar-crete, and you can't spare a lot of air. You pile up sandbags and put a roof over them. Luna has no shortage of sand, all you have to do is bring a lot of empty sandbags. Ohell, even pantyhose will do. It's more labor intensive, yes, but it's cheaper because the only moving parts are humans.

You fill your pantyhose with Lunar dust and lay them down like sandbags all around the hole you dug the dust out of. You put a grid of carbon-fiber triangle-beams across the top of the wall, and it supports two more layers of pantyhose or sandbags to make a roof. You spray a centimeter of polymer inside to seal the floor and the walls, so you don't end up inhaling a lot of gritty dust, you install a pre-fab airlock, and the resulting hut is airtight, self-insulated, micro-puncture resistant, and uglier than a Martian lawyer. But for the fuel cost of a couple kilos of stockings and some hardware, you can build a tiny little home for two or more colonists—or even as many as six if they're willing to hot-bed.

And that's Shanghai Station.

It would never be Nova Hong Kong, but here on the high equatorial plains of Luna, someday it would be a great observatory. Or a factory. Or a launch catapult. The politicians were still arguing with the engineers and the scientists and the accountants. And they'd continue arguing for far too long while Shanghai Station finally grew into its own inevitable destiny. Everybody had opinions. We even argued about it ourselves.

Immediately after splat, the first shift, we slept in the transit pods. As much as we wanted to get out and do the "giant leap" thing, both our seniors insisted that we follow the manual and take at least two hours of rest. We'd have plenty of time later. In fact, according to Senior Cheung, after we got over the novelty of being on the moon, we'd find that the whole experience was mostly hard work and mostly boring and if we expected anything else, it would be mostly disappointing.

But we were on Luna. Most of us had been in the Vision Quest program for at least two years, some as long as five. We'd been training for this opportunity for 18 months. We were here and we were going to build the Turtledome. Our part of it, anyway.

Our youngest member, Jang, had just turned 18; our oldest, Jasmine, was 24. We were mostly male now, at least physically; although when we'd started out, we'd had at least five different sexes among us, possibly seven if all of the different stories about Slipstick were true; but for the purposes of this mission, we'd been required to transition to standard male form because most of the body maintenance was easier. At least, that was the reason given.

I wasn't the only one, of course, and among ourselves, we speculated what the real motivations might be for requiring the transition, not the least of which was having the whole team aligned on the same thing at least once in our Vision Quest career. And even though most of us had already admitted genuine curiosity, anticipation, enthusiasm, and impatience to experience sex in free-fall, or even in one-sixth gee, we had all taken suppressants anyway just before launch, so that we could focus on the more immediate tasks at hand—completing this mission in excellence and earning our team merit badge. But there was still a lot of boyish flirting and grab-ass, mostly so we could pretend that we were just too masculine (at the moment) for the suppressants to work completely. Besides, if we hadn't spent some time speculating about micro-gee positions, the Troop Leaders might have worried about us. Lacking any real experience, I kept my mouth shut and listened with no small amount of puzzlement. What was the big deal about a penis anyway? Most of the time, it just feels like it's in the way.

I guess that's the reason that most people think scouting is about gender-shifting, body modding, augmented telepathy, the technology of extended consciousness, transformational training, and all the other stuff that energizes the rad-bloggers; but there's a lot more to it than that, more than most people realize. As scouts, we had to learn our own history, all the way back to Lord Baden-Powell. Some of it wasn't very nice.

Scouting started out as a way to prepare young men (and later, young women, and eventually just young people of whatever gender they happened to choose at the time) for the responsibilities of adulthood. For most of the first century it served as a useful career path through adolescence that often led to ROTC and then from there to a military career.

But after the reformation, everything changed, especially the definition of adulthood, so young people have to be trained differently. Now, it was recognized that adulthood doesn't just happen, it's the result of the intentional pursuit of a goal or a vision. Hence, Vision Quest. Yes, the merit badges in joyous sexuality, compassionate nurturing, and gender-consciousness are important, but the underlying skills of flash-construction, geocaching, fabbing, and even poly-cracking are still as important as they were in grandpa's day. The day before we left, Auncle Norm did twenty minutes about how the whole thing was silly; building a functional Lunar dome is better left to bots, human beings shouldn't do dirt-work. Of course, she was right, but we weren't doing it for the dirt.

We weren't going to the moon to help build Turtledome; that was just the mechanical expression of the larger goal. We were contextually challenging the inherently intransigent nature of physical reality—a long-lost and too-often overlooked skill, but every bit as important as poly-cracking. Not everything is virtual. Sometimes you have to know how to boil a *real* egg. Sometimes even a centimeter can be a big thing—especially if it's the difference between a close fit and a secure fit. Or as Senior Whitlaw once said, "The vacuum in your helmet starts between your ears."

After the sleep-shift, we suited up, checked our greens, and stepped out into the Lunar night. It was dark and bright at the same time. The dust glowed faintly with the light reflected off the half-Earth low on the horizon, but the stars above were a splash of brilliance from one end of the horizon to the other. I'd seen this display often enough, but never in real-time, never in meat-life. It was somehow different. Not as spectacular as the big display down at the Wal-Mall, but a lot more *real.* And maybe a lot more, I dunno, meaningful...?

Mission Control gave us fifteen minutes to savor the moment—to bounce around, plant our flag, take our group pictures, and sink our prints into the crunchy Lunar grit.

For the first few moments, nobody said anything. We were just too...

Excited? Awestruck? Wonderwhelmed?

We made it! We were on the moon!

It was....

Just not describable. I won't even try.

But it's true, what they say. Once you've been there, you're different. And you can't understand what kind of difference it is until after you've been there. And all the words that have been written about it will never be enough. You have to go yourself.

Of course, we took pictures of each other. We all wore bright-colored starsuits; each one of us sporting a different color and design. And even though we had been specifically warned not to see how high we could jump, we did it anyway. We bounced around the landscape like cartoon characters superimposed on a black and gray diorama. The trips were all in green and yellow; when they stood side-by-side, they formed a triptych that spread across all three of their suits. Jasmine had an orange suit, which clashed with Libby's bright pink display. Mariko Bailey was a shimmering blue, almost like the sky on Earth, only brighter. Of course, all the suits were capable of full-video, front and back, but that had long since been demonstrated as too distracting, so we only had the video for our chest and back displays. So others could read our trendlines. Which were a little jacked up now, at the high end of optimal, but otherwise normal.

—so that meant it was time to get to work. We jacked the pods up into position and opened the external lockers. We unpacked the wheels first, six for each pod. They were circular honeycombs, bright yellow, fat and rubbery, three meters in diameter. After they were installed, they'd hold the pod-vehicles high above the roughest Lunar terrain. The wheels had six times more flex than would have been practical on Earth, so they were pretty good shock absorbers too.

After the last piece clicked in green, we stopped for a pee-break. And that experience was sufficient to demonstrate the difference between theory and practice, as well as the difference between practice and actual application—but it also gave me a reason to appreciate the above-mentioned mission requirement. We also had our milk-and-cookies—that's what we called our in-suit liquid and solid refreshments; nutrient-rich something that we could sip and nutrient-richer something that we could chew.

Before resuming work, we checked each other's greens. On this shift, my buddy was Rocklyn. Our personal readings were good, close enough to optimal to keep going for at least another hour, so we jacked the axles into place and mounted the wheels onto the engine hubs. Everything was lighter than we'd practiced on Earth, but it still had the same mass *and* inertia—so it wasn't easier than we expected, it was harder—at least until we learned how to compensate for the discrepancy between weight and momentum. But it was mostly a snap-and-click job, then you run the tests, wait for the confirming greens, and give each other a high-five/low-five.

Then we unlocked the dragonfly wings—the solar panels that would provide both shade and power when we hit dayside, or when dayside caught up to us, whichever. We had 96 hours until dawn; we'd already sorted ourselves into shifts so that whenever one person was sleeping another was working. We'd be hot-bedding the entire tour, one per bunk supposedly, but maybe not. We weren't all sexual, but some of us liked to cuddle. The twins and the trips, maybe because they'd been raised that way; but not me. And I don't talk about why I'm a singleton either.

After everything was triple-confirmed, we climbed back into the pods—except they weren't pods anymore; now they were horizontal and on wheels, so they were trucks. We popped off our helmets and waited for the go/no-go from Mission Control.

Of course, we were being monitored. On Earth, there were at least a hundred other troops in training for their own missions to Turtledome. They were probably huddled or clustered or more likely lounging in front of video-walls, watching the multiple feeds from our helmet cameras, analyzing, commenting, judging our every move. Just like we'd done when we studied the 23 previous Lunar Quest missions—all the teams who'd preceded us.

But those were just the lookie-loos. Our primary was Vision Quest Control at Salt Lake and our secondary was Shanghai Station, about thirty klicks over the horizon.

There was an old launch catapult in Utah, purchased by General Transport a few years ago and now used mostly for boosting cargo, mostly international transports, but occasional low-Earth orbits as well. The control galleries had been refitted and were now among the very best in the western hemisphere. Vision Quest Control had an internship agreement; we used whatever spare galleries were available for monitoring Lunar Quest Expeditions and General Transport used the missions as training sessions for their own tech teams as well as ours. The relationship wasn't just symbiotic, it was incestuous.

Luna-side, Shanghai Station only monitored us in case of emergency, and only until we passed into Turtledome jurisdiction. Shanghai kept three trucks on standby whenever scouts were in the Sea of Screams. In the entire history of the program, they'd only come running once, and that was for a case of unscheduled menstruation.

Turned out the fellow was pregnant and hadn't told anyone. He miscarried in his suit. Rumor had it that the suit was ruined. I didn't want to think about it. And why does anyone want to get pregnant anyway when it's so much cheaper, safer, and easier to put the embryo in a bottle for ten months? But I guess some people are just old-fashioned stupid. The real problem there was that none of his buddies had noticed—and you had to ask, what was wrong with those relationships that he didn't trust anyone enough to say anything until it was too late? I guess he was afraid that if he'd told, he'd have been dropped from the mission; but according to rumor (the files were sealed) he said he didn't know he was carrying. Right.... And I didn't notice this thing in my panties either.

While we waited for our congratulatories and go-aheads, we took a primary meal-break. I hadn't realized how hungry I was; I put away a whole meal-pack and probably could have eaten two more. Low-gee work is exhausting; it puts you into a real energy-debt. It's not just the labor itself, it's the effort of moving the suit as well. Starsuits are made of workflex, multiple layers of nano-weave and exo-muscles. It's kind of like wearing an old-fashioned wet-suit, like some of the reenactment surfers still do, only one that works with you instead of against you; but there's still a lot of resistance, and while you don't feel it outside, after you get back in and unpeel, that's when you find out how stiff you are. Not to mention how much you've outsweated the suit's ability to absorb and recycle. The first thing to do is rehydrate with oxygenized water, at least a pint. Two is better.

Mostly, you're naked inside your starsuit. So when you unpeel, the first thing you do is wipe down—or you wipe your buddy down and he wipes you down, all the places that you can't easily reach by yourself. It's like being in a hot sweaty shower room, only without any water. And in an enclosed place like a pod, there's a lot of intense body smells. We use aloe/vitamin E scrubbing towels. Lunar vehicles and habitats are only pressurized to 5 psi, so your skin dries out quickly, and when it dries out—it flakes. And human skin-flakes are the primary source of dust in an enclosed environment with human hair coming in a close second. The one thing you really don't want is dust building up in your filters and machines. So we vigorously scrub each other's arms and legs and backs and fronts to remove dead skin and keep the living cells moisturized and the hair follicles retarded. You end up feeling as smooth as a baby. The first few times it's embarrassing, then it's interesting, then finally it's boring—except sometimes, like when my buddy is Mariko, it starts to get interesting again. But it's one of the few times we *don't* talk about sex. Go figure. You'd think that with all those naked young bodies in such close proximity—but no. I'm sure there must be a reason.

It's a Loonie thing. Dirtsiders, of whom I used to be one until just a very short time ago, don't get it. The ones who talk about Luna even though they've never been here and never will get here, no matter how much they talk about it—they're talking from the land of the untrained. What Whitlaw calls the arrogance of ignorance. They look at the facts and only see their opinions. Like clothes. There's all these porn-stories on Earth about how clothes will be unnecessary in space, we'll have such a perfectly tuned environment, we'll all float around naked. That's just silly.

Just like the starsuits are tuned nano-weaves designed for outside, we have much lighter and softer nano-weaves for inside. Some of the dirtsiders make really expensive lingerie out of the same material, which is a waste of good nano, because it's not really designed for that, but some idiots call it starcloth or space-cloth and charge other idiots a premium for it. And then other idiots wonder why Loonies have to wear expensive lingerie all the time. But it isn't. It's specifically designed for maximum utility and comfort. It only looks like underwear, but it's really just very lightweight T-shirts and shorts. The soft weave of the material is partly for comfort and protection—when your skin is being kept that smooth, it's no fun bumping up against stuff; partly for color—so you have immediate identification of people by their color designs; partly for enclosing and maintaining a stable air temperature close to the skin as well as wicking away excess personal humidity; but just as much so you have a place to put your pockets—because unlike some of those silly shows you see on video, you still need pockets in space, or at least some kind of utility-belt. Because, really, where else are you going to put your lucky marble?

But there's also the more important part that dirtsiders don't understand. It's nano-weave, with all the strength that implies—when you don't have a mall next door, you need your clothes to last; but more important, in an emergency, there's a lot of things you can use a nano-weave T-shirt for. During our training, we were given three of them to examine and told to come up with 100 things we could do with them. My favorite was tie them together and use them as a sling to kill Goliath.

Mission Control waited until we'd finished eating and our heart rates had returned to something approximating normal, then informed us that our buggies were good to go. That was the good news. The bad news was that they wanted us to take a four-hour sleep shift first. After the usual groans and protests, we slung our hammocks and settled in. In one-sixth gee, a hammock is almost luxurious. In fact, just about any bed on Luna is a lot like floating. There's no such thing as bedsores on this wannabe-planet. There are, however, other circulatory effects, like light-headedness and perpetual erections that have nothing to do with full bladders or full libidos, just blood flow. Or maybe it's psychological. Or adolescence. Or just another thing to whisper about after lights-out.

This time, for some giddy reason, it was euphemisms about mastur-bation. Someone said, "Keep your hands in your own pants!" and some-one else shouted, "Tickle your own pickle." And someone else replied, "In your case, jerkin' the gherkin." And in short order, we also heard, "adjusting the antenna," "exercising your right," "five-knuckle shuffle," "badgering the witness," "white-water wristing," "flogging the beagle," "loading the cannon," "flying solo," "deconstructing Longfellow," "rel-ishing the hot dog," "charming the snake," "man-milking," "launching the morning missile," "firing the staff," "squeezing the squirter," "drop-ping the kids off," "liquidating the inventory," "committing spermicide," "freeing the hostages," "spackling the ceiling," "helping put Mr. Kleenex's kids through college," and "running in single-user mode." And from those who'd recently been persons of the vaginal persuasion: "finding your niche," "auditioning the finger puppets," "rubbing the ruby," "riding the unicycle," "tickling your fancy," "patting the robertson," "pounding the pebble," "slapping the tribble," "playing the slot machine," "tiptoeing through the two lips," "flossing the cat," "checking for squirrels," "drilling for oil," "triggering the gusher," "spelunking in the mystery cave," "fill-ing the pink taco," "spearing the bearded clam," "getting a stinky pinky," "digging the stench trench," and "attacking the Death Star." Until finally Senior Cheung lost his patience and hollered something in Cantonese that sounded like a fishwife's curse. Whatever a fishwife was. We didn't need translation. Shut up and stop behaving like a bunch of giddy *poke-gai gwei-lohs*. You're going to need your sleep.

Except in my case, sleeping was the last thing on my mind.

See, we re-buddied almost every shift, which usually wasn't a prob-lem, except this rotation put me opposite Mariko Bailey, which meant my hammock was elbow-close to his, and that meant knowing smirks from Jason and Jonah and Jorge. Despite the fact I'd never said anything at all, everyone had figured it out anyway that I had a crush on Mariko. Everybody except Mariko who mostly, sort of, ignored me.

Mariko Bailey was the most beautiful boy in two worlds. He was a chocolate redhead. His skin was the purest deepest shade of Hershey I'd ever seen on any human being. His father must have been a tall muscular African because Mariko was all chest and muscles. He had a waist that other people can only aspire to, even with corseting. His mother must have been Chinese because he had perfectly angled eyes that accented his grin with a permanent twinkle; but his third parent must have been Irish, because he had naturally auburn hair. His tight curls were trimmed back in exquisite corn rows. I'd fallen in lust with him the first day I'd met him; he was the best argument for staying a girl I could imagine.

So of course, I assumed that everyone else saw how beautiful he was too. When Jason made the inadvertent remark that Chinese eyes didn't match either red hair or chocolate skin, I made the mistake of arguing that the combination was exquisite. I guess that's how it started. I got so embarrassed, I wouldn't stay in the same room with Mariko. I just didn't want to deal with the smirks.

So there I was, floating next to the curved wall of the pod, with Mariko Bailey's warm body hanging only inches from mine. He smelled so good, I had to roll over—do you know how hard that is to do in a hammock? In one-sixth gee?—to face the bulkhead.

After a moment, I felt a gentle touch on my arm. "Shan...?" he whispered. I tried to ignore him, but he repeated the touch, this time shaking me gently.

I rolled back to face him. In the dark, I could just make out his eyes. He hooked his fingers around the net of my hammock and pulled us close together so he could whisper directly into my ear. "It's only for one shift."

Huh? What the hell was he talking about?

"We've gotta talk."

I was too startled to say anything, I didn't know what to say.

"Look, I am what I am." His voice was so low I could barely hear him. "Get over it already. I'm a triffid, so what? It doesn't mean anything. I'm still your scout-brother—"

"Shh!" I said, maybe a little too fiercely, a little too loud. I hated myself almost immediately. I realized I had my hand over his mouth. I let go, embarrassed. I wanted to touch his face, I wanted to whisper to him, "How could you think that, you idiot? I think you're wonderful—" But then what? I love you? I hardly knew him. We hadn't exchanged ten words in as many days. The last thing he'd said to me was, "Yo? The ketchup? Over here?" Shit.

"I don't care if you're triploid, lots of people are—" I stopped myself, I lowered my voice, I struggled to figure out what to say next. How could I get from here to there?

"So why do you hate me then? Because I'm Chinese brown? Because I was an occupation baby? That war ended 19 years ago. Can't we just get along for one shift?"

"Stop it," I said. I put my hand on his mouth again, this time gently. He shut up.

Now what? I could hear the silence between my heartbeats. How do I tell him anything? How do I tell him he's too beautiful to be real? And that I'm so silly-stupid I can't stand to be in the same room with him because I just want to stand and stare? Oh, fuck, I can't even ask those questions yet. How do I get him to stop hating me because he thinks I hate him? Oh, fuck—

"I'm sorry," he said abruptly. "I shouldn't have said anything. Just forget it. Let's just get through the shift. And I'll stay away from you after that." He pushed away, rolled over in his hammock, and pulled his blanket up around his ears. Great. Just great.

I faced the bulkhead again and thought about crying, but maybe that was just hormones again. Or moon madness. Or maybe…I don't know. Somehow this wasn't anything I'd expected. We were supposed to be a team, and I was screwing the whole thing up.

What passed for morning in the pod was loud noises and bright lights, followed by disorientation and someone toppling me out of the hammock into a low-gee, slow-motion tumble of huh-where-the-hell-am-I? Oh, the moon. Right. Thump. Caught on the first bounce by Mariko, who let go of me as soon as I had my footing. Without ever meeting my eyes. Dammit.

I could have enjoyed a shower, but we weren't scheduled for another twelve hours; first we had to get to Turtledome. We rehydrated, had a couple of cookies each, then lit up our stations and rechecked everything.

Mission Control gave both pods a green light, so we released the parking brakes, powered up, and rolled.

We cheered as the pods lurched into motion. We even hollered a bit, letting off tension, and then we quieted down just as quickly. This wasn't a bus trip to the snow-dome; this wasn't a simulation, there was real work to be done.

The pod-ride was bouncy and light, like rolling over a rutted road in slow motion. You could feel the bumps, but they didn't feel real. Part of it was the one-sixth gee, part of it was the oversized wheels, and the rest of it was the magnetic suspension of the undercarriage. It wasn't the same as driving on a highway, but the dark rides on King Kong Island have rougher bounces.

Occasionally, we'd hit a bigger than usual bump and we'd float for a second. That surprised us the first time, after that we just shouted, "Air-time!" Because "Vacuum-time" didn't really work.

Top speed for a Lunar truck is supposed to be 30 klicks. We knew that some experienced drivers had hit as high as 70 or 80—but they were traveling on known routes. And unofficially, some had hit as high as 120 on short straightaways. So we figured we were doing somewhere between 40 and 50 kph once we hit "Route 66."

Route 66 isn't a road, it hasn't even been bulldozed or flattened. It's just a series of bright orange pylons marking the route between the Sea of Screams and Turtledome. Follow the pylons carefully and you probably won't roll into a crater. Get sloppy, you can embarrass yourself in front of nine billion viewers.

We all took turns driving, each one of us spotting for our buddy. Mariko navigated while I piloted, then we switched off. Our conversation was so formal we both could have been bots. We're lucky the rest of the troop didn't open a window and toss us out.

Every thirty minutes, we did something just like that. We popped a survey-bot into a release tube and dropped it behind us. The operative lifetime of a bot was 5-7 years, but some bots roving the Lunar surface were almost 15 years old. There were over a hundred thousand working bots on the moon; for more than half a century, every piece of rolling stock was mandated to drop a bot every twenty klicks. The bots looked like bright orange spiders and their job was to roam the terrain, pho-tographing, sniffing, scanning, sensing, looking, listening, performing all kinds of terrain and mineral surveys, and phoning home every few days. Supposedly, the bots were so sensitive that if you dropped a fork at Asimov Station, the nearest thirty bots could correlate the seismic shock waves and report what flavor pie you were eating.

Eventually—sometime between next week and the return of the Centauri probe—we'll have a complete Lunar map, detailed down to the last millimeter. Satellite mapping is useful, of course, but it's incomplete. See, Luna is covered with dust—gritty gray dust that sticks to everything as if it's statically charged. Actually, it just hasn't been eroded. Down on Terra, every little piece of sand has been pushed back and forth by the wind and the waves, ground around forever by the restlessness of wind and gravity, tides and weather, every little grain rubbing against every other little grain. Do this for a few million years, and you rub away the sharp edges, turning them into little polished marbles. But on Luna, everything just sits there—no wind, no waves, no nothing. The nature of Luna is that there isn't any nature. Put Lunar sand under a microscope and it's all hooks and sharp edges. That makes it great for lots of different kinds of industrial uses, polishing grit and sandpaper, but it's hell on machinery, starsuits, and lungs—especially lungs.

As hard as everyone tries to keep it out, a little bit sneaks in through the airlock every time someone comes back inside. There's lots of stuff we can do—plastic coatings, filters, electrostatic fields, micro-blasts, nano-sweeps, and so on. But the eenth percent that still squeaks through is still a nuisance, which means eventually, it's a problem. One of many.

But we still have to know what kind of surface lies underneath the dust-crust. Tin? Nickel? Ice? Copper? Especially copper. Or just plain old rock. I'm not a selenologist, have no desire to be—but even I can understand the need for a good map of the available bedrock. Someday soon, they'll be putting up cable car towers. That's why Turtledome is where it is—because it's a junction. Someday, it'll be a city. Or not. It depends on whether or not we can finish the dome. Once there's a dome, we can argue for a line. Without a dome, there's no need for a line.

Meanwhile, there's just this gray uneven surface, rolling out to an impossibly-close horizon. Low hills and wide valleys, everything sloping this way and that, everything pocked with craters and strewn with rocks and rubble. It's not unreal or surreal—it's hyper-real. It's like a simulation ride, only not.

See, lots of people have said lots of different things about Luna—that its desolation is magnificent, that it's got a stark poetic beauty, that the terrain is silent and brooding and mysterious, and so on and so on and so on. All of that is true, but at the same time, it isn't. It's like what Gramma said to me, "You won't see the moon. You'll see yourself. The moon will be your mirror." Everything everyone says—it's not how it really is, it's only how they saw it.

So, how is it really—? You'll have to go and see for yourself. That's the only thing that's true about Luna.

To my mind, the big mystery about Luna is how anything so monotonous and boring can be so exciting at the same time. Luna is all scenery and no rest stops. Every place is different and everyplace is the same. It's almost completely colorless—everything is either black or dazzling bright. Or dark gray, or gritty gray, or fuzzy gray, or soft gray. Or just plain old gray. It's ugly and pretty at the same time.

And after a while, twenty minutes or forty minutes, or three hours, it's mostly boring. Once in a while, the truck has to go up a long slope, or around the edge of a wide crater, or down through a stark valley, but most of the time it feels like everyplace on Luna is just a variation of every other place. That isn't true, of course. We've all seen pictures of the Southern Jumble, and the Lunar Appenines, and the Levine Ravine. But we're still just scouts, and there's places we're not going to be allowed to go, because we're still just scouts.

But that doesn't stop us from speculating. When boys aren't flirting, they're gossiping. Or making stuff up. Worse than girls. Or maybe there's no difference at all. (Everybody talks about the differences—especially the way it was in the olden days, when the differences were important, but what if all those differences are just different ways of doing the same thing? Just like there are lots of different ways to masturbate. Or say "masturbate.")

Anyway…there are over a hundred thousand permanent residents on Luna, more than enough for a Lunar culture, of sorts. So there are stories and rumors and legends and mysteries enough to keep even a confirmed gossip like Slipstick chattering for weeks. He slid easily from the imported Russian mythology of the impish Rock Father to the more ominous mystery of the extra footprints found at Tranquility Base. Who had secretly visited the site before the Americans returned? The usual suspects included the Chinese, the Japanese, the Russians, the British, the Israelis, the Emirates, and the Australians. Slipstick said it was really Bigfeet—the mysterious aliens whose accidental sightings had triggered the Rock Father mythology. And furthermore, that was the real reason for dropping bots everywhere—the government knew that the Bigfeet were secretly watching us, all over Luna, so the bots were counter-surveillance. But the Bigfeet were as skilled at avoiding our bots as they were at avoiding us. So that's why we hadn't caught any video of them yet. Besides, they probably had some kind of cloaking technology that made them invisible to our sensors. And so on.

Jang said that the bots were really about establishing a total-monitoring environment, because some of the people on Earth were terrified that Luna might someday declare independence. They were already convinced that the Loonies were secretly building a hidden civilization—"Invisible Luna." That's where all the cost overruns and inflated budgets were really going. And that's who really left the footprints.

Mariko, who normally didn't respond to even the wilder speculations, just rolled his eyes, and said, "Do the math. How much air, water, food, and energy does it take to sustain one body on Luna. The annual Lunar numbers have enough wiggle room for maybe twelve people, maybe fifteen, certainly no more than twenty. That's not enough for a real conspiracy."

"You think so? Even nineteen people can be a conspiracy—"

Mariko was sharp, he caught the historical reference, but he still shook his head. "That was a century ago. Things are different now. Everybody's implanted with locaters. Every moment is monitored, including us. And every monitor is synched. You can't pick your nose, you can't wipe your ass, you can't even make a baby on Luna without an audience."

"Ohell, you can't make a baby on Luna, even *with* an audience." That was Libby. "It's all male up here."

Jonah laughed. "—which is exactly the way you like it."

Jason added, "Why do you care? Are you planning to get pregnant?"

"Not with you—"

After the rest of the jokes died down, we talked about how all the old predictions about life on other planets had gotten so much so wrong. Rocklyn reminded us of a silly old movie, based on an even sillier old novel, from way before the age of colonization, where the author had described three untrained brothers bouncing across the surface of the moon in giant plastic bubbles. While it wasn't technologically impossible, the author had conveniently ignored a few things about dealing with the Lunar terrain—like radiation, heat, cold, solar blinding, headlights for areas of shadow, humidity within the bubbles, air refreshening, and so on. And those were just the obvious ones. Or maybe he'd just assumed that the readers would assume he'd thought of those things and didn't have to describe them.

After that, we speculated about what sports might be possible on Luna after the dome was finished. Assuming we had a large enough playing environment, what would one-sixth gee do to golf, football, baseball, volleyball, tennis, ping pong, and Frisbee? What about high-diving? And if we had large enough wings, would we really be able to fly? Maybe, if the air pressure was high enough. Rocklyn promised to do the math on that one. But it all depended on whether or not you could build a big enough interior space.

Luna already had a few domes, less than twenty, but none of them large enough to have enough space for any kind of a playing field, not even a tennis court. The largest dome on Luna was still less than a city block—the limiting factor wasn't the production cost of the dome, but filling it with enough air and water and soil to make it livable. Do the math yourself. Compute the volume of a hemisphere and how many packages of bottled air it takes to fill it.

That was the real challenge of Turtledome; when finished, the dome would enclose a space three kilometers in diameter. It would be huge. Big enough for a small forest, a lake, a meadow, and a couple of golf courses. With space left over for a few dozen football fields and baseball parks. Some people were already saying that filling it would be impossible—that Luna would never have a real "outdoors." Or whatever you wanted to call an environment safe enough to take your clothes off and go skinny-dipping.

But the real reason for Turtledome was much more important. The dome was intended as an inhabitable reservoir, a giant self-sustaining store of air and water and nitrogen. Her most important products would be soil and earthworms. Right now, most of the organic support and supplies still had to be imported from Terra, one cargo pod of air and water per day, per thousand inhabitants. Once there was a local sustainable supply, the cost of living on this rock would drop by twenty percent, or more. More important, once Luna could produce her own resources, she could be independent. She could be the architect of her own growth.

After two hours of lightly bouncing the trucks along the unglorious road, Rocklyn and Jonah relieved us. Mariko asked me if I wanted tea, I said yes and followed him to the back of the pod, where the galley and the lavatory were situated.

"I would have brought it to you," he said.

"I wanted to talk to you. Privately."

He made a face. There's no such thing as privacy. Not on Luna. And certainly not in a bus full of scouts.

"About last night—"

"Forget it," he said. He busied himself with the hot water, clumsily fumbling with the nozzle and the injection port of the mug. He was annoyed.

"I can't forget it."

"I can—"

"We're supposed to be buddies—"

"Only for a few more hours." He shoved the mug into my hands. A sudden bump pushed him against me for a moment. My heart bounced in my chest, I grabbed onto him—as much from instinct as desire. "Sorry," he said, embarrassed, and pushed away. He pulled open a cold-locker and grabbed a squeeze-bottle of milk. He popped the top, but before taking the first pull, he turned to me, "You want some?"

Wordless, I held out my mug. He pushed the spout into the socket, and gave me a couple of squirts. "That enough? Or you want more?"

"More, please."

A couple more squirts and he pulled out. It was the most intimate exchange we'd had yet.

"What?" he looked at me, puzzled, almost annoyed.

"How can you be so nice to me and so mean at the same time?"

"You're asking that of *me*? I should ask you the same thing."

With difficulty, I met his gaze. His expression was curious, but his eyes were hard. Finally, I managed to say, "I don't want you to hate me."

"I don't hate you," he said. But then he added three fatal words. "Actually, I'm indifferent." After a couple of sips of milk, he continued. "Just like you. You're a machine."

"I'm not indifferent," I said, tried to say—I croaked. "I'm not a machine. I just...." Oh, fuck. How do you tell someone something you don't even understand yourself?

He didn't wait for me to answer. He pushed past and back into the main cabin. I sipped my tea and shuddered. Too much milk.

There's this article I read, about this thing called maturity. According to some researchers, the natural hormones of adolescence are so strong that they overwhelm the functioning of the frontal lobes. What that means, is that you have no facility for critical thinking. The pubertal suppressants are supposed to counteract this effect, and I guess they do. The graphs in the article showed that the sublimation of sexual energy results in a 10-20 percent boost in applied intelligence, and a stability of perspective that many adults don't achieve until the exhaustion of old age. But some of the side effects included a decreased ability to bond, a retardation of social skills, and a higher proportion of gender identity confusion. Among other things. At least, I knew the technical reasons for what was wrong with me. And maybe Mariko as well. Maybe all of us. I wished I could open a door and just take a long bounce over the nearest dark hill.

I wouldn't be the first one to do that. According to everything I'd ever seen about Luna, it happened a lot. Too many times. Like two or three times a year—somebody would open an airlock without first putting on a starsuit. Or he'd put on a starsuit and just start bouncing in whatever direction he was pointed.

I guess sometimes that happened by accident. People still get starstruck, so enchanted by the never-changing wonder of Luna that they just forget to come back inside. But maybe, just as often, maybe it's deliberate. I'd read a lot of articles about it. We all did. It was part of our training. Luna is exhilarating—but when it's not exhilarating, it's depressing. It's a monotonous, gray and gritty wasteland. You get desperate for a bit of greenery, for a flower, for the sound of a dog barking or even a real wind. Most of all, you miss the fresh smells of spring, and the warm smells of summer, and the icy crisp bite of autumn. You miss the seasons.

In response to that, the Loonies say that they do too have seasons. Despair, Grief, Suicide, and Hell. Terrific.

Some of the doctors say it's because your internal clock misses its natural biological cycle, finally it breaks down, and you lose all sense of time. Everything just stretches away into blazing gray emptiness. So one day, you just put on your starsuit and head out the lock and go off in search of whatever is out there beyond this rill, beyond that crater, beyond the next near horizon, until you've gone past your point of safe return—and you no longer have enough air to make it back. Now that we were here, now that I was seeing it for myself, I could believe it. Why do people choose to live up here? Why did I want to?

I stared out the port and thought about nothing. There was certainly a lot of nothing to look at. And not a lot of words to describe it. After you've used up empty and barren and desolate, after you've said bright and dark and dazzling and grim—after you've said all that, you're pretty much done. Magnificent desolation. Period.

I wondered what it would be like to live here all the time. Being able to leap tall boulders at a single bound was fun, but it could also be as dangerous as it was exhilarating. And giving up blue skies for black was a whole other question; even the most mundane details of existence were different here. One-sixth gee affected the function and shape and construction of everything. Toilets. Ladders. Beds. Chairs. Even ceilings—permanent dwellings had foam ceilings, or the ceilings were carpeted with half-inflated air-bags. Think about it.

But those were the obvious things. Not-so-obvious, Luna might also be a great place to slowly starve to death.

As big as Luna was, did she really have the resources to sustain an independent civilization? Or was the cost of extricating those resources too high? With Terra looking over your shoulder, wouldn't it be a whole lot easier to just drop all the air and water you needed off the beanstalk?

Well, yes—and no. Eventually, you hit a ceiling, and this one wasn't padded. You can only lift so much. The beanstalk has a limited capacity, and somewhere in that number is the limit of Lunar growth—the amount of air and water that can be imported from Earth. So Luna has to develop its own resources, or forever be a satellite instead of a world.

Ultimately, it's all about process. That's what I thought about most—and that's what I was the best at. Everybody said that my meatware was overclocked. And even though they didn't say it where I could hear it, I knew they thought I had no real feelings either; because mostly I hardly ever said anything about how I felt. And that was mostly because I didn't trust most people with that information. So I concentrated on process. Because when I'm thinking about process, I'm not thinking about the *other* thing. So—process.

The Loonies could easily crack oxygen out of rocks, all they need is a little heat. The closest furnace is only 172 million kilometers away. Focus a large enough array of mirrors on the target zone and you can vaporize anything for its component elements.

Luna also had a sizable store of ice at its southern pole, and a little less at the north, and by the time that was used up, we'd be catching comets and bringing them down.

But as good as those plans were, at the moment, it was still cheaper and easier to deliver the stuff direct from the Big Blue Brother, dropping unmanned cargo pods onto empty gray deserts, of which Luna had an endless supply. The pods could be put down right on the customer's doorstep.

So there was no incentive to invest in Luna's own resources. The limiting factor wasn't the cost of production. Power is free on Luna. But if you were cracking air at the equator or melting ice at the pole—you still had to deliver the product to the consumers, some of whom might be half a world away. It was the cost of transport that made Luna an economic hostage. Terra could prefab cheap cargo pods, send them up the elevator, and toss them across for a lot less per package than it would cost to truck the same cargo across a few hundred klicks of grit.

It wasn't just the cost of trucks and fuel. It was also the larger job of surveying safe roads across an area larger than North America. And you'd need trained drivers too, at least until you laid out a route for the bots to follow. Taken altogether, the investment looked prohibitive.

And that's why the Turtledome reservoir was critical to Luna—because, it was the first important olive out of the bottle. Once finished, it would be convenient to half of Luna's northern hemisphere, and would function as a source of life-sustaining services to nearly a third of Luna's permanent bases.

Turtledome operating at capacity will be a biosphere. Anyone within a few hundred klicks—would be able to drive up with a train of pods and trade garbage and sewage and raw waste for clean water and fresh soil.

But right now, most of Luna's primary organic reserve was piling up unused, sealed in plastic bags, and stacked up high behind various small stations everywhere. The growing mountains of trash were an embarrassment to the new settlements, but they didn't have refiners on site to process the waste into useful fertilizers and fuel. Or they didn't have the distillation equipment to recover all the water. Most of them didn't even have functioning farms yet. So Luna's most valuable resource—her garbage—sat unused.

Finished, Turtledome will be the largest processing facility on Luna—but the dome itself was only part of the solution. It wouldn't be practical without a cheap and easy way for Loonies to transport their resources to and from. They needed the cable lines too.

It's all process. And I was determined to stay focused on process.

As part of our training for this mission, we spent a month grinding the numbers on Luna's economy. There wasn't a lot of pie in this sky, unless you baked it yourself. And you had to bring your own bakery.

The immediate answer would be trains of trucks—you put wheels on six cargo pods, and pull them behind a seventh. This would work for some stations, the ones that were close enough, but it wasn't a long-term solution. As an economic entity, Luna was still ranked somewhere between "undeveloped" and "impoverished." Luna's trucks were still needed for too many other jobs, much more immediate, and she needed most of her cargo pods for housing and labs. Even if she could convert enough pods into trucks, there wouldn't be enough drivers, and even if they let the trucks drive themselves, they'd use up almost as much resources making the trip as they would bring back.

Don't even talk about pipelines. You don't even have to grind the numbers to see why. A pipeline requires a processing plant at the sending end to reduce the product to a sludge-like consistency, and pumping stations along the way to keep the product moving. Too many moving parts. Maintenance would be a bitch. And you'd need one set of pipelines for pumping sewage in and another for pumping air and water and soil-sludge out. And then you'd need a new set of lines for every station you wanted to service. No. An impossible engineering job. An even more impossible investment.

Somewhere in there, a Hong Kong company suggested a light rail line. In one-sixth gee, you could have a transport system that was lighter and faster than its Terran counterparts, and you could use it for transporting people and other kinds of cargo as well. But even with those advantages, the cost of building such a transport system—even using bots—was still higher than ten thousand trucks. I never thought that grinding numbers could be fun; but the answers we got sometimes surprised us.

It was a Swiss company (of course) that demonstrated the feasibility of a network of cable cars. The towers could be assembled in Earth orbit and dropped anywhere on the Lunar surface they were needed. One-sixth gee was the advantage; the towers could be taller and lighter than their Terran counterparts and still strong enough to carry the load. If they were tall enough, they could be spaced ten or twenty kilometers apart. You wouldn't have to carve roads or lay track and you could create a vast transportation network in years instead of decades. And a key component of the system already existed—the gondolas. Every gondola on the line would be a reconfigured transport pod, the same way that trucks and shelters were converted from pods after landing. A steady stream of gondolas would create a de facto pipeline for humans, cargo, and raw materials, wherever Luna wanted to string cable.

Best of all, instead of going around otherwise impassable mountains and craters, the cable cars could go over or across—incidentally providing some spectacular access to terrain that humans couldn't get to any other way. So…that was one of the big reasons why we tossed bots out the window every thirty minutes—so they could roam the surface looking for what passed for bedrock on Luna. An optimal tower site required a strong place to stand, access to sunlight, and a convenient source of Lunar dust—for making Luna-crete.

The interesting thing—after we finished grinding all the numbers—was that the cargo capabilities of the lines would end up being far more important to the Lunar economy than the ease of travel they would provide to humans. As Senior Whitlaw had pointed out, more than once, humans tend to be anthro-centric; which means, we take everything personally. "If I tell you that the sun is going to burn out in five billion years, the first thing you're going to think is, 'What's in it for me?'"

And he was right. Here we were, on the threshold of the second greatest frontier in human history—Mars had the number one spot—and it didn't matter how much I tried to focus on process, because after all that, still the only thing I could really think about was the bulge in Mariko Bailey's pants. What's in it for me? I was certain the answer was nothing. I felt like the guy in the dirty joke who smelled so bad that even the sex-bot refused.

One of the things the trainers had told us, over and over: "You're not going on an adventure. The last thing you want is an adventure. Do you know what the definition of an adventure is? It's when things get interesting because your life is at risk. We don't want you putting yourselves or your buddies at risk. We want you so well trained that you *don't* have adventures. We don't want your trip to be exciting. We want it to be productive. The only excitement you want to have up there should be the satisfaction of a job well done."

But here I was, distracting myself (again) with stuff that should have been resolved long before we got to Ecuador and rode the beanstalk up. I'm supposed to be a genius. I'm supposed to know how to figure this stuff out. I'm supposed to be…well, like…a hero. So what was so wrong with me that I couldn't focus on the job in front of me—

Oh fuck.

I touched my communicator. The buddy-channel. "Mariko, I need you. Please come back to the galley."

In the forward cabin, I heard movement. A few seconds later, he stuck his head in. "What is it?"

"Check my readings for me?"

He looked annoyed, but he complied. He studied my chart on his personal display. Then he grunted. "Well, I s'pose that explains it. Some of it, anyway."

"What?" I already knew the answer, but I needed to hear him say it.

"You're going through puberty."

"But what about the pubertal suppressants—?"

He was silent a moment more, paging through the displays. "Um. Maybe they've cut out. Maybe it's something to do with your transition to male—a translation effect. It's probably temporary. Only for a week or two."

"Oh, no, no, nooooo."

"It's not as bad as you've heard. Some of it is even fun."

"But not *heeerre*. Not *nowww*."

Dispassionately, he asked, "Have you started having erections?"

"No," I shuddered. "And I'm not going to. I already decided that. It's just too—you know, icky." The whole subject was embarrassing. I was very sorry that I'd paged him.

"Um." He lowered his head toward mine, he put his hand on my shoulder, he lowered his voice. "You do know, don't you—sometimes they happen by themselves. You don't really have that much control."

It was too much. I started to cry. That old thing about big girls not crying didn't count anymore. I was a boy now, and boys cried all the time. Or did I have that backward? Who cares? I cried. Not hard, but enough. I don't know if he pulled me into his arms, or if I threw myself at him, but somehow I ended up with him holding me, patting my back, and comforting me, and I didn't even know why I was so upset or what I was upset about.

I stopped, pulled away, sniffled—he wiped my nose with a tissue. Kind of like a big brother. I looked across at him, suddenly me again. "Do you really think I'm a machine?"

He shrugged. "All you talk about, all you ever think about, is the tech stuff. You never tell jokes, you never say anything unless it's about the job—"

"I have to. I don't want to fail—"

"Nobody does." He wiped my face again, even though it didn't need it. "This is the first human thing I've ever seen you do. "It's almost cute—"

My face felt suddenly hot—

"Even cuter when you blush."

"Stop that—" I felt like I was going to cry again.

He grinned, delighted. It was the first smile he'd ever meant just for me, and it was so intense, I almost passed out.

"You're doing that on purpose!" I accused.

"Doing what?" he asked innocently.

"That!" He had one of his huge hands in the small of my back, gently tickling me with his fingers. "You're playing with my hormones."

"Yeah," he admitted. And lowered his voice to a whisper. "And you like it. You really like it." But he stopped. "There," he said. "You see? You can be human. If you want to be."

"No, I can't—" I said it automatically, without thinking. "I can't be efficient *and* human at the same time."

"Sure you can. It just takes practice." He gave my nose a cursory wipe. He held me until I finished sniffling, finished wiping my face. "You feeling better now? Ready to come join the rest of us?"

I nodded, then— "Wait? Shouldn't I tell the Seniors about…you know?"

He laughed. "They already know. Everybody does. Relax. We've all been through it. We're on your side. Come on, 'Little Brainiac.'" That was the first time he'd ever called me by my nickname. It almost felt good. Reluctantly, I followed him back into the forward cabin. At least my heartbeat was finally returning to something like normal.

Nobody said anything as I took my seat. Not much of a seat, just a flat shelf that unfolded from the wall; but that's another one of those things about Luna—the furniture. Furniture is about gravity. The less gravity you have, the less furniture you need. Something like that. I forget where I read it.

The ride to Turtledome was long. We drove straight through the night—what would have been the night if we were on Earth, but was still night on Luna and would be for another few shifts. Splat-down was 160 kilometers from Turtledome, as the crow flies, if there were crows on Luna that could fly in vacuum, but we weren't driving in a straight line; the marked route weaved through a minefield of craters, all sizes, and there were some up- and downslopes we had to navigate as well; so it was an estimated 36 hour drive. We staggered our shifts and drove straight through. Halfway there, Shanghai Station passed local monitoring over to Turtledome, so we gave a cheer of self-congratulation. We'd been on Luna almost a full Earth day and hadn't killed ourselves yet.

Theoretically, we could have landed closer to Turtledome than the Sea of Screams, there were a lot of other optimal sites; but the terrain closer in was considered too rocky and too uneven for safe landings. Plus, I think, they wanted us to have a couple of days experiencing Luna on our own, before we arrived at the dome. Something about getting our "Luna-legs" before we were in a place to do any serious damage. Just long enough to get bored with the novelty of pouring coffee out of a cup and being able to catch it in the same cup before it splashed across the deck. Nobody needs a bunch of playful puppies bouncing around the worksite. So this was our chance to play—to get some of the excitement out of our systems.

The Seniors decided we should keep our current buddies for another shift, which sort of pleased me. Mariko and I exchanged a glance and he didn't look unhappy either. Maybe he was feeling big-brotherly toward me, which was kind of strange because I was 18 months older than him—but he'd been a boy for a lot longer than me, so maybe it wasn't all that strange. I dunno. I could tell my thoughts were scattered. When I had a job to focus on, I was okay—but as soon as I went into downtime, I would get very conscious of feelings that I didn't have a name for yet.

Mariko and I had two more driving shifts before we arrived at Turtledome. The terrain had gotten progressively rougher, and by the time of our last shift, most of it was upslope. Luna isn't perfectly round, nothing is, but the little gray pearl is a lopsided mess, with mascon bulges on the side facing Terra, and other deformations leftover from a couple billion years of cosmic smackdown. You can't really see it from space, you have to drive the surface and experience it. The land isn't flat, it's lumpy.

Ahead, the terrain tilts up toward nothing. Behind, it rolls down into the same dark empty. Except when it's the other way around.

The horizon is always too close, the edges are too sharp, you get the feeling something is lurking just behind this rock or that hill. You can't help it, you're descended from creatures that used to be lunch for larger creatures. Large open spaces are intimidating. It is a magnificent and ultimately terrifying desolation. Beautiful and ugly at the same time. Or maybe, as my Gramma said, that's just me looking in the mirror.

But finally, we rolled up a long slope, forever to the rocky top—the dark gray lip of the hill rolled away as we approached. We crested and a marvelous view spread out before us, all sparkling and wonderful.

Turtledome Station.

A bright sprawl of light and pattern etched across a great curving darkness. It looked like someone had dumped a giant bag of miscellaneous technology into a giant bowl, scattering little pieces across the landscape in a seemingly haphazard jumble of towers and lights and machines. Floodlit fields of machinery dotted the bottom of the crater, spider-like gantries and cranes loomed like invaders, mechanical mantises preying on the dozers and excavators and trucks. There were clustered installations, webs of scaffolding, and scattered cargo pods everywhere; some of the pods were lit up, people were living in them. And there were greenhouses—lots of greenhouses, growing food and producing air for a growing population. And of course, domes, lots of domes, all kinds and colors—*bright* colors—and bigger than the ones at Shanghai. Everything was connected to everything else by plastic tubes that snaked everywhere across the dirty gray surface—inflatable tunnels, all lit from the inside. It was a Lunar fairyland technological fantasy.

We saw trucks everywhere, making their way between the various structures. There were dozens of bot-piloted trains, each one glittering with light to stand out against the darkness. Most of them were painted in garish shades. They crept across the crater floor and worked their way up the vast sides of its walls. The trails were dozed and marked with orange cones. From here, the trucks looked like cartoon ants following pheromone trails faintly etched in color.

Turtledome crater was three kilometers across. And deep. Bigger and deeper than Barringer Meteor Crater in Arizona. It was visible from Earth with a good pair of binoculars and a tripod, though a telescope would be better. With a telescope, you could even see the glitter of floodlights within the darkness. We'd done it more than once. We'd been closely following the progress of construction for years, even more intensely the last 18 months. There wasn't a spot on the floor of the bowl we weren't already intimately familiar with—at least, in theory.

And now we were perched high on the rim, overlooking all of it.

Seeing it laid out beneath us like a glittering black picnic basket, I don't know how anybody else reacted, but a bright thrill of recognition and fear and overwhelm flooded up inside of me. It was another terrifying reminder that all of this was frighteningly real. I felt a painful pressure inside my pants, finally I stopped pretending and shifted around, slipped my hand into my pants and adjusted it—*oh no!* And then, to make it worse, Mariko saw and nodded. He leaned over, touched my shoulder, whispered, "It's okay, baby boy. You're not the only one." But no, that didn't make it any better.

Before we could call hello, a voice came from the dashboard speaker. "Elephant One, we see you." And a second after that, "Elephant Two, we have you as well. Welcome to Turtledome. We have hot soup and showers waiting." That received cheers from all of us.

Getting down to the bottom of the crater wasn't hard, just intimidating. The dozers had carved wide roads spiraling all the way around and down to the floor of the basin. It wasn't dangerous, but it required close attention on the part of the driver. You had a sloping wall to your right, and a daunting emptiness to your left. It took us four hours to wind our way down, including the three rest stops we took. There were turnouts every klick or so, and if a pod-train was coming up, you wanted to pull off to the side to let it pass. Most of the pod-trains were carrying workers and supplies to the tower construction sites, where they'd stay for a week at a time.

Almost immediately after we descended past the uneven rim of the crater, we saw the demarcation line where the shelf was eventually going to be installed—the foundation of the dome that would someday cap this bowl. A line of bots was patiently carving a deep sloping trench into the shallow slope of the rim. We passed one crew that was installing an anchor-strut. It didn't look big enough to me, but I'm not an engineer.

Most people on Earth think that Lunar domes will be held up by the air inside. Well, yes—eventually. But first you have to build the dome. And you have to hold it up while you build it. The trick is to build the dome like a suspension bridge—hang it from cables. You could do it with three towers, but Turtledome was so large, they were double-engineering everything. They were putting up six towers, spaced equidistantly around the rim. When the towers were complete, they'd string a vast spiderweb of cables and lattices between them—using almost enough cable to build a Lunar beanstalk. And then, when the web was complete, they'd turn the weaver-bots loose. The bots would crawl back and forth across the gigantic web, slowly, painstakingly laying down nets of carbon fibers, then broad sheets of foam-filled honeycomb-polymer, then more fibers and more polymer, over and over again, until they had tented the entire crater with a meter-thick, self-sealing surface. It would be a semi-rigid tent—springy and solid at the same time. It would be puncture-proof and self-repairing. If the sealant hardened properly, if the glue held, if the tent was airtight, then the crater would have a working dome. If not, they'd have a dome needing constant maintenance and repair—and they were already developing the tools for that.

For additional safety, the inside of the dome would be partitioned into seven distinct habitats—a large hexagonal central district, surrounded by six equal-sized trapezoidal chambers. Each of these neighborhoods would be its own airtight, self-maintaining domain, each one dedicated to a specific primary function, but also capable of long-term, exportable self-sufficiency. The design specifications for the habitats required that every individual section be able to provide life support for the total population of the dome, if it became necessary; like if a catastrophic meteor storm were to hit the dome and puncture the seals of the other six habitats, the remaining one would still be a safe sanctuary for the survivors. And if a disaster bigger than that were to occur—well, no physical structure could be built strong enough to withstand a disaster that big.

But it would take years to produce enough air to fill the dome. It would take at least eighteen months to fill a single section, even pressurized to the equivalent of 7,000 meters altitude on Earth. Air-cracking was another one of those limiting factors—how many plants you could build, how much oxygen they could produce; not to mention the issue of nitrogen and various trace elements. Nitrogen can be manufactured, sort of, but the process is energy-intensive.

When everything was finished, when all the separate sections were operational, and when the dome was lit from within, the whole thing would look like a giant turtle sprawled helplessly on its back, with its legs—the towers—sticking up in the air. The head of the turtle was the main access tower for the cable car line, situated in a smaller crater breaking the rip at the north; the tail was the secondary access, following a twisted rill to the south. "Turtledome" was only a nickname, but nobody on Luna called the settlement by its real name.

There was some controversy about that. Some people felt the person who the dome was going to be named after hadn't really earned the honor, but had taken most of the credit for the work of others—most of whom had mostly been overlooked or forgotten, like Coon and Fontana. But there were others who said it was appropriate to honor the dream, if not the man identified as the architect. One blogger had written that either way it was still appropriate because both the dome and its namesake were large and round and safely in the ground.

Apparently, naming stuff on Luna is almost always a political battle. People on Earth say, "Well, it's *our* moon, we should get to name our craters whatever we want, honoring all the great men of history." But people who live on Luna have a much more compelling argument, "It's our *home*, and we're going to honor the men *and women* who made it happen, who built it, who lived and died here." (With the implied, "If you don't like it, you'll have to come up *here* to change it.") And then, to complicate the matter even more, there are all those other people on Earth who think that God wants them to name all the craters after prophets and saints. Some of these craters have six different names; it depends on your religion.

And that's another part of Loonie society that's really different. On Earth, people can afford to have imaginary companions who rescue them from tornadoes and send hurricanes and floods to punish their enemies. Most Loonies leave their imaginary friends on Earth, before they ride the beanstalk. They have to. If you're in trouble on Luna, help isn't coming from anywhere else—you have to help yourself. The best kind of help is being so well-prepared you don't get in trouble.

I guess that kind of thinking is too hard for most Terrans. That's why so many folks flunk the emigration exams. Most of the scouts, almost ninety percent of those who apply for Lunar training, don't make it. Terries don't get it—it's a whole other way of thinking and the shift from there to here is such a break in their reality, they can't always make the leap. The best they can do is pretend they understand.

Like the dome itself. It almost wasn't a turtle, it was almost a mouse—until they figured out that the ears were really lungs. I guess I should explain that. During the Lunar day, the sun scorches the bright side, so the air in Turtledome will heat up and expand. So for two weeks, for 336 consecutive hours, the air pressure inside the dome will steadily increase. During the Lunar night, the reverse will happen—the air will cool, the pressure will drop. Do the math. It'll flex the dome enough to shatter its structural integrity.

So the dome needs a pressure valve, actually two of them. During the Lunar day, you pump expanded air out into a large inflatable; during the Lunar night, you pump it back into the dome, and that's how you keep the internal pressure of the big dome equalized.

Turtledome crater has two smaller adjoining craters along its northeastern side that provide perfect staging sites for its lungs. One crater is just under a klick in diameter, the other is just a little bit over. From above, they appear almost the same size. Now, if you could light up all three craters at once, you'd have a pretty fair approximation of a certain, very famous, corporate trademark. So that very big, very famous corporation was pretty keen on sponsoring the development. There was even talk of putting theme parks in the ears. But that meant they'd have to have the two adjoining craters domed and lit as well. And that would pretty much defeat their usefulness as lungs; and they'd have the same expansion/contraction problems as the main dome. And they'd still need to build lungs, only now for three domes.

And later on, when Turtledome was a fully functioning habitat with a real lake, the lungs would also be used as heat-sinks. Water heated almost to boiling during the Lunar day would be pumped out into the lungs and replaced by cold water stored in underground tanks; that would help keep Turtledome's temperature down. During the Lunar night, they'd do the reverse, pumping hot water back in to help keep the dome warm. There's a lot of engineering needed to make a habitat work, and you can't cheat the laws of physics. (The best you can do is negotiate with them a little.)

The big corporation's engineers understood that. Engineers always understand engineering. But the executives of the company don't understand engineering; they only understand marketing. So they blinked in confusion and kept saying, "Why not?" And, "Why can't you?" And, "If we're paying for it, we get to decide—" And the Loonies just kept on explaining why not and why they couldn't and why it would be a waste of money to even try until the whole deal fell apart. And that's why the turtle will have lungs and the mouse will have no ears.

It's all process.

And—I guess I really am a Brainiac. I guess it's true that the pubertal suppressants create a sublimation of energy into other pursuits. But I like knowing how things work, I like understanding and explaining. I like the whole process of putting things together to produce a result. I like the feeling of control—that I can make things happen, that I can plan and design and build—and make even a little part of the universe work the way I think it should.

And yeah, I admit it—I don't understand dancing. Two people holding each other and walking around in time to music. I don't understand why people sing to each other. Or even why anyone would want to share a bed with anyone else—all that grunting and farting and shoving for space. All of which is my way of admitting, I really don't understand people. That's why I like machines. Machines are understandable. People aren't.

Like why don't the trips see how beautiful Mariko really is? And why do I see it and nobody else? And why don't I get it about women? Or men, for that matter? The whole man/woman thing, or man/man, or woman/woman—do people *really* want to do that stuff? And why? Isn't masturbation a lot less messy, a lot less troublesome?

The last time I tried to have this conversation with someone, they looked at me like I wasn't from any known planet. The best answer I ever got was, "You'll understand when you're older." Well, I'm older now, and I still don't understand.

We finally rolled down onto the floor of the crater and found ourselves on Broadway, so named because it was wide enough to pull a six-car pod train around in a U-turn and still leave plenty of room for two more lanes of traffic in each direction. Orange cones delimited the actual boulevard. We took Broadway southeast, through Times Square, until we hit Vine, then we turned south and drove for a klick and a half until we got to Hollywood Boulevard. We'd be staying at the Turtledome Hilton—no relation to the actual hotel chain—just a local name applied to a cluster-phuque of sandbag huts used for transients like us. It was walking (bouncing) distance from Turtledome Center, a half klick away.

Turtledome Center was a towering lacework of lights and antennas, sitting atop a glittering tinkertoy assemblage of sausage-shaped pods, connecting tubes, and inflatable chambers. It was the base of the whole operation here, and it was installed at Oxford Circus, where Via Appia collided with the Champs Elysees. On the opposite side of the crater, the main storage and construction depots were located in the Ginza and Tienanmen Square.

By comparison, the Hilton didn't look like much—it was the Lunar equivalent of a mud hovel tenement. But just the same, having your hotel at the corner of Hollywood and Vine is a lot more exciting than staying at the corner of Mickey Drive and Goofy Way. Nobody was complaining.

We were still 18 hours away from dawn, so the whole crater was on the ass-end of stored power. For obvious reasons, Turtledome Authority doesn't like using up hydrogen or methane unless they have to. The fuel cells are held for emergencies and the renewable resources are used up first, so most of the power at night comes from batteries and fly-wheels and Stirling engines tapping into stored heat. But at the rate that Turtledome's population keeps expanding, the need for power grows faster than the hardware can be fabbed or imported.

And it's not just power, it's everything. Air, water, food, medical supplies, starsuits, ancillary life support gear, everything necessary to support a single human being—you can put a man on the moon, no problem; it's keeping him there that's expensive.

Okay, this is the bottom line of Lunar economics. The limiting factor isn't the machinery to get folks up here. And it isn't the cost of finding and training qualified people either. No. The limiting factor is mainte-nance—the supply line doesn't have enough bandwidth.

Here's how Whitlaw explained it to us when we were training. He told us that the Turtledome project was likely to take thirty years to com-plete—that's if it stayed exactly on schedule, which simply wasn't going to happen. Ask any bridge builder. I asked why they didn't just send up more people.

"No, that won't work," he said. "Imagine a very tall building. Imagine you have only one elevator that goes all the way to the top. It takes fifteen minutes to load the elevator, fifteen minutes to ride it to the top, fifteen minutes to unload it, and fifteen minutes to bring it back down again. If you have ten people living on the top floor, you only need one elevator a trip per day to supply them with food and water. The elevator is tied up for an hour, you can send it up at three in the morning and not inconve-nience anyone. The elevator stays available for everyone else.

"Now imagine that you have a hundred people living on the top floor, you need ten trips to supply them. That's ten hours that the elevator is tied up. Now it's starting to be a problem. You have to schedule your trips throughout the day, still leaving time for others.

"But what if you want to put a thousand people on the top floor? You can't. The most you can put up there is 240, and the elevator is busy 24/7. You can't even afford downtime for maintenance or people start missing meals upstairs. And God help all of you if there's an emergency. So somewhere between 100 and 200 people, there's your limit in that circumstance. If you want to put more people on the top floor, you can either build another elevator—or the people upstairs need to make their own power and grow their own food. There's a limit to how many elevators you can put in a building, so there's really only one answer."

And that's why we had to wait until sunrise for our showers. But we did get the hot soup.

The Hilton didn't have a hut big enough for all of us to gather at the same time, but they did have an inflatable they used as both a meeting hall and a dining room. I have to admit, it was kind of spooky sitting on the moon with nothing but plastic between us and vacuum. But the Ranger, his name was Hunt, who led us into the dining room, assured us that it was perfectly safe; they hardly ever had punctures. And the advantage of an inflatable this big—the size of a small house—was that even if you did get a pinpoint puncture, the air wouldn't go out in an explosive rush; it would still shoot out, but slowly enough that there would be time for most of the people in the bag to get out safely. No need to worry.

"*Most* of the people?" Libby asked.

"Yes, that's what we project," Hunt said deadpan.

"Has it ever happened?"

"Are you volunteering to test it?"

"Can I wear my starsuit?"

"Then that wouldn't be a real test, would it?"

Dinner was hot tomato-vegetable soup, as promised, and homemade bread. Plus fresh salad and steamed carrots and broccoli; the main course was soy-patties in tomato sauce. Yeah, we noticed. But the entire meal was from the Hilton's own farms—nothing from Earth at all. The bread was different than we were used to; it was sourdough, but it was so light and feathery we called it cotton-candy bread, and aerogel bread, and ghost-bread, and bread-impersonator. That's because on Luna, even when you adjust the recipe, bread still rises three or four times as high as it does on Earth. It ends up so light, you can't even butter it unless you soften the butter to the consistency of pudding. But it was still pretty good anyway.

We found out the Hilton was one of the few private establishments here at Turtledome. Hunt had been up here too long—rehabilitation for Earth gravity would have taken years. Instead, he took over the "hospitality suites" and tended his own greenhouse, providing local services for the construction companies. It worked out well for both sides. The bread was his own recipe; in his spare time, he was working on a Lunar cookbook. "You'll never get bread like this on Earth, not even if you bake it upside-down."

For dessert, we had fresh berries and syrup over pink cotton-candy ghost-cake. There were chefs on Terra who would have cried to see how fluffy a Lunar cake could be. It was like eating a cloud. Later on, we found out that Hunt could bake heavier breads and cakes if he wanted to, but apparently that first night he was subtly reminding us just how different things really were up here.

It was a perfect moment. We were celebrating the completion of the first step of our adventure, congratulating ourselves for arriving safely at Turtledome. We felt like we'd accomplished something, and we were already looking forward to the next step. It was a perfect moment—until the argument broke out.

It was Jasmine and Libby, of course. Jasmine had been in the other truck, Libby had ridden with us, so they hadn't had any real opportunity to strike sparks until now—when Whitlaw accidentally, or maybe accidentally-on-purpose, assigned Libby to Mariko as buddies for the next shift. Jasmine protested that this was out of rotation, and he was supposed to be Libby's buddy for the next shift—and that's when the trips snorted and laughed, and that just made Jasmine angrier and more insistent—but Hunt interrupted harshly. "This is Luna," he said. "Deal with it."

Right. The short version: Luna doesn't care what you want, doesn't care what you feel, doesn't care what you think—Luna just doesn't care. Deal with it. If you deal with it, you breathe, you eat, you survive. If you don't—well, that's another way of dealing with it too. Luna doesn't care.

And the really silly part about the whole thing was that it wasn't about anything at all—until it was about everything. We were having another of those endless adolescent speculations about sex, except we weren't talking about sex, we were talking about everything all *around* sex, so even though we weren't talking about sex, we really were talking about sex. You have to be going through puberty to get it, and not everybody does—Rocklyn, for instance, is permanently neotonic. Not everybody wants to go through puberty. According to the news, almost a fourth of the population of Terra has chosen or will choose to be permanently asexual. Maybe that's a good thing, maybe it isn't, but the Population Authority encourages it, and they're projecting a population plateau sometime in the next two decades. I've thought about it myself.

The argument started innocently enough. Jorge was sitting opposite me, he glanced over at Mariko, then turned back to me and made a not-very-subtle remark about how this trip was turning into a terrific opportunity for some old-fashioned male-bonding.

Mariko's gaze flicked across to me, then quickly back to his cake. I could almost hear him thinking, "Don't react. Don't buy into it."

I didn't have to. Jason and Jonah chimed in immediately, had they set this up beforehand, or were they just naturally stupid? Or did they just seek out opportunities to stir the shit whenever they could, because they couldn't stand being bored? My Gramma used to say that boredom is just evidence that you can't stand to be alone with yourself; people who like themselves don't get bored. I had to think about that one for a bit. She also said that people who like to stir the shit usually end up licking the spoon.

Jonah said, "I think male-bonding is just sublimated sexuality. What do you think, Jason?"

Jason shrugged, his usual performance of non-committal detachment. "Isn't *everything* sublimated sexuality?"

"Well, see, that's my point," Jonah said, "Why do we all have to be male for this trip? Yeah, I know about the plumbing thing, but come on, that's really not that big a problem—is it, Shan?"

I shook my head, shrugged, pretended to be more interested in a particularly bright berry stuck inside a cloud of cake. "Dunno."

But escape wasn't going to be that easy. Jorge picked up the conversational ball and dribbled it around my head. "I think it's because they want to turn us all monosexual. Of course, that's not that big a turn-around for Jasmine. She's already there. Aren't you?"

Jasmine looked annoyed. "Don't ask me. Ask Shan." Everyone's attention flicked immediately to me.

I was already turning red. "Um, actually," I flustered, "I haven't thought that much about it."

Jonah snorted. "Yeah, right."

Mariko interrupted then. He glanced toward Jasmine. "The way I understand it—" he said dryly. "The real point of having us experience both sides of the sexual equation is so that we can escape the simplex personality model engendered (pun intended) by single-sex psychology. Transition provides opportunities to experience complex, even multi-plex gender perspectives, thereby creating a wider empathic model of human behavior for the individual." He stopped, then looked directly at the trips. "In other words, it's about social skills. Something all of us could learn—" He stirred his coffee (Lunar-grown, of course) and lifted it to take a sip, prematurely popping the lid. Unfortunately, he hadn't really gotten his Luna-legs yet, and a dollop of coffee went floating up in front of him, splashing him first in the face, and then splattering down the front of his shirt and all over the table as well. So that was the end of all serious discussion for a while. I passed Mariko all the paper towels in front of me and then bounced to the galley-wall, looking for a towel. So I missed the transition from clumsiness to jealousy. Apparently, I wasn't the only one trying to mop him down. Libby had been sitting on the other side of Mariko—

—and when I got back, Libby had his hands full of paper towels and Mariko as well, "—just a big mess, I told you Shan was off the rails—" and Jasmine was screaming incoherently—not at Mariko, *at Libby*. And that's when it all suddenly made sense. Libby liked Mariko too. Libby was *jealous* of me—? And Jasmine was jealous! Jasmine and Libby—? Of course. That explained everything. And I felt like a triple-ass for not figuring it out before.

Puberty is hell. Especially when it's delayed for a few years, and then explodes messily all over everything. That was the real mess.

Fuck.

When we finally pried everyone apart—have you ever had a fight in one-sixth gee? People really do bounce off the walls, and a few of us even hit the ceiling once or twice. In the inflatable, it would have been fun—except with all the yelling, it wasn't. It was scary. We knew the walls couldn't rip, but who wanted to take chances?

When we finally pried everyone apart, two of the tables were bro-ken—they were easily reparable, most Lunar furniture was, but the evening was effectively over. Senior Cheung wasn't happy. Neither was Senior Whitlaw. We had not made a good first impression on our hosts. Whitlaw and Hunt went back down into one of the adjoining huts for what was supposed to be a private discussion—but we could hear most of it anyway. Hunt was angry with Whitlaw for bringing a bunch of unruly, untrained, unprofessional, *feral dirtsiders* to a high-pressure construction site, and how the flaming fuck did we manage to go for eighteen months of training without learning how to control ourselves, and furthermore, we were the worst bunch of fuckups he'd ever seen, and for a while there, it sounded like we were going to be turned around and sent back to Earth immediately.

"They can't do that!" and "We just got here!" were insufficient responses. But all of us were shouting in protest now. Yeah, we knew we'd behaved badly, but couldn't we at least have a second chance? Now that we're already here? We've worked so hard! It was only a stupid mistake! And of course, the inevitable, "The rest of us didn't do anything!" and "We tried to stop them!" This went on for several minutes until it became obvious that no one cared. Luna didn't care. We petered out.

Cheung glanced off to the other room. He just shook his head sadly, "'Sorry,' is not an eraser."

A moment later, Hunt came back, followed by Whitlaw. They both looked grim. Oh, shit. And we hadn't even unpacked.

Whitlaw spoke first. "I'm embarrassed by your behavior. I'm disappointed in all of you. Whatever you've got going on, handle it." He glanced to Hunt.

"That's all?" Hunt asked.

"That's all I need to say," Whitlaw replied.

Hunt shrugged. Okay.

He cleared his throag and looked around at us. When he finally did speak, it was with enormous deliberation. "Luna doesn't care," he said. "Neither do I. I do *not* care if you want to risk your own lives. But I *do* care about you risking the lives of everybody else working here in the crater. Your mission is cancelled. I'm not going to baby-sit you. Neither will anyone else. You're going home."

He waited until we stopped. "Yes, it is too fair," he said. "What the fuck do you think we're doing up here? Luna demands consciousness. You were supposed to be trained, but you arrived here still acting like blue-sky zombies, bouncing around in a blue-sky trance, just a bunch of fucking tourists. We can't afford that here. We're not baby-sitters. We need professional behavior. Apparently, your seniors didn't get their jobs done—because you're still just a bunch of spoiled, hormone-infused adolescents. All of you. There's no place for that on this worksite. And I want you gone." Then he added, "But here's the bad news. Bad news for me, that is. Transportation to the dust-off site won't be available for at least a week, maybe three. So you're stuck here until we can create an alternative."

He took a breath. "Don't relax yet. And wipe those stupid smiles off your faces. Here's the first lesson of Luna, 'Nobody breathes for free. Nobody eats for free.' You're still going to work for your bread. There's some shitwork that needs to be done, that nobody else has had the time to do. You can do that. But if there's another incident like this, the next job you'll get will be digging your own graves—"

I didn't think he heard Jorge's whisper. *"He's just saying that to scare us—"* But he whirled around and said, "I'm not kidding about the graves. If you doubt me, look up the charter. The Commanding Officer of this operation has the same authority as the captain of a ship. We have the legal authority to shove any one of you out the nearest airlock—or the whole sorry pack if we feel like it. I don't need any reason more compelling than 'freeloader.'"

"But you wouldn't—" Jonah started to say. "I mean, there'd be protests all over Terra."

"Probably," agreed Hunt. "But you'd still be dead. And we'd be back on schedule. We're Loonies. We don't listen to Terra. We listen to Luna." He turned and left.

Jason made a face at Jonah and whispered, *"Yeah, we're Loonies—"*

"Knock it off," said Whitlaw, so quiet and so deadly that the room went instantly silent. "Mariko, go change into a clean jumpsuit. The rest of you, here's your permanent buddy assignments. Until further notice. We're putting you with people you can pretend to get along with. Libby, you'll buddy up with Mariko—"

"No," said Libby. "I'm staying with Jasmine."

Jasmine looked startled. Whitlaw's face was unreadable. He blinked twice. Maybe nobody had ever defied him before. "We'll talk—" he said.

"There's nothing to talk about," Libby replied. "My buddy needs me. This is what I choose."

Whitlaw nodded slowly, as if sorting it all out. "All right." He turned to me. "Shan, you'll buddy up with Mariko again. Apparently, he's the only one who can stand you. And vice versa." He'd never spoken to me that way before and I felt like he had punched me in the chest.

Whitlaw left, probably to go see Hunt again, and now it was Cheung's turn. One thing we all knew—you didn't want Cheung angry with you. Or as, Rocklyn had quietly explained it once. "There are Italian mothers. There are Jewish mothers. And there are Chinese mothers. Cheung is all three." Cheung stored it all up and waited for the right moment. I didn't hear all of what he said. I was already ripped open by Whitlaw's remarks, and I just went off to a corner by myself so no one would see me crying. I sat down at a table and put my head down in my arms and sobbed to myself about what Whitlaw had said.

Normally, Cheung would have dragged me back and I knew he'd get back to me soon enough, but right now, he was focused on Jasmine and Libby, heaping most of the blame on them for jeopardizing the whole program. Pretty soon he'd start in on the rest of us for letting them get away with it.

But surprisingly, he didn't go on long at all. He made some bunk assignments and sent everyone scurrying off through the inflatable tunnels to their respective cabins—huts—whatever. I stayed at the table, head still in my arms, waiting for Mariko to come and get me. It felt like he was taking forever.

That was when I heard the conversation I wasn't supposed to hear. Or maybe I *was* supposed to hear it. Hunt and Whitlaw and Cheung were in the next room over. Their voices were too low to carry. But I turned my hearing up, did some internal signal processing, stripped away the background hum of fans and machinery, and *listened*. They must have forgotten I had augments—or maybe they hadn't forgotten. Maybe they just didn't care.

"That could have gone better," said Cheung.

"It's our own fault," said Whitlaw. "We're the ones who put the pot on the stove. We shouldn't be surprised that it boiled over."

"It's a mess," agreed Hunt. "But it's not irreparable. We'll just have to rearrange the schedule. Give them their sleep-shift, but no shower. Tell them we're not going to waste water on freeloaders; they'll have to earn their showers. Have them suit up when they wake. They're going straight to work, but they can't use the tubes. The tubes are for real Loonies. We'll bounce them to the new greenhouse domes, but we'll take them the long way around and that'll be their first orientation. But we'll do it harsh— stay away from the air-plant, we don't trust you. That's the reclamation dome, if you ever earn a shower you'll go there. And so on. No public feeds, of course. Not until we have these kids actually working. That's so dull that only the die-hards and the trainees actually watch. We'll give the boys a few shifts shoveling soil. Tell them the bots are down for mainte- nance. After a couple of shifts, they'll be muscle-acclimatized enough that we can trust them around real people. That's when they can have their showers. We'll let them spend a few days in their own stink and that'll give us time to reconfigure. We'll need it, in any case. But you know how to handle that one too."

Whitlaw said quietly, "This complicates our public relations problem."

"And maybe this could work to our advantage."

"We should have caught it. But it happened so fast, it caught us by surprise. We didn't turn off the feeds until it was too late. It went out live. We'll be getting calls from downstairs pretty soon." He must have glanced at his watch. "As soon as dawn hits the east coast."

"We knew we were going to take some fire anyway," said Hunt. "'Why didn't you train those boys better?' 'What are you people doing up there?' That kind of thing. But that's why we scheduled this when we did. The Super Bowl is three days away and most Terries don't have the attention-span to think about us and a football game at the same time."

Cheung said, "The dirtside office has already prepared the talking points. And we've got enough public graduates in high visibility who can speak to the issue—that you can't train adults to be perfect, but you can train them to learn from their mistakes. But only if you give them a place to make mistakes. That's the Vision Quest program."

"You think they can sell that—?"

"That's what our people are paid for."

"All right," said Hunt. "Then let it be their problem. Luna doesn't care. So now—let's talk about the real fuck-up here. Look at these trendlines."

Another silence. Finally, Whitlaw said, "They caught us by surprise."

"They caught *both* of you by surprise? I'm really disappointed."

"And we're really embarrassed. We watch their lines pretty carefully We've been doing it for two years; by now, we know their physiologies better than our own. We were green all the way up the beanstalk, and even in the leap-across in the pods. We didn't see anything out of the ordinary until we rolled the trucks. Shan was the first one off the chart. At first, we figured it was just her—him now—and the rest of them were getting a contact hard. We didn't expect the fight—at least not this soon. We didn't think we were going to see anything more than some boyish giggling over each other's Lunar erections.

"But it showed up in their lines a couple hours after we hit the road. After the first sleep-shift it was obvious. They've *all* gone pubescent at the same time." Whitlaw's voice went low and dark. "Obviously, we've got a much bigger problem than one little bitch-fight. We've got synchronization. We knew there was a possibility that one or two might react. We didn't expect anything this intense. They never knew what hit them."

"All right," said Hunt. "How do you want to deal with it—?"

There was silence for a moment. Cheung broke it. "If we were still on Earth, I'd flush them with pheromones, lock them all in a room, and let them fuck themselves into desperate exhaustion for as many days as necessary…until they beg to be let out. After a week of relentless sex, most boys—most *normal* boys—will eventually get tired enough and bored enough with the old in-and-out to start asking what's for dinner."

"That's an idea too," said Hunt. "Not what you said—but we've got a few horny riggers up here. Normally, we don't let them date the scouts until the last two weeks. I wonder if…no, let's not. I have a better idea."

"What's that? Put them back on the suppressants?"

"No. Their systems are already in uproar, and some of them are still in post-transition syndrome—Shan, for example. Let's not overload their livers. We'll have to have the team deal with puberty the old-fashioned way. By living through it."

"Ugh," said Whitlaw.

"*Oy, veis mere,*" said Cheung. "On the moon."

"It won't be that bad," Hunt replied. "Most of human history, we didn't have bio-technology, and the species still got sentient anyway."

Whitlaw's voice, I could almost see his skeptical expression. "Any sensible reading of history shows that we're still not sentient, we're just pretending."

There was a break then, an interruption. Whitlaw said, "Mariko, are you all right?" He must have been coming back from changing.

A muffled grunt in reply. I couldn't make out Mariko's response.

"Yes, well, stop exuding pheromones. That's half the problem. The other half—well, you're still buddied with Shan. We'd better talk—"

I strained to hear, but then Cheung came out to talk to me. "You and Mariko will be in Shelter Six. It's one of the oldest ones, and it's one of the smaller ones, but it's also one of the most livable. It's got a few amenities. Now listen—" He put his hand on my shoulder and bent low to my ear. "You need to focus up and stay on purpose. You're still on Luna. Never forget, there's only a very thin line between you and vacuum. Don't get sloppy, don't forget your procedures—"

Why was he telling me this? I thought I was the most attentive to detail of all of us. Some people even said I was obsessive compulsive—which isn't a bad thing to be if you're committed to integrity. As Whitlaw always says, "Your integrity is your starsuit. How many holes are you willing to poke into it?" For me, the answer is zero. Except sometimes, how are you supposed to know what's *really* going on?

A couple minutes later, Mariko came out of the other room, looking not very happy. "Come on," he said. He didn't sound friendly. I picked up my starsuit and helmet. He picked up his. He scooped up both our duffels where they'd ended up after they finished bouncing, after we'd tossed them aside. He shoved mine into my arms, took me by the elbow and led me out into the tubes.

The inflatable tunnels snaked all over the crater floor. From above, they looked like a network of glowing white veins. From inside, they looked too bright; outside was only ominous darkness, and a vague gray grittiness.

Every hundred meters, we pushed through a pop-lock. Push and it pops open in front of you, step through and it pops closed behind. There were also a few push-locks and one revolving door lock too.

It was too easy to bounce, and with Mariko half-dragging me, I felt like a balloon. We finally slowed down and half-floated half-jumped our way along. We came to a junction marked by signs—follow the green stripe, follow the red stripe, follow the blue stripe—Mariko pointed and pushed/dragged, and we found our way to shelter six. He hadn't said two words to me and I was afraid he was angry, though I couldn't figure out why.

Shelter six had an old-fashioned cycle-pump lock, leftover from the first days of Turtledome. That's how old some of these structures were. The two of us were pressed face to face in the tiny lock. It had never been designed for two at a time. The original designers had engineered it for only one man at a time, they'd assumed he'd be wearing a bulky-suit; they'd never imagined form-fitting starsuits made of workflex, but the two of us could just fit into this lock—if we were friendly. Or pretending to be friendly. Or just putting up with each other.

I could feel Mariko's body pressed against mine, but I didn't know if that was intentional or because he had no room to back up. I took advantage of the moment and pressed just as hard against him, the whole time staring unashamedly into his eyes. He met my gaze. Any moment, I expected him to smile—I hoped he would—but the inner door popped open first and he moved abruptly sideways, almost pushing me out with him. I tripped, but before I could fall—

He turned, caught me in mid-air, and pushed me hard against the padded wall of the tiny hut. I dropped everything I was still holding. His expression was—unreadable. He pushed in close. I could feel—everything.

Then he kissed me. It wasn't icky at all.

It was...wonderful.

And then, Mariko moved his lips to my ear, not even whispering, just barely mouthing the words. I still had my ears turned up, I heard every word clearly. "I wish I had more time, so I could fall in love with you."

I said something like *urk* and lost all physical volition to a flush of surrender. I think that even if I had wanted to protest, I was too exhausted to do so. I just let go and let it happen. I remember at some point, probably about four seconds after Mariko's whispered words, I had wrapped all my arms and legs around his upper torso and he was standing there holding me, and even though we were both still dressed, I was already realizing that one of the opportunities of one-sixth gee was a sexual position that had always struck me before as untenable for periods of longer than a minute or two, at least without external support. Now, I was contemplating the hydraulics involved, and despite my lack of practical experience, I was beginning to appreciate the vertical possibilities with curiosity, eagerness, and enthusiasm. But first, we'd have to get our clothes off—

That didn't happen.

Mariko carried me over to one of the bunks—an inch of foam on an inflated mattress and bounced us both down onto it. He held me close, intensely. One of the nice things about nano-weave is that you can feel things through it. Very intimately. This penis business might not be so bad after all.

Abruptly, he stopped. He lifted himself up and stared down at me. I couldn't tell what he was thinking. *"This is hard—"*

"I like it hard," I said, giggling. Good grief! Did that come out of me?

"Yeah, me too," he said. He lowered himself back down onto me, I loved the pressure of his body on top of mine, light and strong at the same time, and we kissed for a while. Kissing is nice. I don't know how anybody could imagine it as icky. Kissing Mariko is especially nice. We did that for awhile. I lost track of time.

And then we were whispering again.

"Do you trust me?"

A very strange question to ask—

I'd known Mariko for almost two years. No. I hadn't known him at all. I'd hidden from Mariko for almost two years—even all the times when we'd been buddied up in training. And now here I was, with my legs desperately wrapped around his waist, and whatever I'd been using for logic was completely turned around. I liked this rubbing-our-stuff-together business a lot. But how could I trust him while he was doing this? My feelings were all turmoil. But how could I *not* trust him? Was he feeling the same as me? Or something else altogether? How is a girl-boy supposed to know anything?

—I didn't answer. I pushed him up off me. Not hard in one-sixth gee. I could have carried him in my arms, if I could have imagined something to do in that position. I stared up into his face. I could feel the tears welling up in my eyes. What was going on here anyway? I could feel that old familiar hurt gathering itself, just in case it was needed again. *"Tell me—"*

He looked pained. But he lowered himself close and whispered, "Over a year ago, I knew then. You have a great smile, when you let it out. First, you were this very sweet little girl. Now…you're an even prettier boy. But I couldn't—oh fuck, I didn't know it was going to be like this—" He stopped and buried his face in my neck for a moment. Was he crying?

Just about the time I was going to say something, he raised up again. *"I'm sorry, sweetheart. I am so sorry—"*

"No, don't be—"

"No, stop—" He touched my lips with his fingers, to keep me from talking. *"Don't say anything."* He studied my face as if he was memorizing me. And then, after a Lunar eternity, we pulled each other close and held on tight. And we didn't say anything else. Not for a long time. We just quietly made love. And the only sounds were the occasional gasp or sigh or giggle. It was…everything it was supposed to be, except when it was even better than that.

In the morning, or what felt like morning, we washed each other. Two or three times. Technically, the washcloths are supposed to be as good as a shower, if not better. But I still like the feeling of running water on my bare skin. And even though my head knows I'm clean, sometimes the rest of me still insists that I'm not. But today, here, now, I didn't want a shower, I wanted to rub the feeling of Mariko into my body and keep him there forever.

He traced his fingers up and down my body, taking extra time with what remained of my breasts and nipples; even underdeveloped, I couldn't believe how sensitive I still was. I felt so good all over, like I was filled inside with hot chocolate pudding. I felt stretched and alive in a way I'd never even imagined was possible. I tingled, I glowed, I was flushed with feeling. I started to say, *"Promise me something. When I'm a girl again—"*

But he stopped me. *"Please, don't—"* He had the strangest look on his face. As if he knew something terrible was going to happen. He didn't speak much as we dressed. He helped me suit up. He was so tender, it was scary. He checked everything three times, and I had the impossible feeling that he was saying goodbye, and that this might be the last time we'd ever see each other.

Then it was my turn to help him. His blue-sky starsuit made him look like a superhero, and I admit it, I let my hands linger across his skin a lot longer and a lot more tenderly than I'd ever done before. I was all over him, loving the job of dressing him and hating the distance the two starsuits put between us. I liked being naked with my lover.

My lover. What a curious, delicious, wonderful phrase—

We clicked our helmets into place, we blanked our face-plates, we brought up our displays, we checked each other's readings, three times over. We waited for teleconfirmation, then we cycled the airlock. Mariko turned me so I was against the inner door, and that was the last thing I remembered clearly. He turned away. The outer door popped open and the next thing I knew I was lying on my back, floating on an inflatable bed, staring at a soft blue sky with puffy rectangular clouds, which eventually resolved into a painted ceiling with white air-pillows for padding. The smells of antiseptic told me I was in a medical bay. And then Hunt's face swam into view and he looked very concerned, "Do you know where you are?"

My throat felt impossibly dry. "In the morgue? Am I dead?"

"No, you're not dead. Do you have any pain?"

"I don't think so—" I patted myself. Someone had peeled off my starsuit. I was naked under a soft blue blanket. My tits hurt. My legs hurt. I was stiff all over. But most of it was a good stiffness. The overwork of last night? The most enjoyable pain in the universe. I wanted to drift back into the memories—

"Shan. Don't go away—" Something fizzed near my nose and I smelled peppermint.

After a moment, I blinked. I opened my eyes again. "I'm still here." And then I came awake. "What happened?"

"There was an accident."

"I already figured that part out. *What happened—?!*"

"The seals on the connecting tube failed. The monitors said there was air, but there wasn't. When Mariko popped the lock, there was an explosive decompression. You were slammed back against the wall. He was blown outward—

"Where's Mariko? *Is he all right?*" I started to lift myself up—

Hunt pushed me back down onto the bed.

"Just tell me!"

"His helmet cracked. His air bled out. It was quick. And he was probably stunned or unconscious, so he wouldn't have felt anything—"

I don't remember what I said after that. It was probably incoherent. I remember only disbelief and denial and rage and fear and grief and anguish and then a whole lot of other feelings that don't have names yet, but are a lot more horrible than disbelief and denial and rage and fear and grief and anguish. But then something else fizzed, some different smell, and I went out again

and this time when I came back, I couldn't feel anything, I was floating on a different kind of cloud, this was a cloud of not caring, almost like being dead, maybe better, and the nice thing about this cloud was how much I didn't care. I didn't even care that I didn't even care. I could have stayed here forever.

And maybe that was a good thing and maybe it was a bad thing, but whatever it was, it was the thing that was there. Maybe it would have been better to let me rage and scream and fling myself at the walls for awhile until I exhausted myself physically and emotionally. And maybe it was better to leave me numb for awhile too. And maybe it didn't matter, because I hadn't been given any choice in the matter.

And. And. And. It's all ands. It's all words. Just a lot of sentences and noise. It didn't change anything. Mariko was dead and I wasn't. Even while I floated alone, not-caring, I knew that my life was over. There was nothing left for me anywhere. Mariko had gone away and I wanted to follow. Wherever Mariko went, that's where I wanted to be. Even if it meant not-being.

Sleep-shifts came and went. The lights went down and then came up again. From time to time, people came in and looked at me. Their mouths moved. They made noises. It didn't matter. I didn't care. I didn't want to hear any of it. I didn't want to listen. What if one of them actually said something that made a difference? I'd have to give up not-caring. And not-caring was starting to be comfortable. Numbness wasn't an acceptable substitute for feeling—but it was a lot less painful. And I'd already had enough pain, thankewverymuch.

After a while, I went from horizontal to vertical. I moved around. I put food in my mouth. I chewed. I swallowed. I drank liquid. I sat on the toilet and made plopping sounds into the depths below. I peed. I didn't care. I put on a starsuit. I went and shoveled shit in the greenhouse. I came back. I took off my starsuit. I stood naked in the shower and wondered why my nipples still had feeling when I washed them. I didn't have a buddy, or maybe I did. There was always someone watching over me, but I wasn't watching anybody, just the vacant space ahead of me.

And one day—yes, it was day; the sun had finally risen over the sharp eastern horizon—one day, when nobody was watching me, I put on my starsuit and triple-checked my safeties, even though there was no real need to, and opened the nearest airlock, and bounced out onto the naked Lunar plain. I was going to find Mariko.

I'd finally figured it out. Luna was the country of the dead. It's empty, it's barren, it's gray and lonely. Nothing happens here. No wind, no weather, no sound. It's dry hell, gritty and endless. Every part of it the same as every other part, different only in the quality of its monotony. I crunched across the crater floor heading toward the darkness in the south, a forgotten jumble of useless detritus. I turned my suit display off—I went black. The best color for a dead boy. I'd be invisible.

From above, there's an obvious plan. Concentric rings of glowing tubes and dark utility trenches. Someday, those trenches would be sealed over. They might even become tunnels under the habitat. But right now, they were just little chasms to leap across. I passed the last orange cones and started bouncing up the long road toward the rim. Whenever I saw a truck approaching, I went motionless. I crouched down and pretended to be a shadow. Nobody stopped. Nobody noticed me. I felt hurt by that. Even angry that no one cared. But it just confirmed the rightness of what I was doing. I was alone and I was going to stop being alone the only way I knew how. All I had to do was keep bouncing, no matter how long a way it was, and eventually I'd be with Mariko.

After a while, I lost track of time. I remembered cresting the rim of the crater, then striking off at right angles to the road. I headed toward the east, toward the still-rising sun. If Mariko was anywhere, he'd be in the light. My suit started making noises in my ear. From time to time it sounded like Jang or Jonah or Jasmine. When it started to sound like Cheung, it got annoying, so I turned it off. I turned off all the monitors too. I didn't need to know. I'd know when it was time to sit down. Or lie down.

I drank some milk. I ate a cookie. I peed into my bladder-bag, knowing it would quietly recycle through layers of miracle membranes. I climbed a little slope, I bounced down a steeper one. I thought about stopping, but I was on the downhill side now. Nobody walks on Luna, it's almost impossible. Walking is a function of gravity. You lean ahead until you're falling forward, then you put a foot in front of you to keep yourself from falling all the way down—that's what walking is. But on Luna, there isn't enough gravity for walking. You fall too slowly. So to get anywhere at all, you have to spring. You bounce across the land like a human balloon in a wind. Except there's no wind, just you. And the crunching dust. And the glittering horizon. And the sharp-edged shadows. And the rocks. All the painful rocks. And you bounce. Bounce and bounce and bounce again through time and gravity and despair.

And then, finally, I did stop. For no reason at all.

I looked behind. I couldn't tell which way I had come. I turned around a few times, but every direction looked the same as every other. If the sun's glaring brightness hadn't still been low in the east, I wouldn't have known which way I was pointed.

I checked my suit-readings. They were blank. Oh. Right. I turned my monitors back on. But it didn't matter now. I was too far out. My displays told me what I already knew. I didn't have enough air left to make it back, even if I wanted to. Which I didn't. But at least, now they had a signal. They could come and find my body. If they wanted to. My recorder was on, of course; that's automatic. I could have said some words. If I wanted to. Which I didn't. I was finally ready to let go.

So I sat down. And waited.

I realized that some of the not-caringness I was feeling was an afterflush of the drug, whatever it was, they'd been pumping into me. But it was wearing off now. Just enough for me to notice that I was starting to get uncomfortable. My diaper itched. My penis felt uncomfortable, but there was no way for me to adjust myself in a starsuit. My nipples itched too.

I started to cry. I couldn't even say what I was crying about. It was just everything. Luna wasn't wonderful, it was horrible. It was a dreadful place for anybody to die, let alone live. It was no place for human beings. It killed us and it didn't care. So why should anybody else? So I cried because I didn't care either.

And while I was sitting there, crying and not caring, I noticed stars twinkling on the horizon. That was odd. Stars don't twinkle on the moon. No, it wasn't stars. It was something flickering. And it wasn't on the horizon—just in the distance. Something tall and spindly. After a minute or two, I actually started to wonder what I was seeing. I shifted to telescopic view, but it still didn't resolve. It was just something tall and spindly. Maybe it was the Rock Father. Maybe it was one of the Bigfeet. That would be funny. What if I actually met one of the Bigfeet, but died before I could tell anyone? I wondered if that had already happened to anyone else. I almost laughed. If I hadn't still been feeling so sorry for myself, I would have.

The thing, whatever it was, was coming closer. It was headed straight toward me. Maybe it was even coming for me. Now I could see its eyes. Or maybe they were headlights. Though why anybody would need headlights during the Lunar day I couldn't figure out. Not headlights, all kinds of lights, constantly shifting, making it hard to focus on the thing. It looked like a heat shimmer in the distance—except, of course, you don't get heat shimmers in a vacuum.

And then, abruptly, recognition clicked in. It was a ten-meter strider, spidering over the land. It had three long spindly legs, which moved sort of like a stilt-walker and sort of like a Martian war machine. A single stride was ten meters, that's how it got its name. At the very top was a cargo capsule turned vertical and converted into a control pod with living quarters and supplies and tool bays. It wore a hat of scanners and antennas, and from its back sprouted a tangled cluster of arms, folded and unfolded. That's where its legs were anchored too.

I tried to look like a shadow again, but its three spotlights swiveled around and speared me with light. Even with my faceplate fully shielded, I still couldn't make out any details through the glare. Image-processing didn't help. The strider was flickering its external displays to confuse the auto-correlator. I'd studied equipment specs for months—I thought I knew all the striders working at Turtledome. As near as I could tell, this wasn't one of them.

And then—one of the strider's arms unfolded, reached up and over and down, and plucked me off the ground. It held me up before the window of the control pod for a moment—I couldn't see in, it was shielded—then swung me around to the externally-mounted airlock on the side. The door popped open and I pushed myself in. Maybe it was just an automatic reaction on my part, and maybe I'd decided I really wasn't ready to die. And maybe I was genuinely curious. Was this really one of the mysterious Bigfeet?

Inside—I popped my faceplate open. Only then did I realize how stale was the air I'd been breathing. The air in the strider was crisp and cold and fresh. And it felt a lot more solid than anything I'd been breathing in Turtledome. My head cleared quickly. I started to wonder what I'd been thinking before and why.

There were two people sitting in the strider's control chairs. Both were suited, both were belted in. Both their starsuits were black. The pilot of the strider did something and the huge machine swung around and began loping easily across the airless desert. The motion was as gentle as the rocking of a boat, but I had to grab for a handhold anyway. I glanced around, unfolded a seat from the wall, and strapped myself in.

The pilot swung around in his chair, and popped his faceplate. He was a moonburned man with long silvery hair. "Not bad, kiddo—not bad." He nodded toward his panel. "You covered nearly forty klicks. I've seen Lunar fugues before, but this just might be a record-setter."

"So what? Do I get a trophy?"

"Maybe. It depends on your answer to the next question. Do you really want to die today? Or at some point in the unknown future?"

"Um. I don't...understand...the question."

"You are now a guest of Invisible Luna. This is your invitation to join."

"What if I say no?"

He shrugged. "If I thought that would be your answer, we wouldn't have picked you up."

"Oh. But—I was trying to commit suicide."

"No, you weren't." He nodded. "You were just...overloaded. But if you really are determined to kill yourself, then can put you back on the ice and this will be nothing more than the delusion you experienced as your air ran out."

"Oh." I considered my options. Did I really want to die today? The inside of the strider had a strange familiar smell. I still wasn't thinking clearly. This was all happening too fast. I said, "But you don't know if I'll be any good to you—"

"Oh, you will." He grinned. "Here's what you stepped in. Dirtside, and this is the real reason that we call them *dirt*side, doesn't want Luna going independent. So they don't allow females to emigrate. That's why everyone coming up has to transition to male first. If we can't breed, we can't build a real society. We'll always be dependent on the marble."

"Oh," I said. "That stinks." I thought about it. "But can't people translate back to female once they get here?"

"Most of the workers get rechanneled, so they don't want to switch back, but even if they did, they can't. Terra won't send us the meds."

"Why don't you just import fertile eggs and bottles?"

"*All* the meds related to transition and reproduction and gestation are interdicted. They're contraband. And most of the fabbers we get are strictly limited to construction items. They won't even let us have organic fabbers to grow steaks, they're afraid we'll grow a couple of uteruses too. We can't even get some of the basic tools for building gestation bottles."

"But—" I shut up. There must have been a lot more to all this than I was capable of understanding right now.

"So, here's the rest of it. Mariko wasn't a boy. Well, not completely. He was smuggling a full load of fertile eggs. So was Libby. It's a tricky job. We fumbled it once. At some point in the mission, probably triggered by the shift from Terra-gee to free-fall to Luna-gee, or maybe just triggered by the excitement of splatdown, he went into estrus. His body started signaling a readiness to breed. In a closed pod, that would have been pretty intense."

"Um. Yes." I was remembering the wipe-down after our first workshift.

"That would have been more than enough to trigger a pubertal breakdown in some of you. You were the first. Jasmine was certainly the second. What we call puberty isn't a natural phenomenon anymore. When it's controlled, it's a lot easier for everybody involved; when it explodes, there's a lot more drama."

"So does that mean it was all hormones? And Mariko and I weren't really in love?"

He shook his head. "I'm pretty sure that Mariko loves you. More than you know—"

"How can you say that?"

"Because it was Mariko who demanded that we come out here after you." He nodded toward his copilot—who swiveled around to face me in a starsuit that had suddenly turned bright blue.

The next few moments were confused as hell. I remember screaming, crying, and launching myself at Mariko. I felt a rush of emotions so confusing it was painful. I felt betrayed. Ripped open. I think I slapped his face. He had tears running down his cheeks. He didn't notice. "I'm so glad we got to you in time, we almost didn't—" He realized he'd been slapped. "You're right. I deserved that. We didn't know what else to do. I'm so sorry, sweetheart—" Then he scooped me up and I fell into my lover's arms and held on as tight as I could for as long as I had the strength. I remember we spent a lot of time kissing, but just as much time looking into each other's shining eyes and reassuring ourselves that we were both still alive and this was really real—and not the hysterical delusions of a dying teenager. And then finally, we were laughing and I was saying, "I want to be invisible too. I want to be invisible with you forever," and we kept on laughing.

Somewhere in there, Mariko held my face and whispered, "Are you sure?" and when I nodded eagerly, he said, "But I don't know if you'll ever get to be a girl again. Or me—" It didn't matter.

I said, "It's all right, sweetheart. It's all right. I can still be useful. Maybe I can fertilize some of those eggs." And for some reason that struck as both as funnier than anything else. And we laughed all the way to… well, that place that doesn't exist on any map, but it's called the future.

THE DIAMOND SKY

The hull of *The Martian Qheen* was diamond-plated. By design.

A seemingly-endless field of panels reflected the distant starlight with a plated sheen halfway between metal and ice. She looked more like a careless array of solar collectors than the spacecraft she really was.

Captain Adam Neace reviewed the vessel with a critical eye. He wore a VR headset and he rode *Little EVA*, one of the external spider-bots, up and down the long rows of panels, quietly inspecting. He didn't expect to find anything, the spider-bots were more thorough and more relentless than any mere human could ever be, but Adam Neace wasn't a mere human and he was old enough to remember a time when bots were merely extensions of human effort, not independent agents. He liked to look for himself. Despite his own augmented being, he still believed in human intuition; that sometimes the human mind could sense possibilities and connections that a simple intelligence engine might overlook. But mostly Captain Adam Neace rode the bots because he liked being "outside" more than inside.

…another successful breeding season at the Auckland Seaqharium. Alex is the largest giant squid living in captivity, nearly six meters in length. In the wild, giant squids can grow to 16 meters or more. The Auckland Seaqharium covers an area of sixteen square kilometers and is the second largest land-based ocean laboratory in the southern hemisphere. The South African and Australian seaqhariums also have breeding programs for…

The Martian Qheen was eleven years old, built to standard design: a kilometer-long keel, speared through the axis of a mandatory habitat-centrifuge. To an external observer, she might have seemed an unwieldy conglomeration of panels, struts, guy wires, pipes, engines, tanks, sensory gear, ancillary thrusters, and life-support modules; but in actuality, she was a carefully balanced machine, a space-going laboratory as well as a precision vacuum factory. Although she was capable of interplanetary leaps, for most of her life, she'd stayed in perpetual eclipse, riding the shadow of Mars; a tricky but not impossible orbit. It was a necessary maneuver to keep the vessel's isolated so that the delicate fabrication processes of her factories would not be contaminated by stray solar radiation. Solar storms could be violent even this far out from the hearth.

...evolutionary advances in digital archaeology have made it possible to cross-correlate multiple time-data frames, allowing researchers to track the interaction of real-time trends across multi-dimensional matrices, including economic, political, ecological, and sociological causitives. Cusps of chaotic potential appear as three-dimensional spikes in the strata...

"Captain?"

Neace put the bot on auto and flipped up his VR goggles. First Officer Mark Ensley came floating forward into the bridge. "We've got mail. From Admiral Palmer." Ensley pulled himself down into the copilot's seat and belted himself in. Neace touched his display and brought up the message. The first sentence told him everything he needed to know: "Congratulations, Captain Neace." The rest of it was formality: "The Review Board is satisfied that *The Martian Qheen* and her crew have met or surpassed all requirements. The Board is pleased to certify *The Martian Qheen* as ready for service. You may proceed with the next phase of your mission immediately."

Neace scratched his neck thoughtfully. The message wasn't unexpected, as the ship had been prepared for several days. They were already testing the long-range laser-links off the asteroid-belt repeaters. But bureaucracy had to be served—for two reasons. First, bureaucrats needed to feel important, and second, you always had to have enough paper to cover your ass. Just in case. Even so, the official confirmation felt good.

...announced the successful insertion of the ice-asteroid into a close approach orbit, timed to coincide with the Summer Olympic Games in Dallas-Fort Worth. Comet Janisian will have a red, white, and blue tail stretching across one-third of the sky and will be visible for nearly three weeks...

"I'll have the Venus link up as soon as we move out of shadow," Ensley reported. "And we'll have direct acquisition of Earth-Luna at 0803. Not quite the optimal triangle, but it'll give us a baseline."

"IRMA, secure the bots; begin your checklist, please."

"Working...."

...high point of the all-robot revival of Hello Dolly is the astonishing "Waiter's Gallop" sequence, with over a hundred glimmering metal bodies leaping and dancing in pinpoint synchronization, juggling trays of full glasses and pitchers, all without spilling a single drop of...

For most of her life, *The Martian Qheen* had been one of several orbital facilities producing large form diamond-substrates. Working in the universe's largest clean room—the universe itself—her external factory bots vacuum-layered pure crystalline carbon onto panels several meters across to create the largest *and flattest* diamonds possible. The resultant sheets were the ideal substrate for optical and electrical chips, for display panels of all sizes, for precision collectors and reflectors, and for a thousand other industries that needed atomically flat surfaces—for example, mirror arrays for radio, optical, and X-ray telescopes.

As each panel was completed, it was measured and graded. Any panel that failed the "flat as ancient Kansas" test could not be certified. Although there existed a considerable market for these lower grade diamond sheets, shipping them wasn't cost-effective for a ship in Martian orbit; local suppliers could provide the panels cheaper; but this was understood long before *The Martian Qheen*'s keel had been drawn. It had been planned from the beginning that Captain Neace would install the castoff pieces around critical components of the vessel as ablation shields against strikes by micro-meteorites.

...ethics of animal implants remain unresolved. Meanwhile, Sparky has added another thirty words to his vocabulary. As you can see, Sparky enjoys meeting new people, and he speaks his thoughts enthusiastically, as our onsite reporter discovered. <Sparky:> "Maya smell good. Maya mate, yes?"...

But the fabrication and sale of A-grade panels was only a sideline for the *Qheen*—a very profitable sideline, but a sideline nonetheless. Her very best surfaces were reserved for a much more ambitious task. Not all the panes she produced were pure diamond, and not all were flat. Many were doped with layers of other materials to provide specific physical properties, many were subtly curved to fit into a precise design. *The Martian Qheen*'s sole job been the construction of several thousand diamond mirrors, the most optically precise reflectors ever made, all components of the largest distributed array ever constructed.

Her certification had never been in doubt, for the most part, she was constructed with "off-the shelf" technology, but now that she was officially online she could assume her duties as the third and final coordinating station for the Dispersed Array Space Telescope. Two similar ships rode in the orbits of Earth and Venus. Other vessels were planned for the future, but at least three were necessary to coordinate.

...in a limited decision, the court declined to rule on the ethics of Klingon-deprogramming. However, the court did agree that Acht-Facht had not left the Enterprise orbiting hotel voluntarily and that the lawsuit could continue. Representatives of the Klingon Church petitioned to the court to compel The Human Adventure to reveal Facht's whereabouts...

DAST was an inevitable idea, an outgrowth of Arecibo and Paranal and Farside. Spaceships carried telescopes—all kinds—optical, radio, microwave, X-ray, gamma-ray, gravitational, deep-resonance, and stress-field. Link up several telescopes, point them all in the same direction, collate their separate images, and you create a virtual telescope as large as the distance between reflectors. The proof of concept was over a century and a half old, dating back to the days when all astronomy was Earth-bound. The four linked lenses at Paranal had eventually produced pictures even more spectacular than the orbiting Hubble eye.

In the early 21st century, this idea had been exported to space. Four identical planetary probes were linked by laser to each other. All four focused their telescopes on the same set of objects and synchronized their separate exposures. Even as a proof of concept, the results were staggering; the detail of their deep space imagery left astronomers hungering for more. The Distributed Array Space Telescope had been an ongoing project ever since. Almost every ship in transit between Earth and Mars linked its onboard telescopes to the Lunar Coordinating Base at Gagarin; long-range lasers transmitted a steady stream of timing and position data; each ship synchronized its exposures to the nano-second, and returned its images along the same laser beams it used for position-referencing. It was not only the largest virtual telescope in existence, it was also the most cost-effective, using existing observational tools already in place. Even the software was off-the-shelf. All it required was a coordinating station.

...dead at 187. She was the last living survivor of the...

But as humanity pushed outward, to the asteroid belt, to the moons of Jupiter and Saturn—as more and more ships and telescopes came on-line, synchronization became exponentially difficult. Management became the essential problem. *The Martian Qheen* and her two sister ships were intended as a triangle of anchor points, providing precision synchronization data; each one linking to and coordinating all participating ships within her own sphere of influence. The projected increase in resolution was expected to be at least three orders of magnitude.

Each of the *Qheens* needed multiple laser-units and reflector panels for every ship in the linkage. Additionally, to provide a baseline for comparison, each of the *Qheens* carried one of the three largest telescopes ever dispatched to space; when fully opened, the array would be several hundred meters across. From the outset, each of the *Qheens* had been designed as a space-going factory, each one fabricating all of her own delicate reflectors.

…said that the quake, measuring at least 6 points on the Maslow-Richter scale, would be centered in the San Fernando Valley, and would occur in the first week of February. Voluntary evacuations are recommended for the area. FEMA will be sending in over a thousand quake-readiness consultants to advise residents…

"We're out of the shadow," Ensley reported. "We've acquired *The Venus Qheen*."

"Right," said Neace, studying his own displays. "Let's say hello. Three beams." He pressed record and whispered into his microphone, "Peek-a-boo—" The beams were effectively invisible in the vacuum of space; at one part per godzillion, there wasn't enough dust to illuminate them; but 12.3 light-minutes away, *The Venus Qheen*, in the center of the targeting cone, would be able to distinguish three specific pinpoints of color—red, green, and blue. The subtle differences between the beams would allow *The Venus Qheen* to calculate Doppler shift, precise distance, and timing for synchronization.

Allow three minutes for Captain Radley Nakamura to receive the message and record an acknowledgment, *The Martian Qheen* should receive its reply no more than thirty minutes after sending its initial message; once the first laser-links were in place, the primary synchronization could be completed in a matter of hours; even allowing for slippage, no more than eight hours should be required to establish the first backbone channel for the DAST network. At these distances, however, mostly the job involved waiting.

—which is why the ideal candidate for long-term space missions was an immortal.

...largest ever expansion of a sea-going environment, Atlantis will add 20 square kilometers of pontoon-based platforms over the next seven years. Construction will cost 1.7 billion plastic dollars and will increase the sea-nation's surface area by 20%. In off-market trading, share prices went up a half, with further increases expected when the market formally reopens after the weekend holiday...

Neace hadn't set out to be immortal, but as he aged, it had become more and more convenient—and necessary—to augment his biological processes with biotechnological aids. By the time of his 80th birthday, he was nearly 80% augmented; and at the present rate of accretion, his centenary would see the completion of the various processes. He was neither impatient nor apprehensive, merely resigned to the inevitability. He wanted a berth on the first interstellar expeditionary fleet. Non-immortals need not apply. At one-quarter light-speed, the journey to Sirius and back would take 66 years.

His primary motivation, however, had involved Captain Nakamura. He'd been fascinated by her from the first, although he hadn't recognized it as infatuation until later. Their romance had been passionate, but all-too-often interrupted by the exigencies of career. A variety of assignments had sent them careering across the solar system, only occasionally allowing them to match orbits. When she had gone immortal, as most starsiders eventually did, he had followed her lead. Ideally, he hoped they would both secure assignments aboard the same ship of the Sirius mission. But even if not, as an immortal, he now had time to wait. One of the lesser advantages of immortality was the ability to downshift; to place oneself into a slower time-speed—relative dormancy—and thus transform long periods of imposed inactivity to shorter subjective experiences.

...found the stock certificates almost by accident in a stack of fanzines. Purchased for only twelve dollars a share in 1987, the certificates now represent holdings of more than...

"Laser linkage acquired." IRMA reported. "Incoming message." Radley Nakamura's voice whispered a near-flirtatious response: "—I see you!" To an immortal, the twenty-seven minute interval was negligible.

Neace nodded dispassionately. "Initiate calibration." The two ships would ping-pong a complex set of signals and tests, triangulating on each other as they moved through their separate trajectories, and ultimately establishing precision-predictive-positioning data accurate to a tenth of a millimeter, plus or minus an error below the ability of the measuring equipment to detect.

There wasn't much else to report to *The Venus Qheen*. Despite the fact that this was the first time in eleven years that the two ships had achieved direct line of sight, they had never really been out of contact, relaying their messages via whatever satellite and ships-in-transit links were currently available. Bouncing messages off relays always added delays, and depending on the number of intermediate steps, it could easily double transmission times. Direct acquisition meant that the time lag between message and response was now appreciably shorter.

...announced that she will again change gender, this time to play the role of Seth in the BBO production of A Season of Passion. The change will take four months, and filming will begin in the spring. Although no casting has been announced for the role of Diana, producers are said to be in negotiation with Ric Carliss, the only other performer to have won awards for both best male performance and best female performance...

"Peek-a-boo" was almost a six-decade-old joke between the two Captains. In his first year at the Academy, Neace had installed a digital camera on the terrace of his student apartment. The unit had a self-synchronizing motorized mount, automated motion-detection-and capture, holographic lenses, 6-color correction, UHD resolution at 120fps, and a telephoto ratio of 375x. As an exercise in engineering, he'd written software for it to monitor all the visible windows of two facing dormitories, zooming in for close-ups wherever motion was detected. He wasn't the first student to have done this—it was one of several real-world assignments handed out to freshmen. Neace's addition to the software included multi-spectrum collation, extrapolated removal of obscuring artifacts (such as window glare and curtains), digital image enhancement and noise reduction, clothing detection (including lack of), sorting all retrieved data by amount of skin revealed, followed by additional sorting based on conformation of body mass to selected optimal characteristics—including breast size. The video display in Neace's apartment automatically updated to play a repeating slideshow of the most interesting images captured.

Radley Nakamura did not show up in any of these scans, which singular fact was enough to reduce Neace's grade on the project from A+ to merely A. Due to her short hair, her propensity for wearing sweatshirts and sweatpants, the recognition algorithm had erroneously classified Ms. Radley Nakamura as a boy. Already in her junior year, and well familiar with the prevalence of cameras in the buildings opposite, Ms. Radley Nakamura did this deliberately. The instructors, equally familiar with Ms. Radley Nakamura, included her as a test of the recognition abilities of the Neace's software project.

...repair of the three atmospheric-turbines damaged in the last Martian sandstorm is expected to take...

This being a tiered assignment—with final grade dependent on the student's ability to implement improvements and corrections—Neace focused exclusively on Radley Nakamura's window, determined to fix his gender-recognition algorithm. He began correlating a weighted value system, based on Adam-apple size, wrist size, complexion, general softness of features, center of gravity, motion characteristics, body-fat ratios, generalized behaviors, and other characteristics with specifically measurable differences between the sexes. Very quickly, he realized that the problem stemmed from Ms. Nakamura's commitment to her career. Having decided that gender identity was an inconvenience, she had gone androgynous, preparatory to becoming immortal. The androgynous part was reversible, of course; but not the immortality augments. Neace had to rewrite his recognition algorithm to allow for androgyny superposed over gender. It wasn't a trivial problem, and he aimed his camera directly at her balcony to gather sufficient observational data to establish a personal baseline for Radley Nakamura to measure against the statistical norms.

Unfortunately, the video software failed to update any motion from Ms. Nakamura's balcony. Reviewing the capture in real-time revealed why. Ms. Nakamura had hung a curtain across her balcony, blocking any further intrusions of her privacy. Even more to the point, she had set up her own camera, pointed directly back at Neace's.

Neace got the point immediately. He hand-lettered a sign and hung it below the lens of his camera. The sign said, "Peek-a-boo."

...presented a new plan for shadowing Venus. Based on their preliminary results, researchers now believe that Venusian temperatures could be reduced in less than 150 years...

A day later, Ms. Nakamura's camera displayed a matching sign. "I see you."

Neace hung a new sign on his camera. "Dinner?"

She replied. "Diner. 7pm."

Over dinner at the diner, Neace discovered—among other things—another reason why his recognition algorithm had failed. Nakamura was genetic male, female by choice, and as previously determined, temporarily androgynous. Neace wasn't old-fashioned, he'd dated members of several genders with enthusiasm, and varying degrees of success; he was simply annoyed with himself that he hadn't included this possibility. After briefly debating with himself about a possible appeal of his project grade, he decided instead to recode the recognition algorithms and win his points fairly.

… encyclical from Pope Maria Theresa reaffirms the church's stance on the sanctity of all sentient life, whether it's carbon-based or silicon…

Nakamura found Neace amusing. He was intrigued by her unusual insights, a product of her peripatetic gender identity. Although their mutual schedules allowed for only the occasional hurried meal at the diner, they kept in constant touch by e-mail, and by displaying increasingly cryptic messages on their respective balconies, each one a puzzle. If the recipient couldn't solve the problem, he or she had to pay for the next dinner. Neace ended up paying for most of their meals.

It wasn't that she was smarter or that he lacked puzzle-solving skills; rather, he was methodical and determined where she had grown up outside the lines. He knew why he was fascinated by her; but for a while, he couldn't understand what she liked in him. Eventually she had to tell him. "It's the strength of your determination. Determination without genius got more ships launched than genius without determination." For Neace, it was a moment of sheer *aha!* The two them complemented each other.

Which was why, even 12.7 light minutes apart, they were still able to play "Peek-a-boo, I see you."

…representatives from Roma, Cathay, Nubia, and Babylon again failed to reach agreement with the World Health Organization on the issue of vaccination. Health care has always been a sore point for the historical simulacra, with extremist factions decrying modern health measures as anachronistic influences that distort or destroy the accuracy of the recreated cultures…

"We've got Earth/Luna," said Ensley. "Just coming up over the horizon. We've got radio tracking."

Neace glanced up at the high resolution display. A highlighted frame expanded to reveal a bluish pinpoint, imperceptibly sliding out from behind the shield of the red planet.

"And we've got incoming—"

"Nice timing on their part," Neace noted.

The hearty voice of Manda Sahir boomed from the speakers, with just a hint of single entendre. "Gotcha! Enough with the peek-a-boo. Let's play pattycake."

"I love you too, Manda," Neace replied, even though it would be 6 minutes before Captain Sahir heard his response.

... tourism to Bradbury is projected to increase with the completion of the third phase of the Grand Canal project, with other Martian cities expecting to benefit as well. Burroughs will increase its Thoat-breeding programs, and Wellsopolis will make the Invasion of London-1890 an annual event. (That's Martian-annual, not Earth-annual.) Bookings will need to be made at least two Martian-years in advance...

Captain Manda Sahir had always been aggressive, so much so that she'd earned several astonishing nicknames during her career, "scream-and-leap" being the least objectionable. But in truth, her attitude was far more playful than passionate; she wasn't flirtatious, she was just "kidding around with the guys" and she'd calculatedly rebuffed several who misunderstood where the boundaries had been drawn. Neace had been one of the lucky ones, caught between missions. The affair had been affectionate, playful, friendly, and ultimately noncommittal. Nevertheless, Neace now regarded himself as the hypotenuse of the farthest-spanning triangle in human history, although it would have been more geometrically accurate to consider his position acute angle—at least until the movements of the several planets and their orbiting *Qheens* altered the shape of the triangle.

...spokesman for the Reich predicted a seventh consecutive victory over the Allies in the upcoming replay of World War II. The simulation is expected to attract over a million players, and nearly that many observers. The ReichsKampf also released further information about the Vaterland-1936 enclave, now under construction at...

"We've got RGB from *The Lunar Qheen*," said Ensley. "Right on target."

"Did you expect less?" Neace grinned. "Light her up. Initiate calibration, let's see what we've got." Neace waited until the displays flashed
green, then half-turned to his first officer. "Congratulations. We're online. Let's take some pictures. Earth, Venus, Jupiter and Saturn. Then I
want a long shot of Sedna. After that, the standard celestial repertoire.
Horsehead, Crab, Orion Anomaly, the whole package. We'll need the
shots for comparison after we've established first collation."

"Working," said Ensley. The program had been written months before. All he had to do was call it up and check off the appropriate targets.
The computer would do the rest. Indeed, the program was as much a
test of the synchronizing software as it was of the telescope itself. They'd
already had a dozen test runs while still in the shadow of Mars. There was
no significant importance to this shoot, except that for the first time, it
was an *official* test.

*...super-clustering over thirty million subscribers, with a projected real-
time decryption matrix...*

IRMA beeped softly. Incoming messages arriving. The first of thousands that would arrive over the coming weeks, as various ships in transit
sought to establish their own linkages. Aside from their individual partic-
ipation in the Dispersed Array Space Telescope, there was a much more
immediate objective—accurate mapping of the solar neighborhood, accurate positioning within that map, predictive analysis of gravitational
rumpling and mascon perturbation of smaller space objects.

Ensley briefly reviewed the ship's e-mail. Most of the requests for
connection would be auto-replied over the next few days, but no additional connections would be made until the *Qheens* established their own
baseline. The big problem here would be correlating massive amounts
of data in real-time. Once the DAST was online, that problem would
expand exponentially. It wasn't that the ship didn't have the processing
power—it did—the problem was throughput: the allocation of bandwidth resources.

But several of the messages did require human attention and Ensley
began working methodically through them. It was the commentaries in
the science journals he was most concerned about. Occasionally, someone
or other would so totally misunderstand the workings of the Dispersed
Array Space Telescope that it required an immediate response, before a
whole mythology of ignorance was inadvertently allowed to take root—
like that most notorious of all scientific misunderstandings, dating back

to the early 20th Century, that a rocket couldn't work in a vacuum because there was no air to push against.

...breaking the record for the longest sustained (non-fatal) orgasm ever recorded, Yates credited all three of her partners...

Some of the questions raised about DAST included, "How can it be a telescope if it's mostly space and very few mirrors?" and "How do you focus a virtual reflector 400 million kilometers across?"

The more literate objections dealt with parallax and resolving power. "Won't parallax issues make collation of the separate images problematic, especially for objects close to or within the solar system?" "Isn't the ultimate resolving power limited by the resolving power of the individual reflectors?" "Aren't existing space arrays sufficient? Doesn't this take us way beyond the point of diminishing returns?"

There were answers to all of these. Ensley had already authored several articles and a short book addressing the various issues in language as accessible to the lay reader as possible. But even he acknowledged that in some regards, astronomy had gone way beyond the proverbial "rocket science." The simple process of scanning the diamond sky now required technology that even many astronomers did not fully understand. As one wag had put it, the gap between theory and engineering was now estimated to be several light hours and expanding exponentially.

...but that argument still doesn't address the legal issue; if an adult rejuvenates to an adolescent or even a pre-pubescent body, is he or she still an adult capable of informed consent? When individuals choose to become infantiles, dependent upon others, how can they still claim adult privileges and responsibilities? Should sexual encounters with infantiles and rejuveniles be considered acts between consenting adults with body-mods—or are we seeing a new form of statutory rape? We have to ask if those who seek out and engage in such relationships are expressing a pedophilic intention. Does this create an environment that ultimately endangers all sub-adult beings...

When the first high-resolution pictures of Earth and Luna finally came up, both Neace and Ensley breathed a sigh of relief. Neither man had realized they were holding their breath. The resolving power of *The Martian Qheen*'s array was at the high end of optimum, almost approaching the theoretical limits. It was better than expected, more than was hoped for.

...documentary on the completion of Mons Rushmore, including interviews with the descendants of...

The next few shifts kept both men busier than usual and left little time for flirtations, long-distance or otherwise. The pictures of Jupiter and Saturn were excellent, and the project shifted easily into its next phase.

All three *Qheens* synchronized on schedule and their first collated image was of far-distant, frozen Sedna, once considered Sol's tenth planet. First discovered in 2004, Sedna wandered in an elliptical orbit as close as 76 AU's, as far as 1000 AU's, taking over 10,500 years to complete a single orbit. Sedna was moving away from Sol now, and would continue to do so for several millennia, looping out again toward its home in the Kuiper belt. These were not the first or even the best pictures of Sedna; several robot probes had already mapped the planetoid's bright red surface; but the pictures of Sedna were still important. They would be used to gauge the resolving power of the DAST coordinating stations.

During the same period, each of the *Qheens* began receiving pings from ships-in-transit, robot probes, orbital stations, and all three Lunar observatories. Once the Sedna test was completed, the *Qheens* began assembling an intricate web of laser connections; the assignments were made on the basis of bandwidth and telescope-size. Although, other planetary networks existed, none of them required the same nanosecond-precise synchronization. That most of the separate pieces of the network existed light-minutes apart complicated the job enormously. Each and every node had to predict the Doppler shift of every node it was connected to.

...defense department has awarded the contract for the 4-meter S-14 mobile infantry powered armor to the Lockheed Skunk Works. The Secretary also announced the purchase of an additional 500 R-60 Patton Attack Bots, to be built by Toyota-Boeing...

This distant from Earth/Luna, Neace and Ensley were somewhat insulated from the flash crowd of distant interest—that proportion of the twelve billion human beings on the home world that actually wondered about the marvels hidden in the night sky. Had they known that their fifteen minutes of fame had also created a moment of system-wide breathless anticipation, it might have unnerved them; they considered their work important because it was *their* work; they hadn't considered that the human race as a whole might share some of the same fascination.

So the reaction to the Orion Anomaly caught them mostly by surprise. The first pictures of the Horsehead and Crab Nebulas and other familiar visions were remarkable for their depth of detail and resolution, but unless you were viewing them on a wall-size display capable of Extreme Definition, they did not appear significantly sharper than the previous observations of various space-based observatories.

The Orion Anomaly, however, was something else entirely. Behind the Orion Nebula lay a star system that had always photographed fuzzy and uncertain. Even the smaller proof-of-concept dispersed array space telescope projects of the past had failed to resolve the object or objects. Computer enhancement produced unsatisfactory results because the computer had no idea what it was enhancing. Whatever it was, it was as large as the solar system, possibly larger. Too large to be an exploding or fragmented star—and not enough mass anyway. A whirligig of orbiting bodies? A cosmic whirlwind? There were more theories than facts; but whatever the theory, the evidence refused to abide. The Orion Anomaly remained one of the more tantalizing mysteries of the sky.

...despite the lopsided gender ratios, the Chinese birth rates remain strong as increasing numbers of males choose to carry their own embryos to term; because a majority of the male-borne fetuses are also male, this will exacerbate the problem for the next generation of Chinese husbands. Until China and other Asian states learn to recognize that female children are as valuable as males, the imbalances will continue...

By the time the DAST was ready to focus on the Orion Anomaly, several thousand ships, probes, and orbiting stations had linked up to the three *Qheens.* Because of the wide dispersal of the participating components, collation of the images took several hours. But the resolution of the image was high enough to finally reveal some of the details of the Anomaly. The Extreme Definition display revealed it as a scattering of thousands of small fairly-bright objects in irregular orbit around a midline star. Not comets. Something else—something that still defied explanation. The mystery wasn't solved, it was only deepened.

Unfortunately, further observations were interrupted by a flurry of solar storms which disturbed the linkages between the various ships. The slight but continuing perturbations of orbit confused the predictive synchronization of the coordinating stations, effectively destroying the synchronization necessary to accurate surveillance. During the interregnum, the DAST components would still continue mapping the local distances between planets and asteroids and ships-in-transit. Most of that monitoring did not require predictive calibration. It was routine work and the bots would handle it automatically.

...mixed reactions in the community of body-mods. Most people still view modding a cosmetic enhancement or fashion statement, but more serious modders disregard casual modding as little more than fad-chasing. Tigerman adds, "modding isn't about the look, it's about the experience. That's why the sensory augments are so important. All the new tastes, smells, colors, sensations..."

Neace spent much of his down-time meditatively jogging. The ship's centrifuge turned slowly and the uppermost levels provided a mere one-third gee, which allowed for a languid, almost thoughtful stride; the jogger spent most of his time airborne, barely tapping the floor to stay aloft. For many runners, the experience was close to flying. In fact, the jogger had to lean so far into his stride that he appeared almost prone, like an oversized road-runner, but bouncing from point to point instead of racing.

The long, slow strides provided a time-stretched aerobic workout and Neace could submerge himself into the rhythm as comfortably as if he were floating in an isolation tank. He could run for hours at a stretch, keeping himself physically balanced at a level of exertion simply unachievable at Earth-normal gravity. The result was a zen-like state of endurance and health that most human beings never realized. It was during such workouts that Neace often had his most remarkable insights—many other starsiders had also reported their own experiences of centrifugal nirvana or "jogging eurekas."

Neace had already calculated that the crew of the first starship to Sirius would spend at least one-third of their time jogging, possibly more. They would be able to brag that they had sprinted to Sirius and back. Nowhere would the unbreakable relationship between time and space be more evident than aboard a long-range starship. Even the shorter hops among Sol's family of planets could take weeks or even occasionally months. It was no accident that a large number of exceptionally thoughtful books and articles had been written in transit. Authorship remained the best offense against boredom.

*...most serious breach since Stan-18's tell-all book, **It Only Hurts When You Laugh**. A spokesman for the Laurel-Hardy company said that the situation was a personal and private matter between the clone-families,*

and would not interfere with the upcoming production of "Laurel and Hardy on Mars"...

This day, however, Neace's thoughts came inevitably back to his Radley Nakamura and Manda Sahir. Among starsiders, most relationships were not only long-term, they were also long-range. Perhaps part of it was a physical byproduct of immortality, and part of it was an emotional adaptation to the accretion of age—the underlying assumption that with immortality, now "we have all of time and all of space." But Neace felt that explanation was too easy, and therefore insufficient. Researchers had long since proved that human beings were chaotic events, a cross-section of processes and intentions, pressures and needs, expressing from moment to moment as an illusion of consciousness, only occasionally achieving exercises of actual sentience. But the illusions of consciousness were still useful, because it was on the shoulders of such illusions that the moments of sentience stood.

No, Neace's own theory about the languid pace of starside affairs was that it was an essential adaptation to the expanded time-sense of orbital existence. It was a recognition that every human being is on an individual trajectory, sometimes parallel, more often not. You have no choice but to live inside the moment as it occurs, or as Jarles "Free Fall" Ferris once put it, "Breathe here now."

There wasn't anywhere to go with the thought. It didn't inspire a course of action. And that, too, was part of the adaptation—that thoughts could be complete in and of themselves, without requiring immediate expression or eventual deed. It was simply part of the larger construction of the ground of being on which true identity would later stand.

...although this solar probe lasted 8 minutes longer than any previous close-approach vehicle, the photosphere still hasn't given up all of its mysteries. Next year's Magenta series, however, will be the first test of hyperstatic shielding and should allow the probe to penetrate...

Neace was successful because he was meticulous; a skill he had discovered in school and honed to near-perfection throughout his career. He didn't just plot a course, he plotted consequences. But while the mechanistic approach worked well for creating opportunities for passion, it did not create passion itself. Neace had come to that understanding somewhere between "Peek-a-boo" and "Gotcha."

Thereafter, he had planned his affairs so as put himself into matching orbits with women who were aggressive enough to take the initiative in sexual relationships. In that sense, they completed him, providing the triggers for passion that he himself had never quite mastered. This particular insight was not new to Neace, he revisited it frequently while meditatively jogging. He was neither satisfied nor dissatisfied with the realization. He had accepted it as part of his internal construction.

But this day, the moment of insight that came to him as he purposed methodically through the air— that identity is the construction of self. And that everything he had done up to this point in his life, every problem he had taken on, every challenge he had accepted, had ultimately been about nothing more than his own satisfaction of achievement. He was *self*-centered.

Adding Radley and Manda to his personal equation hadn't ever been about constructing a triangular relationship—it had been solely about completing the structure of his own identity. For a moment, Neace felt guilty.

...four more cases of hyper-chocolate poisoning, bringing the total number to 73, with 9 known fatalities. All-Mart Industries has ordered all hyper-chocolate products removed from store shelves until further review...

But the moment passed, the sense of guilt eased. What *other* kinds of relationships were possible in space? And didn't Radley and Manda equally use him as adjuncts to their own constructions of being? Of course, if he approached it from that perspective, he considered, then he was committing the error of methodical analysis again—and he'd already had this conversation with both of women; that some human interactions were beyond both method and analysis, particularly those of the heart.

And then he got it.

...each of the new plastic coins will contain V-70 ultrawave circuitry. While the long-term goal is to create a more accurate cross-sectioning of economic flows, consumers will experience immediate benefits. Each coin will also function as an independent node in the wireless web, providing 22% packet redundancy at GBS rates and expanding available mobile bandwidth to...

Intellectually, he'd had the answer for the better part of a century— that the condition of love, beyond the mechanics of trust and intimacy, existed only where the other person's well-being was essential to your own. He'd known that as an equation. He'd never quite realized it as an *experience*. Until now. For no reason at all.

Except perhaps that for a moment, a single overarching moment, a breathless pause, while his body continued to pace methodically, languidly, gracefully through the centrifuge—for that single moment, he actually felt *lonely*.

He missed Radley. He missed Manda. The graceful curve of Radley's neck, the breadth of her shoulders and the muscled strength of her legs—the voluminous sensuality of Manda's embrace, the delicious pressure of their bodies together. He'd once wondered if it was possible to love two women at the same time—then surrendered to the inevitability of the truth.

And now, in this moment, with no apparent trigger except the silence in his own head, he *understood*.

He continued jogging, savoring the transformative knowledge. The sweat beaded on his body. He had a joyous grin on his face. He had an erection.

...critical threshold of processing for constructed sentience on a super-cluster. Below that threshold, holes in the processing matrices reduce confidence to the organic level, which is unacceptable for accuracy in...

Later, he knew he'd have to share the insight with both of his lovers. He wasn't quite certain how he would phrase it—and on some level, he understood that this message would be best delivered in person, with skill, delicacy, and of course all the passion he could generate.

But he also knew that this bit of self-knowledge wasn't about what existed in himself as much as it was a recognition of what *didn't* exist within. It was the realization of the need to rebuild a sense of identity that was beyond his own control—an identity that existed as a partnership, as a fusion.

He wondered if that were even possible in a starside environment. Then moved immediately from there to the acceptance of the challenge. It was now something else to be invented.

Laughing, he both women the same message. "I get it. I've been a jerk. That's why you should marry me. Because I finally get it."

...expected to issue its report on the financial costs of the solar flare by the end of the week. Reassembly of the DAST array has already resumed, with optimal calibration expected in the next few hours. Included among the targets scheduled for closer examination, the Orion Anomaly has had astronomers arguing...

Later—everything aboard a ship is always *later*—on the bridge, waiting for their separate replies, now more than an hour overdue, Captain Adam Neace sifted impatiently through all the separate images that had accumulated since his last review. The targeting scopes stayed focused on the other *Qheens* but the latest pictures showed both ships looking different now, so he directed one of the larger arrays to capture clearer images.

A few moments later, the enhanced views came up on his display and he began to laugh. Arrayed in lights along the side of *The Venus Qheen* was a simple message: "Peek-A-Boo." *The Lunar Qheen* displayed, "Gotcha."

Neace opened a channel and said, "I see your sign, Radley."

Half an hour later, the message came back. "Yes, we'll marry you, Adam. But the sign isn't for you—it's for them."

Them?

Who?

Them—!

And in that moment, Adam Neace became the second human being in the solar system to understand the Orion Anomaly.

JUMPING OFF THE PLANET

"Ask him, if you don't believe me," my weird brother whispered. "He's kidnapping us."

"Thpffft," I said.

"Think about it, Chigger. Why do you Dad is bringing us all this way?"

"It's a vacation, stupid."

"Up the Line? And then he's going to bring us *back*?"

I didn't answer that. Weird was 17, almost 18, and he was starting to think like a grownup—stupid. My stinky brother was only 7, almost 8, and he didn't think at all. I turned my back on both of them and stared up at the Line.

Maybe Weird was right. Dad and Mom hated each other. And Mom was always calling her lawyer, screaming about visitation and child support and how he couldn't have one if he didn't supply the other. I don't know what the lawyer said, but it never made Mom any happier. The best part about a vacation with Dad was that it was always a lot quieter. Sort of. Stinky made up for it with his whining. That was why I was sure Weird was wrong—why would Dad want Stinkenstein?

Weird and I had our stuff in backpacks. Dad lugged his in a rollaround. And Stinky had half his clothes in his own backpack and the other half in a smaller one on the electric monkey. Dad bought the monkey for him in Arizona, hoping it would keep him quiet on the trip. Wrong again. Stinky held the monkey's hand and chattered at it like they were married. It waddled beside him like an obedient child with a full diaper. I said they looked like twins, which got a protest from Stinky, a laugh from Weird, and a dirty look from Dad.

Maybe Weird was right. We'd come a long way to Terminus dome—all the way from El Paso to Ecuador on the Super-Train. That wasn't a normal vacation for Dad. I didn't know what to think, so I leaned out over the edge of the balcony railing and gawked. Weird lifted Stinky up so he could see too.

The three cables of the Line plunged straight down from the very top of the Terminus Dome into separate holes in the floor of the station. They were as big around as buildings. Bigger. As we watched, an elevator car slid down one of the cables into a reception bay; at the same time another one popped up on the other side of the same cable.

Dad came back with our tickets then and herded us down the ramp to the boarding level. The cars were shiny blue metal with silver trim. There was a row of them, all creeping toward the Line together. The edge of the platform was a moving slidewalk, rolling at the same slow speed, so boarding the elevator car was a lot like getting on a car in an amusement park ride, only you stepped in through a triple-layered hatch. After we boarded, they slammed it shut with a scary *thunk*. Like once it was closed we couldn't get out again.

Our car was filled to capacity—not exactly crowded, but you had to watch where you were stepping. There weren't that many tourists aboard; it was mostly locals. There was a big tropical storm moving inland and a lot of the folks who lived around the base of the Line were going up to One-Hour to wait it out. They said it was the safest place to be. There were hotels and restaurants and theaters up at One-Hour, so they were probably going to make a party of it.

At last, our car was in the number one position. There was a gentle bump and then the car was locked into the launch tube. That's when I started getting scared. I wanted to ask if I could get off, but I didn't want Dad and Stinky and Weird to know how scared I was. So I just grabbed Stinky's hand tighter and said to him, "Any minute now. Don't be afraid."

He looked at me with a funny expression. "I'm not scared. It's only an elevator."

There was a chime then and everybody else who hadn't yet found a spot at the windows, came pushing in behind us to look. At first we didn't feel anything, but the cable-wall next to us started sliding down and then we rose out of the launch cradle and up through Terminus station—and my heart did one of those sudden flip-flops like it does at the top of the roller coaster when you realize you're strapped in and it doesn't matter what you want to do anymore because *this* is what you're *going* to do, *whether you want to or not.*

We were on our way.

Up.

The One-Hour platform is called that because it takes exactly one hour to get there. It's also the legal limit of the atmosphere, so anyone who visits One-Hour can say that he or she has traveled into space.

One-Hour is also one of the biggest of the platform cities. Seven stories thick, it's suspended from all three cables; it fills the space between them and extends quite a ways out beyond as well. It's a city floating in the sky. You're high enough to see the curvature of the Earth in all directions. You can see as far as Mexico to the north and Peru and Bolivia to the south. To the west, the Pacific Ocean slopes away.

Directly below us was a humongus storm—except it wasn't a storm anymore. Now it was a hurricane. It was a great whorl of white, so big it covered more than half the world below us. From up here it looked as peaceful as a swirl of whipped cream on top of a big lemon pie, but if you watched long enough, you could see the banks of clouds moving slowly around a common center. Almost a hundred klicks an hour. They were calling it Hurricane Charles. I didn't feel honored.

Then Stinky asked the important question. "Can we call Mom now? And tell her where we are?"

"I thought we were going to wait until we reached Geostationary," Dad said cautiously.

"But I wanna talk to Mom *now*." There was something real frantic about the way he said it.

Dad looked uncomfortable. He glanced to both Weird and me as if looking for help—but Weird just said, "It might not be such a bad idea, Dad. Mom might be a little worried about us. We should let her know we're out of the storm." This made Dad even more annoyed, but he finally sagged and assented in that way he does when he's giving in to something he doesn't really want to do.

Stinky had already run to a phone booth, one of the ones with glass bottoms, so you can see all the way down. He was already punching for Mom. "I wanna show her my monkey!" He'd put his phone-home card in the slot so there was nothing for Dad to do except step sideways out of camera range. Me, I studied the walls, the ceiling, anything but the floor, until the screen finally lit up. First it showed a map of the US, and then it zoomed down in as it tracked her location. Mom wasn't at home; she was in San Francisco. She answered almost immediately; she looked tired but happier than we'd seen her in a while. Behind her we could see somebody's apartment, and out the window, we could even see what looked like trees or bushes. In the background, I got a quick glimpse of someone—a woman, Mom's age—but I didn't see her clearly.

"Hi, Mom!"

"Bobby! Where are you calling from?" At first her expression was surprised—as if she hadn't expected to talk to any of us for a while, but then her eyes flicked down as she read the information at the bottom of her display. And her expression darkened immediately. "Put your father on!"

Dad stepped into view then. "Hello, Maggie," he said grimly.

"You're doing it, aren't you!"

"I told you I would. It's the only way to be fair."

"You son of a bitch! The court said no."

"The court said not without your agreement."

"And I said no! So that means the court says no too!"

"Maggie—" Dad was keeping his voice deliberately calm. "I will not let you abuse the children as a way of getting even with me. They are old enough now, they're entitled to make up their own minds." Douglas shot me an *I-told-you-so* look.

"I'm going to stop you, Max—I'll see you in jail, you lying pig!" Abruptly, she remembered that Weird and Stinky and I were there too. "You kids—Bobby, Charles, Douglas—why did you let him do this? You stay where you are! Don't you go *anywhere* with him. I'm calling the police." Behind her, a woman's voice was asking, "Maggie? What's going on—?" And then the screen went blank.

There was silence in the phone booth for a moment. Finally, I said, "So this wasn't such a good idea, was it, Dad?"

"Shut up, Chigger!" said Weird.

"I wanna talk to Mommy!" Stinky wailed.

I realized then that after her hello, she hadn't said a thing to any of us kids, except to order us to stay put. For some reason, that made me feel really angry at her. If she really cared about us as much as she said she did—why was she yelling at us? At least, Dad didn't yell. He just went silent.

He was silent now. He looked uncertain. Actually, he looked old. Beaten up.

"Dad?" asked Weird. "Are you all right?"

"No," he said. "Look. I need you to understand something. All three of you. Your Mom didn't want me to bring you on this trip. So I did it without her permission. Maybe it wasn't the smartest thing to do. But I have to do this. I really do." Dad dropped to his knees in front of Bobby and me and put his hands on our shoulders. "I've made a lot of promises to you kids and I haven't been able to keep all of them. Just once in my life, I wanted to do something out of this world for you. And this is it. And I wasn't going to let anybody say no."

He looked so sad and vulnerable—and for a moment, he even looked *old*—that I couldn't help myself. I flung myself into his arms. And so did Bobby. And Douglas. Not because he was right, but because he was Daddy. And he *needed* us. And suddenly it was very scary, the whole thing, and I guess *we* needed him too, and then Stinky started crying. And I have to admit, even I—

Dad pulled back and looked me in the eyes. "Are you all right?" I guess he'd felt me trembling.

"Yeah," I said. "I'm fine. I just don't like her yelling at us all the time. That's all."

"Me neither," said Stinky petulantly.

Dad looked at Weird. "Douglas?"

Weird shrugged noncommittally. "It's just Mom. That's just the way she is."

"Do you want to go back?"

"She's going to call the cops on you."

Dad sighed and nodded. "I hope she doesn't. For your sakes—" he added sadly. "Because then we could both lose custody. And you guys would end up in foster homes. And that wouldn't be good for anyone." He looked sorry he'd said it, but it was too late to take the words back. Foster home? I'd never thought of it.

Abruptly, he looked at his watch as if he had an appointment to keep. He straightened up. "So? Are we going to Geostationary? Gotta make up your minds now."

I looked to Weird. He gave me a half-and-half expression, and finally said, "Well, it'd be silly to come all this far and not go all the way."

"Yeah!" I said. Because I really did want to go, no matter what Mom said. And so did Stinky.

We were going up again.

Our cabin attendant was named Mickey and he looked so shiny and clean he could have been a robot. He had one of those perpetual smiles that wouldn't quit and he acted like he was genuinely glad to see us. He kept trying to make friends with me and Stinky and Weird as if he'd been waiting all his life for this moment.

Our cabin was up at the top of the car. This car was bigger than the one we'd caught at Terminus. It was ten levels and each level was big enough to hold ten cabins. The level we were on, there were only four cabins and they were all big. We had a wall of windows with drapes that were secured at both the top and the bottom, and a big overhead window too, so we could look straight up.

What was weird was the way everything looked. Even Weird said it was weird. Mickey just smiled and explained that this was because the inside of the car was built to rotate around its central axis, so that it could be spun like a top as we approached micro-gravity. Then the outer walls would become the floors, and all the furniture and appliances had to swivel; that's why they were built the way they were. He said they'd spin us up to one-third gee. It would feel almost normal.

There was a chime then and Mickey said, "I've got a launch station to attend to." He bounced out, leaving us in a cabin that was bigger and more comfortable than our living room back home in El Paso.

Below us, the Earth was bathed in ghostly sunlight. The storm clouds shone so cold and white and bright that it was hard to believe how ferocious the winds must have been underneath them. I was glad we were out of it. Someone said that the storm was likely to disrupt passenger traffic up the Line for as long as three days.

The last chime sounded, and the car started sliding upward. We hardly felt anything, but out the window the beanstalk started moving downward. Actually, it looked more like One-Hour was falling down the Line while we hung motionless in place. As we watched, it dropped away faster and faster until finally it disappeared into the distance. We weren't just leaving One-Hour; we were leaving the Earth behind. Our next stop was (approximately) 22,300 miles above. 35,770 klicks. Compared to that the distance from Terminus to One-Hour was insignificant.

I felt sort of *squooshy* inside. For a lot of reasons. My stomach felt as mixed up as my head. I looked to Weird and said, "Well, are you going to ask him—or not?"

Dad said, "Ask me what?"

Weird cleared his throat and managed to stumble over a whole paragraph. "Well—it's about you and us and mom. Chigger and I were talking—and well, I mean—are you kidnapping us, Dad?"

Dad didn't answer right away. He sat down, nodding his head as if he had been expecting this conversation for a while. "I guess we should talk." He sighed. "You know that your Mom and I aren't on very good terms. I'm sorry about that. I wish it were different."

"Mom always maintained that the divorce was your fault—"

"I asked for the divorce, yes, but I think you should know why. I found your mother in bed with someone else—"

"That woman we saw on the phone?" Weird asked.

Dad shrugged. "I don't know if she's the same one or not. It doesn't matter. I've had a lot of time to think about this, Douglas. I've been paying the price ever since, because I don't get to be with the three people I love most in the world—you kids."

"Yeah, Dad, we've heard this part before," I said. "Every year, when we go on vacation. You always spend the first three days trying to make up for everything. Except it can't be made up."

He nodded his agreement. "Charles, I think you're the one who's been hurt the most by all this, and I wish I knew what to do for you to make it all right. It isn't easy being the middle kid. You're always getting overlooked and taken for granted and I don't blame you for feeling the way you do—"

"Yeah, Dad, yeah," said Weird. "We've all heard that speech before too. Tell us what's going on now." I was mad at Weird for interrupting. I had thought for a moment that Dad was finally going to say something that would make a difference. But maybe not, because he just let Weird change the subject without even noticing how unfinished I still felt.

"I've been thinking about this for years," Dad said. "Leaving Earth. It's something I've always dreamt of—going out into space and never coming back. But I was never sure where I should go. There were too many possibilities, and I could only have one of them. And then one day, I realized that not choosing meant I wasn't having *any*. So I made a choice. And then I started thinking—if I leave, I'll never see you boys again. And if you hated me for not being there when you were growing up, you'd hate me all the more for abandoning you. And I just couldn't stand that thought. So—" He stopped to take a breath and to figure out how to say the next part.

Weird filled the silence. "So you decided to just grab us and take us with?"

"No." Dad shook his head. "No, that's not it at all. I do have tickets for you, but they're refundable. I'm taking you only as far as you want to go. I'm trying to give you two things here, Douglas—the trip I've always promised you, and the choice you never had before on how you want your life to turn out."

Dad turned back to me. "You said something once, Charles, that has stayed in my head like a ball-bearing bouncing around the inside of an empty steel drum. You said that it was your family too and nobody ever asked you what you wanted. Well, this is me asking you. All of you."

"Do we have to decide now?"

Dad shook his head. "No. There's time enough when we get to Geostationary. You can go back down if you want. Or you can come on out to launch point with me. From here on in, whether you come with me or not is all your own decision. But at the very least, you're going to get an out-of-this-world vacation. I asked your mom—I said I wanted you to come with me up the Line, and then I'd send you all back home again. She said no. She was sure that I was going to try to steal you. And then she threatened to go to court and I realized just how angry she was and that she was going to try to hurt me any way she could. Even if it meant hurting you too. And that's when I started thinking that if jumping off the planet was a chance for me to have a better life than is possible on Earth, well then maybe it might be a chance for you kids too. But I promise you, Douglas, I won't take you anywhere against your will. I just want to spend some time with you before I go. Is that too much to ask?"

"Why didn't you tell us this before?" I asked.

"If I had, would you have believed me? Would you have come?"

I thought about that. He was right. I wouldn't have believed him. Would I have come? That was a harder question. Not believing him, I don't know what I would have done. In reply, I shrugged.

Stinky had been silent the whole time. I wasn't sure how much of this he understood, but he'd been listening carefully and suddenly he piped up, "Aren't we going home? I wanna go home!"

Dad and Douglas and I exchanged looks. Dad scooped up Stinky and held him on his lap. "Hey, kiddo. You're going to go home real soon, if that's what you want. But Daddy's going away for a long time, and I wanted us to have some time together before I say goodbye, that's all."

"Where are you going?"

"Very far away. So far away that you can't even imagine it."

"Why?" demanded Stinky. "Don't you love us anymore?"

"I love you more than anything, sweetheart."

"Then why are you going away?"

"Because it's something I have to do."

The frustration on Bobby's face was evident. He began to cry. "*But why...?* It isn't fair!"

"I'm not sure I understand it all either, kiddo. This is just the way it is." Dad hugged Bobby close, probably because he didn't have anything else to say.

Douglas gave Dad a weird look then—one of those looks that got him his nickname. He shook his head over some personal annoyance that maybe only the two of them understood and headed for the door.

"Where are you going, Doug?"

"Nowhere. Out."

Yeah. Like where *could* he go? And then he was gone anyway.

About three hours later, Weird came back. Without a word, he went straight to the bathroom. He was in there for a long time, and when he came out again he looked weird. Weirder than usual. Even for Weird. He looked flushed and upset and scared, but he also looked excited about something—kind of like the time he got off the roller coaster and discovered he'd crapped his pants.

Sometimes Dad can be very smart. He put his book down, went over to Weird and put a hand on his shoulder. Very quietly, he asked, "Do you want to talk about it, Douglas?"

Douglas gulped and nodded. He couldn't even talk. He managed to say, "I just joined the Elevator Club."

Elevator Club—?! Huh? I wondered who the unlucky girl was.

Stinky was already demanding— "What's the Elevator Club? I wanna join too!"

I stared at Douglas in amazement—suddenly realizing my big brother had just crossed a line and even though he was still my big brother, he was finally and irrevocably a grownup too. He had the secret handshake. And Bobby and I were still children. I turned to Bobby and said very calmly, "You have to be eighteen to join. It's like a driver's license. I can't join either."

Dad gave me an appreciative glance. "Thank you, Charles," he said. He patted Douglas on the shoulder. "You want to talk privately?" Douglas nodded and Dad and he went into the bathroom and shut the door behind them. I thought I heard Douglas stifle a sob, but I couldn't be sure.

After they were gone, Stinky looked at me. "Well, what kind of a club is it—?"

"It's a secret. You have to be eighteen."

"Well, what do they do that's so secret?"

"That's the secret."

"But that's not fair!"

I shrugged. "You're finally starting to get it, Bobby. Nothing is fair. Grownups make the rules—and they make them for grownups, not for kids. And that's the way things are."

"When I'm a grownup, I'm not gonna be like that."

"Oh, yes you will. So will I."

"No, I won't—"

"Yeah, you will, and I'll tell you why; because when you're a grownup, you'll have waited all your life for your chance to make your own rules, and you aren't going to give it up when you get it. Nobody does."

"It's still not fair."

"Yeah," I said. "It sure feels that way." But all of a sudden, I could see Dad and Douglas's point of view a lot clearer than I could see Bobby's. I wondered if that grownup thing was starting to happen to me. It's that thing that Dad is always talking about. Personal responsibility. Is this what it feels like? I said a bad word.

"Umm," said Bobby. "I'm gonna tell."

"Go ahead. I don't care. Maybe I'll even tell Dad myself."

Dad and Douglas were in the bathroom for a long time, and when they came out, neither of them looked like anything had been settled—but they were smiling, so at least I knew they were talking to each other again, and that was something.

*

"*Señor* Dingillian?"

Dad turned around to see who had called his name. It was a fat man, a very fat man. He looked Mexican, but he could have been from anywhere. "Yes, I thought I recognized you. I am Doctor Bolivar Hidalgo of Mexico City. I am an Associate Representative for Baja to the SuperNational Congress." He strode over and pumped Dad's hand enthusiastically, as if they were old friends.

Dad looked worried, but *Señor* Hidalgo reassured him quickly. "Oh, please, sir, have no worries. I don't think anyone else on the car is aware of your...ah, circumstance, I wouldn't fear. Here, come sit with me—no, please, I insist. You will be my guests for dinner, I will not take no for an answer." He indicated a booth in the corner.

Dad tried to beg off, but *Señor* Hidalgo insisted, and he had a firm grip on Dad's arm. *Señor* Hidalgo—"

"*Doctor* Hidalgo," he corrected. "Doctor of Political Science."

"Since when is politics a science?" Weird asked.

Hidalgo laughed. "I've often wondered the same thing myself. Here, you sit next to me, *muchacho*. Roberto, correct? No? Bobby, *si*. And you are Charles, yes? And of course, this handsome young man, so tall and skinny, must be Douglas. You have fine sons, *Señor* Dingillian."

Dad shrugged off *Señor* Doctor Hidalgo's inquiries with noncommittal answers, but I could see him mentally counting his pennies. Despite the wad of cash he was carrying, he had to be worrying about expenses. He accepted with a nod and dropped into a chair, but not before turning to the rest of us and cautioning us not to eat like pigs, we were guests.

"Don't be silly, *Señor* Dingillian. You are my guests. Order anything you like. I'm not paying for it anyway. I will charge it to, let me see..." He pawed through a fistful of credit cards. "Ah, here we are. These people owe me many favors. And I owe them nothing. They shall pay for your dinner tonight." In explanation, he added, "I have many sponsors. Politics costs money—especially when you are on the side of the poor. The rich can buy as many politicians as they want; the poor have only the leftovers and the castoffs." He laughed, as if this were funny. "Nevertheless, do let me recommend the ceviche. Or the —"

After a while, Dad finally interrupted. "Your courtesy is welcome, Dr. Hidalgo; but you barely know us. I can't help but wonder—"

"Forgive an old man his vanities—"

"You're not that old," Dad said.

"Old enough to be working on my second bottle of Tabasco," Hidalgo said. "You don't believe me? Cut me in half and count the rings. I'm old enough to have seen Lucy in first-run—"

Weird shook his head. "Now, I know you're teasing us, Dr. Hidalgo. "Lucy was born before the First American Civil War."

"Ahh, the *first* Lucy—I was thinking of the second one. And you're thinking of the Second Civil War. But yes, you're right, I'm not quite that old, but almost. Nevertheless, please accept my hospitality. I have no one else to share my table—now, let's have a look at this menu and see if they have an old-fashioned chocolate soda for Roberto here. You do like chocolate, don't you? I'm sure you do not get very much of the real thing. It's quite expensive, you know. Trust me, the chocolate sodas here are very very good."

Dad was curious about Dr. Hidalgo's intentions, and some of his impatience was starting to show, but the old man just kept chattering away about inconsequential things, refusing to let politics—or anything else—interfere with a good dinner. And it was a good dinner. There were things on the menu that I couldn't even pronounce, but the *Señor* Doctor ordered them anyway, and when the waiter put the plates in front of us, they looked and smelled delicious, and tasted even better than that. So for a while I didn't care what Dr. Hidalgo wanted. I was too busy eating. And Dad too, finally gave in to the inevitable and ordered himself a steak so thick you could have insulated a wall with it.

For dessert, the waiter rolled a big cart up to the table covered with cakes and puddings and things even Dad didn't recognize. I'd never seen so many different kinds of fruits in one place before in my life. And chocolate! Stinky's eyes went as wide as saucers, and I guess mine did too, and I think for the first time, I began to realize just how poor we really were.

I didn't know what to pick, and even Stinky and Weird were over-awed too because everything looked too good to eat. Weird actually smiled at me. It made him look almost human. All three of us—four, counting Dad—just stared at all the desserts so long that Doctor Hidalgo just started pointing and ordering. "Apparently, the boys cannot make up their minds, and neither can I. So we'll have it all. Just the best. We'll start with some of those fat red strawberries in cream and definitely the fresh grapes on a bed of thick rice pudding—and a big slice of the Chocolate Death, *por favor*, we shall all share that. Bring extra forks."

"Doctor Hidalgo—" Dad began slowly, "I appreciate your generosity, almost as much as my boys do, I'm sure, but it makes me very uncomfortable—as if you're trying to get to me through my sons."

Hidalgo wiped his mouth with his napkin. "Ahh, *Señor* Dingillian, a thousand apologies. Sometimes my generosity overwhelms people. I am used to giving. Sometimes I forget that other people are not used to receiving. I meant no offense. I only wanted to share some time with you— a man so committed to his sons that he will risk his freedom for them. I think I understand your situation, sir. And I think I might be able to help you. Conversely, you might be of some use to my people too— in your situation, you are probably going to need some useful friends, *comprende?*"

Dad sighed. "Doctor Hidalgo—"

"Please, call me Bolivar. Or Bollie. We have broken bread together." He waved at the table. "A great deal of it, indeed."

"Doctor Hidalgo—" Dad tried again. "I want you to understand something. I'm *not* kidnapping my children. I'm giving them the choice that their mother tried to deny them."

"Yes, I'm certain that's what it looks like to you, and I'm not so big a fool as I seem, that I would try to argue that with you. And that is not the discussion I want to have with you anyway." Hidalgo stifled a belch, wiped his mouth again, and conveniently looked at his watch.

"Oh *Madre de Dios*, look at the time. I have a very important conference call that I must be a part of. *Mucho importante*. It starts in five minutes. I must rush. Thank you so much for your company tonight, all of you—you have been very kind to an old man. No, no, sit down, finish your desserts. Do not leave the table until all of these plates are clean—" He shook hands all around. "I shall see you again before we reach our destination, I'm sure of it. *Señor* Dingillian, we do have much to talk about, and let us connect with each other tomorrow. For breakfast, perhaps? Or lunch? Please. Your company has been most gracious. *Au revoir.*"

Douglas giggled. "*Au revoir—?*"

Dad smiled. "Perhaps he forgot he was supposed to be Spanish." He glanced at his own watch. "That certainly was a convenient departure on his part. Just when he was getting to the punch line."

"Do you think he timed it that way?" Doug asked.

"I think *Señor* Doctor Hidalgo is way too good a snake-oil salesman to leave anything to chance. Yes, I think he timed it that way."

"Snake-oil?" Stinky asked.

"It's what you buy when your snake gets squeaky," I said, wondering what it really meant. Mostly, it meant another trip to the dictionary.

"Right," said Dad, heaving himself up from the table with a satisfied grunt. "And right now, it's time to get our squeakiest snake into bed—"

When we woke up in the morning, the gravity was completely sideways. Except it wasn't gravity—it was centrifugal force. We were so high, the pull of the Earth was insignificant. While we were sleeping, they had spun the car on its vertical axis, just enough to give the feeling of one-third gravity. We all wanted to see how high we could jump, but after Stinky bumped his head, Dad told us to stop, so we did—at least while he was watching. Instead we practiced walking back and forth for a while. It felt weird to be that light.

The door we had come in by was now on the ceiling— "How're we going to get out?" wailed Stinky. Weird went to one of the side walls and opened a circular hatch. Last night it was locked, because it would have opened onto a vertical shaft; now it was a horizontal corridor so we could walk the length of the car; except Dad wanted us to stay in the cabin.

Mickey brought us breakfast. He didn't say much; he just pushed the cart into the room and laid out everything on the table and then left quietly. Dad eyed him warily. Douglas looked like he wanted to say something, then went into the bathroom until he was gone. Dad made a show of turning on the video.

Hurricane Charles was still all over the news. The winds were still too high for the cleanup and the rescue crews to go in, and there had been a lot more damage at Terminus than they'd expected. They were already calling this the hurricane of the century. They expected Line traffic to be disrupted for weeks.

While we were watching, the door chimed—it was *Señor* Doctor Hidalgo. He looked flushed and impatient. "*Señor* Dingillian, I apologize for interrupting your morning, but I must speak with you. I had hoped to see you at breakfast, but that did not happen. The attendant told me that you were keeping to your cabin—good morning, *muchachos. Buenas dias.* Please, may I come in?"

Dad let him in and offered him a seat. "Would you like some tea, coffee? Something to drink? We have a bar."

"No, no—*muchas gracias*, anyway. I appreciate the thought. But you cannot afford to feed me or give me drinks in the style to which I have become accustomed. Even *I* cannot afford the style to which I have become accustomed. Never mind that—we must talk frankly. Can you send the boys out?"

"Out where—?"

"Yes, there is that. Very well then, I shall have to speak candidly in front of your sons. May I?" He pushed Stinky's monkey out of the way and sat down on the couch. He sank down into it, although he didn't sink as far as he would have the night before. Even in micro-gravity, he was still heavy. Dad sat down in the chair opposite him. I notice he didn't sit too close.

"Please forgive my bluntness, *Señor* Dingillian. There isn't much time—the people I work for know that you are carrying something of some importance. These people would be willing to pay you very handsomely—much more than your present employers—for the package. Two times, three times as much. Plus whatever other protections you need."

Dad stood up. "Thank you for coming by, Doctor Hidalgo. I appreciate all your courtesies." He offered his hand—whether to shake Dr. Hidalgo's hand or help him out of the couch, I wasn't sure. Dr. Hidalgo took the hint and levered himself up to his feet.

"I am very sorry you feel that way—I had hoped we could negotiate."

"There's nothing to negotiate. I don't know who you're working for, and I don't much care. I'm not carrying anything. And I'm offended at your offer. I'm not the kind of person who sells property that is not his to sell."

Hidalgo sighed. "Yes, I see. Of course. In that case, I must tell you—please do not take this the wrong way, I am not threatening, but I mean this in the sincerest sense—I am seriously worried about what will happen next. Money does what it wants. Money buys whatever it has to. I am afraid that the money will try to stop you, may even try to hurt you or your sons. Please reconsider—I will be available to you, wherever you are. If there is anything that I can do to help you, I would consider it an honor and a privilege to be of service—"

Dad was standing at the door, holding it open for Dr. Hidalgo. I sort of felt sorry for him, for both of them. I'd never seen Dad looking so grim. I know it hurt him to behave rudely toward anyone.

"We have nothing else to talk about, Doctor Hidalgo. Thank you for your courtesy and your concern."

Dr. Hidalgo looked very upset, like he was going to have to go tell someone some very bad news. He shook his head and sighed and pushed himself through the hatch. Dad sealed it behind him.

"Okay, Dad," said Douglas. "If you're not carrying it, where is it hidden."

"I don't know what you're talking about, Douglas. I'm not carrying anything."

"Uh-huh. Right. And our Christmas presents weren't hidden in the closet behind your file cabinets either."

Dad looked startled. "How did you—" He shook his head, exasperated. "Never mind. Just drop the subject, okay, Douglas?"

"He threatened us, Dad."

"I'm not deaf, Douglas. And I'm not stupid."

"Neither are we, Dad. What's going on?"

Dad turned to Douglas and took both his hands in his own. "If I ask you to trust me, will you?"

Douglas gave him that sideways look he does so well—the one that translates out to, "Excuse me? Did you really just say that?"

"Douglas, please—?"

"The money for the trip, right? That's where it came from."

"I can't talk about this. And you mustn't either."

"Uh-huh. Right. It's our lives too—and we're not allowed to know. You did it to us again, you son of a bitch, didn't you?" Douglas pulled his hands free and started toward the door, but he pulled free too hard and both he and Dad bounced in different directions, which would have been funny if it hadn't been so scary at the same time.

"I'm trying to protect you—goddammit!!"

"I don't want your protection! I want the truth." And Douglas was out the door—

We were traveling upward at 1600 klicks per hour, so the car started slowing thirty minutes before we reached Geostationary. By the time Mickey came by again, we were already packed and waiting. He had a serious expression on his face.

"Station Security knows you're here. Yes, Douglas told me what's going on." Dad gave Douglas a furious look, but Mickey interrupted him. "Mr. Dingillian, even if he hadn't, I already knew. I was only waiting for Douglas to ask me for help. There are officers outside waiting to take you into custody. They can detain you until proper paperwork is filed dirtside. And they will."

Dad had that perceptive look on his face. The one he wears when he's just figured out you're lying about something. "Go on," he said.

"Do you have a colonial sponsor?"

"I had one when we started. Sierra Corp."

"Had?"

"It was withdrawn this morning. My wife's lawyer filed some kind of a claim and Sierra withdrew. Some kind of protection clause in their boilerplate."

"Actually, that's a bit of good luck," Mickey said. "I have a friend who can get you a placement. It might not be a great one, but it'll be better than most. If you want it."

I spoke up then, annoyed—"Why the hell should you care, you're just a sky-waiter." Both Mickey and Douglas glared at me.

"Charles—" Dad warned.

Douglas answered for Mickey. "The Elevator Club. It was Mickey. That's why."

"Huh—?" And then I got it—*Oh!*—I didn't know what to feel. Angry. Or jealous. Or hurt. Or curious. Or just disgusted. Mickey? I didn't know what to say—so I said something to my brother I'd never said before. At least not like this. "I'm sorry, Douglas."

He reached over and put his hand on mine. "There's nothing to be sorry about, Chigger. I've sort of known it for awhile. Now you do too." He sounded like every other grownup.

I shook his hand off, and turned back to Mickey. "I don't understand —what does a sponsor do?"

"A sponsor gets you off this car safely and legally and puts you in the custody of a major corporation. At that point, you become their investment, and your mother—your wife, sir—will have to contest your status against a battery of very expensive lawyers who are perfectly willing to tie the legal system in knots rather than let the precedent be established that their indentures can be invalidated by decisions made in dirtside courts."

"How do you know all this?" I demanded.

"I learned it at my mother's knee." He picked up my backpack and shoved it into my arms. He turned to Dad. "Your sponsor is waiting outside. Are you coming or not?"

Mickey led us down the corridor toward the aft hatch, located at the former bottom of the car. "This is the cargo access. Service goods are brought aboard and waste is removed through this hatch."

"Are we going out in a dumpster?" I asked.

"Nothing that dramatic. Watch that light. As soon as it goes green, I punch this button and that door opens. There'll be a woman standing there holding a document. As soon as your dad signs it, you'll be under the full legal protection of Partridge Colonial Enterprises."

The green light went on, and Mickey hit the button. All three doors of the hatch whooshed open and a stocky older woman carrying a big business bag stepped in. "I'm your new lawyer. Call me Olivia. You're Max Dingillian? Pleased to meet you. Sign here, here, and here. She pulled a camera out of her purse.

"You kids, up against the wall. I need your pictures." Snap, snap, snap. Dad too; one more snap. "Raise your right hand. Do you solemnly swear that the information provided in these documents is true to the best of your knowledge, so help you God? Thank you. Congratulations, you are now clients of Partridge Enterprises. Would you thumbprint this, please? Right here. And here. Thank you. You kids too please?" She folded the papers and stuffed them into her purse, then turned to Mickey, wrapped him into her big arms, and gave him a hug that I thought would crush him. "How're you doing, sweetie?"

Mickey grinned at Dad. "Mom's the best. She eats human flesh. Raw, if she's really hungry. She can strip a full grown cow to the bone in seven minutes."

Olivia directed us into the transfer pod and hit the go-panel. Nothing happened at first; then we felt like we were getting lighter and lighter. "The pod-drum has disengaged from the cabin. It's slowing down now. As the spinning slows, we lose pseudo-gravity. Just hold on." For a moment, we were weightless, or close enough that the difference was insignificant. It kind of felt like we were falling, but not quite. After a moment that sensation went away and we weren't falling at all, we just kept feeling like it. Stinky started giggling. I felt like I was going to puke.

Something outside thumped softly and Olivia said, "We're connecting to the disk now. You'll have the feeling of weight in a second or two. Main level gives you one-half your normal weight, just a little more than the elevator car." Even as she said it, we were already sinking down to the floor.

The door popped open and we were staring at a hallway long enough that we could see how it curved up in the distance. "We're here," said Olivia. "Come on, I'll walk you through customs. Got your ID's and passports? Now, listen—you're going to be stopped by security agents. You've got to let me do the talking. Don't say *anything*. Nothing at all. They'll be recording everything." She looked to me, Douglas, and Bobby. "Look determined, okay? Like this is what you want."

"There they are—" The ugly little man saw us first and came advancing like an attack Chihuahua. He wore a wrinkled suit; it looked like he'd gotten it from his older brother and still hadn't grown into it. Two security guards came following after with bored expressions. A fourth man came running with a multi-lens vid-cam aimed at us. I said the word again.

Olivia saw them at the same time they saw us. She put on her biggest smile and said, "Howard, how nice to see you again. I understand they're getting an ambulance up here for you to chase."

"Don't be nasty, Olivia. I have a court order—" He held up an official looking document I guessed was a subpoena.

"Fold it and stuff it, Counselor. I have a Colonial Contract." She held up a paper of her own. Our contract. For a moment, the two of them faced each other like they were about to start a sword fight—only with folded documents instead of swords.

"I'm filing a complaint with Judge Griffith. You had unfair and unauthorized access."

"My clients requested that I meet them as soon as possible precisely to guarantee their rights of residence. That's all the authorization I needed. Why don't you try another line of work, Howard? You're not very good at this."

A crowd was starting to form. Olivia turned her attention to the guards, incidentally making sure that she was facing enough toward the man with the vid-cam that he would have a good angle on her. "My clients are under the protection of Partridge Colonial Enterprises. Whatever claims any groundside agency has against any of these individuals must come through me. I will receive service of summons forthwith—" She plucked the subpoena from Howard's hand and stuffed it in her purse. "But please be aware that under the terms of the Singapore Convention, custody of my clients may not be transferred without a hearing before Judge Griffith. You may not arrest, detain, or otherwise hinder the movements of these four people. Do you understand?"

Apparently they'd heard the speech before, because they looked bored as she went through the recitation. "Right. We know the drill." One of the guys didn't look happy; but the other said, "Are you going to be at Lemrrel's party Saturday, Olivia?"

"Of course, wouldn't miss it for the world. See you there." She stuffed her papers back in her purse and started to push forward—

"Hold it, Olivia. Not so fast. There are minors involved this time!" Howard stepped in front of her. He motioned to the guy with the camera. "Get in close for this, will you?" He stepped up in front of us and said, "Which one of you is Charles?"

Olivia nodded to me and I held up my hand politely.

"Thank you, Charles." He stepped in closer. He had bad breath. "Now I want to ask you a question and I want you to think very carefully before you answer. You don't have to answer for anyone except yourself. Are you going with your father of your own free will?"

I looked to Olivia, as if to ask her if I should answer. She held up a hand to stop me from speaking. "I take exception to this, Counselor."

"Nevertheless, Counselor—" Howard said right back. "For the purposes of this case, the court has seen fit to require evidence that the children are not being held against their will." He handed her another folded paper. She unfolded it and looked through it quickly. She nodded. "Well, I'll be damned. You got one right, Howard. This is all in order." She handed the paper back. "All right, Charles, you may answer the nice man."

"What was the question again?"

"Are you going with your father of your own free will, or are you being forced? You don't have to go with him if you don't want to. That's why these agents are here. To protect you."

"Oh," I said. "I think I'd rather stay with my Dad."

Howard frowned. He looked to Stinky. "You must be Douglas—"

"No, I'm Bobby. That's Douglas."

"Ah, thank you." Howard turned to Weird. "Douglas—are you accompanying your male parent of your own free will?" Douglas didn't like being pressured, but he nodded slowly. Howard leaned in toward him. "What was that? I need you to say it aloud. For the camera."

"Yes," he said loudly. "I'm going with my father of my own free will. And you need a better mouthwash." The crowd laughed.

Howard ignored it and turned to Bobby. "And you, young man—are you going with your father too or do you want to go home to your Mommy? You know she misses you *very* much."

"Watch it, Howard—" Olivia said warningly.

"I'm going with Chigger and my monkey," Bobby said. "Wherever Chigger goes, I go."

"The monkey?" Howard looked momentarily confused—

Stinky put the monkey down on the ground. "Show this man a 'farkleberry.'" He pointed toward Howard. The monkey immediately did a funny little dance in a circle, ending up in front of Howard, where he turned his back, yanked down his pants, and made a horrendous farting noise. The crowd roared. Some of them even applauded. Olivia guffawed like a horse.

Howard was not amused. But instead of losing his temper, he turned to Olivia and waggled his finger in her face. "Judge Griffith's, first thing tomorrow morning. The child did *not* indicate a preference for the male parent. We're calling in Social Services for a Protective Custody Interview. 9:00 am. It's already on the docket."

"As you wish, Counselor," Olivia said, calmly. She pointed us toward the Customs' officer. "Pick up your monkey, Bobby. I don't want it getting any fleas from the lawyer. See you in court, Howard."

Olivia guided us into her apartment and pointed us at chairs, with a brusque, "Get comfortable." Then she headed straight for her work station. "Power up, Betsy. Momma's got work to do. First things first. Do you want Italian or bleu cheese on your salad? You kids, what do you want on your pizza? Let's get the important decisions made first—then we have a lot of paperwork to review. I'm afraid your case has just gotten a little more complicated." She surveyed all of us on our likes and dislikes for dinner, finished punching the order in, then turned back to us expectantly.

"Is there a problem?" Dad asked. He looked worried.

"Yes and no. Your ticket's one-way, isn't it?"

"Yes. Mine is. The boys' aren't."

"Good. Then there's no problem. As long as you're not coming back any time in the next seven years. Statute of limitations."

"Huh?"

"Let me look over your resumes, your insurance, your tickets, all your paperwork. The problem is I'm going to have to void our contract. Or rather, you are."

"I don't understand."

"You're going to have to fire me for unsatisfactory representation. I'm going to have to advise you against that."

"But then they'll arrest us."

"That's why you can't fire me just yet—not until you get back on the outbound elevator." She hesitated. "No, I have a better idea. Don't fire me. I'll quit. If you get on the outbound elevator, I'll have no choice but to refuse to represent you anymore. Yes, I like that. It'll prove I have some integrity, and the result will be the same. And Howard will be *really* pissed at me. Judge Griffith will have a good laugh. She doesn't like Howard anyway. But I don't know how she feels about *this* case. We'd better cover our asses with a lot of paper tonight." She patted her ample butt. "And that's going to take a *lot* of paper.

"Now, hmm. How're we going to get you out to Disk Seven? Howard will have his goons posted by now."

"What about Dr. Hidalgo?" Douglas asked. Dad had told Olivia of his offer and his threat.

"He's not a problem. Not yet. Whoever's behind him, it's going to take them some time to organize. And I really think Dr. Hidalgo would rather negotiate. That's his style—I've seen him in action. Next time around, he'll offer you ten times what you were paid. If you refuse, then we'll have to worry about your life expectancy." She pulled her chair up to the computer and started typing and talking at the same time. She frowned and slapped the side of her monitor. "Come on, Betsy—get your fat ass in gear." Apparently Betsy didn't, because Olivia swiveled in her chair to face Dad. "Y'know—it's risky, but I could put you on the out-bound without a firm bid. That way I could get you out of here—wait, let me check." She swiveled back. "Betsy, how soon would Max and his children have to leave to catch the earliest possible lunar launch?"

The computer answered quietly, "The midnight car is the earliest one with open bookings. Should I make a reservation?"

"Yes. Use the Goodman account. If it's not overdrawn again. Two rooms for six people. Cancel two of the people just before boarding and sell the other four tickets to the Dingillians." To Dad, she said. "That should confuse Howard. He'll be watching for any booking for four, es-pecially in your name." She turned back to her keyboard. "If I can get you out of here and on the way to Luna, that gives me two days to find you a placement." Abruptly, she pushed herself back from the keyboard. "I've got another idea. Betsy, get me Georgia."

Almost immediately, there was a chime and a woman's voice an-swered, "Olivia, how are you?"

"The pizza's on it's way, Georgia—where the hell are you?"

"Pizza? Tonight? I thought we were getting together on—" The voice stopped, then came back laughing. "Oh, that's a good one, Olivia. Very good. You almost caught me. What do you need?"

"I need you for dinner. I have some people I want you to meet."

"The Dingillians, right? Howard was just here."

"I want you to interview the kids, sweetie. This is a beautiful family. They don't need a Protective Services evaluation."

"I'd rather do this through channels, Counselor."

"Georgia, so would I—but these people have already had one bid withdrawn because of this publicity. And there aren't going to be any more bids for them until this is resolved, we both know that. This is a delaying tactic by Howard—"

"Acting on behalf of the mother—" Georgia put in.

"Nevertheless, it's a delaying tactic designed to keep my client from his freedom to emigrate."

"Downside sees it as a custody battle."

"Yes, that's true. And starside sees it as a freedom-to-emigrate issue."

"Either way," the unseen Georgia said, "it comes back to the rights of the child."

"Precisely," said Olivia. "That's why I think you should meet the children. Tonight if possible. Not in a court of law. You need to see these kids as people, not specimens."

Georgia sighed. There was a pause. Then she asked, "What's on the pizza?"

"Your favorite. Mushrooms, onions, tomatoes."

"No Martian anchovies?"

"Have you seen the price of Martian anchovies lately? Next year, when Mars gets a lot closer, we'll talk anchovies. Can you be here in fifteen?"

"The distance has nothing to do with the price. You're just a cheapskate. And I'll be there in ten. Open a bottle of Lambrusco and give it a chance to breathe."

"Yes, your honor."

"This call is adjourned." Judge Griffith clicked off with a sound like a gavel coming down.

✳

The pizza arrived then, filling the apartment with thick tomatoey smells. I didn't know pizza could smell so good. At home, pizza is an industrial product, little squares rolling out of a machine. But this one was round and Olivia said it was hand-made. I couldn't imagine that.

Before Olivia could finish laying out plates on the table, a laughing woman in a wheel chair came rolling in. Judge Griffith. "I hereby declare this dinner officially in session," she boomed. And rolled right up to the table to put a small vase of flowers in the center. "From my own garden, Olivia. You always liked the blue roses, didn't you?"

Her chair had a built-in swivel, she wheeled around to face us. We were both staring at her open-mouthed. "You must be Charles and

Bobby. Douglas? Pleased to meet you. Max Dingillian? Wish I could say the same. You've sure stirred up a fine kettle of worms. Made a lot of extra work for all of us." She looked around, blinking. "Where's Mickey?"

"Late as usual," Olivia said. "We can start without him. Come on, everybody to the table—did you kids wash your hands? No? Well, hop to it. The pizza's getting cold. More wine, Your Honor?"

"How can I have any more when I haven't had any yet?" Judge Griffith held out her glass impatiently.

"Excuse me?" Dad said, when we were finally all seated and Olivia was passing out thick slabs of fresh hot pizza. "But am I the only one who sees a possible conflict of interest here? The lawyer and the judge and the defendants all having dinner together?"

Olivia and Georgia exchanged glances. And laughed.

Georgia said, "If this were a trial, yes, there would be a conflict of interest. But you're not defendants. Not yet. Tomorrow's hearing is investigatory, not evidential. My coming here is to obtain background information on the case, at the request of your attorney. And just in case you haven't noticed—" Georgia pointed toward two of the corners of the room where vid-cams were mounted. "—your kindly old Auntie Olivia is recording everything. For her protection, and for yours. When did you start the files, dear?"

"When you rolled in, Your Honor. All of the discussions we had before you arrived are in separate files, private-coded. These recordings are being made with grade-three authentication."

Georgia turned back to Dad. "This is upside law, not downside. We do things differently up here. You may have noticed that already. We don't have time to spend a year or two on a legal matter that should be resolvable in a couple of days. Nobody benefits from that. Justice delayed is justice denied. And pizza delayed is asphalt. So eat before that piece cools off in your hand."

Dad took a bite. Thoughtfully. Then another. He looked uncomfortable and he kept looking back and forth between the two women at the table. We'd just met the both of them and suddenly our lives were in their hands. How had we stumbled into this? Was this going to turn into a bigger mess now?

Olivia noticed first. "Max," she said, almost conversationally. "Do you have community standards classes in your town? Seminars?"

"Sure, doesn't everybody?"

"What's the stated purpose?" The way she asked, there was obviously more to her question than curiosity.

"To establish stability for the entire community. The most good for the most people."

Olivia looked to Georgia. "Sounds good to me—for dirtside. How about you, Your Honor?"

Georgia shrugged and spoke around a mouthful of salad. "Yeah, sounds good for dirtside."

I was starting to get the feeling that "dirtside" was a nasty word. A rude way of talking about people who lived on the ground.

"Well, it is good," Dad said. "There are seventeen billion people on the planet. You can't have everyone running around making up their own rules and setting their own standards. The, uh—the social contract and all that. The common good requires that people have a common context."

"That sounds pretty common to me," Olivia nodded.

"Yep," agreed the Judge. "Me too."

Dad finally got it. He narrowed his eyes. "Is there something wrong with the idea of the common good?"

"Nope," Olivia said innocently. "Not if you don't mind being common."

Judge Griffith leaned forward then to explain. "Max, downside, you can talk about things being common, because for most people, that's exactly how they are. Common. Ordinary. But up here—" She waved her hand to indicate not just the room, but everything beyond it. Geostationary. The Line. The moon. "Up here—*nothing* is ordinary. *Everything is extraordinary.*

"People don't come up here looking for more of the ordinary, they come up here because they want to get away from the ordinary. That's what space represents, the last chance for the *extra*ordinary life. This is a lifeline for the human race—a way out of the trap."

Dad shook his head. "The last report I saw said that there are still three million babies being born every day, something like that. The Line would take eight months to boost that many people into space. Assuming there would even be a place for them to go. The beanstalk isn't a way out. It's a luxury."

"No, it isn't," said Olivia abruptly. "It's a lifeboat. And there weren't enough lifeboats on the *Titanic* either."

That made for a moment of uncomfortable silence, until Judge Griffith rescued the conversation. "The point is," she said, "we're trying to get as many kids into the lifeboats as possible. And world-builders. And people who know how to make a difference. We might lose the Earth, yes—but this way at least, we won't lose the game."

✳

Mickey showed up then, looking very unhappy. Without a smile, he didn't look like the same person.

"I told you not to be late," said Olivia. "Your pizza's cold."

"I'm not hungry—" He sat down at the table and picked up a piece of pizza anyway. "I got terminated."

Olivia sat down opposite him, immediately all business. "On what grounds?"

"No grounds." He nodded in the direction of Dad. Or Douglas. "Getting involved." Mickey looked embarrassed.

Silence in the room for a moment. Olivia looked around, saw that Douglas looked particularly embarrassed, pretended she didn't notice, then looked back to Mickey as if she wanted to say a whole lot of things to him, but didn't dare.

"It's not Mickey's fault," Douglas blurted abruptly. "I asked him. He didn't ask me. And he said no the first two times I asked."

"Thank you for that, Douglas—but it still doesn't change Mickey's responsibility in the matter. How old are you, Doug?"

"I'll be eighteen next month."

"Close enough. No problem there. It's consenting adults," said Olivia.

"Line policy," countered Georgia. "They have a case. Tell me, did you do it on your own time?"

Mickey nodded.

"Well...at least they can't get him for neglecting the customers," Georgia said, then laughed at her own inadvertent joke.

Olivia turned to Mickey now. She lowered her voice. "Just tell me one thing—"

Mickey already knew the question, even before she asked it. "Yes, Mom. He *is* special."

Olivia gave Douglas a friendly smile, then turned back to Mickey. "That's all I wanted to know." She patted his knee. "Just so long as *you're* sure." She made me wish our Mom were as understanding. She started to turn back to Georgia—

"Mom," Mickey stopped her. "We've gotta talk. Things are getting really bad downside. You haven't seen the traffic we're getting. I don't know if I want to keep doing this."

Olivia looked pained. "Mickey, please—you're too valuable where you are."

"Mom, you said I could say when. Well, I think I'm finally saying when."

Georgia interrupted then. "Tell me about the traffic, Mickey. What's going on?"

"We're getting too many rich emigrants. Whole carloads. Groups. They all know each other, and they're very tight-lipped about where they're going. It's that thing Mom's always worrying about—people bailing out. Well, I think it's happening."

Georgia nodded. "We've noticed the traffic through here. We have some idea where they're headed. It's legal. And you could probably find a lot of other reasons to explain the increase—like having three new brightliners, the new catapult, the shift in immigration policies, the changes in the transportation laws—"

"Yes, but isn't it interesting that all that stuff fell into place at the same time, Aunt Georgia?"

Georgia rubbed her cheek thoughtfully. "I'm not willing to rule on it yet, Mickey. I'm still hearing evidence."

"Okay, here's a couple more for you. Last month, we had a family come up, you know what was in their luggage? Industrial memory. Nothing else. Forty bars of it. Probably three or four billion dollars worth. They had to pay a surcharge for the extra weight; they didn't even flinch at the cost. Georgia, they had enough raw memory for a small government. Or even a corporation. Whose data were they carrying offworld? And why? And *where*?"

"There's nothing illegal about transporting memory."

"No, there isn't. But on this big a scale? Doesn't it make you a little bit suspicious? What if it were bars of gold?"

"It wouldn't be worth as much—"

"That's right. And this is the fourth time this year we've had a passenger like that. At least that I know about. I'm only on one car. There are 95 other cars a day between dirtside and here. If what I've seen is one percent, then what would it mean if there were 380 more passengers like that?" Mickey spread his hands wide. "I'm just telling you what I've seen, Your Honor. You be the judge."

Georgia smiled. Obviously, it was an old joke.

Mickey turned to his mom. "You know that booking we've been talking about? I think it's time to use it."

Olivia's face clouded. She said, "We'll talk about it later."

Judge Griffith looked at her watch. "Your mother's right. That's a subject for later, Mickey. Right now, we've got a more immediate matter to attend to. The Dingillian kids." She wheeled her chair over to where Douglas and Bobby and I were sitting. "Okay, Munchkins, let's talk. Douglas, I saw Howard's tape. You're certain you want to go with your dad, right?"

Douglas frowned. "If you'd asked me last week, I'd have probably said I'd just as soon like to stay on Earth. But that was before we came up here. I dunno. Maybe Dad has the right idea. I've learned a lot in the past couple days." He looked to Dad and smiled slightly. "I think...if I have to decide tonight, then I'll stay with Dad."

"You *think*?" Georgia asked. "This is the rest of your life we're talking about."

"I know—you want certainty. Everybody always wants certainty. And you want me to say I'm sure about this—but who's ever sure of anything? Based on everything I've seen and heard, this is what looks best to me. I hope I'm not wrong."

"For a young man as confused as you are, you are very eloquent." Georgia laughed. "Listen, you're close enough to adulthood that I can separate your case out anyway. You can do whatever you want and I don't need to know why. Just be aware that the decisions you make here today are going to stick with you for a long long time." She turned to me. "Charles, let's talk."

"I want to stay with my Dad," I said.

She blinked at my certainty. "Why?"

"Because—well, I know this might not make sense to you, but my Dad lets me listen to my music. He doesn't interrupt. He *understands*."

"What about your Mom?"

"I still love her—I guess. When she's not fussing or nagging or screaming, she can be a pretty funny lady. But...she hasn't been very nice to be around for a long time. I'd like to say goodbye to her, but I'm afraid to. Last time, all she did was scream."

"Ah, I see," said Georgia. "What if you knew how much your Mom was hurting today and how much she was going to miss you and how much you were going to miss her? Would that affect your decision?"

I swallowed. Hard. I hadn't thought about it that way. Not really. Tears started to come up in my eyes. "If I do this, I'm never going to see her again, am I?"

"No, you won't."

"But if I go back to Earth, I'll never see Dad again either, will I?"

"That's right."

"So you're asking me to choose between one parent and another, aren't you? For the rest of my life."

"Yes, I am. I know it's a tough decision. But this is a lot more decision than you had last time this battle was fought, isn't it?"

"No. Last time wasn't for keeps."

"I guess not," Georgia said. "Nevertheless, this is the decision you have to make. So what's it going to be, Charles? Do you know?"

I wiped my nose, my eyes. I tried to imagine what life would be with Dad, wherever we were going. I couldn't, because I didn't know where we were going. I did know what life would be like if we went back— if *I* went back...

If I went back, I'd be going without Douglas. And maybe without Stinky too. And even though I always used to joke about wanting to be an only child—or even an orphan—now that I had the chance to decide who I wanted to live my life with, it was suddenly a much bigger decision than I'd realized. This was like running away from home. Only worse. Because we could never go back again. This was a one-time deal.

"Charles?"

"I don't want to leave my Mom," I whispered. "But I don't want to lose my Dad either. I don't know."

Georgia sighed. She turned to Olivia. "I've heard enough."

"You haven't talked to the little one."

"Do you think that's going to be any better?"

"No. I guess not."

Georgia patted me on the shoulder. "You did well, Charles. You told the truth. You made my job a little harder, but that's okay. We'll try to find a way to sort this out."

"Listen, wait—" I said. "If I could just *talk* to my Mom. Just to say goodbye. Just to tell her that...well, you know...that I love her and not to hate me, please. That would...I think that would make it all right. Maybe. 'Cause I do want to go with my Dad."

"I understand," Georgia said. She patted me on the shoulder one more time, then wheeled her way over to Olivia. "I'm not going to vacate the order. Howard has a case. At least enough for a hearing. You'd better be well-prepared tomorrow, Counselor."

Olivia stood up and pulled her chair out of the way. Georgia wheeled backward and swiveled toward the door. "Mickey, give me a hug. Nice meeting you, Douglas, Charles, Bobby—under different circumstances, I might say the same thing to you too, Max. See you in court tomorrow." She wheeled out and the room was painfully silent.

Nobody looked at me, but it was my fault. What I'd said to Georgia hadn't been good enough. I'd screwed up everything.

Olivia said a word. The word. The word that Dad keeps telling me not to use, and I keep using anyway. "All right," she said. "Let's try something else." She went back to her console, while Mickey began clearing the table. Douglas got up to help him and the two of them exchanged sad smiles.

Stinky had fallen asleep on the couch. The monkey was beside him— picking its nose, pretending to examine imaginary boogers, and then flicking them at me. Ha ha.

After a while, Dad got up and walked over to Olivia's desk. "Now what?"

She looked at him, almost startled, as if she'd forgotten we were all here. Then she snapped back to reality and said, "Okay, we go back to Plan A. We get your ass off this station as fast as we can. You'll have to fire me—sign that—and then you can hire Mickey as your agent instead. The placement will be on his license and he'll collect the fee. I'll be out of it. Here's his authorization, only don't date it until tomorrow. Otherwise, you'll be putting him in violation of the law too when you leave the station."

Dad looked to me. And Stinky. "What about the kids?"

Olivia shrugged. "They're your kids. You know them better than I. Will they be all right with it? Probably not. They're going to have a lot of anger to work out—just like before—only this time *you'll* get the brunt of it."

Dad didn't answer that. He just nodded in acceptance of the truth. Finally, he said, "I suppose I should tell you that I really appreciate what you're doing for me, but—"

"I'm not doing it for you," Olivia snapped. She looked up from her keyboard. "I'm doing it for the children."

She stood up to look Dad straight in the eye. "I hate cases like this. I hate family kidnappings. Even when they're justified. And this one isn't. This one is about you being selfish enough to think that you know better than everybody else. The fact that I agree with some of your conclusions about Earth and about what's best for your kids still doesn't mitigate the appalling selfishness of your actions. So don't assume that I like you. I don't. I just don't want to see your kids thrown back down the Line. That's the only thing you're right about. There is no future left down there." She glanced up. "Mickey? How long will it take you to pack?"

"Huh?"

"You said you wanted out. Well I've got six reservations on the midnight elevator, and Betsy is holding reservations on the next lunar shuttle. Make up your mind, right now—"

"Uh—" Mickey looked to Douglas. Douglas didn't look like Douglas anymore. He nodded shyly. Mickey turned back to his mother. "I'll go."

"Good. Then that'll settle the Dingillian placement too. I'll file it right now." She looked to Dad. "You are a lot luckier than you know. You'd better spend some serious time thanking Douglas *and* Mickey." She dropped back down onto her chair and rolled up to her keyboard. She started typing immediately, and whispering instructions to Betsy as well.

"Where are we going?" Douglas asked.

"As far as you can go." Abruptly Olivia turned to her son. "Mickey? What's the rest of it? The stuff you didn't tell Aunt Georgia? The part that panicked you so badly?"

Mickey looked very unhappy, but he stepped over to his mother and spoke quietly to her. "We had a meeting downside, yesterday morning. Elevator Security. They wanted to brief us about our responsibilities should the, uh...cable have to be shut down. Someone asked if they were thinking about it and they said that the corporation was currently examining all of its options if civil unrest should break out. The first step would be to restrict all passenger travel except to corporate passengers, which they're already doing—"

"Rats leaving the ship?"

"And their lawyers—sorry, Mom. The second step will be to restrict all travel entirely. Nothing at all will move between Terminus and One-Hour. The uh...the third step would be—more drastic."

"What's more drastic than shutting down traffic?"

"Breaking the cables at Terminus and letting the beanstalk pull itself off the planet altogether—"

"What?!!" Olivia came out of her chair so fast, it went flying backward and ricocheted off the wall. "You can't be serious—no, *they* can't be serious."

"Yes, they are, Mom." Mickey's voice was deadly quiet. "The Line has been self-sustaining for nearly a decade. There's enough farms up and down the Line, there's enough supplies stashed in the various pods—if we had to break free, we could. And apparently there are plenty people dirtside who see the Line as the perfect target. Break it in the right place and you get a wire wrapping itself around the equator of the Earth with an impact velocity of 40 kilometers per second. Nothing within 150 klicks on either side of the equator would survive. Counting passengers in transit, at any given moment there are almost 100,000 people on the beanstalk. There are six thousand permanent residents here at Geostationary alone. We've got two and a half percent of the world's wealth tied up in the Line, and the economic sphere is at least three times that large. Rather than risk that destruction of property—and the valuable shareholders who went up the Line—the corporation is prepared to pull anchor and hang free for as long as it takes, and not reestablish a ground base until Earth's governments can guarantee Line security."

"It'll never work!"

"It's already happening, Mom! They're using the hurricane as a first-stage drill. They're already moving the balance pods down the Line. They have this thing all planned out. I'm telling you, they briefed us on it—on what we would have to do in every eventuality. And the briefing officers looked scared, as if they knew more than they were saying. If we go to stage two, every elevator attendant automatically becomes a member of the Line Security force. There are stun-guns on every car now, and they're going to start stun-gun training immediately. You don't make plans that detailed and you don't brief that many people as a readiness exercise or a thought experiment. It was scary, Mom. Some of the women were in tears. The briefing officers made it sound like it was going to happen any day now and we had to be prepared."

"Why didn't you tell this to Georgia?"

"Mom! Think about it. Georgia has to know already!"

"Don't be silly—" But she stopped herself and turned to her keyboard.

"What are you doing?"

Olivia shook her head. "You don't need to know the details." She typed in a last command, then whirled to the wall behind her. She slid a panel sideways and unclipped three memory cards from their stations. She put one in her business bag, handed one to Mickey, and the third one to Dad. "Stash that in your luggage. Don't worry what it is. It's not illegal, and it's encoded. Your courier fee equals my legal fees. We're even." To Mickey, she said, "Get packed and get out of here. If I'm not at the station tonight, go without me. Can you get aboard through the cargo access?"

"If Alexei's on duty, we can board in a cargo bin—"

"Eh?" She raised her eyebrow.

"Mom, an empty cargo bin can be very useful for...you know."

"No, I don't know. And I don't want to hear any more. At least not now."

"Excuse me?" said Dad. "What's going on?" He waved his hand to indicate he meant *the whole thing*.

"Nothing, I hope," said Olivia. "And I'm too old to be taking these kinds of chances." She stopped long enough to look at Dad, "You picked a *lousy* time. You're trying to leave town in the middle of a corporate war. And this could be particularly bad for you because Security is going to lock down the entire Line. Even if we get you on a car, it's going to be tricky. It depends on how screwed up things get."

Mickey came out of the other room, carrying a silvery briefcase-purse thing over his shoulder. He looked like he was on his way to the gym or the skating rink; he was all scrubbed and shiny again. I could see why Douglas liked him so much. Even though I still didn't.

"All right," Mickey said. "You're going to have to do exactly as I say. There isn't time to explain everything. Is that all your luggage? Just those backpacks?" He made a face. "That's still too much. Take only what you would carry if you were sightseeing. If you can't put it in your pocket, don't bring it. Douglas, here, take this shopping bag. Anything that you really need, that you can't fit in your pocket and you can't replace, put it in here, so it looks like you've been souvenir-buying. Mr. Dingillian, that memory card that Mom gave you, toss it in here too. This is all the luggage you've got. Anything else you need, you'll pick up later. Doug, you'd better carry Bobby. No, leave the monkey—we'll get him a new one."

"Uh-uh, no way—" I said. "You've never seen a Stinky tantrum. *I'll* carry the monkey. I'll pretend its mine." I was already opening it up to switch off all of Stinky's programs. "Hey," I said. "Give me that memory bar. There's room in here for one more. The monkey's a perfect place to hide..." I stopped in mid-sentence and looked at Dad. He'd gone as white as a scream. "...stuff," I finished lamely. I looked to Doug. He'd gotten it too—at the exact same time. We both looked to Dad. He saw the expressions on our faces and he knew that we knew. And we knew that he knew that...

Douglas recovered first—neither Mickey nor Olivia had noticed, or if they had they were better actors than we were. They were talking about Olivia's connections; she'd be traveling separate. Doug tossed me the memory card and I shoved it into the last socket and closed up the monkey again, and we both pretended to busy ourselves with other stuff for awhile. Dad too. But for a few seconds, it was very uncomfortable.

Mickey delivered a running commentary as we walked, pointing things out as if we were nothing more than tourists. Douglas looked to Mickey curiously. Mickey smiled guilelessly. "Come on, let's get some ice cream."

Almost on cue, Stinky woke up, rubbing his eyes and looking around. "I didn't get dessert—" he started to whine.

"We know," said Mickey. "See, we're already here—this is going to be the best part of your trip. I know, the desserts you had on the elevator were good, but most of them are too rich and too sweet to be really enjoyed. You practically have to wear protective gear."

Dad spoke up then. He'd been very quiet ever since Doug and I had realized the truth about the monkey. "Excuse me—*why are we stopping for ice cream?*"

Mickey didn't answer immediately. He was studying the menu. After a minute, he said, "I think you should have the banana split. Bananas get more expensive the farther out you go. This might be your last chance to enjoy a banana split." The waiter arrived then and Mickey looked around the table. "Okay, are we all decided?"

We ate in silence. There was no sound except the clink of spoons against glasses and Stinky making bubbles at the bottom of his chocolate soda. Mickey looked up abruptly, "Ahh, Alexei—*dos vidanya.*" He pulled out a chair for the newest arrival, a tall skinny geeky-looking guy, all arms and legs. He looked like a spider. He gangled. He wore a Russian-looking turtleneck, shorts, and sandals—except for the shirt, it was pretty standard station wear. To the rest of us, Mickey said, "Alexei is a native Loonie, down here for college and muscles. How go the exercises, Alexei?"

Alexei grinned and made a muscle. There wasn't much to show, but he seemed proud of it. "I shall be a muscleman when I return home. The girls will flock around me at the beach." He grinned and laughed. I stared at him, so did Douglas and Stinky. We'd never met a *real* Loonie before.

Mickey must have seen the expressions on our faces, because he made introductions then. Alexei stood up and bowed to each of us, then offered his hand for a handshake. He shook hands with each of us, grabbing our hands in both of his own to do it. He turned to face Mickey and said casually, "So? You said you had packages?"

Mickey nodded toward us. "Four. Five if you count me."

Alexei glanced at us again, his face darkening. "I don't know, *Mikhail.* I'm not equipped for a job like this—this is a little big for me. You know the whole line is locking down?"

"I know," said Mickey.

"It's going to be expensive."

"I have information. *Big* information."

Alexei pursed his lips and frowned to himself. He was thinking it over. He steepled his fingers in front of his chin and nodded thoughtfully. "How big?"

"The biggest. It *will* affect your business." Mickey lowered his voice and said, "Listen, Alexei—Max here has pissed off one of the SuperNationals. Do you know Hidalgo? Yes, that one. He threatened Max—oh, not directly, of course—but there was no doubt about his intentions. This might very well be a matter of life and death."

Alexei glanced at Dad, with new respect. "I like you. You make powerful enemies." To Mickey, he said, "All the more reason why I shouldn't get involved in this."

Mickey stared right back. "You really want to hear what I know."

"Don't do this to me, *Mikhail.*"

Mickey leaned over and whispered in Alexei's ear. Alexei's eyes widened and he pulled back to stare at Mickey. "You're crazy."

"No—*they're* crazy."

"They'd have to be—good God." Alexei put his hand over his mouth, shocked. It was like he didn't want to let himself say anything else. It took him a moment to find his voice again. "I have phone calls to make, lots of phone calls," he said. "I wish you hadn't told me—no, that's not true. I'm glad you told me. But now I'm obligated to do this stupid thing for you, aren't I?"

"That's why I told you." Mickey smiled sweetly.

"You have the soul of a viper. Your mother trained you well."

"I love you too, Alexei." Mickey glanced at his watch. "Come on. We'd better get going." Mickey slid his card through the table's reader. "Okay, we're paid. Let's go."

Alexei pulled out his phone and started calling people. Most of his calls were in Russian, he spoke in thick rabid phrases, shouting almost hysterically at whoever was on the other end. Each time as he broke the connection, he smiled at us. "You've got to talk to them in their own language: Stupid. Is not to worry. They will do what I tell them. There is too much money at stake." He looked to Mickey. "This is going to be very expensive—for everyone. Especially for me, not for you though. You are already paid. The information you have given me—I will make millions of dollars today. Already I am having some wonderful ideas. *Mikhail,* I hope there is time for them all. I am most grateful that you called me—I will name my firstborn child after you, even if he is a girl." He popped his phone open and started hollering into it again.

Still roaring into his phone, Alexei fumbled a pass card out of his shirt pocket and used it to unlock a wide hatchway; we followed him into a service bay and boarded a cargo elevator. Alexei gestured impatiently at the walls, and we all grabbed handholds—he hit the go-panel and we rose "up" toward the axis. Pseudo-gravity faded out. Dad and Doug and Mickey took turns carrying Stinky who hadn't quite fallen asleep again, but was content to just rest in the arms of whoever was carrying him. In micro-gravity, he wasn't as much of a burden, but he was still an awkward bundle.

Alexei closed his phone and looked at Mickey. "I am going to make too much money today, *Mikhail.* I will have to give you some of it or my conscience will trouble me—not too much, though. I do not have a very large conscience. You will share some of it with your new friends, *da?* That gives me another idea—later." He opened his phone again and yelled into it.

When we got to the top—we came out of the tube into a narrow service corridor, the floor here had the steepest curvature of all. The pseudo gravity was too light for real walking, so we sort of bounced forward, caroming off the walls for a bit until Alexei slowed us down and suggested we conserve our energy. He pointed to handholds spaced along the walls. "Use those. Pull yourselves along. Pretend you're swimming. I will carry the little one—" I wished he hadn't said that about swimming. I was already having trouble remembering up and down. This wasn't as much fun as it looked. Stinky thought it was fun. He wanted to try bouncing by himself, but Alexei promised him that it would be more fun to ride on his back, so he decided to try that instead. How often do you get to piggy-back ride a Loonie in free fall?

We passed a whole bunch of KEEP OUT, THIS MEANS YOU! and AUTHORIZED PERSONNEL ONLY! signs, but Alexei ignored them. Whenever we came to a locked hatch, Alexei would pull out an appropriate clearance card and pass us through. "How do you have all these cards?" Dad asked.

"What do you think I came here to study? Domestic Ecology. I am on a work-study plan. I earn my education with hands-on experience. I am three years here, I have clearances everywhere. I can go anywhere on the station. It is the perfect job for a young smuggler, *da?* Do not worry, Mr. Dingillian, I do not abuse the trust of my employers. At least, not very often. And usually only for a good cause. This is a good cause. Besides, if what *Mikhail* tells me is true, I think that my usefulness here has just ended. I am returning to Gagarin very shortly. I will visit my money."

"When?" Dad asked.

"Tonight," laughed Alexei. "On the very same elevator as you. We go out together. Ahh, here we are—"

Here was a thick hatch into a triple-sealed room—an airlock? Inside was a ladder up into a hatch in what would have been the ceiling if there were any gravity. Alexei passed Stinky into Mickey's arms and pulled himself up the ladder. At the top, he put his card into a reader and punched an entry code. He looked back down to us. "You must be very careful here. We are at the hub. The axis. The Line passes through the center of a pressurized core. As you come through, you'll see that the top is moving. Don't be afraid. Hold onto the railings, you'll be fine. I'll be right here to help. Any questions? Let's go."

Alexei tapped the go-panel and the hatch slid open. He pulled himself up through the opening and disappeared for a moment. Then his head reappeared. Hokay, Douglas, you come next please?" Douglas jumped and floated right up to the hatch, grabbing onto the handholds near the top. "That's right," Alexei coached. "Now just pull yourself through. Hokay, Charles—you come next. This is very easy, *da?*" I swallowed hard. For some reason, up and down and sideways had suddenly decided to stop being up and down and sideways and were all changing directions on me. I felt dizzy. I squeezed my eyes shut. Sometimes that helped. This time it didn't.

"Charles? Are you all right—?" That was Dad. I didn't answer.

"*Charles*—!" That was Alexei. "Open your eyes and look at me. Do it *now!*" His voice was so hard it startled me. I opened my eyes. He was holding his hand out toward me. "Look at my hand, see? Just grab my hand, hokay? I'll do the rest."

Before I could shake my head no, I felt Dad lifting me up to take Alexei's hand. Alexei grabbed my arm and pulled me gently through the hatch. "See, that wasn't so bad—here, grab this railing and hold on. Douglas, hold him, please? Thank you. Move down now, just a bit. Make room for the others." I was still uncomfortable—almost close to tears, I didn't know why—but then Douglas put his arm around my shoulder and held me close and I didn't feel quite so bad any more.

"*Mikhail*, I am ready for the little stinky one. Pass him here. That's it. Come to me, Bobby. Here, stick your head through. Look around— see? Nothing to be afraid of. The only monsters up here are your brothers. Hold onto this railing, please. *Mikhail*—? Send up Mr. Dingillian, please."

Dad came next, and Mickey followed. Alexei sealed the hatch behind him. Now, we were all clutching handholds on the inside of the steepest curve yet. Three meters away, the curved wall of the core whispered by. We could hear the air whooshing as it passed. We watched a steady progression of warning signs and arrows and numbers and access panels. There were tracks along the surface—and on our side too.

"Ahh," said Alexei. "Here it comes." *It* was a bright red platform sliding toward us on the rails. It slowed to a stop directly next to the access panel. It had handholds and equipment boxes mounted all over it. Alexei pulled us all aboard, and then pushed a green go-button. The platform began moving spinward, faster and faster, speeding up until we had matched the speed of the inner wall, opposite a panel marked **One-Gamma-Three**.

Alexei unfolded the collapsed contraption in the middle of the car. It was an extensible ladder and it went all the way across to the inner wall. "Hokay, let's go." He grabbed Stinky in a bear hug and started scrambling across like a pregnant spider. I shook off Dad's help, but not Douglas's. When we were all safely across, Mickey hit the release on the top of the ladder and it folded back down. Now the ceiling felt motionless and the floor was rolling past. Below, the car we'd ridden on began slowing down; pretty soon, it disappeared around the curve behind us.

Alexei was already opening the One-Gamma-Three panel and pulling us through. First Douglas, then me, then Mickey—they passed Stinky through—then finally Dad and Alexei. Inside the core—I levered myself around to look and nearly lost it—"*Douglas!*" I wailed. My brother caught me and held me tightly with his right arm. "It's okay, Charles. I'm right here. I'm not letting go. Just hang onto me—we'll be fine. Really."

I buried my face in Douglas's shoulder. I could sense that both Mickey and Dad were hovering close, but I didn't want to have anything to do with either of them. Only Douglas.

What I'd seen...was the largest interior space I'd ever seen—well maybe not *the* largest, maybe Terminus was larger—but definitely the *deepest*. It was like the inside of a giant pipe, filled with humongus wires, cables, tubes, conduits, vents, catwalks, ladders, platforms, machinery, and *stuff*. And it all looked *up* and *down* and *sideways* —all at the same time!

"Are you okay, son—?" That was Dad. I didn't answer. Douglas pulled away just enough look at my face. He tilted my chin upward so we were eye to eye and nose to nose. I couldn't remember the last time we'd ever been this close. Maybe we never had. "I'm not going to let anything bad happen to you, Charles. I promise."

"What's wrong with Charles?" I heard Stinky asking.

"Nothing. Please be quiet, Bobby. Charles has an upset stomach. He'll be okay in a minute. Go back to sleep." Douglas looked back to me. "Just tell me when you're ready."

I shook my head. I didn't want him to let go. I liked having his arm around me. I felt safe. I swallowed hard. "I don't want to lose you, Douglas," I whispered, so only he could hear. "Not to anybody—" I sort of nodded toward Mickey.

"You're not going to lose me. I'll always be your brother, no matter what."

"Is that a threat or a promise—?" I half-joked.

He half-smiled. "Yes." He nudged me. "Come on, the others are waiting. And we don't have a lot of time. Are you ready?"

"Yeah. Just stay close, okay?"

"*Hokay*," he said. Just like Alexei.

It was like being on the inside of a giant pipe that kept changing its orientation. But as long as I kept focused on the wall and pretended that I was swimming and it was the floor, I was okay. If I had to look away from the wall, for any reason, I pretended that everything else was *up*. It sort of worked, but I still felt dizzy.

Alexei pointed around the curve of the wall toward a cluster of pipes and a vertical platform on which there were some storage lockers. We pulled ourselves along a line of handholds, and when we got to the platform, we anchored ourselves against its railings.

"Do you see this pipe?" Alexei pounded on one of the thicker pipes next to us. "Put your ear next to it. You can hear the water rushing through it. Very useful stuff. We use it for ballast. We use it to balance the rotation of the disks. Sometimes we even turn it into oxygen to breathe and hydrogen to burn. And of course, we also use it for drinking and bathing and growing our crops.

"But—" he interrupted himself. "—these pipes are also very useful if you have to go somewhere and you don't want anyone to know that you are going or how you got there. And so, while we respect the water, sometimes we ride it too." Alexei opened one of the storage lockers. Inside was—scuba gear?!

"Huh? Are we going swimming?" Stinky asked.

"You? No," Alexei said. "Them. Yes." He pointed. We looked up—every direction was *up*—and saw four, no five, teenagers diving out of the center toward us. Three boys, two girls. They were wearing shorts and T-shirts and looked like they had fallen off a runaway picnic. They were laughing like they were diving into a party.

As they approached, they began waving and calling to us. They caught themselves easily on the platforms and ladders and railings around us and they shouted things at Alexei in Russian that made him blush with embarrassment. They passed him a backpack and a pair of canteens. They had a third canteen of their own, which they passed around among themselves, each one taking deep swallows of whatever was in it. From the way they acted, I didn't think it was water.

Alexei took the flask when it came to him and took a deep swig of his own, then he pocketed it, much to their dismay. "You have all had enough," he said. Then he bawled them out in Russian. Or gave them instructions. Or told a dirty joke. Whatever. When he finished, they all laughed and started pulling on the various pieces of diving equipment.

Alexei explained, "These are my fellow students and colleagues. The swimming equipment is part of our service. Sometimes we have to inspect the pipes from the inside. Sometimes there are air-bubbles. Sometimes we have to retrieve a broken robot or a piece of something that has caught somewhere. We do not have to do that very often. In fact...I can't ever remember having to go into the pipes at all for anything a robot couldn't handle. But, nevertheless, we have our responsibilities. We have to keep ourselves ready and able to handle any possibility, any emergency at all. So we practice and drill and keep ourselves focused on our responsibilities to the water of the community. Today—ah, today we get to put into practice what we have practiced. They shall be...the *decoys*."

"So this is how you do it," Mickey said. "I've always wondered about that."

"Wonder no longer," Alexei said. "Sooner or later, somebody was certain to figure it out anyway. No matter, I already have three other ways to move things from here to there—just not as exciting. I leave it to you to figure them out, *Mikhail.* I will bet you a day's interest that you cannot."

"I can't afford that bet," Mickey laughed.

Alexei laughed with him and clapped him on the shoulder. "You are smarter than you act. This is a good trait." To the rest of us, he said, "We have to assume you are being watched. At the very least, monitored through station security. There are those damnable little cameras everywhere. They saw us coming up the service elevator. They know that an access hatch was opened. That was why I used my *own* card. So they could monitor our progress. Very shortly, they will be monitoring the progress of five divers through the pipes—and one of them will be carrying my locator. Five divers, not six, we will keep them wondering what happened, *da?* They will meet the divers on the topside of Disk Seven. But by then, we will be somewhere else, and they will have lost us. I am too clever for my own good." To his Russian comrades, Alexei shouted, "What is taking you so long? Do you think we have all night? Look at the time. We have less than an hour—"

"Alexei," said one of the men, a dark brooding fellow with eyebrows like furry caterpillars. "The deposits are made, *da?*"

"*Da.*"

"This is good. We have made our own reservations, we will be on the one ayem car. If what you say is true—"

"You have told no one else?"

Caterpillar-brow shook his head. "I think the word is already spreading. But no, we have told no one. Go now. Godspeed!" He glanced around. "Godspeed to all of you." Then he grabbed Alexei and the two of them exchanged kisses on each cheek, the way they do in Europe. I'd never seen men do that before, kiss each other—even friends. It sort of freaked me. I looked at Douglas and Mickey and tried to imagine them kissing. It didn't seem right, but it didn't seem as wrong anymore either. What the hell did I know?

We were going up the Line—*by hand.*

From an Earth perspective, we were going up. From the Geostationary perspective, we were going sideways—starside—outward toward Disk Seven.

From our perspective, we weren't going any direction at all. Just *forward* along a never ending pipe. There was water on the inside of the pipe; we could hear it. There were handholds running the length. We were climbing to forever. I wondered how long it would take to climb the whole Line—

"How come we can't take a maintenance car?" I asked. "Look, there are lots of tracks along these pipes. And there's a car over there."

"The maintenance cars are monitored." Mickey said. "We don't want to leave any evidence of where we started and where we got off. Most of all we don't want anyone showing up to meet us. Just keep pulling yourself along."

Alexei showed us how to do it. "Don't try to hurry," he said. "You'll tire yourself out. Slow and steady does the job. Do like I do, hand over hand, counting like this—like music—and one and two and three and four...like that. That's how to make the best time over a distance." He added, "If you did this all the time, you would know how to go faster, but I need you to conserve your strength. We have a long way to go. Almost two kilometers."

I concentrated on watching the handholds passing in front of me. I pulled myself steadily forward, left hand over right, right hand over left.

It took us more than an hour. We stopped once to pass a canteen around and catch our breaths; this canteen had water in it and a nipple over the opening; I sucked at it thirstily. Doug whispered to me, "Slow down, Chigger—don't pull a Stinky." He was right. I passed the canteen on. It was a very short rest; as soon as everybody had had a drink, we were on our way again.

At the top, or the far end, we exited the core the same way we had entered. It could have even been the same access panel; the only thing different was the number painted on it. **Seven-Gamma-Three**.

We transferred across to the rotating part of the disk without incident. It was a little bit easier for me this time, because I knew what to expect. We climbed back down into the service corridor, but instead of heading toward the elevator, Alexei led us in the opposite direction, looking for a specific hatchway. We passed several before he found the one he wanted.

"Okay, comrades," he said. "This is where you must each make a prayer to Saint Vladimir—"

"Saint Vladimir...?"

"I made him up. He is the patron saint of smugglers. I smuggled him into heaven. Now let's see if he is appropriately grateful." Alexei took out his clearance card and swiped it through the reader slot. He inhaled. He exhaled. The panel turned green and when he tapped it, the hatch popped open.

"Thank you, Saint Vladimir. I shall light candles at your altar." Alexei said to the ceiling. "As soon as I can find candles. As soon as I can build an altar." We passed through—into the top of a brightly lit shaft lined with machinery. It was deep and slot-shaped, and the walls were lined with tracks and service bays. On one side, we saw seven or eight elevator cars, each one docked and surrounded by lights and equipment and service gear. From our perspective, they looked like they were stacked sideways. None of them had the cabin spinning; all had their lights on.

"Ahh," said Alexei. "I have done good. Very good. And Saint Vladimir has done good. I was afraid I was going to have to replace him. See there? We are almost at the beginning of your journey. This way, citizens. We must not be seen."

We entered 1187 without incident. It was a lot like the car we'd ridden up in. We pulled ourselves in through the left-side hatch; it was the cargo hatch, the bottom. I wondered which way it was going to spin—clockwise or counter-clockwise? Would it make any difference?

We pushed and pulled ourselves into our suite and bounced into chairs. Mickey showed us how to latch the seat belts, and we belted ourselves down. Douglas wrapped a blanket around Stinky, who promptly curled up and fell asleep wrapped around his monkey. The monkey snored softly for a moment or two and then fell silent.

Alexei was already pulling rations out of his backpack. "I thought you might like a snack while you wait. I have cheese, sausage, bread, grapes, little tomatoes, carrots. Eat hearty. *Bon appetit.*" He bowed from the waist, difficult to do in micro-gravity. "I must return now—they will be looking for me. I must not disappoint them. Otherwise, it spoils the game. Besides, I need to collect some things. Including my alibi." He handed the backpack to Mickey. "*Mikhail*, please make sure my father gets this. If I am not able to deliver it myself. Hokay? Thank you." And with that, he was gone.

"Where's he going?"

"Back down."

"The same way?"

"He can do it in fifteen minutes. He was a finalist in last year's no-grav Olympics. It's those long arms of his. And all the practice he gets." Mickey explained, "He'll probably go back to the ice cream place or walk around the promenade for a while, whatever it takes, until he's sure that whoever is watching knows that he's not with us anymore. Then he'll disappear again. At least, that's my guess. Charles, do you want some grapes?"

"No thanks." I pushed the plate away. "All the grapes I've ever gotten have been sour."

"Yes, and you've done a fine job making sour whine." It was the first time Mickey had ever said anything rude to me. I looked at him surprised. He looked right back at me with a hardness I'd never seen before. "Don't you ever put a cork in it, kiddo? Do you know that you are *no* fun to be around?"

"So what?"

"So look around you and stop acting like a spoiled brat. Your family is coming apart—"

"It came apart a long time ago."

"Shut up, stupid. Try listening for a change. You might learn something. In case you hadn't noticed, your brother, Douglas, is having a very difficult time of this. And your dad isn't doing too well either—he hasn't spoken two words since we left my mother's. The only reason Bobby hasn't thrown a tantrum is that we slipped a sedative into his chocolate soda. We should have done the same for you. You're not doing anything to make this easier for anybody."

"Nobody's trying to make it any easier on me," I snapped back.

"Excuse me—?" Mickey pushed in close, getting right in my face. "Douglas wasn't there for you when you got free-fall panic? Your dad didn't lift you up when you needed it? Your dad hasn't been trying to reach out to you all evening? Or was I hallucinating? You're acting like a selfish dirtsider, Charles. And I don't like you very much, right now."

"So what? None of this would have happened if you hadn't—"

"Don't *go* there...." he warned.

"Mickey, please—" That was Douglas. "There's more to this than you know." He stepped/bounced over to Mickey and put his hand on his shoulder; they looked at each other and something unsaid passed between them. Mickey looked frustrated, but he nodded and backed off. Douglas turned to Dad then. "Okay, Dad," he said. "What's in the monkey?"

Dad shook his head. "I wish you hadn't found out about that."

"Yeah, well—it wasn't too hard to figure out. Is there anything else you want to tell us?"

Dad shook his head. He looked beaten, frustrated, angry, unhappy. "No, there's nothing else. I just thought—that maybe we could have some time together that wasn't a fight."

"Why would you think that?" asked Douglas. "Every time we get together, it's a fight. That's all we ever do. Why would you think this time would be different?"

Dad looked across at Doug and his expression was as straight as I'd ever seen. He spoke slowly and it was hard for him to get the words out. "I thought that because it would be...the last time we'd all be together as a family...that maybe we'd all try to make it something good to remember."

"Why should we? What do we owe you? Or mom? You've both been using us—and using us up. Between the two of you, Mom and her tirades, you and your passive-aggressive bullshit, you've turned Stinky into an incontinent little pissant, and Chigger—well, he's well on his way to becoming a sociopathic hermit with surgically attached earphones. I'm sorry, Chigger, but Mickey is right. You can be a royal pain in the ass sometimes."

He turned back to Dad. "And me—? Well, just look at me, Max. I'm your son. This is how I turned out. I have the social skills of a virus. Chigger is right, I am the geekoid from hell. We're all of us screwed up, Dad—and this...this isn't an answer. It's more of the same. It's you running away again. Only this time, you want us to run away with you. But how can we run away with you when it's *us* you're been running away from all this time?" I couldn't believe what I was hearing from Douglas. He was almost in tears. And Dad—poor stupid Dad—he just sat there and took it.

Douglas stopped, exhausted. For a moment, he just floated limp. Finally, he drifted down toward Mickey's lap. He bounced off Mickey and started to push himself up again, but Mickey pulled him back down and held him with one arm firmly around his waist. Douglas looked uncomfortable for a moment, but Mickey whispered "shhh" at him, and Douglas finally let himself relax. He leaned his head back and closed his eyes for a moment, not caring if we saw.

"Charles?" Dad looked at me. "Do you have anything you want to add?"

I thought about the opportunity. Yeah, I had a lot to say. But it wasn't necessary anymore. "No. Doug said it all."

"Is it my turn now?" Dad asked. "Do I get to say anything?"

I shrugged. "I don't care." Douglas shook his head too.

Dad took a breath. He was gathering his strength, and his words. Then he said, "I remember when you were born, Doug—when Charles was born too. And Bobby. How proud I was of each of you, how much I cherished you. I used to wake up in the morning, promising myself every day that I'd be the best dad I could for my boys. And I really did try. I really did. Now I wake up every morning wondering how I screwed up so badly. And what can I do to make it right? It always comes back to money. I don't have any. I'm a million and a quarter in debt. And no matter how hard I work, I just keep getting deeper and deeper. And nothing is fun anymore. Sometimes even taking the next breath is a chore.

"So when they offered me this chance to be a courier and get off the planet and make some money—and give my sons a second chance too—I didn't have to think about it too hard. It was a way out. I was drowning. What would you have had me do, Doug? Charles?" He took a deep breath then and added, "I don't know what's in the monkey, I don't even care, but someone is paying for this trip, so it must be something valuable and we'll deliver it and we'll be done. Then you can do whatever you want to. I'm through trying. I'm beaten."

Doug didn't say anything to that. Neither did I. There wasn't anything to say. And I was through trying to figure things out.

We ate, we dozed, we waited. Pretty soon, the car started sliding along the track to the departure bay. We felt it thump into position, and then we heard the soft clunk of the transfer pods moving into place too. A little bit after that, the car started spinning and pseudo-gravity returned. A while after that, we heard people moving around outside in the corridors.

When he deemed it was safe, Mickey ducked out of the cabin—"I'll be back as fast as I can. I have to get your tickets validated. Otherwise, this cabin will show up as empty and they'll give it to someone else." To Douglas, he smiled. "Save my place, huh?" And then he was gone.

He was back almost immediately with an odd expression on his face. "Come with me," he said. "All of you. Quickly."

"Huh? Why?"

"Just come—" He was already picking up Stinky. I grabbed the monkey. Douglas shouldered the backpack. Dad picked up his worries and we followed Mickey out the hatch and up the corridor to the transfer pod. Mickey wouldn't answer any questions. "I'll explain later," was all he said.

The transfer pod dropped us down to the boarding level. Actually, there are two boarding levels. There's the public boarding level and the Very Important Person boarding level—Mickey took us to the VIP level.

We stepped out of the hatch into—

—I didn't see the room at first. It was about the size of a classroom or a lounge, I guess, but directly in front of us was Judge Griffith in her wheelchair and next to her, but not too close, there was Olivia, looking unhappy, and a couple other people I didn't recognize, but very official looking, and also that stupid lawyer, Howard. He still wore that stupid suit that didn't fit right, only now he looked like he'd slept in it, and he had a very smug look on his face, like he'd caught us with our pants down and our hands on our dicks. I was tempted to give him my own farkleberry.

"Ahh," said Judge Griffith. "Thank you all for joining us. Mickey, did you have any trouble?" Mickey shook his head. Douglas glared at him, but Mickey didn't meet his look, so Douglas stepped over and took Stinky out of his arms, then he moved away from Mickey, as if he didn't want to know him anymore. Mickey looked miserable.

"All right, if everybody will take their places, we can get this business handled once and for all." Judge Griffith wheeled backwards, moving out of the way. She pointed with her gavel; she held the head of it in her fist and used the handle as a pointer. The chairs and the tables of the lounge had been moved into positions like a courtroom. "Olivia, if you'll sit over there on the left. Mickey, you too. The Dingillians—thank you. Howard, I want you on the right. Court officers, here beside me. And...yes, that'll do it, thank you."

Dad whispered to Olivia, "What the hell is going on? What did you do to us?" Olivia just shook her head and pointed us toward the chairs. "I can't advise you," she whispered. "You're on your own now." Dad looked as angry as I'd ever seen him in my entire life.

Douglas laid Stinky down on a nearby couch. The rest of us sat down in chairs that were much too comfortable for a legal procedure. But Judge Griffith put those doubts to rest immediately. She wheeled up to a small table that was to serve as the bench; her clipboard was already open and propped up so she could see it. She reversed the gavel in her hand and rapped it sharply on the table. She glanced over to her assistant. "Joyce? Are we missing someone?"

The woman nodded. "Godot called. He'll be late."

Judge Griffith raised a questioning eyebrow. "I assume he has a good excuse?" She glanced at her watch. "Was the shuttle delayed?"

"The shuttle docked on time, the paperwork was delayed. Last I heard, he's waiting for customs to clear."

"Never mind, we can still take care of the preliminaries. And if he can't get here before we finish, then the hell with him. This Court is not on call." She turned forward again. "The Third District Court of The Orbital Space Authority, serving GeoSynchronous Station and Allied Domains, Judge Georgia Griffith presiding, is now in special session, this session being mandated by the attempted flight from jurisdiction of the following individuals..."

Olivia stood. "Beg pardon, your honor, but no one has actually fled jurisdiction yet—"

"Don't nit-pick, counselor. We caught them with the tickets in their hands." She looked exasperated. "Listen up, folks—I don't like working late. If I could think of a good reason to justify tossing all of you into the cooler for a week or two, I'd do it." She continued, with a dark glower in Dad's direction. "We're here because Max Dingillian and his three kids somehow ended up on the midnight elevator to Farpoint. I presume the destination was Whirlaway. Correct? This, in spite of the fact that a court hearing was ordered for nine in the ayem, tomorrow morning. So I am left with the not unreasonable assumption that you, sir, Max Dingillian, were attempting to evade the authority of this court."

She leaned forward in her chair, aiming her remarks directly to Dad. "However, the Court *chooses to ignore*—for the moment, anyway—the evidence of your attempt to evade jurisdiction. Sit down, Howard! I'll get to you in a moment!" She turned back to Dad. "At the very least, I should hold you in contempt of court, but it is not in the best interests of your children to do so, and it does not serve the goal of a speedy resolution. Let it be known, however, that the court views your conduct with extreme displeasure. Let me translate that for you: you've exhausted whatever good will you had here. Do you understand?"

Dad nodded. "I understand completely. And I thank you for your... uh, mercy, your honor."

Judge Griffith ignored Dad. She turned to Howard-In-The-Wrinkled-Suit. "All right, Howard, now you may object...." Howard started to stand up, shrugged, sank back down in his seat, spreading his hands helplessly.

"Right," Judge Griffith agreed. "Objection overruled. Thank you. The Court appreciates your efforts to help move this process forward as fast as possible." She turned to Olivia. "Counselor, you no longer represent the Dingillians, is that correct?"

"That is correct." Olivia's voice was unemotional. Detached.

"Nevertheless, you were planning to leave on the midnight elevator with them. Is that correct too?"

"Yes, your honor. That is correct."

"Do you have an interesting explanation for this?"

"Conflict of interest. My son has a relationship with Douglas Dingillian."

"*Had*," corrected Douglas. Judge Griffith gave him a curious look, but otherwise ignored his interruption.

"Did you advise the Dingillians to evade jurisdiction, Counselor?"

"Of course not. I'm an officer of the court. That would be unethical."

"Nevertheless, was it among the options you discussed—?"

Olivia nodded reluctantly. "Yes, it was."

"Well, Olivia," the Judge continued, "we have here the evidence that you booked the tickets yourself under one of your shadow accounts. So although you recused yourself from this case, you still managed to be a participant in an action that would have damaged the court's ability to function. The Court finds you in contempt and fines you..." The Judge consulted her clipboard, tapping at its surface as she looked something up. "...and fines you one thousand chocolate dollars." Olivia didn't react to that. Judge Griffith continued, "Sentence suspended in recognition of your assistance in arranging this special session."

"Thank you, your honor," Olivia said quietly.

"The same thing I said to Max Dingillian goes for you too, Counselor. Your store of good will is exhausted in this court. Remember that."

Now, Judge Griffith turned to Howard-The-Smug. "Any objections? No? Overruled anyway. Don't worry about your store of good will, Howard. The court's opinion of you remains unchanged." To the rest of us, she said, "The issue here is simple, and if we can resolve it in the next two hours,"—she glanced at her watch—"then the Dingillians, or at least Max Dingillian, depending on the ruling of this court, can continue their—*or his*—journey." By the emphasis she put on "*or his*," she made it very clear that she had not yet made up her mind whether Dad was going to go to the moon with us or *without* us.

*

Judge Griffith looked to her assistant. "Any word yet?"

"The last of the passengers have cleared customs. Godot is on the way up. Five minutes."

"All right," said Georgia. "Fifteen minute potty-break." She banged her gavel once, and wheeled toward the restroom, her assistant following.

Dad leaned toward Olivia. "Who's this Godot?"

"I don't know," Olivia whispered back. "That's what the Judge calls anyone she has to wait for." She added, "I'm sorry we got caught—but I don't think Georgia had any choice in the matter."

"*We*—? *You* got a suspended sentence. I'm likely to lose my kids—! There's not a lot of 'we' in that, Olivia! You turned us in, didn't you?"

"I didn't have a choice, Max." She sounded just as frustrated as Dad.

"Oh, terrific. You told us to go out on the limb—and then you sawed it off."

"I don't think you should say any more," Olivia said quietly, with a meaningful nod toward Howard-The-Brooding.

"You've put us in a really bad situation, Olivia."

"I'm sorry. I miscalculated."

"Apology noted. Now what are you going to do to help clean up this mess?"

"Nothing. I can't! I'm not your lawyer anymore, Max."

Dad shook his head in disgust. "I can't believe this. Why did I trust you?" He sank back down in his seat, not looking at Olivia anymore. She looked just as unhappy. Now all that was left was a fight between her and Mickey, and we'd be complete. Everybody would have fought with everybody. I couldn't think of anyone else we could fight with—

And then Godot arrived.

Godot was Doctor Bolivar Hidalgo. And following him into the room was...*Mom?!* And that other woman behind her.

Just about everybody came to their feet then. Douglas, Dad, me—even Stinky woke up, rubbing his eyes again. This time, crying, "Stop waking me up!"

Mom went straight to Dad, she moved across the room like a missile—and slapped him across the face. Hard. Dad was knocked back a step; he put his hand to his jaw and blinked. "It's good to see you again too, Maggie," he managed to say.

And then Stinky saw her for the first time and yelled, "Mommy!!" And flung himself into her arms like an automatic monkey. He grabbed hold so tight she almost fell backward. "Mommy, mommy!! Are you going with us?"

"I came to take you home, sweetie —"

"But I don't wanna go home! I wanna go to the moon!"

Mom gave Dad a dirty look and moved away from us, cooing softly to Stinky and patting his head. Now it was Doctor Hidalgo's turn. He waddled over and bowed to Dad. "My compliments, *Señor* Dingillian."

Dad just glowered.

Dr. Hidalgo pretended not to notice. Instead, he took Dad by the arm and made as if to lead him off to a corner. "Can we talk?"

"You can talk," Dad said, not moving. "Do I have to listen?"

"It would be better if we could talk alone...?"

"Anything you have to say to me, you can say in front of my children, Dr. Hidalgo. I'm not going to hide anything from them. It's their lives too."

Douglas and I exchanged a look. We came and stood next to Dad. The monkey climbed up onto my back and made faces over my shoulder. Doug hissed at me, "Turn it off, Charles," so I did.

We followed Dad and Doctor Hidalgo over to a corner of the lounge. Doctor Hidalgo plopped himself down onto a chair and started talking immediately. "If you think about the organizational effort involved and the money it takes to get someone onto a shuttle on such short notice, you might begin to understand just how important your package is. It's important enough that a great deal of money is going to be spent on the effort to intercept it and prevent its delivery. Are you convinced yet?"

"What I told you before still stands," Dad said.

"It affects the lives of your sons. How do they feel about it?"

"Whatever my Dad says, goes for me too," I blurted. "Right, Douglas?" I poked him.

Douglas didn't need to be poked. "We're a family, Doctor Hidalgo. We might be having problems, but that's our business, not yours. We don't sell each other out."

"Admirable. Very admirable." Doctor Hidalgo grunted his approval. "Not very smart, but still admirable. The smart man recognizes when he can't win and cuts his losses early. So..." He levered himself to his feet. I figured he must have massed two hundred kilos. He sure looked it. Even in low-grav, he was having problems getting out of a chair. "...so I guess we have nothing further to discuss. Let the games begin." He waddled back to the other side of the lounge.

Dad looked to me and Douglas like he wanted to say something. But there wasn't anything that needed saying, so he just clapped Doug on the shoulder—he was closer—and said, "Let's go."

Judge Griffith called the session back to order then, with three sharp raps of her gavel on the table. "All right, people, we've got a lot of work to do and not very much time to do it in. I've made a promise to some folks here to be finished before midnight so they can catch an elevator, and I intend to keep that promise. Would everybody please take their seats and settle themselves quickly?" Judge Griffith nodded to her assistant. "Joyce, please make a note of our new arrivals. Godot is here. Finally."

Mom and the woman who had followed her in sat down with Dr. Hidalgo on the other side of Howard-The-Malignant. She leaned over to confer with him. They shook hands quickly, so I guess this was their first face-to-face meeting. She held Stinky in her arms and he appeared to have fallen back asleep. He woke up just long enough to stick his tongue out at Howard and then he laid his head back down on Mom's shoulder again. Whatever they'd given him, I wanted a lifetime supply.

Judge Griffith was already moving along. She meant it, about finishing quickly. "Dr. Hidalgo, the Court appreciates your interest in this case; however, if it is your intention to complicate matters with extra-curricular issues, let me warn you ahead of time that the Court will take a dim view of any such matters that do not *directly* affect the issue at hand."

"Your honor," Dr. Bolivar spread his hands wide in an oily gesture. Obviously, someone's snake was squeaky. "I am here only as a friend of the court. I simply wish to see justice done."

The Judge snorted. "Bollie, you and I both know that you have no interest in anything except your own stomach. You brought the boys' mother up for reasons that have nothing to do with justice or friendship. Consider this a warning. Your friends have no authority over this—" She waved her gavel at him.

Judge Griffith turned to Mom, now. "Mrs. Dingillian—"

"Campbell. It's Campbell now. I've gone back to my maiden name, Your Honor."

"Fairly recently? Ah, yes, here it is. Thank you for the correction." She looked to Mom and said, "Ms. Campbell, I've spent the past several hours reviewing the records of your divorce and custody hearings. I wish I could say it makes for interesting reading. Unfortunately, it does not. It is a tiresome and petty matter, and I think both you and your husband have a great deal to be ashamed of. This is not a case where one side is right and the other is wrong. It is a case where both sides are wrong— and this Court has no interest in trying to determine which side is more wrong. The *only* issue here is the welfare of the children. Events have clearly demonstrated that *neither* of the parents has provided an appropriate commitment to the welfare of these children. Therefore—"

"Your Honor, I object to that—" That was Mom, leaping to her feet.

Judge Griffith sighed. She could see where this was headed. "Ms. Campbell?"

"I am *not* a bad parent, and I do put my children's welfare above everything else—"

Judge Griffith tapped her gavel gently to interrupt Mom. "Your husband came home and found you in bed with someone else. I suppose that down on Earth, you might be able to justify it in your mind that this was a generous and unselfish demonstration of commitment and dedication to your family, but this isn't Earth and *this* court is having a very hard time viewing it that way. This situation—this entire avalanche of errors in judgment—was all triggered by that first little pebble—"

"Your honor," Mom started to protest, "with all due respect—we *had* a working custody arrangement, until *he*," —she waved her hand angrily at Dad—"went and violated it! All I want is for you to return my children to me so we can go home!"

"Sit down, Ms. Campbell. That's *not* going to happen. At least not because you or anyone else demands it. You pushed your husband into this situation. It's all here in the history." She tapped her clipboard meaningfully. "You kept challenging his visitation rights every chance you got—you gave him no rational choice. That doesn't excuse what he did, but neither did you provide an environment in which your separate disagreements could be worked out rationally. This court has absolutely no interest in providing an arena for one more round of legal spouse-bashing. If you want to hurt each other, if that's the kind of post-marital relationship you both want, that's fine with me—I'm just not going to let you use my court for it."

Judge Griffith poured herself a glass of water. Her hand trembled slightly as she drank. She put the glass back on the table and looked from Mom to Dad and back again. She said, "In other words, Mr. Dingillian, Ms. Campbell, based on everything that has happened so far, this Court cannot justify awarding either one of you custody of these children. Do you understand what I am saying? The decision cannot be based on your credentials as parents. Neither of you deserves that consideration. This court is going to have to look *elsewhere* for guidance in this decision. It's time to let the children vote...."

She looked around the room as if daring anyone else to speak. No one wanted to. So she rapped her gavel sharply. "Douglas Dingillian, as you are only a month shy of your eighteenth birthday, this court sees fit to declare you an independent adult. You are hereby granted autonomy. You are no longer under the custody of either of your parents. Do you understand?"

Douglas nodded. He looked a little scared, but he nodded.

Judge Griffith continued. "You are free to return to Earth, either with or without your mother; you are free to continue your outbound odyssey, either with or without your father. However, before you make *any* decision, we still have the matter of the custody of your brothers to resolve, and the court will appreciate your input on that."

Douglas nodded again.

Now Judge Griffith turned to me. "Charles, I want you to understand, ordinarily I would not ask a thirteen-year old to make the kind of choice that I'm about to give you. But under these circumstances, I think this is the best way to do it—and I'm satisfied that you're up to the challenge. So here's the question—"

I could already see it coming. And I was already formulating my reply.

"—Do you want to go back down the beanstalk with your mother, or do you want to continue outward with your father?"

I stood up. "Neither," I said.

Judge Griffith shook her head, smiling gently. "I'm afraid that's not an option, Charles."

"Yes, it is," I said. "*I want a divorce.*"

Almost immediately, both Mom and Dad were on their feet, shouting:

"Your Honor—you can't allow this!" and , "Charles, have you lost your mind?" Douglas looked surprised, though he shouldn't have been. Even Stinky was awake now. "Whatever Chigger gets, I want one too!" he yelled, screeching above the tumult. Judge Griffith banged so loudly with her gavel that the head popped off. She had to wait until her assistant, Joyce, went and got it and brought it back to her.

"Everybody settle down, dammit!" she shouted over the noise. "And *sit down*! I'll handle this." She banged a few more times until everyone sat down again, and then she turned back to me. "Charles—" she started to say gently.

I didn't let her finish. "I want a divorce," I repeated.

Judge Griffith looked very unhappy. "Charles, do you know what's involved in that kind of action?"

"Yes, actually, I do. At least as much as I could find out from reading about it."

"Somebody should hang a warning sign on you, Charles. Caution, contents will probably explode in your face." She smiled wryly, to let me know she was joking, but I could see she meant it too. "Why do you want a divorce?"

"Do I have to have a reason?"

"Not really. You and your brothers are the only ones who *didn't* promise to love, honor, and etcetera. And if that's not a promise you want to keep, you shouldn't be held in a situation where it's a requirement. But it would help if you did have a reason. Otherwise, children would be announcing right and left that they want a divorce every time they get sent to bed early."

I pointed at Mom. I pointed at Dad. "Those are my reasons."

The Judge nodded. "Those are two pretty good reasons. And considering everything else that's happened, the court would ordinarily be inclined to grant your request—but let's look over the edge of this cliff before we jump, okay, Charles?"

"Sure," I said. "Whatever. But it's not going to change my mind. I've been thinking about this for a long time."

"Charles—" Mom called across the room. "You don't have to do this. If we could just sit down and talk things out—"

"Leave him alone, Maggie! Haven't you done enough damage already!" Dad shouted across at her. "Look at the poor kid—!"

Judge Griffith rapped her gavel only once. Without even looking up: "Any more outbursts and I'll put the both of you in jail. In the same cell!" The threat worked. They both sat down again, glowering at each other. "Howard?" Howard-The-Troll looked up. "Are you still representing the interests of the mother?"

Howard looked to Mom, she nodded, and he said, "Yes, Your Honor."

"Would you like to question Charles Dingillian?"

"Uh—I haven't had time to prepare."

"Neither has anyone else here. Perhaps giving lawyers time to prepare is why justice always takes so long. Maybe in the future, in the interest of producing results, I should deny all recesses and continuances. Don't panic, Howard, it's a joke."

Howard came over and stood in front of me. "Well, you're the reason we're here, Charles. It all revolves around you. Let me ask you—do you think running away is going to solve anything?"

"Some people do."

"Do you?"

I knew what he wanted me to say. No. Running away never solves anything. But...sometimes running away buys you time to think.

He held my eyes with his. He didn't look nasty. He looked like he was trying to be friendly and it was a strain. He said, "Charles, do you think your parents have a responsibility toward you?"

"That's what they teach us at school. Don't have babies unless you're willing to make a lifelong commitment."

"Yes. I know that it hasn't worked out the way you think it should, but don't you think that your parents have your best interests at heart?"

"Yeah? So?"

"My point is, Charles, you've received a lot from your parents. You owe them something in return. Do you think this is the right way to repay it?"

And when he put it that way, something clicked. "Can I ask you something?"

"Yes, Charles—what is it?" He seemed genuinely interested.

"Well, when I was in school—I don't know if it's the same way up here—we had classes about social responsibility. My teacher taught us that everybody is part of society. We're all connected to each other lots of different ways. We all make work for each other, so we need each other for jobs. And we all make messes—like garbage and pollution and sewage and crap—so we all have to clean up after ourselves. And sometimes, like during flu season, we're all infectious. And stuff like that. And even if we like to think that we're individuals, we really all depend on each other. My teacher said it was Thoreau's ax."

"I beg your pardon?" said Howard-The-Puzzled. "Thoreau's ax?"

"Yeah. Thoreau was this guy who thought it would be a good idea to go out in the woods to Walden Pond, and commune with nature. He thought worldly goods distracted people and kept them from getting in tune with everything good."

"Yes, I know who Thoreau was. What about his ax?"

"Well, that's the point. Where did his ax come from? If he wanted to build himself a shelter, or chop a tree for firewood, or stuff like that, he needed an ax. Where does the ax come from?"

"From a...blacksmith," offered Howard.

"Uh-huh. That's why Thoreau was a dope. You can't just go off and live by yourself. You need the stuff that other people make. And they need what you make. And even if you think you're not connected to everybody else, you really are, because even if you're going out to the woods to live, where are you going to get your ax?"

"Judge Griffith is looking at her watch again, Charles. What does all this have to do with *your* situation?"

"Well...I can see what's going on. Some kind of evacuation. People who can afford it are leaving the Earth. Like guests leaving a party where they trashed the house. They're taking their money and they're going up the Line to the moon and everywhere else. Isn't that right?"

"Yes, Charles. I won't lie to you. There are people who afraid of the possibility of war and disease and economic turmoil —"

"That's my point—if you grownups can't keep your promises, if you can't keep your part of the social contract to the whole planet—if grownups are running away from the problems they made, then how can you ask a kid like me to stay behind with the mess? I don't know that running away solves any problems, but I don't see that I accomplish anything useful by staying either."

For a moment there was silence in the Court. A lot of people looked real uncomfortable. Dad. Mom. Judge Griffith. Olivia. Mickey. Howard. Dr. Hidalgo. Finally, Judge Griffith said, "I think he's pretty well nailed the lot of us to the wall."

But Howard wasn't finished. He said, "I can think of a reason to go back."

"What?"

"Because you love your Mom."

I looked over at Mom, she looked hopeful. Her eyes were shining. I looked to Dad, he looked kinda proud. I looked at Douglas, who flashed me a quick nod and a smile.

"Yeah," I said to Howard-The-Duck. "That's a good reason." Mom smiled at me—until I added, "But it's not good enough. Not anymore," and her expression collapsed into grief. I should have stopped there, but I didn't. "I love my Mom. I really do. I love my Dad too. But I don't like being in the middle anymore. Love's a good reason for lots of stuff—but not for doing something stupid. And going back to either of them is the stupidest thing I can think of."

Howard sat down, defeated.

Judge Griffith glanced at her watch and made a face. She turned sideways in her chair to face me. "Thank you, Charles. That was very nicely argued. Have you ever considered becoming a lawyer?"

"Only once. Dad threatened to strangle me in my sleep."

"And he's probably right. Never mind. Do you still want a divorce?"

"Yes, Judge Griffith. I do."

"Hmm." She frowned. "You know, I can grant it, right here and now. It's irregular, but so is this whole situation. So it wouldn't be out of line to resolve it with an unorthodox decision, particularly in light of some of the other pressures on us." She sighed, glanced at her watch again, and began to explain. "But I'll tell you honestly, I'm very reluctant to just bang the gavel and be done with it."

"Why?"

"You see, Charles, we have a problem here. You and I in particular. I can declare Douglas an adult, because he's only two months shy of his majority. And I can ask you what you want to do, because even though you're not yet old enough to be independent, you're still old enough to have a say in what happens to you. And if you want a divorce, I can put you in Douglas's custody. But I can't give the same choice to Bobby, can I? Do you think he's capable of making an informed decision? Do you think so, Douglas?"

I shook my head. So did Douglas.

"So you see the problem here. We have to make a decision about what's best for your brother, you and I and Douglas. I already know what your mother and father are going to say. They're going to fight over custody of Bobby, even more ferociously, because he's all that's left; so I need to hear what someone else thinks—someone else who knows your Mom and Dad, and nobody knows them better than you and your brother. So what do you two think I should do? Charles? Douglas?"

Douglas and I looked at each other. I searched his face for a clue, even a hint, of what he was thinking. He shook his head slightly—a signal to be careful? Or that he didn't know either.

"Well...first of all," I said slowly. "I want to go with Douglas." I looked to him for reassurance. He gave me a quick nod of okay, and I smiled tightly and blinked fast before any tears could come.

"What happens if Douglas chooses to go someplace you don't want to go?"

"I can't think of anyplace like that, Your Honor. I want to stay with my brother. We're family. We've always been together. I know how to live without my Mom and without my Dad. I've been doing that almost all my life. I don't know how to live without Douglas, and even though he can be real weird sometimes, I still want to go with him."

"You're sure about that?"

"As sure as I can be."

"Hm. Well. I see." Judge Griffith mulled that over. "I could probably do that. As I said, I can grant Douglas acting custody over you, subject to the approval of the jurisdiction you end up in; in the absence of any other contesting relatives, they'd probably confirm it. Your problem is going to be—or rather, it'll be Doug's problem—supporting yourselves. I understand that you're looking for an indenture, Douglas?"

"Yes, Ma'am."

"Mm. Be careful. Make sure you have an agent review the contract. But you should be able to get an indenture that covers Charles as well. He can take on a delayed indenture that doesn't kick in until he turns eighteen, and the two of you should be able to find a colony that can use a couple of fairly intelligent warm bodies. So it's doable, and I can sign off on it. But that still leaves the problem of your younger brother...?"

"Yeah, Stinky's a problem," I said. "But he's *our* problem. Douglas and I have spent more time taking care of him than Mom or Dad."

"Are you suggesting that you and Douglas also take custody of Bobby as well?"

When she put it that way...I had to hesitate. But Douglas didn't. He stepped forward. "Ma'am, I'm not saying it'll be easy. In fact, it'll probably be the hardest thing I've ever done. But I've been thinking hard about this—not just tonight, but for several days now. I think it'd be the best for Bobby. I think it'd be best for me and Charles too."

Judge Griffith sighed. She was doing a lot of sighing tonight. She steepled her fingers in front of her mouth and thought for a moment. "You have your tickets?"

Mickey stood up then. "I have their tickets, Your Honor. And unless they've cancelled my contract, I am the agent of record for this family. I can guarantee delivery to Luna and a 70% probability of an acceptable contract. I have three possibilities already. We have insurance in place against failure to contract, so the family will not end up a drain on the resources of any starside facility."

"Fair enough. Is it my understanding that you are also emigrating, Mickey?"

"Yes, Aunt Georgia."

"I'm going to miss you, sweetheart. Is it your intention to accompany the Dingillian family?"

"Uh—" Mickey looked to Douglas, uncertain. Douglas...hesitated, then nodded. Okay, so that fight was over. "Yes, your honor."

"Are you willing to accept co-responsibility with Douglas Dingillian?"

"Uh—yes, I'm prepared to accept co-responsibility up to and including such time as I can guarantee financial security through an appropriate colonial contract, and for as long after that as the Dingillians are willing to accept my support."

"Mickey—?" The Judge looked at him sternly. "You just met these folks—what is it? Two days, three days ago? Are you willing to take on this kind of a commitment on such short notice—especially now, after you've seen them at their worst?"

"Aunt Georgia, I admit that...there's a lot of dirtside crap going on. But I think these are good people. And they wouldn't be in half the trouble they're in if it hadn't been for me...."

"And your Mom," Judge Griffith added.

Mickey shrugged in acquiescence of the point. "The thing is, I like them in spite of themselves. I owe them. I want to do it."

Judge Griffith cleared her throat gruffly. "Well, that sort of settles that. The younger generation has come of age. All that's left for us old broads is to find a nice warm grave and get someone to throw some dirt over us. Olivia, you did a good job on this boy. He has a conscience." To the rest of us, she said, "All right, I'm now prepared to hear arguments from the parents. I assume you are both going to protest a ruling of divorce here—?"

Both Mom and Dad stood up at the same time; they both said yes. In unison. It was the first time I'd ever seen them agree on anything. They looked at each other in surprise. Dad made a waving gesture to Mom. "You go first."

Mom didn't spare any words. If there's one thing Mom can be counted on for, she always lets you know what she's thinking. "Is this the way justice up here works? Is your culture up here so morally bankrupt that you have to steal other people's children—?"

"That's the way, Mom," Douglas said. "Butter her up. Make her like you."

"Shut up, Douglas," Mom snapped at him. "I heard about your— misadventures. I can't tell you how disappointed I am."

"Yeah, me too," said Douglas. He looked meaningfully at the woman next to Mom.

"Douglas," said Judge Griffith. "It's your mother's turn. Sit down, please." To Mom, she said, "I assume you have an argument to present?"

Mom turned to Howard-The-Repugnant. "You're a lawyer! Do something!"

He shrugged, looked through his briefcase, pulled out a folded paper, and passed it to her.

"Huh? What's this?"

"My bill," he said. "The minute you walked in the door, you destroyed my case. Not being here was your best chance. As long as you were still groundside, I could make the argument that the children were being taken away without your opportunity to be present and have your side of the issue heard. It would have justified pushing the case into a Liaison Court, which handles mixed jurisdiction disputes. But now that you're here, this constitutes a fair hearing and all I can do is restate what's already in the record. So there's nothing I can do here, except enjoy the show. Please pay that within thirty days." Howard leaned back in his chair, grimly satisfied. He looked almost human.

Olivia grinned over at him. "I may have misjudged your intelligence. You finally found a way to avoid losing a case—stay out of it. And present a bill anyway. My compliments, Counselor."

"Belay that noise, Olivia." This was punctuated with a rap of the gavel. I was beginning to wish I had a gavel of my own. It was a great way to get people to pay attention. "Ms. Campbell, do you have anything else to say? Anything to justify awarding you custody, that is?"

"Your honor, I already have custody. You have the case in front of you. The El Paso District Court awarded me custody of my children. These hearings are illegal. This is a kangaroo court. You have no authority over me or my children. I demand that you affirm the rulings of the groundside court."

"Thanks for the demonstration of how to put the tact into tactical, Ms. Campbell. But this hearing is *very* legal. I suggest you ask your attorney to explain the limits of groundside jurisdiction and the farther reaching authority of starside courts. You are certainly free to appeal this case to the World Court and I'll be disappointed in you if you don't—but once I make my ruling, it's going to be implemented immediately."

The woman next to Mom stood up. "Your Honor, may I speak?"

"Why not?" Judge Griffith sighed. "Everyone else is going to insist on having their say tonight. Your name is...?"

"Bev Sykes, Your Honor. I think you can understand that my partner is justifiably upset about this situation. She came to San Francisco for a much-needed vacation; the next thing, she's in the biggest crisis of her life—"

"It is a crisis which she helped create, Ms. Sykes. No one is innocent here. Least of all you, if I read this history right."

"The point is, Your Honor, that what you're proposing to do is overturn a stable situation—"

"I've seen absolutely no evidence of stability in this situation, Ms. Sykes."

Mom spoke up again then. "Perhaps if you'd ever had children of your own, you'd understand—"

Oops.

Judge Griffith's face darkened. "I had two daughters of my own, Ms. Campbell. They died in the Line accident of '97. That's when I got this chair. Do either of you have anything useful to add?"

Mom and the other woman whispered together for a moment, then they both shook their heads and sat down. They looked very unhappy. I almost felt sorry for them, but I wasn't going to change my mind, and I didn't think Doug was going to either.

Judge Griffith looked to Dad. "Mr. Dingillian, you had something to say?"

Dad stood up. He seemed strangely calm. "I want to apologize for my conduct in this whole affair. I made a serious error in judgment. I've hurt my children. I've made a lot of trouble for everybody. I know that."

Judge Griffith was studying her watch. "Get on with it, please."

"Your Honor, whatever you decide, I'll still be the boys' father, and Margaret will still be their mother—regardless of how you assign custody, we have the right to spend time with our children. And if our children want to spend time with us, they should have that right as well."

"The Court is already taking that into consideration," Judge Griffith said, typing something into her clipboard.

"Well, that's my argument, Your Honor. If the children end up in a location so far removed that visitation is impractical to the point of being impossible, then those visitation rights are effectively denied."

Judge Griffith raised her eyebrow. "In view of the circumstances which forced this hearing, the court finds it profoundly ironic that you should be making that argument, Mr. Dingillian."

Mom snorted. Loudly. I knew that snort.

Dad remained nonplused. "Nevertheless, Your Honor—if it was wrong for me to consider denying my wife access to her children, then it is equally wrong for the court to allow a situation to occur where visitation is impossible."

"Now that's a good point," Judge Griffith said, gesturing with the gavel. "But it seems to me that if visitation with your children is important enough to you, it's your responsibility to make sure to keep yourself near to them. The problem in this family is that both you and your wife have been attempting to make visitation impossible for each other, she by legal means, you by moving the children around. And the Court finds that behavior an intolerable state of affairs. Not because it is unfair to either of you, but because *it is unfair to the children.*

"You both claim that you are interested only in the well-being of your children, but you have both put enormous emotional burdens on them. Your children need a place to heal, a place to recover from their parents. Considering the abuses of the visitation process in this case, the Court is not inclined toward allowances for the needs of the parents. I won't rule out visitation rights, but I'm not going to make visitation rights as large a part of the final decision as it would be downside. Anything else, Mr. Dingillian?"

Dad looked beaten. He shook his head and sat down.

"All right then." Judge Griffith rapped her gavel. "Here's my ruling. It is the decision of this court that Douglas Dingillian is to be regarded in all rights and privileges as a legal adult. It is the further decision of this court that Charles Dingillian is granted a summary divorce from both of his parents and given to the care and custody of Douglas Dingillian, contingent on the co-responsibility of Mickey Partridge. Charles, this divorce is contingent on review by the legal authority of whatever jurisdiction you and your brother settle in. So choose your destination carefully."

"Yes, Your Honor."

"In the matter of Robert Dingillian, the court recognizes the long history of custody disputes in this case, and acknowledges the already established legal rights of both parents...and sets them aside. The welfare of the child always takes precedence. Because the parents of Robert Dingillian have not demonstrated, in the opinion of *this* court, sufficient commitment to the child to put their own disputes aside, the Court is left with no alternative but to remove the child from the custody of the parents and place him in the care of his elder brother, Douglas. This is also contingent on the statement of co-responsibility from Mickey Partridge, and final review by the legal authorities of your ultimate destination. Mickey, I mean it, choose *carefully*. This concludes the business of this court. And if there are no further objections, I declare this hearing adjourned—"

But before she could rap her gavel on the table, Dad stood up—"Your Honor? Point of order? Um—may I ask for clarification, please?"

Judge Griffith hesitated, the gavel poised above the table. "Go ahead."

"My sons are free to use the tickets I purchased for them, if they wish to. Is that correct?"

"Your sons are free to choose their own destination. Yes, they can use the tickets you paid for. The Court has not terminated your access, only your custodial authority."

"I understand that, I'm just trying to get clear on where the line is drawn. Am I *also* free to use the ticket I purchased for myself?"

"Yes," said the Judge. "You are."

Over on the other side of the room, I heard Mom gasp. "I can't believe this—"

Both Dad and the Judge ignored her. Dad asked, "Even if it means traveling together with my sons? Your Honor, you do understand that if my sons use their tickets to go on to Luna, we'll be sharing the same cabin...?"

"Mr. Dingillian, the Court has no objection to you traveling with your sons, if that's what they want." Something about that last part, I looked over to Douglas. He'd caught it too, but Judge Griffith was still talking to Dad, "You *are* entitled to visitation rights. But you no longer have any custodial authority over them. That's the limit of this ruling—"

"Oh, great!" said Mom. "We're right back where we started! He has no custodial rights, but he still ends up with the kids! What kind of a kangaroo court is this?" She turned to Hidalgo. "You said you could help me! This is the way you help people?!"

Hidalgo wasn't stupid. He didn't even try to calm her down. He was already pushing himself ponderously to his feet, raising his hand for attention. "Your Honor, there is one other matter left unresolved. If I may beg the Court's indulgence...?"

"Just a moment, Dr. Hidalgo." Judge Griffith turned to Mom. She finally laid her gavel down. "Ms. Campbell, please understand, you have the exact same rights—or should I say, lack of rights. If you wish to travel with your children, you may do so as well. Under the same terms as your ex-husband. If the children wish it." There it was again—

"Oh, yeah, right! With what money?! I don't have a SuperNational credit card—I can't go to the moon!"

"Somebody paid for two tickets on the express shuttle...." Judge Griffith left the second half of that thought unsaid. Mom fumed and sputtered, but the Judge was already moving on. "All right, Bolivar. You paid for two tickets to this circus—let's hear what you have to say." She glanced meaningfully at her watch.

"It is the matter of *Señor* Dingillian's financial status. If you will consult your own records, you will see that this man does not have the resources to have paid for even one ticket up the beanstalk, let alone four."

"So?"

"So if he is going to the outbeyond, the Financial Responsibility Act requires proof that he is leaving behind no significant debts."

Dad stood up. "Your Honor, there is documentation on file with the Emigration Authority to demonstrate that not only are all of my outstanding debts paid off, but that there is a fund in escrow to handle any future claims that may arise. Additionally, there is Emigration Insurance to cover any contingencies that exceed the funds in escrow."

Judge Griffith was sitting at her table with her hands folded in front of her chin again. She looked from one to the other, more amused than anything else. "Is there a point to all this?" she asked.

"With the Court's indulgence," Hidalgo said, "I would like, at this time, to present documentation that *Señor* Dingillian's trip has been financed by certain SuperNational interests, and that in return, he is functioning as a courier for them—"

"So what?" said the Judge. "We have private couriers going up and down the Line every day. Many people finance their emigration that way. There's nothing illegal about it."

"Your Honor, may I please direct your attention to Section Four of the Line Authority Transportation Act? There are a number of restrictions on private courier service. It is illegal if the item being transferred is contraband or stolen property or if the intent of private service is to avoid legal obligations, such as liens, claims, custody, or taxation. If a courier is suspected of carrying items in violation of Section Four, the Line—that's you, Your Honor—has the authority to investigate and, if appropriate, require divestment of any and all packages."

"I see you've done your homework, Bollie. As usual. So what is it that Max Dingillian is carrying that you want to get your hands on so badly that you're willing to pay for two premium class round-trip shuttle tickets?"

"Your Honor, it is not for myself that I act, it is on behalf of the—"

"I've heard the speech, Bollie. More than once. Just tell the Court what the McGuffin is."

"Your Honor, six days ago, Stellar-American Resources transferred an extremely large amount of money into an American-Lunar transfer account. The account is a pipeline that may be accessed freely both on Earth and on Luna. It is commonly used for holding funds being moved off-world. Stellar-American Resources has three transfer accounts of their own, all bonded and monitored, which they normally use for off-world access. That they are suddenly using this account to transfer an extremely large resource suggests that they are attempting to avoid transfer taxes, as well as legal scrutiny. Not even the company's own stockholders are aware of this transfer—"

"But you are?" Judge Griffith noted with mild sarcasm.

"There are people who tell me things, Your Honor. Be that as it may, however the information comes to light, there is certainly enough to be suspicious about. And it is my solemn duty to call this to your attention. My people believe that *Señor* Dingillian is carrying one of three password-checks necessary to complete the transfer of funds. The other two may have already arrived on Luna."

"Just how much money are we talking about, Bolivar?"

Hidalgo pursed his lips and looked extremely uncomfortable. "It is over three trillion dollars, Your Honor. Perhaps as much as ten. The money came out of nine thousand different accounts that my people regularly watch, and at least ninety thousand more that we have not yet found a way to monitor. For this much money to move off of Earth so abruptly—"

Judge Griffith rapped her gavel. "The money flows, Bolivar. The fact that you don't like where it goes doesn't make the river a crime. This isn't a McGuffin at all. It's the stuff that dreams are made of."

"Your Honor, I respectfully request the Court to require *Señor* Dingillian to divulge the truth about what he is carrying. If it is a legal transfer, then I shall apologize profusely for taking up his time and the Court's. But if *Señor* Dingillian is carrying a check of such enormous size, I am certain that there are law enforcement and tax agencies both groundside and starside who will want to check that no laws are being broken by such a transfer." Hidalgo folded his hands across his paunch and waited.

Judge Griffith frowned. "I understand exactly what you're trying to do, Bollie. But what you're asking is generally beyond the reach of this Court. I can ask Mr. Dingillian to reveal what he is carrying, but absent of any evidence of a crime, he isn't required to violate his own privacy. If there is no evidence of wrong-doing, I can take no action."

"I understand, Your Honor, but I believe it is in the interests of justice to compel such performance as is appropriate."

"Mm. Yes. Bollie, I know you—you always want the best justice money can buy. So be it." She turned to Dad. "What are you carrying, Max? You don't have to tell me, but if it'll get Bolivar Hidalgo off your back...."

Dad shook his head and spread his empty hands wide. "Your Honor. I am not carrying anything."

The way he said it—with an unspoken *now* attached to the end of the sentence—was enough to raise Judge Griffith's eyebrows. "Have you already delivered it?"

"I have not delivered anything, Your Honor." Again, the same unfinished tone. If you didn't know Dad, you might not catch it; but if you were smart...like Judge Griffith, you could hear that what Dad *wasn't* saying was almost as important as what he *was* saying.

Judge Griffith hesitated. I could see she'd figured it out. But of course, being a judge, she'd probably learned how to tell when people were telling the truth or not. And by now I figured she probably had some game of her own working....

"Well, then," she said. "If you're not carrying anything—this court has no further business with you."

"Your Honor!" That was Hidalgo. "Ask him who paid for his tickets and what he had to do in return!"

She appeared to be mulling it over. I glanced over at Doug, he looked to the monkey in my lap, I shrugged and looked at the ceiling. Dad looked back and forth between us, carefully blank. Despite the Judge's decision, Stinky was still asleep in Mom's lap, and I wondered if we were going to be able to get him away from her.

Judge Griffith unfolded her hands. "Dr. Hidalgo, I think you're asking me to get into an area that is beyond the scope of this session. I told you earlier that I would not get into any inquiries that did not bear directly on the custody of the Dingillian children. I'm not going fishing for you. While the matter you have raised is certainly an important one, we cannot pursue it here. If you wish, you can pursue this in another court." She started to pick up her gavel again—

Almost as soon as the Judge had begun speaking, Hidalgo had nudged Howard, who began fumbling in his briefcase. Now, as Judge

Griffith finished, Howard leap to his feet. "Uh, not so fast, Your Honor, I have a warrant here—"

"And you're just serving it now?"

"I hadn't expected that it would be necessary."

"Pass it up."

Howard-The-Unkempt gave the paper to Judge Griffith's assistant, Joyce, who passed it to the Judge. She unfolded the paper and studied it thoughtfully. She scratched her eyebrow with a fingernail while she read. "Well, this appears to be in order," she said finally. To the rest of the room, she announced, "This is a Line Authority search-and-seizure warrant for the property of Max Dingillian. I'll spare you all the whereases. You're accused of transporting contraband."

Dad stood up, "Your honor, all I have are the clothes I'm wearing. If the court will provide me with something to wear, I'll be happy to give you these clothes."

"It's not that easy, Max. I'm authorized to detain you."

Dad shrugged. "Go ahead, Your Honor." He held out his wrists, as if awaiting handcuffs. "Take me away. I don't have anything—"

"Wait a minute," I said. I stood up, still holding the monkey. "Dad is telling the truth. He isn't carrying anything. I am. He gave it to me. I put it in the monkey."

Dad and Douglas both stared. "Charles—!"

I was already prying the back of the monkey opened. I pulled out the bottom-most memory bar and carried it over to Dad. "Here," I said. "Give this to the Judge."

Dad looked at the card, looked at me, looked at Olivia—she was carefully blank—then handed the card to Joyce, who handed it to Judge Griffith, who turned it over in her hands, examining it. "You were paid to transport this—?"

Dad looked to Olivia, looked back to the Judge. "Yes, Your Honor. I was paid to transport that."

"Well then, the warrant is satisfied." Judge Griffith passed the card to her assistant. "Joyce, seal that. It's not to be released to anyone." To Doctor Hidalgo, she said, "If it can be demonstrated that the intention of this warrant was to disrupt a lawful business enterprise, not only will I hold you in contempt, I will fine you for the full amount of damages. And you too, Howard. Let it be noted that this Court does not approve of the mischievous abuse of litigation."

"Your Honor," Howard-The-Illegitimate said, "We would like to request that the...uh, monkey be confiscated as well. In case there are other memory cards—"

"Nope. The monkey doesn't belong to Max Dingillian. It belongs to Robert Dingillian. Sorry, Howard." She raised her hands in mock helplessness.

He sputtered. "But the warrant—!"

"The warrant says nothing about the property of *Robert* Dingillian. And as he is no longer under the custodial authority of Max Dingillian, we cannot even use that umbrella. Hm, I see you forgot to add an *a priori* clause that would have allowed me to grant your request. You should be more careful when you draft these things, Howard. You left a loophole big enough to drop an electric primate through. Given the wording of this document," she waved it at him, "this Court has no authority to seize the property of any other Dingillian. And I will not act beyond the authority of this document. If I did, the next judge up would have ample grounds to invalidate the warrant anyway. So consider that I'm doing you a favor. If you want the monkey, go get another warrant."

I couldn't help myself, I surreptitiously switched the monkey on—and whispered into its ear. It leapt down from my lap, ran over to Howard-The-Stupid and gave him a double-chocolate hot-fudge farkleberry with whipped cream and a cherry on top. Plus a noise like an elephant fart. Then it came scurrying back to me. Howard looked like he was going to explode.

Keeping her face carefully blank, Judge Griffith picked up her gavel and rapped it once. "We're adjourned." She looked at her watch. "And just in time. You have an elevator to catch, Mickey. Get your butt in gear. They're holding the gate for you—"

And then a lot of stuff happened all at once. Dr. Hidalgo waddled over and stood in front of Dad. "You have been very lucky, *Señor* Dingillian. Very very lucky. I hope for your sake and your children's sake that your luck holds out."

Dad shook his head and laughed. "And you've been very stupid, Dr. Hidalgo. Very very stupid. You never figured it out, did you?"

Dr. Hidalgo raised an eyebrow. "Enlighten me?"

"You and your people—I was never carrying anything. I was a *decoy*. Do you really think they'd trust that much money to my care? Even I'm not that stupid. Whoever it was, and even I don't know for sure, you probably know more than me, they wanted you looking in the wrong place. So they hired me. And I guess it worked. While you were busy chasing me up the Line, you weren't hassling a whole bunch of other folks—"

"That's an assumption on your part."

"Maybe so, maybe not. But I got my job done. Thanks again for dinner." Dad offered his hand.

Surprisingly, Dr. Hidalgo took it. He held Dad's hand in both of his. "You may yet need my help, *Señor*. I do not think you know what you are playing with. You keep my card. You call me if your new friends don't work out. *Adios. Vaya con dios.*" And he turned and waddled over to confer with Howard-The-Unhappy.

Dad turned to look at me. And Douglas. We were whispering together. Dad must have seen the look on my face. And on Douglas' too. He said, "*What?*"

And I said to Douglas, "You tell him."

And Dad said, "Tell me what?"

So Douglas swallowed. Hard. "You sure, Charles?"

"Yes." I nodded.

Douglas turned to Dad. "We don't want you to come with us."

Dad looked confused. He looked from me to Douglas and back again. So I added, "Judge Griffith said we don't have to take you if we don't want to. Well…we don't want to."

Dad went pale. "Charles? Douglas? Are you sure—?"

"We have to go, Dad." Douglas hugged him quickly. "Maybe we'll see you on the moon. I hope so."

I went to Dad to hug him too, but I didn't say anything to him. He looked like he'd been stabbed—and was still waiting to fall down. He didn't hug me back, so I let go and followed Douglas over to where Mom was standing. She was holding Bobby, rocking him back and forth on her shoulder.

Douglas stopped before her, silently and sadly. Joyce, the bailiff, stood at a respectful distance, watching. Mom was holding Bobby as hard as she could. She glared over his shoulder at Douglas, and at Joyce too, and she held onto Bobby for the longest time, rocking him, stroking his hair, whispering into his ear, telling him over and over how much she loved him and how she was going to come and get him, not to worry—but at last, Douglas leaned over to take him, and she let him slip out of her arms. Tears were running down her cheeks and I was starting to feel real bad about this whole thing. Doug bent his head to kiss her, but she just turned away.

So Douglas turned away from her and she was standing there by herself, just looking at me—and I didn't know what to say or do. She walked over to where I was standing alone and when she spoke it was like being dragged naked over nails. She just shook her head and asked, "Why, Charles—why?"

I shook my head, helplessly. "I—I'm sorry, Mom. I didn't do it to hurt you."

"Was I really that bad a mother to you?"

"Mom, you're angry all the time—"

"Well, don't I have good reason to be? The way you treat me. The way your father treats me."

"Mom, this isn't about you—"

"Well, then *who* is it about—? Answer me that!"

"Mom, you don't listen! You don't *ever* listen—you're not listening now."

"Charles, I have a right to know. You're breaking up our family—"

"No, Mom. It was already broken. You and Dad broke it up a long time ago—"

"Is this really what you want—to hurt me like this?"

I wiped the tears from my cheeks. "Mom, what I want most—" It hurt to say it. My voice cracked—"What I want most is...to get away from you, right now. I can't stand it when you talk to me like this. It isn't *my* fault!"

"Go ahead then! You're just like your father, you little bastard! I hope you're happy!" And then—she slapped my face! For an instant, I saw stars.

I didn't know what to do or say. I was too shocked. She hadn't ever hit me before. I couldn't believe it—everybody was staring at me—so I just turned to go—and then she was grabbing at me, crying, "Oh, God, Charles—I'm so sorry, I didn't mean to do that! Charles, please—wait! Wait! Charles!"

There was one thing she could have said that might have made me stop, and I was listening as hard as I could to hear her say it, and maybe she *was* saying it in her own way, but I was listening for the words, and she never said them. She never said the words. So I kept going.

And then Doug put an arm around my shoulders and I started sobbing as we followed Mickey to the hatch of the transfer pod. Dad looked uncertain, then Olivia grabbed his arm and held him back so he couldn't follow us. I looked back to see Dr. Hidalgo and that Sykes woman rushing to Mom's side, and then Doug steered me into the waiting pod and then the door closed and they were gone—

"So what happens now?" I asked, still wiping tears from my eyes.

"I have an idea," Doug answered, shouldering Bobby with one arm, and hugging me with the other. "Let's go to the moon."

RIDING JANIS

If we had wings
where would we fly?
Would you choose the safety of the ground
or touch the sky
if we had wings?
　　　　　　　—Janis Ian & Bill Lloyd

The thing about puberty is that once you've done it, you're stuck. You can't go back.

It's like what Voltaire said about learning Russian. He said that you wouldn't know if learning Russian would be a good thing or not unless you actually learned the language—except that after you learned Russian, would the process of learning it have turned you into a person who believes it's a good thing? So how could you know? Puberty is like that—I think. It changes you, the way you think, and what you think about. And from what I can tell, it's a lot harder than Russian. Especially the conjugations.

You can only delay puberty for so long. After that you start to get some permanent physiological effects. But there's no point in going through puberty when the closest eligible breeding partners are on the other side of the solar system. I didn't mind being nineteen and unfinished. It was the only life I knew. What I minded was not having a choice. Sometimes

I felt like just another asteroid in the belt, tumbling forever around the solar furnace, too far away to be warmed, but still too close to be truly alone. Waiting for someone to grab me and hurl me toward Luna.

See, that's what Mom and Jill do. They toss comets. Mostly small ones, wrapped so they don't burn off. There's not a lot of ice in the belt, only a couple of percentage points, if that; but when you figure there are a couple billion rocks out here, that's still a few million that are locally useful. Our job is finding them. There's no shortage of customers for big fat oxygen atoms with a couple of smaller hydrogens attached. Luna and Mercury, in particular, and eventually Venus, when they start cooling her down.

But this was the biggest job we'd ever contracted, and it wasn't about ice as much as it was about ice-burning. Hundreds of tons per hour. Six hundred and fifty million kilometers of tail, streaming outward from the sun, driven by the ferocious solar wind. Comet Janis. In fifty-two months, the spray of ice and dye would appear as a bright red, white, and blue streak across the Earth's summer sky—the Summer Olympics Comet.

Mom and Jill were hammering every number out to the umpteenth decimal place. This was a zero-tolerance nightmare. We had to install triple-triple safeguards on the safeguards. They only wanted a flyby, not a direct hit. That would void the contract, as well as the planet.

The bigger the rock, the farther out you could aim and still make a streak that covers half the sky. The problem with aiming is that comets have minds of their own—all that volatile outgassing pushes them this way and that, and even if you've wrapped the rock with reflectors, you still don't get any kind of precision. But the bigger the rock, the harder it is to wrap it and toss it. And we didn't have a lot of wiggle room on the timeline.

Janis was big and dark until we lit it up. We unfolded three arrays of LEDs, hit it with a dozen megawatts from ten klicks, and the whole thing sparkled like the star on top of a Christmas tree. All that dirty ice, 30 kilometers of it, reflecting light every which way—depending on your orientation when you looked out the port, it was a fairy landscape, a shimmering wall, or a glimmering ceiling. A trillion tons of sparkly mud, all packed up in nice dense sheets, so it wouldn't come apart.

It was beautiful. And not just because it was pretty to look at, and not just because it meant a couple gazillion serious dollars in the bank either. It was beautiful for another reason.

See, here's the thing about living in space. Everything is Newtonian. It moves until you stop it or change its direction. So every time you move something, you have to think about where it's going to go, how fast it's going to get there, and where it will eventually end up. And we're not just talking about large sparkly rocks, we're talking about bottles of soda, dirty underwear, big green boogers, or even the ship's cat. Everything moves, bounces, and moves some more. And that includes people too. So you learn to think in vectors and trajectories and consequences. Jill calls it "extrapolatory thinking."

And that's why the rock was beautiful, because it wasn't just a rock here and now. It was a rock with a future. Neither Mom nor Jill had said anything yet, they were too busy studying the gravitational ripple charts, but they didn't have to say anything. It was obvious. We were going to have to ride it in, because if that thing started outgassing, it would push itself off course. Somebody had to be there to create a compensating thrust. Folks on the Big Blue Marble were touchy about extinction-level events.

Finding the right rock is only the *second*-hardest part of comet-tossing. Dirtsiders think the belt is full of rocks, you just go and get one; but most of the rocks are the wrong kind; too much rock, not enough ice— and the average distance between them is 15 million klicks. And most of them are just dumb rock. Once in a while, you find one that's rich with nickel or iron, and as useful as that might be, if you're not looking for nickel or iron right then, it might as well be more dumb rock. But if somebody else is looking for it, you can lease or sell it to them.

So Mom is continually dropping bots. We fab them up in batches. Every time we change our trajectory, Mom opens a window and tosses a dozen paper planes out.

A paper plane doesn't need speed or sophistication, just brute functionality, so we print the necessary circuitry on sheets of stiff polymer. (We fab that too.) It's a simple configuration of multi-sensors, dumb-processors, lotsa-memory, soft-transmitters, long-batteries, carbon-nano-tube solar cells, ion-reservoirs, and even a few micro-rockets. The printer rolls out the circuitry on a long sheet of polymer, laying down thirty-six to forty-eight layers of material in a single pass. Each side. At a resolution of 3600^2 dpi, that's tight enough to make a fairly respectable, self-powered, paper robot. Not smart enough to play with its own tautology, but certainly good enough to sniff a passing asteroid.

We print out as much and as many as we want, we break the polymer at the perforations; three quick folds to give it a wing shape, and it's done. Toss a dozen of these things overboard, they sail along on the solar wind, steering themselves by changing colors and occasional micro-bursts. Make one wing black and the other white and the plane eventually turns itself; there's no hurry, there's no shortage of either time or space in the belt. Every few days, the bot wakes up and looks around. Whenever it detects a mass of any kind, it scans the lump, scans it again, scans it a dozen times until it's sure, notes the orbit, takes a picture, analyzes the composition, prepares a report, files a claim, and sends a message home. Bots relay messages for each other until the message finally gets inserted into the real network. After that, it's just a matter of finding the publisher and forwarding the mail. Average time is 14 hours.

Any rock one of your paper planes sniffs and tags, if you're the first, then you've got first dibsies on it. Most rocks are dumb and worthless—and usually when your bots turn up a rock that's useful, by then you're almost always too far away to use it. Anything farther than five or ten degrees of arc isn't usually worth the time or fuel to go back after. Figure 50 million kilometers per degree of arc. It's easier to auction off the rock, let whoever is closest do the actual work, and you collect a percentage. If you've tagged enough useful rocks, theoretically you could retire on the royalties. *Theoretically.* Jill hates that word.

But if finding the right rock is the second-hardest part of the job, then the *first-* hardest part is finding the *other* rock, the one you use at the *other* end of the whip. If you want to throw something at Earth (and lots of people do), you have to throw something the same size in the opposite direction. Finding and delivering the right ballast rock to the site was always a logistic nightmare. Most of the time it was just difficult, sometimes it was impossible, and once in a while it was even worse than that.

We got lucky. We had found the right ballast rock, and it was in just the right place for us. In fact, it was uncommonly close—only a few hundred thousand kilometers behind Janis. Most asteroids are several million klicks away from their closest neighbor. FBK-9047 was small, but it was heavy. This was a nickel-rich lump about ten klicks across. While not immediately useful, it would *someday* be worth a helluva lot more than the comet we were tossing—five to ten billion, depending on how it assayed out.

Our problem was that it belonged to someone else. The FlyBy Knights. And they weren't too keen on having us throw it out of the system so we could launch Comet Janis.

Their problem was that this particular ten billion dollar payday wasn't on anyone's calendar. Most of the contractors had their next twenty-five years of mining already planned out—you have to plan that far in advance when the mountains you want to mine are constantly in motion. And it wasn't likely anyone was going to put it on their menu for at least a century; there were just too many other asteroids worth twenty or fifty or a hundred billion floating around the belt. So while this rock wasn't exactly worthless in principle, it was worthless in actuality—until someone actually needed it.

Mom says that comet tossing is an art. What you do is you lasso two rocks, put each in a sling, and run a long tether between them, fifty kilometers or more. Then you apply some force to each one and start them whirling around each other. With comet ice, you have to do it slowly to give the snowball a chance to compact. When you've got them up to speed, you cut the tether. One rock goes the way you want, the other goes in the opposite direction. If you've done your math right, the ballast rock flies off into the outbeyond, and the other—the money rock, goes arcing around the solar system and comes in for a close approach to the target body—Luna, Earth, L4, wherever. This is a lot more cost-effective than installing engines on an asteroid and driving it home. A *lot* more.

Most of the time, the flying mountain takes up station as a temporary moon orbiting whatever planet we throw it at, and it's up to the locals to mine it at their leisure. But this time, we were only arranging a flyby—a close approach for the Summer Olympics, so the folks in the Republic of Texas could have a 60 degree swath of light across the sky for twelve days. And that was a whole other set of problems—because the comet's appearance had to be timed for perfect synchronicity with the event. There wasn't any wiggle room in the schedule. And everybody knew it.

All of which meant that we really needed this rock, or we weren't going to be able to toss the comet. And everybody knew that too, so we weren't in the best bargaining position. If we wanted to use 9047, we were going to have to cut the FlyBy Knights in for a percentage of Janis, which Jill didn't really want to do because what they called "suitable recompense for the loss of projected earnings" (if we threw their rock away) was so high that we would end up losing money on the whole deal.

We knew we'd make a deal eventually—but the advantage was on their side because the longer they could stall us, the more desperate we'd become and more willing to accept their terms. And meanwhile, Mom was scanning for any useful rock or combination of rocks in the local neighborhood which was approximately five million klicks in any direction. So we were juggling time, money, and fuel against our ability to go without sleep. Mom and Jill had to sort out a nightmare of orbital mechanics, economic concerns, and assorted political domains that stretched from here to Mercury.

Mom says that in space, the normal condition of life is patience; Jill says it's frustration. Myself...I had nothing to compare it with. Except the puberty thing, of course. What good is puberty if there's no one around to have puberty with? Like kissing, for instance. And holding hands. What's all that stuff about?

I was up early, because I wanted to make fresh bread. In free fall, bread doesn't rise, it expands in a sphere—which is pretty enough, and fun for tourists, but not really practical because you end up with some slices too large and others too small. Better to roll it into a cigar and let it expand in a cylindrical baking frame. We had stopped the centrifuge because the torque was interfering with our navigation around Janis; it complicated turning the ship. We'd probably be ten or twelve days without. We could handle that with vitamins and exercise, but if we went too much longer, we'd start to pay for it with muscle and bone and heart atrophy, and it takes three times as long to rebuild as it does to lose. Once the bread was safely rising—well, expanding—I drifted forward.

"Jill?"

She looked up. Well, *over*. We were at right angles to each other. "What?" A polite *what*. She kept her fingers on the keyboard.

"I've been thinking—"

"That's nice."

"—we're going to have to ride this one in, aren't we?"

She stopped what she was doing, lifted her hands away from the keys, turned her music down, and swiveled her couch to face me. "How do you figure that?"

"Any comet heading that close to Earth, they'll want the contractor to ride it. Just in case course corrections have to be made. It's obvious."

"It'll be a long trip—"

"I read the contract. Our expenses are covered, both inbound and out. Plus ancillary coverage."

"That's standard boilerplate. Our presence isn't mandatory. We'll have lots of bots on the rock. They can manage any necessary corrections."

"It's not the same as having a ship onsite," I said. "Besides, Mom says we're overdue for a trip to the marble. Everyone should visit the home world at least once."

"I've been there. It's no big thing."

"But *I* haven't—"

"It's not cost-effective," Jill said. That was her answer to everything she didn't want to do.

"Oh, come on, Jill. With the money we'll make off of Comet Janis, we could add three new pods to this ship. And bigger engines. And larger fabricators. We could make ourselves a lot more competitive. We could—"

Her face did that thing it does when she doesn't want you to know what she really feels. She was still smiling, but the smile was now a mask. "Yes, we could do a lot of things. But that decision has to be made by the senior officers of the Lemrel Corporation, kidlet." Translation: *your opinion is irrelevant. Your mother and I will argue about this. And I'm against it.*

One thing about living in a ship, you learn real fast when to shut up and go away. There isn't any real privacy. If you hold perfectly still, close your eyes, and just listen, eventually—just from the ship noises—you can tell where everyone is and what they're doing, sleeping, eating, bathing, defecating, masturbating, whatever. In space, *everyone* can hear you scream. So you learn to speak softly. Even in an argument. Especially in an argument. The only real privacy is inside your head, and you learn to recognize when others are going there, and you go somewhere else. With Jill … well, you learned faster than real fast.

She turned back to her screens. A dismissal. She plucked her mug off the bulkhead and sipped at the built-in straw. "I think you should talk this over with your Mom." A further dismissal.

"But Mom's asleep, and you're not. You're here." For some reason, I wasn't willing to let it go this time.

"You already have my opinion. And I don't want to talk about it anymore." She turned her music up to underline the point.

I went back to the galley to check on my bread. I opened the plastic bag and sniffed. It was warm and yeasty and puffy, just right for kneading, so I sealed it up again, put it up against a blank bulkhead and began pummeling it. You have to knead bread in a non-stick bag because you don't want micro-particles in the air-filtration system. It's like punching a pillow. It's good exercise, and an even better way to work out a shiftload of frustration.

As near as I could tell, puberty was mostly an overrated experience of hormonal storms, unexplainable rebellion, uncontrollable insecurity, and serious self-esteem issues, all resulting in a near-terminal state of wild paranoid anguish that causes the sufferer to behave bizarrely, taking on strange affectations of speech and appearance. Oh yeah, and weird body stuff where you spend a lot of time rubbing yourself for no apparent reason.

Lotsa kids in the belt postponed puberty. And for good reason. It doesn't make sense to have your body readying itself for breeding when there are no appropriate mates to pick from. And there's more than enough history to demonstrate that human intelligence goes into remission until at least five years after the puberty issues resolve. A person should finish her basic education without interruption, get a little life experience, before letting her juices start to flow. At least, that was the theory.

But if I didn't start puberty soon, I'd never be able to and I'd end up sexless. You can only postpone it for so long before the postponement becomes permanent. Which might not be a bad idea, considering how crazy all that sex stuff makes people.

And besides, yes, I was curious about all that sex stuff—masturbation and orgasms and nipples and thighs, stuff like that—but not morbidly so. I wanted to finish my *real* education first. Intercourse is supposed to be something marvelous and desirable, but all the pictures I'd ever seen made it look like an icky imposition for *both* partners. Why did anyone want to do *that?* Either there was something wrong with the videos, or maybe there was something wrong with me that I just didn't get it.

So it only made sense that I should start puberty now, so I'd be ready for mating when we got to Earth. And it made sense that we should go to Earth with Comet Janis. And why didn't Jill see that?

Mom stuck her head into the galley then. "I think that bread surrendered twenty minutes ago, sweetheart. You can stop beating it up now."

"Huh? What? Oh, I'm sorry. I was thinking about some stuff. I guess I lost track. Did I wake you?"

"Whatever you were thinking about, it must have been pretty exciting. The whole ship was thumping like a subwoofer. This boat is noisy enough without fresh-baked bread, honey. You should have used the bread machine." She reached past me and rescued the bag of dough; she began stuffing it into a baking cylinder.

"It's not the same," I said.

"You're right. It's quieter."

The arguments about the differences between free fall bread and gravity bread had been going on since Commander Jarles Ferris had announced that bread doesn't fall butter-side down in space. I decided not to pursue that argument. But I was still in an arguing mood.

"Mom?"

"What, honey?"

"Jill doesn't want to go to Earth."

"I know."

"Well, you're the Captain. It's *your* decision."

"Honey, Jill is my partner."

"Mom, I have to start puberty soon!"

"There'll be other chances."

"For puberty?"

"For Earth."

"When? How? If this isn't my best chance, there'll never be a better one." I grabbed her by the arms and turned her so we were both oriented the same way and looked her straight in the eyes. "Mom, you know the drill. They're not going to allow you to throw anything that big across Earth's orbit unless you're riding it. We have to ride that comet in. You've known that from the beginning."

Mom started to answer, then stopped herself. That's another thing about spaceships. After a while, everybody knows all the sides of every argument. You don't have to recycle the exposition. Janis was big money. Four-plus years of extra-hazardous duty allotment, fuel and delta-vee recovery costs, plus bonuses for successful delivery. So, Jill's argument about cost-effectiveness wasn't valid. Mom knew it. And so did I. And so did Jill. So why were we arguing?

Mom leapt ahead to the punch line. "So what's this really about?" she asked.

I hesitated. It was hard to say. "I—I think I want to be a boy. And if we don't go to Earth, I won't be able to."

"Sweetheart, you know how Jill feels about males."

"Mom, that's *her* problem. It doesn't have to be mine. I like boys. Some of my best online friends are boys. Boys have a lot of fun together—at least, it always looks that way from here. I want to try it. If I don't like it, I don't have to stay that way." Even as I said it, I was abruptly aware that what had only been mild curiosity a few moments ago was now becoming a genuine resolve. The more Mom and Jill made it an issue, the more it was an issue of control, and the more important it was for me to win. So I argued for it, not because I wanted it as much as I needed to win. Because it wasn't about winning, it was about who was in charge of my life.

Mom stopped the argument abruptly. She pulled me around to orient us face to face, and she lowered her voice to a whisper, her way of saying *this is serious*. "All right, dear, if that's what you really want. It has to be your choice. You'll have a lot of time to think about it before you have to commit. But I don't want you talking about it in front of Jill anymore."

Oh. Of course. Mom hadn't just wandered into the galley because of the bread. Jill must have buzzed her awake. The argument wasn't over. It was just beginning.

"Mom, she's going to fight this."

"I know." Mom realized she was still holding the baking cylinder. She turned and put the bread back into the oven. She set it to warm for two hours, then bake. Finally she floated back to me. She put her hands on my shoulders. "Let me handle Jill."

"When?"

"First let's see if we can get the rock we need." She swam forward. I followed.

Jill was glowering at her display and muttering epithets under her breath.

"The Flyby Knights?" Mom asked.

Jill grunted. "They're still saying, 'Take it or leave it.'"

Mom thought for a moment. "Okay. Send them a message. Tell them we found another rock."

"We have?"

"No, we haven't. But they don't know that. Tell them thanks a lot, but we won't need their asteroid after all. We don't have time to negotiate anymore. Instead, we'll cut Janis in half."

"And what if they say that's fine with them? Then what?"

"Then we'll cut Janis in half."

Jill made that noise she makes, deep in her throat. "It's all slush, you can't cut it in half. If we have to go crawling back, what's to keep them from raising their price? This is a lie. They're not stupid. They'll figure it out. We can't do it. We have a reputation."

"That's what I'm counting on—that they'll believe our reputation—that you'd rather cut your money rock in half than make a deal with a *man*."

Jill gave Mom one of those sideways looks that always meant a lot more than anything she could put into words, and certainly not when I was around.

"Send the signal," Mom said. "You'll see. It doesn't matter how much nickel is in that lump; it just isn't cost-effective for them to mine it. So it's effectively worthless. The only way they're going to get any value out of it in their lifetimes is to let us throw it away. From their point of view, it's free money, whatever they get. They'll be happy to take half a percent if they can get it."

Jill straightened her arms against the console and stretched herself out while she thought it out. "If it doesn't work, they won't give us any bargaining room."

"They're not giving us any bargaining room now."

Jill sighed and shrugged, as much agreement as she ever gave. She turned it over in her head a couple of times, then pressed for *record*. After the signal was sent, she glanced over at Mom and said, "I hope you know what you're doing."

"Half the rock is still more than enough. We can print up some reflectors and burn it in half in four months. That'll put us two months ahead of schedule, and we'll have the slings and tether already in place."

Jill considered it. "You won't get as big a burnoff. The tail won't be as long or as bright."

Mom wasn't worried. "We can compensate for that. We'll drill light pipes into the ice, fractioning the rock and increasing the effective surface area. We'll burn out the center. As long as we burn off fifty tons of ice per hour, it doesn't matter how big the comet's head is. We'll still get an impressive tail."

"So why didn't we plan that from the beginning?"

"Because I was hoping to deliver the head of the comet to Luna and sell the remaining ice. We still might be able to do that. It just won't be as big a payday." Mom turned to me.

"The braking problem on that will be horrendous." Jill closed her eyes and did some math in her head. "Not really cost-effective. We'll be throwing away more than two-thirds of the remaining mass. And if you've already cut it in half—"

"It's not the profit. It's the publicity. We'd generate a lot of new business. We could even go public."

Jill frowned. "You've already made up your mind, haven't you?"

Mom swam around to face Jill. "Sweetheart, our child is ready to be a grownup."

"She wants to be a boy." So Jill had figured it out too. But the way she said it, it was an accusation.

"So what? Are you going to stop loving her?"

Jill didn't answer. Her face tightened.

In that moment, something crystallized—all the vague unformed feelings of a lifetime suddenly snapped into focus with an enhanced clarity. Everything is tethered to everything else. With people, it isn't gravity or cables—it's money, promises, blood, and feelings. The tethers are all the words we use to tie each other down. Or up. And then we whirl around and around, just like asteroids cabled together.

We think the tethers mean something. They have to. Because if we cut them, we go flying off into the deep dark unknown. But if we don't cut them...we just stay in one place, twirling around forever. We don't go anywhere.

I could see how Mom and Jill were tethered by an ancient promise. And Mom and I were tethered by blood. And Jill and I—were tethered by jealousy. We resented each other's claim on Mom. She had something I couldn't understand. And I had something she couldn't share.

I wondered how much Mom understood. Probably everything. She was caught in the middle between two whirling bodies. Someone was going to have to cut the tether. That's why she'd accepted this contract—so we could go to the marble. She'd known it from the beginning. We were going to ride Janis all the way to Earth.

And somewhere west of the terminator, as we entered our braking arc, I'd cash out my shares and cut the tethers. I'd be off on my own course then—and Mom and Jill would fly apart too. No longer bound to me, they'd whirl out and away on their own inevitable trajectories. I wondered which of them would be a comet streaked across Earth's black sky.

Take me to the light
Take me to the mystery of life
Take me to the light
Let me see the edges of the night
　　　　　—Janis Ian

GANNY KNITS A SPACESHIP

"Why do we need a spaceship?" asked Ganny. The question wasn't rhetorical.

Gampy grunted, sucked some coffee from a bulb, left it hanging in the air while he scratched his ear and rubbed his chin and did his whole performance of being thoughtful. "Because," he said. And folded his arms.

Ganny did that side-to-side head shake she always did, accompanied with an expression of bemusement that usually decoded as "If that's the only answer I'm going to get, then I get to live with it." If Ganny waited long enough, eventually Gampy would explain. But by that time, she'd usually figured it out herself. Either way, Ganny knew better than to push. Wise people, she said, respect each other's orbits.

She meant that people who live in space live differently than people who live on planets. I'm not talking about the micro-gravity and the sense of confinement and the recycling of air and water and protein, the exercise regimen, and all the implants and augments, like bone-sintering and radiation-nanos and white-blood infusions, and all the other stuff that dirtsiders think about. That's just mechanics. You live with it.

No, there's something else. Dirtsiders don't notice it immediately, but they notice it eventually. And they notice it a lot more intensely than starsiders do because starsiders don't notice it at all. Starsiders live the way we do because that's the way we live. But dirtsiders say there's an emotional distance, a privacy wall, a cocooning. They say it's because of the isolation and the close proximity and the lack of elsewhere to go. According to dirtsiders, people who live in space are all introverts, socially enclosed, and given to long disturbing periods of self-inflicted privacy. They see it as being shut down. I guess, by comparison with dirtside, maybe that's true.

I've never been dirtside so I have no personal experience of what they're talking about, but I do watch dirtsider videos from time to time and if that's a valid reflection of how they think, I really don't want that experience. They talk too much about nothing in particular. Like, "What did you have for dinner?" and "How was it?" and "How are you feeling?" Like all that stuff is important. I know how I'm feeling, it should be obvious to everyone around me how I'm feeling. Just look at my face, okay? Maybe it's just me, maybe I'm missing something. But from where I am, they look stupid, they talk everything to death like they're incapable of doing anything on their own. And even if they can do it on their own, they don't do it until they've talked it over with at least six people. All that chatter. What's it good for?

Ganny says it's about bonding. They bond differently dirtside. I don't see why that should make a difference, but apparently it does. Ganny should know. Both Ganny and Gampy were born dirtside. I asked them once if there actually was that big a reality gap and they both had to stop and think. Finally Gampy said, "Ayep." And after a bit, Ganny added, "There might be more to it than that." But that was as much as either of them said at the time. So I figured it was one of those things that you have to do for a while before you can understand it. But dirtside isn't something I want to do. Germs and insects and airborne contaminants? Yick. I guess some people can learn to live with it. And if you've never known anything else, then that's what you call normal. It just looks dirty to me.

But I do know some dirtsiders. We exchange almost every day. They don't seem to notice the soup they're swimming in, and I don't mean the air and water, I mean the cultural soup, the context. But we don't talk about that much. That's too much like school. Oh, that's another thing.

Living on the whirligig, everything you learn in school is about survival. Dirtside, you learn all kinds of stuff that doesn't have much application for anything at all, let alone survival.

But James, my dirtside boyfriend asked—well that's what I called him, he was never a real in-the-flesh boyfriend, and that was before I broke up with him anyway—James once asked if it wasn't lonely out here, not having any real friends. I told him I have real friends. I have friends all over the ecliptic and a couple on the long ride. Okay, they're all web-friends, but I don't feel alone. How could I? Web-friends are the best kind because you go to them only when you feel like it. They can't bother you any hour of the night or day like they could if they were right next to you in meat-space.

Okay, so I don't chat in real-time, but so what? Chatting has a lousy signal-to-noise ratio. It's mostly pauses while each person thinks about what they really want to say and what they should say instead. It's easier and more efficient to think things out first and then text it all at once. And when you send it as an email, you not only get to rewrite it a couple times before you click on send, sometimes you can even snatch it back if you have to.

What I mean is that talking is useful, sure, if you're talking it out to yourself, or writing into a journal, because that's how you figure out what you really think, but that doesn't mean you have to inflict that whole linguistic journey of ratiocination on the nearest innocent bystander. Because if you do, then that implies an obligation on your part to listen to them verbalize at length as they work their way through their own fumbling thought processes. Long, boring, tiresome. It's only interesting if it's about you, and if it's about you it's almost always something you really didn't want to hear in the first place, like someone's projection of their personal narrative about you, which is almost always negative and comes with the corresponding implication that because you listened you are now obligated to change yourself. And that's just silly. If it's the other person's narrative, not yours, it's their responsibility to author it in a way that's useful to them. What someone else believes, even if it's about me, is none of my business. I'm not so self-involved that I need to care. There are more important things. The only way information like that is ever useful is when you get it from more than one person because then you're hearing a common perception, but even then it's still only a report on the effect you're having on others. You're only obligated if you choose to be obligated. And most of the time, I choose not to be. That's how it is. No, that's not how *I* think it is. That's how it really *is*. Ganny says I could out-stubborn a cat, I don't know, I've never met a cat. I can out-stubborn a mountain, if that means anything, but that's a different story. When I say something, I mean it, that's all.

Never mind. This is about Ganny and Gampy. Whenever Gampy said we should do something, we all knew it wasn't ever just a casual thought, but that he'd been thinking about it for a few days or weeks, goggling and thinking and probably even arguing with himself. Gampy never said anything unless he'd already decided it needed to be said.

And then, after he'd said it, he knew that Ganny and I and whoever else might be in earshot would go off on our own and ask ourselves why he'd said it and we'd do our own thinking and goggling and thinking some more and probably a lot of arguing with ourselves as well. By the time Gampy's thoughts had finished echoing in the heads of me and Ganny and anyone else around, most of what we would have said didn't need to be said at all. Which is fine, because after you've lived in space with the same people long enough, you know them so well that you know most of what they're going to say before they say it and you really don't need to hear it one more time, so you learn to keep your cake-hole shut unless it's something that actually needs to be said. Like "You oughta come back in now. Your O-mix is getting a little thin."

So when Gampy said it, he wasn't just saying it. He was inviting the rest of us to think about it. Me, Ganny, the blue-crew, and all three of IRMA's personality-units. The Blue Crew worked three to six months at a time, depending on orbits, personal and ecliptic, alternating with the Red Crew. Some came back, some didn't, but Ganny and Gampy had a team of mostly-regulars and we didn't see new faces all that often.

Sunday dinner we always ate in the wheel, where we had real pseudo-gravity and Ganny could cook the old-fashioned way. Usually we had chicken roast, because that was the tradition, but not always. Chicken was just the fastest-growing protein. And most cost-effective. Ganny was a budget-nazi. But we also had goose, duck, swan, ostrich, dodo, pigeon, rabbit, beaver, beef, horse, pork, goat, venison, elk, antelope, moose, mutton, lamb, buffalo, tuna, swordfish, salmon, shark, lobster, sea turtle, clam, squid, snake, alligator, rhinoceros, dinosaur, or any of the hundred different hybrid-proteins Ganny was growing in the meat tanks. We also had synthetic sasquatch, bandersnatch, yeti, and tribble. If you can imagine it, someone has probably already gene-tailored it.

The thing about protein farming, you don't have to worry about flavor too much, because you can add whatever flavor you want long before you start slicing, but you do want to pay attention to muscling, fat content, marbling, and digestibility. All the pieces of the viability equations. And of course, how you exercise the collagen web you grow the tissue on determines the texture and chewability, which is even more important than flavor. When you get all that balanced, then you either leave it alone, because some people prefer the natural flavor of the meat, or you start adding flavor components, genes, enzymes, hormones, whatever, because other people like their meat pre-spiced—but to Ganny it's all about cost-effective protein design. So even before the tissue-starters go into the growth tanks, she's doing targeted gene-splicing and chromosome-braiding and designer-musculature. Starsiders are always looking for better ways to turn CHON into stuff that tastes good, so you have to keep a big library of resources on hand, because you never know when someone is going to invent another new culinary fad, like rhinoceros green burrito or fried buffalo sushi or mango horse fish. On the gig there's always something that needs harvesting and even though most of it was grown to order, it always worked out that there was enough left over for dinner, sandwiches, stews, and snacks. Ganny said it was quality control. She wouldn't sell anything she wouldn't eat herself. Mostly.

Being born on Earth, Ganny and Gampy still had a few dirtside prejudices. Ganny was adamant that she would never grow chimpanzee or any other kind of ape, whale, or dolphin. Also on the list were rat, mouse, squirrel, possum, bat, cat, dog, wolf, hyena, lion, tiger, eagle, vulture, and most other scavengers and predators. No monkeys or elephants either. She did keep all those stem-cells in vitro, in case someone else wanted to buy starters for their own farms, but she wouldn't grow them for our own consumption. She did give in once on whale and dolphin, just to see, but she wasn't happy with the amount of water it took to produce a kilo of flesh, even though the water really didn't go anywhere and we always reclaimed it, but she said the recycling overhead had to be figured in and she felt it was prohibitive. That was what she said anyway. But while she allowed some wiggle room there, she was an absolute wall when it came to chimpanzees and other major primates. "I'm not a cannibal," she said.

"I won't eat my cousins. Not even metaphorically. Maybe some people will, I won't."

Sunday dinner—that was when we did talk to each other. We shared what was important, all the stuff that needed to be said face-to-face. And if nobody said anything, which happened sometimes, because we were all too busy doing the knife-and-fork thing, slicing and stuffing and chewing and swallowing, which was the best acknowledgment of Ganny's hard work we could give her, a lot better than silly verbalizing like, "Mmm, this is good." Of course it's good. If it weren't, we wouldn't be eating it. But if nobody said anything at all, Gampy would start poking. "So, Starling," Gampy finally said to me, "What did you figure out this week?"

"Railroads," I said. "Highways. Trucks. Costs of shipping."

"Mm," he said around a mouthful of something designed to approximate dinosaur, it still tasted like chicken. He chewed for a bit, swallowed, and finally asked, "And…?"

"Well, um. If you own the tracks, you have a monopoly, you set your own prices. But if you don't own the tracks—the roads—then everybody gets to compete, and the market determines the cost of shipping. In the ecliptic, there are no tracks, only orbits. And everybody's got their own. So it's like roads. It's all about intersections. Convenient intersections."

Gampy looked to Ganny. "See? Told you she'd get it."

Ganny swallowed politely before answering. "Was there ever any doubt?"

Gampy looked back to me. "Go on."

"I know we like to say that everybody comes to Rick's, because sooner or later everybody has to come to a whirligig to slingshot into a new trajectory, but that isn't true anymore. Not since whatsisname invented the traction drive. Used to be, they'd come for a slingshot, but now they only come if they want to fill their freezers. And that's only locals now, and only when they need to resupply, and only if they don't have a farm of their own. In ten years, fifteen, everybody will have tractions. Even cargo pods. So whirligigs are like internal combustion engines. Very very useful, but only until people invented something more efficient."

"Good," said Gampy. "You might have been a little too optimistic about how quickly everyone will switch to tractors, but I might be wrong too. The human factor is always a monkey wrench."

"What's a monkey wrench…?"

"It's where you raise Jewish monkeys."

"Never mind, I'll look it up later."

"I'm sure you will." Gampy stuffed another baby potato into his mouth and grinned. That was his answer to almost every question: "Look it up, I'm not going to do all the work here, you're the one who wants to know." Gampy said that the only thing worse than not knowing how to swim in the data-sea was knowing how and never getting your feet wet for anything more than looking at people trading body fluids. I didn't understand that one until I was eight, not because I was slow but because orbital physics was a lot more interesting than looking at boys taking off their underwear. Why do they do that anyway? I mean, okay, it's cute enough, but after a while you have to ask, what's the point? They all sort of look alike. Are those things really that important?

"So, kiddo," Gampy poked again. "Is a spaceship cost-effective?"

"Yes and no. I mean, a traction drive isn't that hard to fabricate. We could even print a couple dozen ourselves. There's enough open-source matrices on the web, we'd only have to choose one, maybe adapt it for our needs, so it's mostly a problem of raw materials and energy. And we wouldn't have any problem fabbing new solar panels, three or four racks and probably a dozen new capacitor farms, so it's only a problem of raw materials and we can cannibalize most of that from the junkyard. I'm guessing we could do it in 24 months or less. Worst-case scenario is 48 months. If we double up on the fabbers, I bet we could cut the production time to 16 months."

Ganny looked annoyed. Gampy covered his smile with his napkin. "What's the no part, punkin?"

"The life support system. We don't have a hull. Unless you're planning to cannibalize modules from the whirligig. But you'd never do that because the gig has to maintain a viability score of 350 or more for a crew of 20 and you won't risk the numbers. I don't know how big a crew you're planning for the spaceship, but even a yacht needs a lot of hull space to be self-sufficient."

"Why do we need to build a self-sufficient ship?" Gampy asked.

I gave him the look. The one that says "Why are you even bothering to ask?" It almost worked. He still gave me the "Come on, answer the question" gesture with his hand.

I took a deep breath, my way of showing him how annoyed I was that I even had to explain. "Because," I said. And folded my arms.

Gampy laughed. Ganny smiled and said to him, "She's got you there."

Of course, that wasn't the end of the conversation. Conversations never really ended on the whirligig, they just spun around for a while, evolving, changing, recycling. Some of the conversations eventually flung off into space, forgotten. Others got winched in for closer examination and winched out again when they were no longer relevant. I expected this to be one of those kind of discussions, I should have known better. Gampy never wasted air. Gampy was famous for that.

Actually, Gampy was famous for a lot of things. He and Ganny were sort of like legends. As near as I could tell, everybody in the belt knew them, or at least knew *of* them.

The way most people know the story, Gampy built the first whirligig. He didn't, not any more than Henry Ford built the first car, but Gampy built the first one that worked well enough to be profitable. You can look it up. Gampy started the first pipeline. And like the railroads, the pipeline made it possible for people to expand outward to Mars, the belt, and the Jovian moons. And the Saturnalias as well (their name for it, not mine).

The pipeline isn't really a pipeline with tubes, although I'm sure a lot of dirtsiders think it is. Once, when Ganny was angry about something, she said, "Never underestimate the stupidity of dirtsiders in large groups, except when they're alone and have to do their own thinking." And even though I know that there some smart dirtsiders, Ganny says not to depend on it. Anyway, the way the pipeline works, cargo pods come up one of the beanstalks, Ecuador or Brazil or Kenya or mid-Pacific, and also from Mars and Luna too. The pods go all the way out to the ballast rock at the far end of the cable, unless they're carrying cargo or passengers that can't stand the gees, and then they go only as far as they can. At just the right moment, the pod lets go of the cable and like a stone released from the end of a sling, it goes hurtling off in whatever direction it was pointing when it let go. Most of the pods go to Luna and Mars. A lot go to the Jovian moons. And a lot go out to the Saturnalias, now that they're getting serious about colonizing. A few more go out into deep space, those are usually long-distance robot probes. The rest come out to the belt where we catch them with the whirligig.

The whirligig is a beanstalk without a planet attached. You get a length of cable and two rocks, a kilometer is a good length, but you can do it with less—or more if you want. It works on any scale. Gampy says you really want a minimum of three cables for redundant strength, but he eventually used six, which gave him strength for expansion.

You start with a construction and a cable. Then you catch two rocks—that's the hard part because it involves wrassling a flying mountain, and that's a lot of delta-vee, but if you can catch the rocks, or better yet, break one big rock in two pieces, you're in business. You catch each rock in a big net. You loop one end of your cable around one rock, you loop the other end around the other rock. If you're smart, like Gampy, you use multiple cables, because no matter how well you plan, you never know what surprises will happen once stress is applied.

Once you've got your rocks securely netted and harnessed and attached to the ends of the cables, you give each rock a push, but in opposite directions, a small push at first, just enough to start them orbiting slowly around each other like a bolo. That's the hard part because big rocks usually have their own opinions about where they want to go. That's what I mean about out-stubborning a mountain. Which is why as soon as you've got them going, you want to get out of the way, because you've probably miscalculated and you're going to have to apply a lot of corrections. That's why you start out slowly at first.

This is the part they don't always tell you about in the engineering books. In theory there's no difference between theory and practice; in practice, there is. The physical universe is going to get sloppy and you have to adjust for it. Constantly. Then you start adding more push, more acceleration, until you get your bolo whirling at the rotation you need to catch and sling cargo pods. Keep making corrections until you don't have to anymore. Wait a few days until they stabilize, then wait a few days more to see if you've miscalculated again.

With all that centrifugal force on the rocks, you want to be certain that they've finished settling. Sometimes pieces decide to fly off, which is why you want to get above or below the local ecliptic, so you're not accidentally in the way. You want to make sure that the whole thing isn't going to suddenly fly apart before you make a commitment. (Gampy says the same thing applies to women too.) Sometimes the stress and strain of applied "space-gravity" destabilizes the inner structure of the rocks, causing them to crack or crumble or simply rearrange themselves in their harnesses, changing their center of gravity and the center of gravity on your bolo. When you're finally satisfied that the bolo is spinning safely, then you proceed. Then the construction harness crawls back and forth along the cable until it finds the exact center of gravity on the line. That's where you start your hub and install your axis.

Okay, so now you've got pumps on both ends of your pipeline. We're at the top end—one of the top ends. The bottom end is the great big whirligig called the big blue marble. A top end is any whirligig near your intended destination, or at least on the way there. You can sling a lot of stuff back and forth between the two lines. The tricky part is catching the pods. There are a lot of different ways to do it. The easiest is to hang a big hook at the end of the catching line. The pod then puts out a big loop of cable, as much as a kilometer in diameter, if necessary. If you're really cautious, you also put a hook on the pod and the gig puts out a lasso as well. The velocity differences at match-up are fairly low, usually less than a few kph. But despite all the course corrections all the way in, you only get one chance at threading the needle. And with cargo pods carrying as much as a half-billion plastic dollars' of cargo at a time, you just don't take chances. And if the pod is carrying passengers, you *really* do not want to let them go sailing off into space, especially if the chance of recovery is somewhere south of impossible. Gampy says that having to listen to desperate calls for help fading off into deep space can ruin your whole day.

Gampy's whirligig outsizes everything else in this part of the belt, ten degrees east and seven degrees west, so we catch all the fastest and heaviest traffic in this slice of the arc. Seventeen degrees. And that's a lot of arc. That's because Gampy had the far vision. That's what Ganny calls it. Far vision is being able to see past tomorrow. A long way past. The way Ganny tells it, Luna got too crowded for Gampy's taste, so he hiked all the way out to the belt with a big roll of cable on his back, picked out the two biggest rocks he could find, hitched 'em together, and started 'em spinning. Then he ordered more cable. By the time the big space exploration companies got out here, Gampy had a giant spinning spiderweb with eight ballast rocks and sixteen stabilizing engines. Cargo slingshots through here for delivery to the local group or slingshots back and forth between Earth and Jupiter, Earth and Saturn, and occasionally even Earth and Mars, depending on everybody's orbital positions. Work it out for yourself. When Mars and Earth are on opposite sides of the sun, it's faster to fling it to us and we fling it on. It's called a double-play. Tinkers to Evers to Chance. I had to look that one up. The allegory isn't exact, but Gampy's a history nut, always peppering his conversations with little nuggets for me to find and research. He does it on purpose. It's the game we've played for as long as I can remember. But no matter how sharp I get, he's still the bear, I'm still the cub.

When a pod gets out here, it doesn't have to slow down. It only has to arrive at the right speed and the right time so that it momentarily matches trajectory with one of the spinning arms as it comes around. There are a lot of different spinning arms, different lengths, different positions, so there's a little wiggle room on the final approach, but not much. And IRMA takes over control of the pod on its way in and manages the entire docking maneuver. (If the pod doesn't let IRMA take control, we don't catch it. No matter what's on board.)

After a pod latches on, after the hooks and loops catch, there's a few moments of load-balancing, because even with all the ballast rocks in place, the whirligig's center of gravity has shifted and we either have to pump some water around or winch some other pods in or out, or both. IRMA manages that.

Some pods we winch down to the hub—and that requires more load-balancing. Others, we just wait for the next convenient launch window and send them whirling off to their next destination. Gampy says it's a lot cheaper for the big money to pay us to catch and sling cargo pods than build their own whirligigs. Gampy says that's how he became one of the first trillionaires in the ecliptic. On paper, anyway.

At any given moment, Gampy had maybe 950 billion dollars' worth of cargo in transit outward and maybe another 125 billion in value headed back, depending on market value. But depending on where the pods were launched from, depending on whether or not they had to slingshot around something, the outbound journey could take as long as three years. Complicating the matter, pods could only be launched when there was an open catching window for them at whatever point in the future they were scheduled to arrive, so the computations could get tricky.

But belters can't wait three years for supplies, not even three weeks if it's air and water they need. So Gampy always bought a lot of stuff on margin against a slice of long-term earnings. What that meant was that technically Gampy owned the cargo until the recipient paid for it. Somewhere, in some dirtside bank, somebody would subtract a few zeroes from one account and add them to another. Out in the belt, nobody starves, nobody suffocates. That's not just the Starsider ethic, that was Gampy's rule. "Out here, the equations are as warm as we can make them. Anybody doesn't like that way of business can go somewhere else." Except for the longest time there was nowhere else.

Gampy never turned anyone away. If he had it to give, he gave. Only once did he have a problem with one family of belters. They didn't pay their bills. Even with all the computerized projections and advisories they had available to them, they always knew better, until eventually they mismanaged themselves into a very ambitious bankruptcy, but they kept on anyway. Because Gampy kept resupplying them for a lot longer than he should have. Until finally, it became obvious they were never going to work their way out of their very deep hole. They wouldn't take any of the little jobs Gampy offered them because they still believed in the big score, the solid-gold asteroid. Those little jobs would have kept them going and Gampy could have recouped some of their debts. But no. They were too proud to take little jobs. So finally, one night, Gampy loaded them up with just enough fuel and almost enough food to get to Mars, and as soon as they were all asleep in their ship, he slung them off to Mars. They made it, but they were really hungry when they arrived. The way Ganny tells it, a lot of other belters started paying their bills on time Real Quickly after that.

Every so often, some dirtsider complains about the amount of product that comes out to the whirligigs, enough to supply a small town for a couple of years, enough to build two or three long-riders. "I thought they're supposed to be self-sufficient. Why are we still supporting them? That money should be spent on the poor? Not on the spoiled starsiders."

But they don't understand. The whirligig *has* to be a warehouse. Maybe it's the way they live, everything is too easy. If you can waddle down to the corner store and pick whatever you want off the shelf, you don't worry too much about how it got there or where it came from in the first place or what it took to get it there because the next day the shelf is full again. Dirtsiders don't have to think about where their next breath of air or drink of water is coming from, so they don't stop to think that the rest of us do. Everyone who lives starside.

But the ones who do understand, the ones on the bottom end of the pipeline, they're even worse. Because every so often, one of those cute little business-school graduates figures that he can boost his bottom line by raising prices on the belters. Charge a dollar more per cubic liter of oxygen, two bucks processing fee for clean water, decontamination surtax for every item loaded into a cargo pod, no problem. It adds up. What are the belters going to do? Take their business elsewhere? Where? Negotiate a new deal? With who?

The last time Gampy got one of those "New Fee Schedule" messages he replied with a new fee schedule of his own. "Service fee for new software processing to prevent returning capsules from accidentally falling into the Pacific Ocean or onto a continental landmass." The service fee was considerable. Enough to offset all the surcharges and processing fees and surtaxes. That was a fun negotiation. It lasted for eleven and a half months. Until a few of the capsules started falling into the Pacific. Including one very expensive capsule with a lot of stuff they really didn't want to lose. Oops. My bad. I told you we needed to update the software. Then they paid attention. Gampy appointed himself the ad hoc negotiator for all the belters and refused to back down until three planetary authorities agreed to regulate cargo launch costs more honestly. Gampy even wrote in a clause guaranteeing a cost of living margin for all the cargo handlers on the ground as well as the ones in space, so that guaranteed popular support from the important people on both ends of the line. A lot of dirtsiders weren't very happy about it. They said words like arrogant and blackmail and terrorism and wanted to stop sending us supplies at all. Obviously, they didn't think that one all the way through.

It wasn't a great relationship, but it worked. Gampy said it was about power. If you have it, sometimes you have to use it—to remind people that you have it. Otherwise they'll think you don't have it. But the whirligigs were important, just too important to the economies of four worlds and a handful of lesser settlements. Nobody could afford to get into a prolonged fight. The alternative was to accelerate things the old-fashioned way, by boosting a lot of fuel into orbit and using half of it to accelerate and the other half to decelerate. And twice as much more if you expected to bring anything or anyone back, because you pay a fuel penalty to boost the mass of your fuel too. So before the traction drive was invented, the whirligigs were the cheapest way to sling things around the system.

It took a while to get the big traction drives out of the labs, but even before the first tractor ships started shooting around the system, everybody knew that the role of the whirligigs would be changed. Probably diminished. To run a pipeline, you need a sling at both ends, but a tractor can go directly from point to point and usually a lot faster. Cargo doesn't care how long a trip takes, passengers do.

So there wasn't any question why Gampy wanted a spaceship. It was the only way to stay competitive. Or we accept a reduced role in the economy of the belt.

Over the next few weeks, Gampy had us all working on the question of life support modules. Not just me and Ganny, but folks on the Blue Team as well. They were the real crew and he said their input was the most important, because they were the guys who had to make it all work. How big a module would we need? Could we afford to construct one? Or would we have to buy a hull from the Martian Electric Boat Company? What would our requirements be? How big a crew would we carry? And what about passengers? Will our payload include cash-carrying customers? How many? And what level of service will we provide?

The problem with that equation was that every time you added a warm body, you also had to expand the life-support systems to accommodate. Above a certain point—twelve is the magic number—there's a certain economy that kicks in. But when you start adding passengers, you also have to add stewards, at least one for every twelve bodies. It adds up.

There's a lot to think about in spaceship design. No matter how good all your software might be, you still have to make hard decisions about how far you want to go, how much you want to carry, who and how many you want to bring along, how you're going to keep everyone alive and comfortable and productive, and most important, how you intend to pay for it all. The irony of ship design is that there's a corresponding relationship between size and comfort and profitability. The more comfort you want, the bigger the ship has to be. The bigger it gets, the more people and cargo you can carry. The more you carry, the more profit you make. So the ultimate question is how big a ship can you afford to build? It's all about the life support module. The traction drive doesn't care. It's null-N, non-Newtonian.

So you can build a starter ship for five and later on add a second ring of cargo pods and maybe a couple passenger payload systems and you only have to add one or two or three traction cores to your basic unit. If you've designed for expansion.

So Gampy's real question wasn't about whether or not we should build a spaceship. It was about what kind of spaceship we were going to build. And that meant he wanted us to think about what we were going to do with it after we built it? Where do we want to go? And what are we going to do when we get there? And after that, then what?

We spent a lot of time on that question. We needed a keel—that was the easy part. But how long? We needed traction drives. But how many? We were already fabbing the fabbers that would let us fab the drives. We needed a ring to hold cargo and supply pods. But we still hadn't decided on the life-support modules. How big? How many people are we schlepping? That was why Gampy started the discussion in the first place. He'd probably figured most of it out for himself, but he wanted to see if the rest of us would come to the same conclusions. It took us a while, but we did.

The most cost-effective way to complete the ship was to buy a hull from the Martian Electric Boat company. It wasn't the cheapest solution, but it was the fastest. It would save us at least 8 months of construction and testing, and that would get us to the return-on-investment point that much sooner. MEBC was popping out certified hulls two a month, whether they had buyers or not, it was cheaper to keep the assembly lines running, but they never seemed to have an overstock problem; they sold everything they produced. Besides MEBC had over a hundred years of quality control, their hulls had already logged several quadrillion kilometers without a fatality, while we'd be starting from scratch, learning as we went and probably making a lot of mistakes along the way. But, as Gampy pointed out, if we did build the hull ourselves, we'd know every inch of it intimately. Maintenance and repairs would be a lot easier. And faster. Because we'd have a much more personal relationship with vehicle integrity.

Of course I shared all of this with my journal. I wanted to share it with my bf James, but Gampy said not a good idea. Never share family business. Never share personal information. The person you share it with doesn't share your investment, doesn't share your commitment, and might not even care very much what happens to you. You can't know what he will do with the information. Don't take risks you don't have to."

"But James says he wants to come out here and work for us when he graduates. He can hitch a ride on a tramp. He's even willing to indenture. A standard seven-year contract."

Gampy didn't answer immediately. We were walking the centrifuge, we did it at least an hour a day, it was our best time for talking. But now he sat me down at the green bench, the one at the 60-degree mark. I think it was more because he was out of breath than because he wanted to be serious. "Starling," he said. "I need to talk to you as grownup now. You need to listen as grownup. This Sawyer boy might be very nice person. I think he is. Ganny thinks he is. Ganny looked over his emails, yours too. And he seems nice."

"You read my emails?"

"Yes, no. IRMA reads your emails, for your protection. She only flags for red-codes. Doesn't flag very often, so Ganny and I don't have to invade your privacy. But sometimes we check anyway. Shh. Let me explain why. Lots of suspicious people dirtside. Lots of fearful people dirtside. They live in fantasyland. Afraid we'll drop rocks on them. They watch us through telescopes. Everything we do, they see. They write, they speculate, they make things up. They get stupid. Living dirtside does that to you. Makes it easy to stop thinking. Dirtside, people can afford luxuries like stupid and crazy and not caring. Dirtside you can walk around wrapped in belief and ignorance and unconsciousness. But starside, no. The universe has an instant response to stupid. Vacuum is the fastest teacher. You're only entitled to one fatal mistake. No first warning, no second chances. So choose your death carefully, kidlet, you'll be stuck with it forever. And forever is long time, especially on the back end. Remind yourself of that. Say it every day. Like praying, but much more useful."

Gampy saw my impatient nod, I'd heard all this before, many times. He put his hand on my shoulder, his fingers felt frail. "Yes, munchkin. You know all that. But I want you to hear it again and again and again, because I want it written on your heart. Up here, this is the next step in human evolution. No, not spacelings or cyborgs, something more than that. It's about who we have to become in *here*, inside our souls. We're learning how to be conscious, awake, aware—truly *sentient*. That's what's important."

Gampy didn't usually talk this much, or this intensely, and I could see it was an effort for him, but Gampy only said what absolutely *needed* to be said, so I waited while he regathered his thoughts. "This is what I want you to know—dirtsiders don't trust us. Because dirtsiders don't trust anyone. Because they don't trust themselves." He made an annoyed gesture and I could tell he was thinking about someone in particular or a whole group of someones. "And they think everybody else thinks the same way—and anyone who doesn't is stupid. So everybody is either an enemy—or prey. That's why they watch us. A lot. To see if we're a threat, or if they can take advantage of us. Not just optical scopes, everything.

They use data-scopes and web-agents and spybots. They want to know who arrives, who leaves. What we buy, what we sell. What we upload, what we download. Everything. The joke is—we have no secrets. Our business is open book. We are transparent. That's why they think we have secrets. They say no evidence of secrets is evidence of deeper secrets. Crazy dirtsiders only see what they want to see, only see what they already believe. They wouldn't see it if they didn't believe it. Remember that. Loonies and Martians not so bad. They have space-legs. But earthlings…? Too much dirt in their veins."

"But what does all this have to do with James?"

"Yes, James. Nothing, everything. Just be careful." Seeing my puzzled look, he took another deep breath. Labored. He had already used up a two-month quota of words and now he might have to borrow against next year as well. He patted my hand. "James seems like a nice boy. I hope he is. But because dirtsiders don't trust us, we can't trust dirtsiders. Not with important stuff. You understand?"

"Not all dirtsiders," I insisted. "Some are okay. Aren't they? You and Ganny were dirt-born. That has to prove something."

"Yes. But we were smart enough to leave. Some dirtsiders are smart. Some might even be trustworthy. But how do you tell? That's the big question. You figure that out, you're smarter than Ganny."

"Smarter than Ganny?"

His face crinkled impishly. "In all my life, I only outsmarted her once."

"You did? When?"

"When she asked me to marry her, I said yes. I don't think she expected that. Don't tell her I told you."

"Promise." I promised.

"Pinky promise?"

"Pinky promise."

Of course, like every conversation with Gampy, it kept me processing for a week. I finally went back and reread a lot of my old conversations with James. How we met, what we talked about. Everything. I didn't see it. I didn't see what Gampy saw.

So I kept looking.

James first howdied me three years ago. Nothing much, just a "Hey." "I said "Backatcha." And that was most of what we said to each other for a long time. Non-communicative communications. "Agreed." "Yeppers."

"Me too." Stuff like that. Somewhere in there, I decided we were simpatico. But looking back on the messages now, I couldn't find a lot of places where he actually said something on his own. Mostly he was restating my thoughts back to me. But so what? I did that a lot too. Whenever I saw something that I agreed with. So there wasn't anything out of the ordinary about that.

Then later, after a few months, he did tell me a little bit about himself. He was the oldest of three brothers. They lived in a container house in Baja, far enough south they could see the Ecuador beanstalk through a good telescope. His goal was to ride it up to the top. Someday. I asked him what a container house was, he explained that cargo comes in on shipping containers, it's too expensive to ship them back empty, so people buy a few, stack them, add plumbing and insulation, power panels and air-conditioning, and move right in. If you do it right, you can put together a pretty nice house. Resistant to earthquakes and hurricanes. Put it on stilts and it's flood proof. Fairly fire-resistant too. According to James. He sent me pictures. So I sent him a picture of me in the centrifuge, standing by the peach tree.

The peach tree confused him. He accused me of lying about living in space. I had to explain to him about Ganny's gardens and send him a different picture, taken from another angle, that showed just how small the garden was and how the hills in the background were really just a display on the inside bulkhead. I sent another picture of me and the peach tree with the background changing every two seconds, just to prove it. He apologized, of course, but....

So I ran the whole thing through IRMA, asking for a six-level transactional analysis with focused emphasis on semiotic dynamics. I'd never done that with a friend before, I'd always believed I was smart enough to judge for myself, but maybe Gampy saw something I'd missed. He wouldn't have said anything unless it absolutely needed to be said.

IRMA said that the peach tree transaction put me on the defensive and that affected subsequent transactions. Additionally, the information transfer ratio was three to one. I gave James three times as much information about my life as he gave me about his. He asked a lot deeper questions too. IRMA said his trust level was moderate, which was probably as good as you could ever get on the web, but she also annotated that sophisticated chatterbots could generate trust-levels that measured moderate to high because they were designed to do that. Even so, chatterbots were still limited in their responses in some specifically targeted domains of human interaction and that was how you could test them.

IRMA also said that some of my messages had been a little too candid, edging into the yellow area. Obviously, my physical safety was not at risk. But as an information channel, I had moderately compromised the integrity of the data-bubble. Even the alternate photo of the peach tree was suspect because it revealed that Ganny's farm was inside a reconfigured Xinhua-Mercedes cargo pod. But anyone with access to a Hubble-6 eye or better could see that from Martian orbit on close approach, and there were already plenty of photos on the web anyway. But IRMA was a skeptic. Naturally suspicious. Not paranoid like a LENNIE, but if an intelligence engine could raise an eyebrow, IRMA would have one permanently arched.

But okay, so Gampy's point was that James might be for real, but he might not be either. Hard to say. If dirtsiders really were as Machiavellian as Gampy believed then it wouldn't be beyond them to create a sock-puppet specifically to make friends with a lonely teenage girl in the asteroid belt, win her trust, and pump her for data about her grandparents' whirligig. Social phishing. IRMA reported that a preliminary goggle of his backstory checked out, but she had no way of testing if that data was seeded, salted, or homemade. Satellite views showed whole neighborhoods of container houses lining the highway from Cabo to La Paz. Street view of James' address showed an old blue Prius parked in front, with a rebuilt solar on the roof trickle-charging the battery. Whoever owned it, they were lucky if they were getting 125mpg out of that thing. With combustible at $545 plastic dollars per liter, it wasn't something you drove every day to work or shopping or errands. Maybe it was a project-car, or some old-timer's fancy, or I dunno. A relic of times past? Maybe dirtsiders didn't feel rich unless they owned a car, even if they couldn't drive it. Or maybe dirtsiders just didn't know better. Or maybe they didn't care. Gampy said that because most dirtsiders never got into space, not even riding the beanstalk up to One-Hour, they had no idea how small the marble really was, so they dropped trash everywhere. That's why they built mommy-bots—so they'd have someone to pick up after them. Stupid. It's cheaper to not drop trash in the first place.

There was more

At first I didn't know who to be angry at. James for pumping me. Or Gampy for making me distrust James. Or myself—for not being smarter.

Gampy once said we're never angry at anyone else. We're only angry at ourselves for not knowing better, for stumbling into the mess in the first place. For being played. Well, yes. I could see that.

I didn't answer any of James' messages for two days while I sulked. Plus we were six hours away because Earth was on the other side of the sun and everything had to relay around the belt, bounce off Mars, ricochet off Luna, and then down to the mudball, and besides it was September so the hurricanes were probably outpacing the sandstorms, which meant communications might be uneven for awhile, and even if not email wouldn't be at the top of their immediate priorities, so James wouldn't be looking for a quick reply anyway and might not even notice if I was sulking, so that gave me time to think.

I could call him a big fat liar, but what if he wasn't? Then I could be losing one of my best-friends-forever. I could ask him to prove himself, but that would be almost as bad. If he was for real, I'd still be hurting the friendship, and if he wasn't for real then he'd know he'd been found out. And then I'd have to start worrying about all my other friends too. And any new friends I might make, because they might be sock-puppies too.

But this is why Gampy told me what he told me. So I would think about it. And what I finally figured out was this. If James Sawyer was playing me, then I would play him back. Oh, I wouldn't let him know I knew. I'd keep on going exactly the same, as if nothing had changed everything was still like it always was. Only now, knowing what I knew, I'd be a lot more skeptical of everything he wrote and a lot more cautious about everything I wrote. And I'd test him, a little at a time, to see if he was a chatterbot or a sock-puppy or just a space-struck nerd. A space-struck nerd would be okay. That's what I thought he was from the beginning—a tall geeky-looking, boney-elbowed, gangly, big-nosed, near-sighted, horse-faced, freckly, redheaded goof with an incredibly beautiful smile, despite the buck teeth, and a terrific sense of humor. Unless he was a synthesized image, because there was always that possibility too. Everybody had at least a half-dozen avatars for social-surfing. And if he wasn't for real, I was going to kill him. Even if it meant going down to the mudball in person. How dare he mess with my head like that? Well I could mess right back.

So I wrote to him and asked if he was all right because I hadn't heard from him in two days and the satellite view showed hurricanes all over

Cabo and how weird it must be to have to think about weather all the time but please write me back asap because I'm worried about you. Okay?

Then I got back to work on Gampy's spaceship. Gampy said to think big, think outrageous. Imagine everything you think should be in the most perfect spaceship you can think of. Then he added, "You can have anything you want. But you can't have everything you want. But start out thinking of everything and then decide what you want most."

At first, I started out thinking I'd like a bigger personal cabin. But then I had to laugh at myself because personals are always high on the list for dirtsiders. A starsider always thinks of the crew first, what makes the community space better for everyone. So I started thinking about a garden-lounge, a bigger recreation area, and a more luxurious galley— things that felt both luxurious and comfortable. Expansive but homey too. I was afraid to want too much because I knew that we had to be practical. I didn't need anyone to tell me that.

James finally answered my email. He said the hurricane had been pretty bad and his parents' house had been shifted off its foundations and one of the containers had been yanked loose from its moorings and fell down and dented, and they weren't sure the insurance would cover the cost of repair or replacement or reassembly, and his little brother broke his leg when a table fell on him, but other than that, nobody was badly hurt. I didn't know how to answer him, except to say, "Mother Nature is a bitch. Father Time is an asshole."

But I knew that wasn't enough. How do you give sympathy to someone who chooses to live in the path of a hurricane? Dirtsiders should know better. You live on the marble, you get weather. The only weather we get out here is the occasional solar storm. And no matter how ferocious a solar storm gets, it can't knock the whirligig off its foundation. The gig doesn't even have a foundation. Just torque. But I sent James my commiserations anyway, I admitted I couldn't imagine how bad it must be for everyone and I wished there was something I could do.

When he wrote back, he said, "Please just keep in touch. You're my lucky star. I look up in the sky and I imagine I can see you up there looking down at me. I log onto the telescope views of the whirligig and I pretend you're looking out the window, looking at the Earth and imagining me looking up. Do me a favor. Go to the window at 6pm my time and wave. I'll be looking at the gig through a scope then and I'll pretend I can see you waving."

So I did, and he did, and it was sweet, so we kept on exchanging messages. Most of his messages were about how upset he was because of how upset his parents were and how every day was the same damn thing over and over again and he hated waiting in line for fresh water, he had to bring his own containers, and he hated how hot it was in the day and how cold it was at night. He said he envied me, living in space and not having to worry about earthquakes and sandstorms and hurricanes and all the other stuff a restless planet can throw at you, only the occasional solar flare, and with the right kind of shielding in place, even that couldn't hurt you too badly. At least it didn't throw you out of bed in the middle of the night and knock your house apart.

Somewhere in there, I thought I could help take his mind off how bad his situation was so I asked him to help me with a project. I said that I had to design...um, the perfect space habitat. It was part of my term project on cost-analysis. My job was to think of the most outrageous things you could put on a space station and then show how or why they were impractical, because these were things that dirtsiders—um, I mean people on the marble, sorry—would ask for, and I wanted to be able to explain why or why not in the simplest possible terms. And do you think you could help me with that? He wrote back yes.

So we started throwing ideas at each other—most of them silly and outrageous, even impractical. He knew a lot more about starside conditions than I thought. Even though he'd never been up the beanstalk, he knew all about the stuff they do for tourists at Geosynchronous Station. And he had an uncle who helped design the L4 Cylinder and even consulted on the L5, so he knew a lot about that too.

Then we talked about some of the bigger things the Chinese built for their permanent habitats on Luna and Mars. For their Dubai partners. Atriums, swimming pools, mile-high towers, jungle-gardens, forests, village walks, plazas, huge wilderness areas, even zoos and aquariums, lakes, rock-climbing walls, endless ski-slopes, full-size concert halls and theaters, Olympic quality gymnasiums, running tracks, shopping malls, enough stuff to fill a dozen whirligigs. James and I came up with two or three new designs every week, I drafted the outlines, he filled in the textures, we collaborated on the math. I didn't tell him that I was bringing each design to the dinner table for Ganny and Gampy to look at.

Ganny and Gampy knew that he was helping me. As long as it was for a hypothetical space station for my fictional term project, it was all right. They wanted me to be ambitious, so they didn't mind a little col-laboration. They were collaborating on some of their own ideas, so they couldn't very well object to James and I working together.

Every night, after we finished dinner, we sat around the table and presented our latest follies. That's what we called them. Follies. In the traditional sense of the word. We only had one rule—the first response to every idea had to be an appreciation of how outrageous it was and how ambitious it was. After we applauded each idea for its sheer imprac-ticality, we would add it to the list of things we would want on an ideal spaceship. Everything was added to the list. Everything. Nothing was ever dismissed as too silly. Not even Gampy's elephant her or Ganny's Hundred Acre Wood. Or my own Wild Strawberry Fields.

Then, after we laid out the parameters of each astonishing addition, we'd give it to IRMA to run the math. How much lebensraum would it need? What kind of maintenance would be required? How much water? Oxygen? Power? Shielding? How much time would it take to construct? How much would it mass? How much payload penalty would we have to pay to include it? Balance all that against projected usage patterns. If we subtract it from the rest of the package, how much do we gain? Or lose? Everything was given a viability rating, a combined score, and we had a growing list of possibilities sorted by practicality all the way from must-have to violates-the-law-of-conservation-of-energy. Ultimately, our final decision would be where to put the dividing line, the cut-off point between yes and no. From day to day, the maybe zone fluctuated in size. Sometimes it was a big purple haze, sometimes a sharp maroon line. Mostly it was just a shallow band of magenta.

I knew what Gampy was doing, but I didn't mind. It was a great game. He was teaching me to regard every choice as a location on a vast map of possibilities. Consider all the overlapping sets, consider the locus of optimal points. Look for a balance between imagination and sensibil-ity, between desire and practicality, and ultimately between capability and cost-effectiveness.

"I know what I want," Ganny announced one night. We both looked over to her. "I want a bathtub," she said with a voice of absolute finality. "A real old-fashioned bathtub. Round. Big enough to stretch out full length. Big enough for two. With water-massage jets. And sonics. And little champagne bubbles too. And…candles. And scented bubble-bath. And flowers." Her face went all dreamy for a moment.

"A bathtub?" That was me. It didn't sound practical. Why would you want a bathtub when a sonic-enhanced shower was proven far more efficient. It made no sense at all to me. Despite our rule against plonking, I asked, "Why?"

"Because," she said. And folded her arms.

Gampy smiled and told IRMA to add it to the design parameters. And rate it as critical-to-survival.

I turned seventeen and we began whittling our list. Practicality ruled. We didn't discard any ideas because they were dumb, only because they were impractical. For instance, we could have a ship's cat, if we wanted— we could afford the oxygen and water and food for a live animal—but it made more sense to fab a mechanical instead. Easier to train, a lot cleaner, and it would give us an extra set of mobile monitors that could get into small spaces; plus we'd get the same affectional bonus, and it would be a lot less expensive than having a tabby shipped out from Mars.

The same standards applied to all our choices. Yes, we could have a bigger lounge, a genuine salon with its own attendant plumbing, but it would have to serve double duty as a theater and a dining hall and a gymnasium with all the attendant gear folded away into the bulkheads, unfolding as needed. Yes, personals could be larger, but that would mean a smaller crew and more dependence on bots and intelligence engines. That was a null-brainer—a smaller biomass-to-biosupport ratio meant an expanded viability envelope, and an enhanced payload window. Better for everyone.

We had a keel. Actually, we had three keels in the junkyard, that mass of pods and leftover parts at the south end of the gig's axis. We even had what was left of Gampy's first boat. But it was obvious that Gampy wanted something bigger than that. Much bigger. He didn't say it aloud, but he was thinking about the old *Lysistrata*. He'd been talking about refitting her for years, ever since he'd claimed what was left of her for salvage. It made sense, the keel was still good and a lot of her internal harnesses still checked out, she just didn't have life support any more. And of course, she'd need new engines, but we had seven decades of new technology to draw upon. We could use a lot of the existing mountings, and where we needed to, we could strengthen her frame with a bigger set of harnesses. We'd end up with a stronger ship than the original designers had conceived.

Once we'd made that decision, the rest of the plan snapped into place like pieces of a jigsaw puzzle.

We had fifty years of stuff hanging in the junkyard and at least another twenty years of resupply for all the old buckets still crawling around the belt. Plus a few items we'd bought on consignment for resale to option-holders. We had an assortment of power plants, all kinds. We had flywheels, solar panels, fuel cells, hot-and-cold fusion reactors, and even a couple of old turbines. Equipment? All kinds. We had pipes and pumps and all sorts of electronics and monitors and bots and sensors. And engines? Lord, did we have engines, more than enough to grab an asteroid and drag it home. We had six different kinds of blast engines and more than enough tanks of high-velocity propellants to drive them. And if that wasn't enough we had solar sails, ion drives, plasma drives, mass-accelerators, and all the different kinds of spare parts necessary to repair those drives. We had all the stuff people used for throwing rocks around, all the stuff we leased to miners and comet-tossers and anyone else who wants to move a mountain. Best of all, we had the raw materials we needed to build at least a dozen traction units. Best of all, the keel of the *Lysistrata* was strong enough to hold them all. That's why Gampy wanted us to think extravagant. We were going to build one of the fastest, most powerful ships in the system.

We were halfway through the final design process, when Gampy died.

It wasn't anything heroic and it wasn't anything stupid. It was just what happened. He was working his way patiently around the centrifuge, using the cane because his knee hurt. He did that every shift after eating. Six times around and he'd stop at the red bench to catch his breath. This time, he couldn't. IRMA rang the alert and we all went screaming down the slidy-poles, scrambling and bouncing around the arc, but it was too late. The medi-bots already had him stretched out on the deck. Ganny pounded his chest and screamed at him. "Don't you dare leave me now, you son of a bitch! Not now!" She was really angry. But not at Gampy. At everything else, herself mostly. The medi-bots pushed her out of the way and did their medi-bot thing, but it wasn't enough. Gampy was already gone. His face was closed.

The funeral was simple. Gampy had friends all over the ecliptic and over a thousand of them logged in and shared their best memories. Rev Morgan holoed in from Mars to conduct the service and she was as eloquent as always. Of course, everybody had to allow for the time lag. Gampy didn't trust the so-called instantaneous transmissions of the quantum-channels, he used to say that the quantum-channels had to include all possible decryptions, so you couldn't really know if you were receiving the right one. I never knew if he was serious about that or not, I always thought it was because the quantum connections were too expensive to establish and too difficult to maintain, but Ganny said it was because Gampy regarded all instantaneous communication as a kind of electronic leash that anyone could yank whenever they felt like it. Maintaining distance in time and space was his way of staying independent of the demands of others. As much as possible. But anyway, there weren't any glitches in the time-delayed synchronizations and the service was beautiful. My favorite part was the requiem.

"For one brief moment, a piece of the universe comes alive, looks around, asks questions, discovers, creates, connects—and in that moment, the almighty universe knows its own beauty. Whatever meaning life has, it is found in everything we create for ourselves and for others. From stardust we are born, to stardust we return. We commend this soul to the eternal sea in the sure and certain knowledge he will find his way safely home…." And then we freeze-dried him for the H2O, reduced the rest to little pieces, and plowed him into the soil beneath the rose bushes in Ganny's garden because that's what he'd always said he wanted us to do. Waste not, want not.

Of course, Ganny and I both sobbed our hearts out and held onto each other and bawled like babies. I remember being surprised at how small and thin she'd become. But she was still a core of strength and energy and I knew she wasn't going to be following Gampy any time soon. So I just collapsed into her embrace and let out all my grief and anguish in great racking screams of rage. And so did she. I was hoarse for two days after.

Three days in a row, we sat up late talking. All the stuff we usually kept to ourselves, only this time we just let it out, over and over. We talked about everything and nothing and how much we were going to miss Gampy and what we should do next, and Ganny even admitted that she felt so much at a loss, she didn't know what to do next. Should we continue building Gampy's spaceship or cut our losses now? Except that Gampy always knew what he was doing and he wouldn't want us to quit just because he wasn't here or we were afraid, but just the same, he wasn't here and we had to figure this out for ourselves. And then we hugged each other some more and cried some more and went on talking, just talking to talk, not because what we had to say was important, but because it was important that we said something. We talked like dirtsiders, but neither one of us cared, and for a while I even understood why dirtsiders talked so much. It was because they were so lonely inside their skins. Surrounded by all those people, they were still lonely. They had to do something desperate to try to connect. I knew we were being just as emotional but it was all right. We had the right to be emotional. Didn't we?

But there must be something about emotions that makes people *Stoo-pid* with a capital *stoo*. Gampy used to tell me that, all the time. Now I wished I'd listened better. Don't ever do anything while you're upset. Don't even make a decision. It's all right to be upset. Upset is a normal part of life. But upset is also stupid-time, so don't do anything or decide anything while you're in stupid time. That was the part I forgot.

Because while I was still so busy being upset about Ganny missing Gampy so badly, I made the mistake of checking my email, and there was a note from Jimmy Sawyer, how upset he was, because everything in Baja was falling apart and he wasn't going to be able to finish college because both his moms were out of work because there was no money to rebuild the hotels and the tourists were going down to Yucatan instead to watch the Howler monkey wars, which were a lot more interesting than watching *Cabaneros* fight over water and the best projections were that it would be seven to ten years before the local economy recovered, if it ever did, and they might have to apply for refugee assistance and move, but if they did that, they'd have to sign over what was left of his college fund and his moms would have to give up their pensions, but he just couldn't see any other way out of their predicament. They only had electricity for a few hours, only at night, and they were down to less than 2000 calories a day per person, they were hungry all the time, and that was on a good day, and none of them could afford to get any skinnier, especially him. He didn't have any energy anymore. Their situation just kept getting worse and worse, so bad that he was thinking about signing up for a mind-wipe/enlistment so his family would get the bonus. The only thing that kept him from doing that was that he didn't want to give up his relationship with me.

I wrote back, begging him to please not do anything stupid. I didn't want to lose him either. I told him what Gampy always said about not making decisions while you're scared or angry or afraid or so caught up in any emotion that you lose all sense of perspective. Please don't give up on yourself, I told him, because things have to get better eventually. They just have to. But I'm not sure I really believed that myself. The people on the marble just keep stumbling from one polycrisis to the next and they've so incorporated it into their way of life that stumbling through polycrises is their new normal.

Maybe that's why Gampy never wanted to keep close ties with dirt-side. He didn't want to get pulled back down into the soup. So all I could do for Jimmy was keep on writing messages of encouragement. It left me feeling futile and helpless, but Ganny wouldn't let me send him any money. We had a rule about that and we'd never broken it, so all I could do for Jimmy was keep telling him how much I cared—and hope that would be enough. And even that made me feel bad, because now I felt responsible for his well-being. Jimmy had just told me that I was the only thing keeping him alive and that meant I was sorta stuck, wasn't I? I had to keep on being his friend, no matter what, because if I stopped caring then he would probably do something stupid. And then that would be my fault. Wouldn't it?

And that's when I made my bigger mistake. Somewhere in the middle of sending Jimmy back my sympathies and my concern and my caring, somewhere in there I told him I understood how he must feel, like there was no future anymore, and then I told him about Gampy dying and how much I missed him every day and how I felt so bad, maybe even the same way that Jimmy must feel about everything, because now my life was floating adrift, and all of our hard work making plans and everything might have been all for nothing, and maybe it was wrong for me to feel like that because it was selfish, starsiders are supposed to take care of each other, what I really needed to do was take care of Ganny because she had to be feeling even worse than me. I told Jimmy I wished he was here so I could cry on his big beautiful shoulder and help me and Ganny figure out what to do next because all the help he'd given me on the spaceship design proved he was good at figuring things out, and even as I wrote that I knew I was starting to sound like a silly dirtsider girl, helpless and stupid and talking way too much. But the point was, and this is what I needed him to hear, no matter how bad Ganny felt, no matter how much she missed Gampy, she was still determined to keep going, no matter how bad things got. And if an old lady like Ganny had that kind of strength in her heart then I should be able to do that too. And if I could do it then a big strong guy like James should be able to find that kind of strength in his own heart as well. We weren't giving up on our plans and neither should he. Because what we say starside is that no matter how bad things might seem, as long as you're still breathing you're surviving. And as long as you're surviving, you're still in the game. And a bunch more stuff like that. Most of it stupid, but you get the idea. I didn't want him to get wiped and I'd say just about anything to keep him Jimmy.

And then immediately after I sent it I realized I'd said way way way too much about what was happening on the gig. I sent an instant-retrieve message right after it and hoped that the snatch-back would arrive in time, but you never know. It all depends on how quickly you send it and which way the packets are routed and whether or not the other person is sitting on the mailbox, opening things as fast as they arrive. Or if they have an agent doing that in case somebody sends a snatch-back. I dunno. There are a lot of different ways. The real trick is catching the message before it actually arrives.

Out among the flying mountains, it can take anywhere from ten minutes to two hours to get a message, depending how many big marbles and tin cans it has to bounce off. Traffic is a collection of ricochets. Anything with an antenna is part of the cloud. Sometimes the message-packets arrive from a dozen different directions, scattered and out of order. We once waited three days for an episode of Derby to finish downloading. Gampy might have liked his independence, but you pay a price for being a hermit-crab. So I didn't know for the better part of a shift if I'd caught the message to James in time. When the acknowledgment finally did come in, I felt like crying all over again, this time from relief. The snatch-back had arrived nine minutes after the target message, which had not yet been read. The target message was deleted, leaving only a stub acknowledging a message had been retrieved. That I could explain. I'd just have to figure out a suitable explanation. Excuse. Story. Lie. Whatever.

Except once I started thinking, the mind-mice started gnawing.

See, if James was really some kind of a data-pumping avatar, like Gampy once feared, then maybe the damage was already done. The message sat in his mailbox for nine minutes. That's more than enough time for a data-trap to capture a copy. And a data-trap lets the recipient examine a message without giving the sender any acknowledgment at all that it's actually been read. And if James really was a data-pumping avatar, then of course he'd have a data-trap, and of course he'd know what I'd said, even if he pretended he didn't. I'd have no way of knowing. Crap.

And that's the problem with being even a little bit suspicious. You start getting a lot suspicious. And then everything is suspect. And at the end, after you've finished distrusting everybody else—even your closest friends and family—you can't even trust yourself anymore. And I didn't know what kind of message to send to James to replace the one I didn't know if he'd seen or not.

But then things got real busy on the gig, because we had a shift change, and Ganny had to pay off some contracts she had been holding on consignment because without Gampy on the gig our credit rating went down a notch or six, which wasn't really fair because it was Ganny who managed the finances, but you can't argue with software because software doesn't listen. And it doesn't help to talk to a human being about it either because most dirtsiders are software-slaves, not willing to disagree with what the machinery says they can or can't do, which is why they're dirtsiders and doomed to stay that way forever. Slaves. "I'm sorry, we're not authorized to think for ourselves...."

And the Red Team, people we'd known for years, people who'd all professed their sincerest and deepest condolences only a few weeks before—they had the chutzpah to demand payment in advance. Ganny had to put a big chunk of liquidity into escrow before they'd board. And that didn't sit well with her. She understood the thinking, but things were strained for awhile. She'd always treated them like family, but now the union-rep was saying, "Yes, we appreciate that, don't take it personal, ma'am. But business is business." For the first couple of weeks, Ganny's menus were a little restrained. Her way of expressing her opinion about putting business above loyalty. Even though she knew they were right. We'd have done the same.

But without Gampy, we had to shift a lot of responsibilities around, so I ended up taking on most of the menu-planning and that helped a little bit. I didn't think it was fair to punish the red team with liver and onions every night, even though I understood why Ganny was miffed. Although I kinda like liver and onions, not everybody does. And there is such a thing as variety. And more important, food equals morale. Everybody knows that. So when I volunteered to take over the cooking,

I wasn't just doing her a favor, I was doing everybody a favor. This was what Gampy would have wanted. Somebody taking care of things while Ganny put herself back together. Especially taking care of the crew.

Ganny would settle down eventually, she always did, but this time she might need a few extra weeks. When she found out the blue crew wasn't coming back—they'd signed a new contract elsewhere—she disappeared for three shifts, not even answering my calls to dinner. When she finally did come out, her face had a new hardness to it. I didn't ask.

I figured she was still hurting a lot inside and because she didn't have anybody to blame, she couldn't help herself, she just took it out on convenient targets. Even me, a few times. I mean, I'd lost my Gampy, but she'd lost the whole other half of her life. So she was powerfully upset—upset isn't even a good enough word to describe what she was going through, but she was upset enough to forget Gampy's instructions about not making decisions while you're upset. She always apologized afterward, but we were both getting used to the idea that things were going to be a lot different now. We were going to have to build a lot more bots to replace the live crewmembers, but in the long run that would probably be better for our bottom line. We could have switched a long time ago, but Gampy had a rule against giving people's jobs to machines, because machines didn't have families to support, but now that the crews were quitting, without even giving us much notice, we weren't really obligated any more, were we? But then, while we were still sorting that one out, preparing to fab three dozen new bots, the rest of the bad news arrived.

Behind Ganny's back, the dirtside sons of bitches at Payload, Inc. negotiated new contracts with half the belters in the arc. Instead of transshipping through the whirligig, they were going to whirl the pods direct to the customers. Most customers didn't have whirligigs or even the resources to create a spindizzy, a spinning tether. So the pods would have to carry fuel for deceleration and that meant a corresponding reduction in payload, but if they threw the pods from a lower point on the beanstalk, that would reduce their outbound speed and also the amount of fuel they'd have to carry for deceleration. But the slower speed also meant the pods would be in transit a lot longer, some as long as three or four or even five years. But the price difference was still enough to be competitive. And it would have been mostly legal, except for the part that wasn't.

See, almost all of that cargo had already been bought on margin by Gampy. It was his. Ours. Ganny's. But the dirt-lovers had simply cancelled their side of the deal. Oh, they'd done it nice and legal. They'd put the Payload, Inc. into receivership, then sold it to themselves at a three cents on the dollar, just enough to pay off the lawyers, and resold the cargo contracts to themselves for even less. Ganny filed claims—on Earth, Luna, and Mars. The Earth court dismissed it, the Luna tribunal refused to hear the case, the Martian judge ruled that Ganny had a claim, but he had no authority to enforce it against an Earthside company.

Meanwhile the new company, Free Ride, Inc., negotiated half-price deals with all of our customers, so low that even our best friends couldn't resist. So nearly a trillion dollars of Ganny's property was now scheduled to go everywhere but here. Free Ride could afford to be generous with their pricing because they were selling our stolen property to our stolen customers. Later on, once they'd driven us out of business they'd own the market and they could raise prices to whatever they wanted.

Ganny knows how to cuss in sixteen languages, including a couple of dead ones, she might be the last person alive who knows how to swear in Pascal, whatever that is, that's something else I have to look up. Ganny can go on for a long long time before repeating herself. I didn't need to know what all those different words meant to understand what she was saying. A certain Mister I-Won't-Say-His-Name-Aloud should have been grateful that he had 330 mega-klicks of vacuum between himself and Ganny, otherwise he would have lost a couple pieces of his anatomy he might have been attached to and was probably very fond of, attached or not. Okay, that's theoretical on my part, I have the genotype, but not the phenotype, which means I never had any, and even if I had I still would have traded them for the parts I have instead which I like a lot better, I mean, I never understood why anyone would even want all that stuff attached and hanging around and getting in the way. What a nuisance. Ganny says she used to feel that way too, but that was before she met Gampy, and someday I'll probably feel different too. She says. That's nice, Ganny, but way out here in the belt, that's about as likely as giant space amoebas eating Jupiter. Again.

Ganny didn't stop cussing. Not this time. Not even when the IRMA unit told her that she was raising the temperature in the main cabin to critical levels and that the refrigeration units were threatening to fail. Sometime before he died, Gampy had programmed the IRMA unit's social interface with a supercharged sarcasm function, that being the only way to catch Ganny's attention when she went off on one of her rants. Usually that kind of interruption was enough. This time no.

Ganny's rants were impressive. When I was little, they terrified me even though I was never the target. But then Gampy explained to me about performance art, and once I recognized that Ganny's tantrums were for her own enjoyment, I would go and make popcorn and Gampy and I would sit back and enjoy the show. When Ganny would finally inevitably run down, Gampy would say something like, "Not bad. I give it a six. You lost points when you recycled your previous extrapolations of mangled DNA in the ancestry of the reptilian cortex. But I did enjoy the stylistic expansions of neo-Germanic linguistic conjugations." And Ganny would reply something like, "Hmp, that was easily a seven point nine. You should have seen it from my side." Then she'd take a deep breath and that usually indicated that she was finished, and then she'd ask him what he wanted for dinner. And while he was saying, "How about something special tonight?" she was already asking, "Okay, so what do we do next?" And then, in unison, they'd both say, "I'm thinking it over...." And after a while, they'd both figure something out together.

But Gampy was gone and Ganny wasn't going to stop ranting no matter how sarcastic the IRMA unit became because this nasty news was pretty much a declaration of war, arriving exactly one year to the day after Gampy's death. The bastards knew exactly what they were doing.

Ganny spent half a shift talking to Gampy's picture. "You son of a bitch. You picked the worst damn time to die. I need you so much. Now more than ever. This is one hell of a mess. You should have told me what to expect, what to do! You knew this was coming. And we promised not to drop any more capsules into the Pacific Ocean, so what am I supposed to do now?" She sent out a few messages to Gampy's most trusted friends, but she didn't find the replies all that encouraging. The dirtsiders were cutting off the money. And they hadn't moved capriciously. They'd spent years setting this up. Ever since the Pacific accident. This was their revenge.

What they didn't know was Ganny. Maybe they figured they were dealing with a silly old space-lady who kept her collection of pancakes in the airlock. Maybe they figured that without a man to tell her what to do, she'd just fall apart. Dirtside males can be so stupid and arrogant sometimes. What they didn't know was that Ganny had her own set of testicles. She showed them to me once, she kept them in the cryo-freezer.

(Some other time I'll explain why it's a good idea to have both an X and a Y chromosome, even if you put the Y on the shelf and never use it. But I'm still not convinced I want a pair of my own.)

Oh yeah, I did a little ranting myself too. I didn't see much point in it, it didn't make me feel any better, but after Ganny and I stomped around the centrifuge a few times, we both felt silly enough to fall down laughing, so that had to count for something. But finally, after we both stopped laughing, we just looked at each other and said, in unison, "Okay, so what do we do next?" And then in unison, we both replied, "I'm thinking it over...." And then we started laughing again, this time so hard I almost wet my panties.

"All right," said Ganny, "Consider this. We finish the spaceship anyway. We can finish installing engines on the keel, attach a few life-support and fuel pods, hunker down in a pod like the old-fashioned astronauts, go to Mars, and pick up the life-support module. And then...we'll go pick up our property, every pod in transit. We'll do a local spindizzy and sling it long way around to the gig. Then we head back to the gig and catch the balls we've thrown."

"Is that legal?"

Ganny shrugged. "As legal as it needs to be. We have the Martian judgment in our pocket. That's our authorization. What are they going to do to us?"

Somewhere in there, the conversation passed *if*, and went straight to *when*. "Can we build the ship in time?"

"All depends on how many bots we can fab. I figure we can put a hundred to work within two months. We can have bots building bots until we pass the point of diminishing returns."

So Ganny and I sat down in front of the big display and studied orbits, trajectories, hyperbolas, parabolas, ellipses, and even what occasionally passed for a straight line. Of course, no straight line ever went unpunished. The shortest distance between two puns is a straight line. The good news was that the damned blue marble was heading around the backside of Sol, so anything they launched could take as long as five or six years to get to our side of the belt. We had a pretty big window to pick off the pods and send them home.

Then the other shoe dropped. I don't know why dirtsiders are always dropping shoes, but they do. And this time it was a pretty big one. The

Martian Electric Boat Company cancelled our order for a life-support module.

They said it wasn't us, it was them. Yeah, right. They said that changing market conditions required them to reevaluate their customer base. They said that the growing needs of their corporate customers required them to focus on standardized modules. They said their heuristic analysis of our readjusted profit position projected that we would not be able to complete the contract satisfactorily. They said everything except "we are not authorized to think for ourselves."

Right.

I knew it was serious when Ganny didn't say a single bad word. She just sank down into a chair and put her head in her hands. She didn't say anything for a long long time. And I knew better than to say anything to her. I got up and made tea. The good kind. I poured two cups and pushed one in front of her. She ignored it.

"Ganny?"

She looked up. She looked broken.

"They figured it out. They can't allow us to bulid a spaceship." She let out a long sigh. She looked at the mug of tea in front of her as if she was seeing it for the very first time. But she didn't pick it up. "I don't know what to do. We're done. All our plans—" She put her head back into her hands.

Somebody, somewhere had figured it out. Ganny did too have the stones to finish what Gampy started. So they weren't going to take any chances. They'd bought up the entire run of hulls from the Martians for the next seven years. They hadn't just stopped us. They'd stopped *all* the potential competition.

Oh. Crap. And double-crap.

He *had* used me.

I sent James an email. "You bottom-feeding dirtsider! You filthy lying phony! If I could get my hands on you, I'd slap your ugly freckly face so hard it wouldn't stop spinning until it was on the back of your head. For all I care, you can mind-wipe your skinny ass into a rainbow brothel, getting happily cyber-fucked by anyone with two plastic dollars for the coin-slot on a public library terminal! I never want to hear from you again! Go frag yourself!" And this time I didn't snatch it back. I put a block on my inbox so he couldn't reply. But I was nowhere near as mad at him as I was at me. This was all my fault. Me and my big stoo-pid mouth. Frack.

After I finished beating myself up, I went and cried in Ganny's arms. I told her everything. I thought she'd be angry, but she wasn't. She just patted my hair, stroked my cheek, and told me not to worry myself about it, the blood was already in the water, the sharks were already circling, it would have happened anyway. And we were going to have to make the same difficult decision sooner or later, might as well be sooner. Then she told me. We were getting buyout offers and she had to make up her mind which one to accept.

I pulled away and looked at her. Shocked. "But where will we go? The whirligig is all we have."

"I was thinking Mars...."

"Mars! No fracking way. Those people are dirtsider-wannabes. You can't trust them. We can't go there. Not after they've stolen our spaceship. They'll all be laughing at us. Or worse. They'll feel sorry for us for not being big strong men. What would Gampy say?"

"He's not here, sweetheart. We have to make up our own minds what's best."

"Well, Mars isn't! No way. Why don't we just stay on the whirligig? We're self-sufficient, we don't need anything from anyone else. And if we do, we just have them put it in the pipeline."

"Sweetheart, that's the point. We can't depend on the pipeline anymore."

"No! They can't do that. Too many people depend on us."

"Only for the cargo still in transit. After that's gone, we're pretty much done. You've seen the schedules. Gampy knew this was going to happen someday, even without the theft of our cargo. That's why he wanted to build a ship. You've seen the projections. The penetration of traction drives in the ecliptic will be 40% within six years. As fast as they can push the pieces up the beanstalks. It'll be 60% for cargo ships. 80% for bot-driven pods. Without a meat-crew, a big-enough tractor could accelerate continuously at 25 gee. If they can get direct delivery faster and cheaper from a tractor, people aren't going to use the pipeline. The whirligig will be just another piece of nostalgia. Like the pony express. That's what this is all about. The people who stopped us, don't want anyone competing with the shipping monopoly they're building. Don't take it personal. It's like the Red Crew. Business is business."

"But, Ganny—!"

"Sweetheart—we can go to Mars. You can go to college."

"I can go to college from here."

"You can meet a nice boy."

"Like Jimmy Sawyer? No thanks. I'm done with boys."

"You say that now—"

"My vibrator doesn't lie to me!"

Ganny didn't want to answer that one directly. Instead she softened her tone and expanded the context. "Starling, there's a whole universe of possibilities out there—"

It didn't work. "I like it *here!*" Okay, so I sounded like a spoiled dirt-sider brat, but it was honest. Right then and there I didn't want any other possibilities. I wanted what I already had.

"Honey, this is the best we can do—"

"No, it isn't. This is giving up."

"Sweetheart, there isn't going to be anything left. We need to get out now, while we can still get out with a little bit of money. And pride."

"And then what? Sit around and knit?"

"Me? Knit? Gampy would come back from the grave just to see that. No, I don't think so. I'm just trying to make the best of a bad situation for us."

"No, you're not. You're giving up. And I won't have it." I pushed myself off and sailed out of the room. It's hard to slam a door in free fall, don't even try. You can't even swim away with an attitude. It just doesn't work. The best you can do is swim away, scowling.

Of course, I knew I was wrong. I was being angry—and stupid. You can't fight the laws of physics. You can't even negotiate with them. Gampy used to say, "The coyote *always* goes splat. Remember that." But I still didn't see why we had to give up our home. Gampy wouldn't give up. And he wouldn't let us give up either. The coyote usually goes a long long way before he finally splats. That had to count for something. There had to be a way. I just couldn't see it yet. And Ganny was probably having the same conversation in her head too.

If neither of us could see it, maybe it wasn't there.

Except I already knew what Gampy would say to that. "If it isn't there, you haven't created it yet."

I went down to the centrifuge. And paced. One good thing about the centrifuge, it's a good place to stomp around in anger. In fact, it's the only place you can stomp around in anger. When I was little, Gampy and I would make topsoil. The bots would dump a mix of manure and compost and mulch and fungus and pureed garbage and mineral dust and asteroid shavings into the pit. We'd add water and then we'd jump in and stomp up a storm. Whenever I was in a big sulk that lasted more than a day, Gampy would suddenly announce a need to make more topsoil. We'd stomp ourselves silly until we were both laughing so hard I'd forgotten why I was angry. Then we'd seed the whole mess with earthworms, shower off and consider it a job well done. I wished he was here now. We'd stomp up enough soil for a wheatfield.

We made soil mostly in the smaller pools. We'd mix in all kinds of grass and wildflower seeds and how high they grew would tell us how good the soil was. Gampy wouldn't plant crops until the soil was good enough. Once he got so frustrated with a particularly stubborn mix, he had everybody defecate into that tank for a week. Two weeks. Until something green finally poked a leaf up.

When we weren't making soil, we raised koi, big beautiful orange and white fish. They shimmered like liquid metal. Water is the most convenient ballast you can have in space. You pump it wherever you need weight. We used it to balance the centrifuge, with tanks of various sizes anchored all around the circumference, but we had three big pools, spaced 120 degrees apart. They were the primary reservoirs and they were almost always full. The only time I saw the levels go down even a little bit was when Gampy pumped a couple thousand gallons into a pod and slung it out to one of the ships prepping for the long ride. Gampy said that the most important thing you ever want to pack was water, lots of it.

The big pools were only a meter and a half deep, and for the first half of my life I was terrified of them. Probably because for the first half of my life I was shorter than a meter. Even today, I don't believe in free range water. Water belongs in tanks and bulbs, not sloshing around in the open like amoebas without skin. Gampy told me that swimming was fun, but the first time he tried to take me in the pool I shrieked like a rabid banshee. (Ganny showed me the video-logs.)

Gampy said that I needed to learn how to swim, but I didn't see the use of it. I wasn't going anywhere I'd ever need that particular skill. But Gampy didn't force the issue. Instead he made me a canoe. He found a bundle of plastic rods and tied two of them together at the ends. Then he put four cross-braces between them, arcing them out to form a canoe shape. Then he wrapped the frame with a wide sheet of transparent plastic wrap and a little bit of ribbon tape to hold the wrap in place. The boat was so light I could pick it up in one hand. He had to put a couple of keel-weights hanging from the bottom so it wouldn't tip too easily. Then he tied a rope to one end of it and the other end to the railing around the pool. Then he put the canoe in the water and showed me how it would float.

For the first hour, I wouldn't even climb into it. Not even with a life jacket and an inner tube around my waist. I just kept pushing it away and pulling it back. I did like how I could see through the bottom and see the koi a lot clearer and that's probably why I eventually climbed in. Not to paddle around, only to get a better view of the fish. I kept a tight hold on the rope and kept myself tightly pulled up against the side of the pool. But after a while, I did let myself drift out a little and then I pulled myself back quickly, and then after a while more, I'd push off and pull myself back again. And then when I thought no one was looking, I grabbed the paddle that Gampy had made—a rod with a plastic-wrapped loop at the end—and paddled myself around.

Of course, Gampy was watching the whole time. Mostly on the monitors in the lounge, just spinward up the arc of the 'fuge, but occasionally he'd stroll by and ask me how I was doing. At first I didn't say anything, not wanting to concede that he was right, but eventually I gave him a grudging "fine." A couple days later, he'd fabbed some fins and a snorkel and a mask and a paddle board, showed me how they all worked and let me teach myself how to swim. Not because he told me it was something I had to do, but because it was a better way to look at the koi close up.

Now, all these years later, walking around the centrifuge, stomping along the deck, the smell of the koi ponds still made me think of Gampy. I still had the canoe. I hadn't used it in years, I had long outgrown it, but I'd hung it up next to the pool with my fins and mask and snorkel as trophies. Or reminders. That's where I was sitting when Ganny finally came after me. She looked so sad I started crying. We grabbed each other in a tight hug and fumbled our apologies out, both at the same time.

"Ganny, I'm so sorry!"

"So am I, sweetheart. I've been so wrapped up in my own pain I wasn't thinking. I should have talked to you before this."

"No. I mean, yes. Okay. I'm sorry for being so emotional. I'm supposed to know better."

We sat down on the bench next to the pool and held hands for a while, neither of us speaking. Ganny looked up at the old canoe, hanging on the rack we used for towels and tools and whatever, and made a chuckling sound deep in her throat. "It's still watertight," I said. "After all these years. I still put it in the water sometimes. And it still floats. Gampy knew what he was doing."

"Yes, he did." She patted my hand. "He knew better than to force you."

We sat there a while longer and finally I said, "Remember when we first talked about the spaceship? The first time? With Gampy and everyone at the table? We talked about building the LSM ourselves. We ran the math on it, it wasn't impossible. It just wasn't as cost-effective. But…well, maybe we should think about it again."

Ganny didn't answer. She was still staring at the canoe. Still thinking about Gampy and all his little tricks. I wanted to distract her, get her back on purpose, thinking of solutions.

"I mean, we can fab all the parts we need, can't we? So who cares if it takes a little longer? We can still do it. We can show those damn Martians. Can't we, Ganny?"

She took a deep breath, one of those deep deep sighs that can mean anything from "I give up" to "I see your point" to "I've made up my mind." Or maybe nothing at all except "I need to catch my breath and think." But she squeezed my hand and I could tell she was thinking it over.

She started to shake her head, then stopped herself. I watched as her face went through a whole series of contradictory expressions. Yes. No. Maybe. Try this on for size. No, that won't work. Maybe. But it's a stupid idea. But Gampy would have liked it. No, I'm being silly. Well, silly is what got us out here in the first place. Remember? No, it's just too big. That never stopped us before. What am I thinking? I'm over a hundred years old. So what? Wouldn't you like to spit in their eye one more time? And wouldn't it be better to go down fighting than give up without a whimper? But I have to think about Starling's future too. This is her inheritance. But what else is she going to inherit from me? Resignation or determination? I don't know. Do I dare? Would it be fair to her? Would it be fair not to? But how would we do it anyway. I shouldn't make any decision until I run the numbers. Again? How many times do I have to run them? I've already run them a hundred times over, I don't have to run the numbers again. It's just so damned— No, it isn't. It's the mechanics of the job that's so frustrating, not the commitment—

Or maybe I was misreading the whole series of her expressions. Ganny brushed her hair back off her forehead, a useless gesture, her hair went right back where it wanted to go. She stood up and faced the rack with the canoe, reached out and picked it off the hook. She turned it over and over in her hands. It looked like she was trying to distract herself from tomorrow by focusing on yesterday. I wanted to scream in frustration. It looked like she was giving up.

Abruptly, Ganny turned to face me. "Go start dinner. I'm going for a walk." Translation: "I have to think about this."

It was a good sign. Or maybe it wasn't. Maybe what she had to think about was how to let me down easy. Maybe she needed to say goodbye to her gardens. Or maybe she really did need to think it over. I couldn't tell what she was thinking and I was usually pretty good at it.

But Ganny hadn't come down into the centrifuge since Gampy died, so it meant something. This was where Ganny and Gampy did their best work, walking and talking and holding hands like puppy-struck tweens. They were so cute when they did that.

I understood why she wanted to be alone now. She wanted to talk things out with Gampy one more time. This time she'd have to do both sides of the conversation, but she knew Gampy so well, she probably could. Ohell, I already knew what Gampy would say and so did Ganny. But she still needed to walk it out and talk it out, because that was the way they always did things. Together. That part, I envied. If I ever met a boy who was good at that, I might reconsider my decision. But it wouldn't be scummy Jimmy Sawyer, the big fat fake, whoever he was. Probably some morbidly obese dirty oldphart, sitting naked at his keyboard, a six-pack on the desk, cackling to himself how he data-pumped a naïve little starflake. What was that line from Shakespeare anyway? Revenge is a dish best served old? I didn't have to get even now, but I would get even. Count on it. Hell hath no fury like a woman, scorned or not. I'd have pictures of his little tiny penis posted from here to Aldebaran if that's what it took.

The centrifuge has four decks, the top one is Lunar gravity and we use it mostly for crops. The next-to-bottom one is Earth gravity, and the maintenance level beneath that is 1.2 gee, useful for exercise, but very tiring. The second level is Martian gravity and it has our living and guest quarters, where we sleep and eat and work and exercise—and sometimes just hang out. The galley is on the second level too. You can make some really marvelous soufflés in 0.38 gee. And angel food cake so light it practically floats. But tonight, I made noodles and green sauce. I like the *al dente*, and I like the way all the different flavors of the different spices mix together, all sweet and tangy and rich to the point of shameful opulence. It's not one of Ganny's favorite recipes, but it's my personal comfort food. One of my personals. For some reason, it always makes me think of… people I was too young to miss when they went missing. Maybe someday I'd figure out why.

Ganny came into the kitchen while I was mixing the sauce, I had a metal whisk that scraped round and round against the stainless bowl with a satisfying rasp. When Ganny came in, I stopped. She had a frown on her face. She looked annoyed. "I almost had it. I almost did. Damn."

"Had what?"

She shook her head. "Nothing, it doesn't matter anymore. I don't have any…knitting needles."

"Huh?"

"I don't have any spokes."

"Spokes for what?"

But Ganny didn't answer. She was staring at…the whisk in my hand. She reached over and took it from me as if she'd never seen it before. She held it up before her eyes, still frowning, and spun it slowly between her fingers. A drop of green sauce separated itself and drifted lazily to the deck.

"Ganny?"

"I am *so* stupid," she announced. "I don't need knitting needles at all." She handed me back the whisk and bounced out.

"Um, dinner will be ready in fifteen—" I called after her.

"That's all the time I need—" She headed up the corridor to her office. I didn't know what she'd figured out, but it had to be something important. Ganny never put work before meals. "Work will always wait for you," she said. "If a problem is that big, it isn't going to go away. Eat first. Take care of your well-being so you can wrassle the problem down with all your strength." And so on. So, seeing her ignore her own advice was worth a couple of raised eyebrows. But the sauce needed stirring, and I knew she'd tell me what she was thinking as soon as she was through thinking it, so I just went back to work.

Over dinner, it was just Ganny and me tonight, Ganny wouldn't eat with the red team anymore, she broke a family rule, she began talking business. I started to correct her, but she shook her head. "Gampy isn't here, sweetheart. We get to make new rules if we want. And besides, this is important. Mm, your green sauce is just right tonight. You did good." She waved at the display with her fork, bringing it to life. "See, here's the problem, and I think Gampy knew it all along—what we have, we have a lot of. What we don't have, we don't have any. So whatever we do, we have to do it with what's on hand. Because I suspect whatever we try to order, it probably isn't going to get here. Here—"

As she talked, the display assembled all of the various pieces of the proposed ship.. The keel of the *Lysistrata* looked like a spear, but now with a shielded bulb instead of a point—the forward observatory and radar disc. The plasma drives and the accelerators were a thick bundle of thinner rods wrapped around the body of the spear. At the aft end of the schematic, the tractors clicked into place, looking like oversized feathers on a shuttlecock. "Now, we've got the raw material. We can spin out a radiation shield—" A large disc whirled into existence just ahead of the feathers. "The only thing we don't have is a doughnut. A life-support system." On the display, colored in red, a doughnut shaped module slid down the spear and parked itself just in front of the disc of the radiation shield. "Without a doughnut, we're not going anywhere."

"We had this conversation already. With Gampy. Remember?"

"Yes, sweetheart. But I wanted to restate the problem so you could see if I left anything out."

I shook my head. "This is where I always get stuck too. We don't have enough raw material to fab a hull or deck plates or bulkheads."

"Yes, we do. We just don't know it."

"All we have is beanstalk cable. A lot of it."

"Yes, that's what I said."

"You just lost me."

"Sorry, sweetheart. Usually, you're half a jump ahead of me. There's an idea that's been rattling around inside my head for a while. Nobody's ever done it, because nobody's ever had to, but IRMA says it could work, the numbers all crunch."

I made the mistake of interrupting. "I was thinking maybe we could put the whirligig on the spear—?"

"No, I already thought of that. The gig has too much mass. The torque would make it almost impossible to turn. Even if we throw away the ballast rocks."

"Put a gimbal in the keel? Put the engines on a swiveling axis—"

"Still too much mass to push. And too much strain on the swivel joint. No, there's something easier. Look—" She pointed at the display again. "We're going to knit a spaceship. Without knitting needles."

"Huh—?" For a moment I thought she'd popped a seal. The strain of everything had finally gotten to her. I was genuinely scared for both of us. But no—

Ganny pointed her fork at the display. "IRMA, show Starling how to knit a doughnut."

I watched as the display ran Ganny's schematic. It wasn't fancy, it was mostly blueprint, but it was impressive as hell. As soon as I figured out what she was thinking, I started getting enthusiastic. It was crazy, but it wasn't *that* crazy. If we did it right, it would work.

"Wow," I finally said when I was coherent again. "I'd sure like to see the look on their faces when we arrive at Martian orbit with *that*."

"Or even Earth," said Ganny. "You want to visit the big blue marble?"

It wasn't exactly a chill, more like a rush of fear and anticipation, but it did go up my spine and then right back down again. So maybe it was a chill. The marble? Hell, yes! And not just because there was a big freckled nose I wanted to punch.

"Ganny, that'll be the biggest ship in the ecliptic. Even bigger than the one Gampy designed. Bigger even than some of the ships going out on the long ride. You could plant a whole farm—"

"Uh-huh. That's the idea. We'll have to start cracking gas immediately. That's another problem. How are we going to get enough air pressure to boil water for soup? But I have an idea on that one too. But I need you to study this. See if I've missed anything."

Ganny hadn't missed much. There was only one big change that I suggested. "We need two doughnuts so we can rotate them in opposite directions—so they cancel each other's torque. That makes us much more maneuverable. More important, that gives us two independent life-support modules. Remember what happened to the *Ballista*?"

"That will double our cost—"

"In materials, yes. But it's not that much when you think about it. And we'll have the bots for it, more than enough, they're already growing in the fabbers. And they'll work 24/7 with Saturdays off for prayers and maintenance."

"Probably more prayers than maintenance." Ganny smiled. "But go on."

"There's another advantage. We can stagger the construction, kind of like an assembly line. Once you configure a bot for a job on one wheel, you already have it configured for the same job on the other. As soon as it finishes its task on one doughnut, it goes to the other. Also, I think we should triple hull. At least. Maybe more. Maybe six times over the engineering requirements."

Ganny was following and nodding until I got to that last part. "Isn't that a little extreme?"

"Uh-uh. See, the thing is—if I were a dirtsider, I'd be terrified of this hull. Even not being a dirtsider, it gives me the cold shimmies. We have to have unquestionable hull-integrity. Everybody who hears about how this ship is built is going to think we're crazy. At least until they think about it. It's like the first time someone said, 'why not drop a cable from space and run elevators up and down?' It defies common sense, or what passes for common sense on the marble. So we have to out-think their disbelief—what Gampy called their visceral-skepticism. And not just theirs. Ours as well. Like when they finally did drop a beanstalk, they had to make it six times stronger than their own math said was necessary. Just to be sure—in case they were wrong."

Ganny held my argument up to the light and looked at it carefully. She turned it over and over and over, much more than she needed to. But she understood what I was really saying. When you're working with human beings, you're not talking about rationality. You're talking about belief systems. Everybody has one. Especially the people who believe they're objective. So you don't just build for functionality, you build for the kind of certainty that goes way beyond what people already believe. Triple hull. At least. Triple-triple hull.

Finally, Ganny nodded. "It makes sense for a lot of reasons, especially the ones we won't know about until afterwards. Let's run it through IRMA and see what she says."

"Ganny?"

"Yes, punkin?"

"Once we start, we're not going to be able to keep it secret. There are telescopes trained on us."

"Yes, I know."

"Is there any way we can flummox them?"

"Probably not." Then she smiled. "But think about this. Once we start the whole thing spinning, that'll be flummox enough. By the time anyone figures it out, we'll be less than six months from completion."

"But what if they try to stop us? They've already hired away both our crews and cancelled our Martian order. What if they...I don't know... threw a rock at us or something?"

"Mm." Ganny put her fork down. She cupped her hands as if she was about to say a prayer and rested her chin in them. Her eyes went far away for a moment or six. "Okay," she finally said. "Try this. We'll attach the keel to the axis of the whirligig, so it looks like we're extending the gig. We'll mate the *Lysistrata*'s forward airlock to the bottom-cluster. To the big cargo lock. Now, when people ask what we're doing, we announce that we're changing our plans. We're not going to build a spaceship after all, it's not cost-effective, that market niche doesn't work for us, but we recognize the growth potential—blah blah blah—for the next fifteen years as more and more ships are equipped with traction drives, so we're going to expand the gig to accommodate that growing market. Tractor ships are going to put the whole solar system within easy reach, so we're building a grand new gambling resort for all the rich tourists looking for an out-of-any-world vacation experience. Plus, we'll also continue to provide supply and slingshot services for colonists. Does that make sense to you, so far?" I nodded. Ganny went on. "So...we build three doughnuts. Two are counter-rotating LSMs, we'll be honest about that, but the third will be a dummy, to hide the engines we're assembling. We'll say it's our new machine shop, our construction base, which won't really be a lie, we just won't say what kind of machines we're shopping. Nobody will know we're assembling a spaceship until we undock, unfold, and light up the engines. What do you think?"

"I like it," I said. "I think Gampy would too."

"I know he would." Ganny looked pleased, even satisfied. She liked having a plan. She liked having a big plan. "We'll have to run the numbers through IRMA. This is going to require some tricky project planning, but it'll work. It will work." She reached over and patted my hand. "You we did good. You did good. We deserve a treat. Chocolate ice cream! With hot fudge!"

We topped it off with a dollop of gleeful dishing at the expense of MEBC. And then some exuberant fantasizing. After all, if we could do it once, we could do it a many times. We could even go into competition with MEBC. Our materials cost would be significantly less, our production lines could be faster, our per-unit cost would be cheaper, our modules would have no size limitations—

"We'll have to file a patent application—"

"But we won't mention shipcraft applications in the first patents, just expansion modules. We'll file a separate set just before we launch—"

Abruptly, we both looked at each other and stopped laughing. If the first one worked, we *could* build more. We could do it. And revenge is a dish best served *bold*. We left the dishes for a bot to clear and headed straight up to the office, giggling like a slumber party looking for a place to happen.

See, the problem was that once somebody does something, everybody else thinks that's the only way to do the same thing. Spaceship design is still stuck in the twenty-first century. Sure, the individual bits and pieces of technology have improved, the materials are better, but everybody still uses the same old-fashioned design. Build a long strong keel. Attach engines at one end, life-support doughnuts at the other. Add supply pods, equipment pods, ballast pods wherever they fit. Your ship looks like a cluster of grapes on a stick, with solar wings sticking out wherever.

Most ships start at the bottom of a gravity well. Earth or Mars. Wherever you can put down a factory without the neighbors complaining about the noise. All the different parts are manufactured in pieces, sent up the beanstalk, and assembled in space. So they're made—designed that way—to withstand gravity as well as thrust. If you build the pieces in space, you only have to design them for thrust. And if you're never thrusting more than a fraction of a gee, your engineering can be a lot different than if your pods are coming up the elevator at a thousand klicks an hour.

In space, you design for tensile strength and connectivity and hull integrity. You don't have to waste a lot of mass on heat shields and heavy plating and cross-bracing and all the other things that gravity and atmosphere demand. That's what Ganny figured out. Looking at the little canoe that Gampy put together for me in an afternoon, Ganny started wondering, "Why can't we build a life-support module the same way?"

Build a frame and wrap it in plastic sheeting. Or even ribbon tape. Instant hull. Cheap. Easy.

What stopped her wasn't the plastic, but the frame. We didn't have one. We didn't have the materials to build one. We'd need to build a great big wheel. Very sturdy. One that would rotate and withstand the strain of centrifugal "gravity." You lay down floor plates and then you put the bots to work, fabbing reels of plastic and wrapping it round and round and round until you had enough layers to feel secure. But we didn't have a frame and we didn't have the manufacturing capability to fab one. And even if we did, we still didn't have hull plates or the way to build those either. Constructing the fabbers to build either of those things could take as long as three years, maybe as much as five. And we'd still need raw materials. Cannibalizing the junkyard—we'd have to build a shredder and a refinery and all kinds of separators and at least three dozen bots to run the equipment. Not cost-effective. Gampy was right. And probably somebody at MEBC had done all the same math and figured out how to put us out of business with a single phone call.

Then Ganny saw the whisk in my hand and she saw something nobody else saw. As Gampy would say, they didn't see it because they didn't believe it. But Ganny was already halfway there. We didn't need to build a rigid frame. We could *spin* one. It was so simple it was embarrassing. What did we have a lot of? Cable, ribbon tape, plastic wrap. And more cable. Lots of cable. Enough cable to rebuild the whirligig several times over. Enough cable to rebuild a couple dozen whirligigs, which was Gampy's original idea. Don't go out mining for gold, just sell shovels to those who do. You'll make a lot more money.

Think of a sling. Whirl it fast enough and centrifugal force will keep the sling rigid for as long as you spin it. Just don't stop spinning.

Start with a hub. It looks like the rim inside an automobile tire. Put the hub on the axis of the keel. The keel of the *Lysistrata* already had a half dozen hubs in place from its previous incarnation, so we were already set for the next step. Attach one end of a long cable to the top rim of the hub, attach the other end of the same cable to the matching spot on the bottom rim. Attach some keel-weights to the cable, space them as far apart as you want your wheel to be thick. Do this at least three or four dozen times until you have looping cables all the way around. Kind of like the kitchen whisk, only loose.

Now you spin the hub. Get it rotating nice and fast. As the whole thing whirls, the keel-weights fly outward to their farthest possible orbits, pulling the cables rigid. Now each cable becomes two spokes with a connecting arc. The keel-weights (mostly) flatten the arc between the spokes, and all the cables, spaced equidistantly around the hub provide the spokes for a great big wheel. Keep the whole thing rotating and you have a rigid framework for your LSM. With no stiff spars at all.

Now send spider-bots down the spokes and have them start stringing cables from spoke to spoke, start at the midpoint of each arc. Connect everything with ribbon tape. Lay a roadbed. It's a suspension bridge without towers, everything joined at the center, turning round and round, and held in place by centrifugal force. Keep stringing cable and ribbon tape. Work your way up the spokes, connecting everything. Round and round all the little spiders go, crawling patiently around the circumference of the wheel, until they've woven a whole great web of wires, a gigantic whirling hoop. Now you start laying down your plastic wrap, unrolling it round and round and round just like the cables and the ribbon tape.

Okay, all that makes it sound a lot easier than it really is. Actually, you have to construct five concentric wheels simultaneously, each one nested inside the other, like little Russian dolls. You do that so you can have multiple levels of gravity, just like the whirligig; but also because that gives you the security of five bulkheads between you and vacuum.

And remember, you have to do it twice, because you need two LSMs. And half of a third one too. The "machine shop." But once you've got everything turning, once you've got your fabbers turning out cable and tape, the whole process is automatic. The spider-bots are patient and uncomplaining. They only come back in when they need another reel of cable and fresh power cells. As they run the webs, a second set of spider-bots installs hatches, monitors, sensors, electrical harnesses, fiber-optic cables, pipes for plumbing and ventilation, accessibility tubes, pneumatic delivery systems, dumbwaiters, elevators, all of the hidden systems necessary for maintenance and viability.

It sounds like a lot, but once you've got those big wheels turning, you can see how much there is and how little there is, both at the same time. With all the lights on, they look like grand empty outlines, amazing and awe-inspiring, every detail of the still-unbuilt wheels delineated like schematics brought to life, rotating majestically against the diamond stars. All the supports and cables, the spokes and interconnections, all the plumbing and wires, the lights and harnesses, everything connected together, rolling and turning; two of them, identical, 10 degrees syncing up in a bright double vision that collapses into a momentary eclipse of synchronicity and then unfolds again like a kaleidoscope as they continue rotating past. A gigantic, flickering, headache-inducing, psychedelic display.

Of course as soon as we started, long distance stills and videos of our wheels started showing up all over the ecliptic. Anybody who had a scope pointed it at us. We were photoed from the super-Hubble, photoed from the Kenya beanstalk, photoed from the 30-meter Lunar Darkside Observatory, photoed from the Phobos Base, photoed from sixteen different traction-drive vessels with near-space trajectories, photoed from around the arc of the belt—all those photos didn't give any sense at all of how beautiful our wheels were. Not until we published our own pictures. We put out a handful of drones to send back real-time views from edge-on, above, three-quarters, and flyby.

Of course, there was a lot of speculation about our wheels, what all the various harnesses and plumbing would eventually connect to, so along with our progress reports, we also posted our intended structural completion dates, certification target, and when we intended to start taking reservations for the first Asteroid Belt Tourist Hotel and Theme Park. Facilities would include picture window viewports, specialty suites with Lunar/Martian/Terran gravities, null-gee full-body shower-massages, asteroid mud baths, solar sunbathing, outings to the flying mountains, starsuit EVAs, bubble-ball, null-gee bridal suites, and anything else we could think of that you would want a luxury space hotel to provide. Most of it we cribbed from the brochure of the *Hotel Enterprise*, that big fake starship tethered to the beanstalk in low Earth orbit, but nobody seemed to notice. Unfortunately, unlike the *Hotel Enterprise*, we didn't have any simulation-rights, so none of our avatars could look like famous actors.

We also announced a contest for people to submit theme ideas for our hotel, the winner would receive a free two-week visit, all expenses paid, including transportation. That part was tricky, Ganny was afraid we could be sued for fraudulent advertising. But I said no, read the fine print. IRMA was very careful. If we didn't open a hotel, the contest was null and void, and we weren't really opening a hotel anyway, we were building a spaceship, remember? But it was fun imagining the hotel anyway. I started out wanting a Stanley Kubrick motif, but after a hundred or so almost identical contest entries, I decided it was overworked and actually a little creepy. Ganny favored a Jules Verne theme for a while. That could have been fun, but the more we played with the design of our lounge, all that varnished wood and dark red padding started to look heavy and wasteful and ultimately oppressive. Ganny and I both agreed that we wanted something that looked light and bright and playful, but at the same time homey. And easy to maintain.

We both wanted light, lots of it, all different colors, warm and cool, depending on the season and the moods of the people in the room. Lots of green plants, flowers, fish, e-candles, fountains, glowing mist-bowls that doubled as humidifiers, sheer hanging curtains to define spaces, and even a few overhead fans, the old-fashioned kind that were operated by turbaned slaves pulling braided cords, only instead of slaves we'd use theme-bots to pull the cords.

We were so engrossed in planning our fictitious hotel we barely acknowledged the red team when they left. There wasn't that much for them to do anymore and the bots were handling 90% of it anyway. So the team had been keeping pretty much to themselves, just running out the clock. I hadn't seen Grillo, the team leader, for a couple weeks, it was almost like he was avoiding me. The few I did see were very formal and polite, nobody called me short-stuff anymore. Nobody even mock-flirted. If I had cared, I would have minded, would have felt hurt, but I'd already started distancing myself from them when they asked for cash up front, so I just grunted in response to anything they needed to tell me.

Even so, we planned the traditional shift-change party for them, even though we weren't changing shifts, we were shutting down, so the party had a funereal edge to it. But Ganny wasn't going to let her emotions show. She put out her best spread, all the traditional meats, ham and turkey and roast beef, all the best fruits and vegetables and cheeses too. It puzzled me, because I thought she was in a "good riddance to bad rubbish" mood, but then I realized what she was doing. She wanted to give them a good case of the regrets. And she wanted the red team to go back to all their wherevers and tell everybody that if we were hurting, we sure weren't showing it.

Even so, after they left, the gig felt kind of empty. Hollow. Even lonely. And we still had to finish shutting down the last of the traffic, diverting most of it to Spinward and the remainder to Anderson-Base. We were only taking contracts that specifically required the orbital advantages of the Whirligig, either catching or tossing—and we charged premium prices for the effort, because Ganny just didn't want to be bothered. Every catch required a human being watching over the systems, a finger poised over the abort button. I'd done it, but only with Ganny or Gampy standing by. One week before my eighteenth birthday, the Big Gig was essentially out of business. We still got the occasional buy-out offer, but most of those were speculators making half-hearted inquiries. Equity sharks looking for a quick turnaround.

Meanwhile we were focusing on the next step of construction—how to wrap the wheels, how to panel the decks and the bulkheads. The problem wasn't that we didn't have a good way to do it, the problem was that we had too many good ways. We were looking for the sweet-spot, what would work best and what we could afford and what we could accomplish quickly. There's an old saying in engineering: "Good, fast, cheap. Pick two." We were trying for all three.

Actually, all that planning, all that designing, all the discussions back and forth, a lot of it was hard, most of it was hard, but it was a lot of fun too, some of the best fun we'd ever had. Except some of it was bittersweet. Every so often, sometimes almost every shift, Ganny and I would just stop and look at each other and one of us would say something like, "Gampy should have been here to see this," or "Gampy would have laughed," or "Gampy would be so proud of this." And sometimes we smiled and sometimes we stopped and cried a little. And sometimes we just got wistful for a minute or two, until one or the other of us would say, "Okay, that's enough. Gampy wouldn't like us wasting time like this. Let's get back to work."

Now, about those decks and bulkheads. That's what made Ganny laugh the loudest. After all those many times she said she'd never sit down and knit, not for anyone, now she was knitting the biggest longest scarves that anyone in the whole ecliptic had ever knit. At least a couple dozen.

Well, actually she didn't do the knitting, the knitting machines did, back and forth, back and forth, shuttling way too fast to see what they were actually doing on each pass, but each time back and forth, back and forth, adding a new row of intricately looped fiber. Back and forth they went, hissing and buzzing, clicking and clacking. Back and forth, patiently rolling out huge rolls of material, endless rolls, great barrels of triple-knit weave that would ultimately become the floors and walls and ceilings of the wheels.

Okay, yes, the machines did the actual knitting, not Ganny—, but Ganny designed the system, so the knitting was hers, all hers, and as all the different cylinders of fabric began to stack up in the "machine shop," Ganny's grin grew broader and broader. "Yes, this is going to work. This is really going to work."

Let's say you're making cloth. The obvious way is to weave it over-under-over-under, the material is kinda like a checkerboard. But it's not the strongest fabric you can weave. If a single strand breaks, you've got a place where there's extra stress on surrounding strands and that's where the rip is most likely to start. No, it's a lot stronger to knit your fabric. Or even double-knit. Or triple-knit. Because you've got your thread all hooked around and through itself, in and out and under and over, to make an intricate fabric of multiple interlocked loops. If you knit nano-fiber, the result is an air-tight material so fine you can't even feel the weave. Well, it's not really air-tight, it's just that the knit is so tight that most large molecules have a real hard time squeezing through; we use that a lot for starsuits. And graphene too. If you knit micro-fiber, you get a soft silky fabric loose enough to breathe and wick away moisture and feeling really nice against your skin, great for underthings, and we can sell it as space-lingerie in our fictional hotel. If you knit standard carbon-fiber, you get a larger scale of knit, lightweight and very resistant, it doesn't wear out. And so on. All the way up to titanium cable, which gives you a very impressive chain mail. You can knit anything, whatever size yarn or wire you want. You could even knit elevator cables if you needed to, if you needed a net strong enough to catch an asteroid. Or an Enterprise fish. But probably not a giant space amoeba. If we ever met one. It would probably ooze through the mesh.

Ganny set the bots to work weaving all these different knits, because she needed at least six different scales of tensile strength: micro-strength for the smallest of assaults, macro-strength for major events on the hull. She had IRMA run all kinds of simulations, and eventually we decided to panel the wheels with lasagna—multiple layers of knit, each layer pumped full of honeyfoam.

Honeyfoam is a generic term for quick-hardening poly-crete. It creates a layered, bubbled substance; if you mix it right and spray it right, you get uniform-size bubbles and an internal structure like a honeycomb. Very strong. Each bubble stays liquid inside. If something punctures the foam, the liquid bubbles out and reseals the foam just as good as new. Plus honeyfoam also helps against cosmic rays and radiation.

A lot of dirtsiders think that metal plating is the best defense against little cosmic bullets, but it isn't. A cosmic bullet hits a molecule of metal and it splits off gamma radiation, which is even worse. Instead, we can dope the honeyfoam with particles of magnetized plastic and when the wheel spins, it creates a strong enough magnetic field to deflect a lot of radiation. Not the stuff that doesn't respond to magnetism, but if we can reduce the overall exposure to what Ganny calls "sea level on a cloudy day," we're okay. Flip the polarities on the second wheel, the one that spins in the opposite direction, and the two magnetic fields overlay and combine instead of cancelling each other out.

Anyway, we let all three wheels spin for a few weeks to make sure they were stable, no wobbles, nothing seriously off-balance, all the stresses and strains equalized across the frames, everything working, boards green, confidence high, viability optimum, 110 percent, five by five, lock and load, surrender Dorothy, and metaphors be with you. Everything.

One night, over dinner—it was Ganny's turn to cook and she was experimenting with breaded hamster nuggets, I don't know why, but they turned out better than I expected—Ganny put her fork down and said, "Starling, I want to tell you something."

The way she said it, I expected bad news.

But no. "When we started this, I didn't believe it would work. No, really. Let me finish. I honestly thought it was a crazy idea, but I figured if I could you get involved in the planning, it would distract you enough to let me focus on the really hard decisions. And also, I believed, you'll laugh at me now, but I believed that when you finally bumped your head up against the impossibility of this whole thing, you'd finally accept the inevitability of the tougher choices we were going to have to make. I never expected to get even this far, but I am so glad we did. Watching you grow into the job has been the most joyous experience since I don't know when. Gampy would have been so proud of you. I wish he could have seen how passionately you've thrown yourself into this job and what you've accomplished so far."

I started to push my noodles around on my plate, trying hard not to blush or cry or fall bawling into her arms. I wasn't used to Ganny being all maudlin like this. But Ganny reached over and pushed my chin up. "No, you. Let it in. All of it. You've done good. And even while all the

math still says we're crazy, still says this won't work, still says we're dancing so far out beyond the skinny twigs we're way overdue for a splat—
even though this has got to be the single stupidest idea since polarized
milk, I want you to know, I am committed to seeing it through. I've
burned our last bridge."

"Ganny?"

"Well, think about it kiddo. Once we launch, what happens to the
Big Gig?"

"Um." I hadn't thought about it. "It'll still be here, won't it?"

"And where will we be?"

I started to answer, then I shut my mouth. We were going to be
all over the ecliptic. I looked around at the galley as if I'd never seen it
before. The gig was...my whole world. The benches, the fish, the canoe,
the rose bushes, Gampy—

Ganny pointed out the window, at the big wheels spinning grandly
only a few hundred meters away. The third wheel wasn't quite hidden
behind them. "That's our new home, sweetheart."

I didn't know what to say. I looked at Ganny. I looked out the window again. I looked back at my plate. I wiped my nose. I rubbed my eyes.

"It really is real, isn't it?"

"That's what I'm trying to tell you. Yes." Very carefully, she began
explaining. We wouldn't be ready for at least eighteen months. Maybe
two years. But we were going to need a crew. Six, maybe as many as
ten. I've set up a dummy site, operating out of a Martian provider. It's
a hiring service, referring crew to open berths, mostly in the belt. It's all
automated, linking in to all the majors, but we get to look at all the best
applications first. Anybody with a rating of 82 or higher. Shipmasters
start filling their cards a year before launch. We need to start making bids
if we want a qualified crew."

Ganny was right. I nodded thoughtful agreement. "I guess there's a
lot I haven't thought about. I've been so busy focusing on the mechanics of construction, I haven't been thinking about...anything else." I felt
like an idiot. I put my fork down. "You said something about burning a
bridge?"

"The gig. Look, I don't want anyone to figure out what we're up
to. They'll find some way to stop us. Maybe they'll try to decertify our
hull before we launch. I don't know. I'm not going to take the risk. So
everything we do, we have to make it look like something else. So I've

changed my will. Just a little bit. It'll look like I'm only rearranging things because Gampy's gone, but it's really something else. I've sold an option to Spinward. It says that if for any reason I am no longer able to maintain operations on the gig, you take ownership. If you're not able to maintain operations, or if you choose to relinquish your rights, then Spinward Station can exercise their option."

"What if they don't want to?"

"Oh, they do. They've already in the process of transferring the full purchase price into an escrow account. They have 24 months to raise 50% of the capital, with a payment plan on the back end for the rest, plus points on all contracts for the first 75 years of operation. They think they're getting a bargain, they think they're doing me a favor, they think I'm planning for your future. And…they think my health might be a little bit more fragile than it really is."

"Ganny!"

"I didn't lie. I just told them my real age."

"You didn't."

"I did."

"You're shameless."

"I am."

Over ice cream, this time homemade peach, we started making plans for our new home. The wheels were not only bigger than the gig, they were wider as well. We would have nearly three times the floor space on each of the gravity levels. That meant we could have bigger farms, bigger lounges, bigger gardens, bigger everything. Even bigger koi ponds. We'd have to make a lot more topsoil. Even so, we'd be stripping a lot of the value from the gig.

"Can we transplant the rosebushes?"

"Already planning on it. And Gampy's bones too. We're not going sailing without him."

"What about Spinward? Won't they feel cheated if we sail off with all the topsoil?"

"They don't want it, they're cleanliness fanatics. They prefer to grow plants aeroponically. But there's a clause in their contract that gives them rebates for any reduction in viability, anything that becomes unavailable due to your actions or mine. The contract does not include any part of our new construction." She nodded toward the window. "Or any of the materials used in that construction. I was very careful about that. They're only bidding on what's left of the gig if we leave, regardless of circumstances. Don't worry, they won't be disappointed. They want the bottom half, not the top. They want the industrial pods."

"Oh, okay."

A week later, we started carpeting. First, the plastic wrap. We made a big deal about that, not for ourselves, but for all the paranoid dirtsiders. We flooded the pipe with photographs and videos and animatics showing how the whole thing was supposed to work. We wanted them arguing whether or not it would work, arguing how ambitious and outrageous it was. We wanted them applauding our audaciousness while they morbidly speculated about how and when we would die and how horrible it would be and if we would be transmitting our last moments live. We wanted them to believe we were tiny and tony, all a little loony. Ohell, we wanted them to think we were flat-out crazy as a revival meeting.

We let them watch for weeks, while the bots trundled round and round the circumferences, laying down "road-beds," the bottom decks of the wheels, unrolling layer after layer of see-through plastic wrap, until we had a surface nearly a centimeter thick, much more than we really needed for this layer, but we wanted the dirtsiders to get bored. Really bored. By the time we started wrapping the spokes, our viewership had dropped to only the most fanatic members of our audience. The ones who believed we were secretly planning to drop asteroids on their heads.

Then one shift, two of our photo-drones inconveniently collided while maneuvering into new positions and went permanently offline. Coincidentally, the very next shift, a whole new set of bots began "laying carpet." Unfortunately, the only available close-ups of this aspect of construction were long shots from drones much farther out and at very inconvenient angles. It made it very hard for anyone offsite to get a good look at the way we made lasagna. Ganny apologized profusely and promised to fab new camera-units as soon as she could.

But that's when we got serious with all the stuff we didn't want anybody getting a good look at. Ganny didn't want people seeing what level of technology we could apply to the problem. What we had was graphene. Large sheets of it. Rolls of it. Lots and lots of it. Enough to wallpaper a planet.

Graphene is one of the strongest substances ever manufactured. It's another one of those things you can do when you convince carbon atoms to behave themselves and line up nice and orderly in one-atom-thick sheets. You could stretch a piece of it over the top of a coffee cup, suspend a pencil over it, put a three mega-kilo cargo pod on top of the pencil, and the graphene still wouldn't puncture. Roll it up tightly in tubes and you have cable strong enough for a beanstalk. Or a whirligig.

The best graphene is fabbed in a null-gee vacuum, shielded from intense solar energy, but even way out here in the belt, you still get microscopic flaws and cracks, so if you're going to make cables out of it, you have to interleave multiple sheets as you roll them up. We had a lot of graphene rolls, we fabbed it even when we didn't need it and sold it to anyone wanting to build a beanstalk or a whirligig or hang a tent over a crater.

In its sheet form, graphene is good for strengthening all kinds of things, and if you could mass produce flawless, uniform rolls of it, it would be one of the best construction materials in the universe. But so far, nobody has managed to produce more than a few dozen meters of flawless. So you have to wrap it in multiple sheets. Or in our case, just keep wrapping around and around and around. And around. The graphene foundation was necessary for what came next.

Now, we laid down layers of nano-knit and carbon-polyfiber-knit and all the others, and of course more graphene sheets too, balancing them for strength and flexibility. That's another thing dirtsiders don't understand about engineering big things. You have to allow for expansion and contraction, stretching and shrinking, crinkling and cracking, material fatigue and fabrication flaws, and then add a dollop of wiggle room for bouncing and bumping. So we balanced heavy-knit and tight-knit and sheets of pure graphene. We sprayed honeyfoam over and under and inbetween everything, and if anything ever stretched or flexed or cracked enough to break the foam, the foam would just fizz for a second, harden, and repair itself. And of course, we also laid down grids of monitors between the layers to measure temperature, radiation, proximity, vibration, movement, flex, stress, pressure, deformation, internal sound levels, impact, leakage, contamination, material decomposition, and the possible presence of ethereal heffalumps and other boojums. And anything else we could imagine. Because we were designing this ourselves, we were going ultra on the specs. And then as all the internal monitors became active and we certified them, we began growing the matrices for an IRMA installation. Our ship wasn't going anywhere without a brain.

Then for a long time, it felt as if nothing was happening. The big wheels kept on turning, the spider-bots kept unrolling. They pushed the cylinders of fabric rolled around and around the decks like prehistoric dung beetles pushing giant dinosaur turds. Other spiders manipulated huge cones, unwrapping great arcs of material around the spokes. Very quickly, the wheels stopped looking like outlines of themselves and started looking like…wheels. And whatever was happening inside, the view rarely changed from one day to the next. We knew that progress was happening, we just didn't feel it.

So we concentrated on other things. We started moving all the necessary support pods into place both above and below the wheels. Raw supplies, processed food, oxygen and nitrogen tanks, gas-scrubbers, fabbers, all kinds of raw material for the fabbers, maintenance and repair equipment, spare bots and replacement parts, anything and everything. We cleaned out the closets, the pantries, the garage, and the attic. Then we started moving the life-support systems too. Aeroponics, hydroponics, meat farms, more oxygen and nitrogen tanks, more gas-scrubbers, more fabbers, solar storm bunkers, lifeboat pods, emergency life-support units, starsuits, rebreathers, hazmat suits, O-masks, airlocks, and more bots. Did I leave anything out? If I did Ganny would catch it. Whatever she missed IRMA caught. And of course, we had all the checklists too. We had a century and a half of modern shipbuilding to draw upon and all the associated recommendations, requirements, specifications, tech manuals and certification sheets. We were pumped.

Inside the third wheel, our engines were taking shape too. The wheel itself was going to be our radiation shield, protecting us from the emissions of our own drives. There wouldn't be much radiation and most of it would be directed aftward, but just the same, starside you minimize every risk, to yourself and to everyone you approach.

The bottom wheel was made of overlapping leaves, not linked at the sides and permanently connected only to the top rim of its hub. Just before launch, we'd release all the cable connections on the bottom rim and the wheel would unfold like a gigantic flower, opening out to become a great grand dish and revealing our engines to space. We'd keep it spinning for a few weeks while the spiders crawled across it, anchoring the separate petals along their edges, linking them together and forcing them into a gently curving concave shell. Then we'd spray them with heavy-honeyfoam, both inside and out, to give them permanent rigidity.

During that whole time, we'd be running final tests on each of the engine tubes. When all that was finished we'd unroll the primary traction drives, big feathery things that would look like three gigantic oversized pistils sticking out of a very small flower. When everything was finally in place, the ship would look like a gigantic shuttlecock with a sharp pointy tip. We'd have the biggest traction engines ever built and 9 small secondary units spaced within.

If we could avoid any serious missteps, then eight weeks after launch we'll have tested and certified every major drive component. Allowing for the usual last minute unforeseen, unpredicted, and unexpected adjustments, calibrations, fixes, and repairs, the entire ship would be all-green in fourteen weeks. I would be nineteen and we would be starborne. We'd have not only the fastest ship in the system, we'd also have the most comfortable crew quarters.

But right now, we had to finish attaching, loading, and balancing the supply and equipment pods that clustered the length of the keel. And after that, we had to build and install the gear to make the habitat wheels viable. Neither wheel had yet been certified as spaceworthy, we hadn't even run preliminary pressurization tests, but if we started viability construction now we could minimize load-up time later.

Once all that was underway, we began to review applications. While we had been focusing on the hardware, the first few inquiries had already begun trickling in. Mostly desperate wannabes, but not all. A couple were interesting, we put them in the "definitely maybe" file.

We'd decided on a total complement of eight. The two of us, at least three more women, three men. We didn't need a full crew for the shakedown. And we could probably run with four if we had to. But Ganny wasn't saying everything she was thinking yet. I knew her moods well enough to recognize this one. I didn't say anything. I figured she was still working something out by herself, having one of those internal conversations with Gampy, and she'd let me know later if she decided it was worth pursuing. Then it would be my turn to chew it over. I suspected she was thinking about ship-families and teams and long-term relationships. She was thinking about me and my future.

This is another one of those starside things that dirtsiders don't get. "How do you live with the same people day after day, week after week, month after month?" But you could ask a dirtsider the same question. "Why do you get married? And live with the same person month after month, year after year?" Except they don't. As near as I can tell, dirtsider marriages are like mayfly mating seasons. Twenty-four hours long.

Starside, you live with people practically forever. Once you launch you're set for the entire journey, both out and back. So joining a crew isn't about taking on a job, it's about joining a family. Yes, you have to have all your tech-skills in place before your application can even be considered, but after that the real question is what can this person contribute to the family? Does he or she play any musical instruments? Play chess? Poker? Warcraft? Can he/she cook? Raise crops, tend a farm, manage a vegetable garden? Does this person have medical or dental skills? (Yes, I know. Every ship has medi-bots, but it's nice to have a human doctor too.) What fields of continuing education is this man or woman pursuing? What research is he/she currently engaged in? Does the candidate have an interesting personal history? A repertoire of interesting experiences to draw upon and share? Is he or she a good teacher? A coach? A trainer? A counselor? Does this person know when to shut up, when to withdraw? What do others have to say about working with this individual? Does the candidate use the ship's gymnasium? How often? How does this person feel about communal bathing? Does he/she practice nudity? How does this person manage his/her personal hygiene? What is his/her sexual orientation? Does he/she snore? And even though we're not supposed to consider it as a job qualification, it still is one—is this person attractive? Do you want to spend time with him or her?

And then...after all that, after you've accepted someone's application, you put in a confidential bid for their services and then they review *your* folder to see if they want to join *your* starside family. But the starside community is a small one and people have reputations, good or bad or mixed. After you've shipped a few times, you learn how to read folders, you learn what to look for. And what to *look out* for. Somebody who's served on a lot of ships might look good at first glance, but what if it's only one tour on each ship? What does that tell you? What if she's served seven years with one crew and then abruptly quit? What does that mean? What does all that psychometry tell you about ultimate compatibility?

The big problem was that neither Ganny nor I had a lot of experience in crew selection. That was usually the crew chief's responsibility, red or blue. Whoever we picked, we would be taking a big chance. There were a few people we knew, folks who had worked for us on the gig in the past, but the ones we would have invited were already booked for the next few years, and most of the ones who were available were people Ganny never wanted to see again. She didn't go into detail. If I had ever met any of them, I didn't remember. When you're little, you form your memories from a much smaller perspective.

Ganny was thinking that we needed to protect our secrecy right up to the last minute. Maybe we could have our prospective crewmembers train for our ship on simulators at Anderson Base. Anderson wouldn't even need to know who the sponsor was, we could run it through our Martian dummy company. Wheels within wheels within wheels. Literally.

And then—in the middle of all this—someone tried to kill us.

When traffic to the gig was at its very heaviest, we would catch and sling as many as a dozen pods in a four-hour shift. After the traction drive made it possible to build very big and very fast ships, slinging cargo into the pipeline was only cost-effective for the lowest priority cargos—things that would be needed soon or eventually, but weren't needed *now* —what the shippers called "futures" but we called "staples." Like extra supplies of air, water, emergency kits, scrubbers, rations, spare parts, fabber components, raw materials for fabbers, toilet paper, stuff like that.

By the time Gampy died we were down to six pods a day—on a busy day. When the red team left, we were doing half that. And after Ganny finished shutting down all but the most essential contracts, we were doing less than that in a week. And most of that was stuff that had been in transit for a while. Some of the owners had been able to course-correct their cargo-pods to Anderson or Spinward, but not all, so we still had traffic.

In past years, there had been a healthy "futures" market in pod-traffic. Speculators would load and launch a pod with all kinds of goodies, but with no specific buyer on the far end—in the expectation that by the time the pod arrived a month or a year later, somebody would pay a premium price for a cargo that was already in the neighborhood. That was a nasty game for a while, with belters bidding against each other for premium cargo, until Gampy organized a co-op, and all of a sudden the auction market collapsed because almost nobody was bidding. Gampy caught over a dozen of those speculative "futures" pods that arrived at the Whirligig without a buyer. That's when the real fun started. He purchased the cargo at a dime on the dollar and resold it to the co-op at forty cents. Then the belters bought what they wanted for fifty percent of original value.

But now—there were no more pods. In only a few years, the market had evaporated. A lot of investors took big losses. And the gig ended up overstocked with everything the buyers had abandoned. There was no longer a futures market, and if we saw more than a few pods a week, we experienced it as an annoyance, not a duty, because it pulled us away from the much more interesting challenges of ship construction. But our rule was that we always had to have a human finger on the abort button. No matter what.

Which was why Ganny and I were both on deck when the assassin pod came in. We were trying to figure out an alternate cargo cluster con-figuration on the keel of the ship, and at the same time fussing over what to make for dessert tonight. We were almost to the point where Ganny was going to win one argument and I was going to win the other when IRMA buzzed—loudly. The pod was coming in fast and its orientation had shifted. Ganny didn't even have to flip the plastic cover off the abort button, IRMA popped it for her. Half a second later, every alarm went off, the pod was firing its course-correction thrusters. It was aiming for the hub of the whirligig—the central control core—us. Hitting us at speed, it would shatter the keel of the gig.

The gig is big—a huge spinning disc—but it's not unbreakable. Imagine a spiderweb twenty kilometers across, with additional strands going out another ten, twenty, or thirty klicks, each with a ballast pod at the end. Or even a much heavier ballast rock on the major spokes. The combined mass is considerable, the torque of the spin even more so. It's pretty much an immovable object, a spinning immovable object. Just below the web, or above, depending on your orientation is the spin-ning doughnut of the living modules and control core. Cargo pods were supposed to link up with the outer ring of the web, or occasionally even the hooks at the end of the ballast rocks, depending on the approach velocity. But this cargo pod suddenly pointed itself at the keel of the gig and accelerated inward, a self-firing cannonball.. We had less than three seconds to impact—

Of course, it never hit. It got caught by the Gulliver nets. Essentially invisible, a network of wires and beanstalk-cables, strung from all over the keel of the gig to thousands of points all over the spiderweb disc of the wheel, hundreds of thousands of strands, covering every degree and each one studded with hooks. They work like arresting cables. Individually, none of them are strong enough to catch a pod, but collectively they're damn near impenetrable to the kind of traffic we get. If a pod comes in wrong, too narrow, too close, it will get caught by the turning wires. We might end up breaking a lot of cables in the process—they're fabbed with different strengths, all the way from a little brittle up to extremely elastic, so if they're hit the breakage is staggered sideways and around—and the contents of the pod are swung into place over a period of several seconds instead of instantaneously. It makes for a more survivable catch, both for the contents and for any passengers who might be riding as cargo.

The assassin pod caught, lurched, swung, almost hung, then caromed sideways and exploded. Most of the shrapnel missed us. One of the empty storage pods in the junkyard took a hit, but it wasn't a pressurized pod and the damage was easily repairable. Less than an hour's work for the bots. We didn't feel even a thump. Neither Ganny nor I said anything for the first few seconds. Not even a curse. Finally, she very quietly pushed the plastic cover back onto the abort button, leaned back in her chair and calmly said, "IRMA, track that bastard back to its point of origin."

Of course, it was untraceable. The pod had been slung to us from a whirligig at one of the Martian LaGrange points. The launch came from a dummy company, contracted by a dummy company, hired by a dummy company, licensed through a dummy company, owned by a dummy company, in cooperation with a dummy company, so many levels deep that even Ganny was impressed. The chain of responsibility was not only old and cold, but most of the links had already been removed. Somebody wanted us dead and we didn't know who. Or why.

The motivation could have been anything from a long-delayed and now-useless revenge against Gampy's co-op to a preemptive strike against the launch of our spaceship—the latter was far more likely. And if so, then somebody dangerous had put a lot of pieces together. Not too hard to do once you figure out that Ganny is both committed and capable. When you understand the circumstances, then you also understand the author of the circumstances—and that defines your options and your choices. Somebody was looking over our shoulder. Somebody was copying our homework.

Ganny thought about all the possible responses we could make, then opened a private diplomatic channel and sent this message: "The next time someone tries to kill us, we're going to drop cargo pods all over the system. Our targets might include Mecca, the Vatican, Jerusalem, Moscow, Washington DC, Beijing, Dubai, New Delhi, Paris, Disney

World, Clavius, Tranquility, Turtledome, Burroughs, Asimov Station, or even the Beanstalk Terminus in Ecuador. Or maybe some other sites we haven't thought to mention. If we do it, we'll sling the pods around the sun so they come up out of the glare, impossible to see until it's too late. It doesn't matter who authorized the attacks on us, we'll retaliate on the most convenient targets, and you guys can sort it out among yourselves who deserves the blame. Or if you're really smart, you'll figure it out among yourselves *now* so that there are no more attacks. And in case you think I'm bluffing, remember the pods we dropped into the Pacific all those years ago? Dropping them into the Pacific was a courtesy. We're through being courteous." She closed the channel, looked at me, and said, "That should do it."

"I'm not sure I understand—"

"It's politics, honey. It's not about playing the game, it's about playing the players. It doesn't matter if we know who did it. *They do.* Or they know how to find out. They'll very politely tell the folks who tried to kill us to knock it off. Or maybe not so politely, I don't care. They're probably not worried about our threat, they know how to track and destroy a rogue pod long before it becomes a threat. They learned how to do that after Gampy taught them the necessity. But just the same, they can't take the chance that we'll fling a heavy load of gravel at them, or something else they can't stop as easily. So they'll spread the word around: *Hands off the crazy lady.* And if somebody tries something again, they'll retaliate on our behalf and we won't have to. It's like playing Assassination Poker, only with real bullets."

We never got an official response to Ganny's message, but we got several unofficial notes. Nobody said anything specific. Mostly it was polite sympathy at our narrow-escape, praise for having such effective safety mechanisms (that they had never known were actually in place), several unconvincing promises that the ultimate ownership of the death-pod would be thoroughly investigated, and only a few vague acknowledgments of anything beyond that—except for one obfuscatory letter suggesting that if somebody was out to kill us, their next attempts would probably not be so obvious. Like we needed to be told that.

Ganny looked at me, I looked at her. She said, "You know what Gampy would say right now?"

"What?"

She scratched her neck gently with the backs of her fingernails. She put on her deepest voice and a thick Italian accent: *"But I didn't know until this day that it was Barzini all along."* To my puzzled expression, she said, "Okay, movie night tonight. My pick. I can't believe we left out such an important part of your education. There's an important lesson you need to learn—oh, and for dessert we'll have cannoli. I'll teach you how."

A couple of weeks after that, almost enough time to start feeling normal again, Ganny got a confidential email relayed through a Lunar proxy. "I am writing on behalf of a private information resource entity. We do focused data-mining in various technological and engineering domains. From time to time, we discover confluences of significant interest. Where we feel it is appropriate, we volunteer our services as agents, negotiating contacts of mutual benefit between entities who might otherwise would never have come in contact. Because we recognize the critical value of personal privacy as well as corporate privacy any information that we gather is treated as extremely confidential. We never release or exchange private information without first paying for the privilege of doing so.

"Recently we have become aware of an entity looking to charter an interplanetary vessel capable of high-speed, high-capacity delivery of cargo and passengers to multiple destinations within the populated ring of worlds, moons, colonies, asteroids, whirligigs, and space habitats. Attached is the list of projected specifications and requirements for cargo and passengers.

"We are writing to you because of your reputation, your experience with long-term starside habitation, and because you are uniquely situated to have knowledge of trustworthy independent contractors willing to work outside mainstream channels. All of our data-projections suggest that you represent a very useful avenue of inquiry. We recognize the unorthodoxy of contacting you this way, but we believe the circumstances warrant it. Our data maps suggest that the possibility of significant mutual benefit is very high. If you are intrigued by this possibility, we would establish confidential and secure procedures to put you in contact with the above-mentioned entity. Even if this is not an opportunity that presently suits you, we still hope to establish a relationship with you for the development of other opportunities in the future. Please reply to this confidential address if you wish to continue this discussion."

Ganny read it aloud, then passed me the e-page to look over. "What do you think?"

I shrugged. "Somebody knows."

She nodded. "Somebody who wants to hire a smuggler. And they think they're being very coy about it."

"Not smuggling," I said. "Freelancing. And not coy. Careful."

"Is that what they call it now?"

"Ganny, this is the free market in action. There's no regulation, no enforcement, and a lot of money to be made."

"Starling! I had no idea you were a libertarian. I thought we kept you away from that antiquated foolishness."

"Ganny! Don't be silly. I'm not a libertarian. I'm a greedy capitalist. Big difference. Real capitalists don't whine. There's a lot of money to be made in freelancing. That's what you and Gampy always wanted to do."

"What we wanted was to give you the career you've been training for all your life."

"I know. So we should talk about that. Where do we want to go? What do we want to do?"

"It probably won't be a long conversation. You've been crunching numbers for six months. I've been waiting for you to tell me what we're doing."

"I thought you'd already figured it out. Saturn."

Ganny raised an eyebrow. "Saturn?"

"We don't have enough gas to fill the wheels. We can only pressurize them to fifteen kilometers. Even if we enrich the O-mix, even if we wear O-masks, we're still going to have side effects—like pre-packed meals, because we can't do any real cooking where water boils at room temperature. We can't steal gas from the gig, that's not fair to Spinward, it violates our deal with them, and it isn't practical to crack gas from an asteroid because that's another year or more sitting around waiting before we can launch. And we lose our window to go collect our stolen goods. So instead, we live in the pods for a couple weeks while we ship out to Saturn, collect ice from the rings, crack it for gas, fill both centrifuges and pressurize them to sea level. Isn't it obvious? And while we're out there, we grab as big a berg as we can and bring it back. Enough to fill the new lake at Luna City—it'll be cheaper than lifting the same mass up from Earth and we can show a profit on our very first trip."

"We might get a better price at Asimov. And it's a lot closer."

"Mars? But that's where MEBC is located and—" Oh. I got it. A dish best served cold. Ice cold. "Okay, that works for me too." Sure. Let's knock the bottom out of their private little water market. That would be a very nice gift to the Martian farmers. "We'll need an agent to resell the water--?"

"Already handled, not a problem." Ganny didn't have to explain. The biggest monopoly on Mars is water-cracking. It's not impossible, it's just slow, tedious, and more expensive than you'd think. Plus you have to pipe it from where the water is to where you want it. In principle, it's easy. In practice, it's a bitch requiring a big investment in heavy equipment. If you have the heavy equipment, it's a seller's market. But if you don't, well then Mars isn't heaven. They've got you by the short and curlies, if you're one of those people who still have short and curlies. If not, they've still got you. Selling cheap water to Martians could overturn the planet's economy. Ohell, if we had a fleet, we could overturn the whole system. Hmm, a fleet....

Ganny must have been reading my mind again. She added, "We've also got agents on Luna and here in the belt. Dark agents. No one knows it's us yet."

"Some people suspect," I said. I'd looked at a couple of the deep data-mining sites, where folks speculate on all kinds of things, in this case, the very slight uptick in employment offers without a corresponding uptick in scheduled ship launches. And various other contract inquiries. "But, Ganny—I don't want to be a truck driver. Saturn is only a shakedown cruise. I want to do something else."

"I know. I've seen how you've outfitted this ship. You want to go for the long ride."

"I'm that transparent?"

"You're that transparent."

"Well, I sort of figured we'd do like we planned from the beginning. We'd pick up our pods, the ones we can get to, allow our unfaithful customers to renegotiate for delivery, you know, finish up as much old business as we can, maybe take another year or maybe two running around the ecliptic, testing ourselves, sorting out our crew, getting settled in, and then...when we're sure we're ready...we grab a load of colonists and head out to...someplace no one's ever been before."

Ganny nodded thoughtfully, taking it all in. "Well, at least you're giving yourself time to think about it. It is a long ride, sweetheart. You'd better be sure. You'll be years away from everyone else." She paused to wipe something from the corner of her eye.

"But you're coming with, aren't you?"

"I haven't decided that part yet. The long ride is a journey for younglings."

"You're still young—"

"Physically, yes. Emotionally...I feel as old as time. Maybe I'd feel different if I still had Gampy." She reached across and patted my hand. "But we don't have to decide that now. Let's take this one shift at a time." She took the forgotten e-page from me and held it aloft. "So, what do we tell this wannabe smuggler?"

"Nothing. It could be a ruse. Like Jimmy Sawyer."

"Ignore it?" She was ready to shake the page blank.

"Um. No. Let's find out what he knows about us. Ask him for more specifics. Don't say why."

The reply came back three days later. It was not what we expected. Ganny's face was ashen as she passed the plastic sheet to me. The bad news was the video. A whole column of video windows down the right side of the page. The entire construction of our ship. The top window showed the keel being moved into place and attached to the bottom of the whirligig's axis. The second showed the bots stringing the first cables. The third showed the hubs spinning and the cables sailing out to form a wheel shape. The next showed the completed frame and the spider-bots layering the first rolls of plastic wrap. The last showed close-ups of the bots rolling out the first layers of knit. Whoever it was—they knew everything. We had no secrets.

I looked at her, confused. "Someone tapped our private channels?"

"No. Look at the camera angles. We never put any drones on that side of the junkyard. Someone got smart. They must have attached a device to the outside of a cargo pod, probably a pod of supplies or equipment that we ordered for our own use, something we'd pull in instead of slingshotting it off somewhere else."

"But we haven't pulled in any pods since—oh, frack."

Ganny figured it out the same time I did. The drone had been attached to the transfer pod that the Red Team arrived in. Either with or without their knowledge. Probably with. As soon as it could detach without being slung off, it must have released and taken up position less than a klick off our axis.

Frack, frack, frack. And double-frack. It wasn't Jimmy who'd told. Now, I felt really stupid. I'd made an assumption. I'd fragged him. I'd shut him out. I'd slagged him with nastiness. I couldn't even apologize. I'd probably hurt him so bad he'd probably given up and gone for the mind-wipe. Googol-frack.

"I wonder how much those bastards made betraying us," Ganny said. Her expression was as dark as I'd ever seen it. "That explains everything. I wonder how many other spybots they planted." She was too angry to waste time cussing, she was already rising from her desk. "We're going to have to sweep—"

"Wait, Ganny—"

She stopped.

"Did you read the text?"

Her hands were trembling. Badly. She reached for the page. As she tried to focus, I said, "I don't think they're trying to blackmail us."

She started reading slowly. "Thank you for your quick response. You will likely see the attached videos as an intrusion into your privacy and for that we sincerely apologize, but we believe the need for contact is urgent. Let me explain.

"Several years ago, we determined that various stations in the asteroid belt would be good candidates for independent surveillance. The attached files confirm that judgment. While you have publicly stated that you intend to build a space-hotel, much of your construction also appears to be well-suited for the assembly of a long-range vehicle. We presume you have already considered that possibility. If the addition of traction drives are indeed a part of your future plans then we have several opportunities we would like to present to you.

"Additionally your construction methods could also have system-wide applications and we would like to discuss this with you as well. We are in an excellent position to explore, extend, and maximize your technology. Recognizing the critical time-factors involved, we want to arrange a personal meeting as quickly as possible. We have an agent who is familiar with your circumstances and can leave immediately. If you agree, we can have our agent at your station within two weeks.

"Please be assured that we recognize the critical importance of protecting your privacy. Even within our own organization, access to the attached files and the details of your construction methods has been severely restricted. Regardless of the outcome of our discussions, we will protect your technological secrets. I hope to hear from you soon. Sincerely, etc."

Neither Ganny nor I recognized the name at the bottom. A quick goggle provided only three lines of information. This company was a dummy for someone or something else. Just like Ganny's Martian and Lunar dummies. Did everybody distrust everybody so much that they only did business through sock puppies now?

We talked it over, we walked it around the centrifuge, we sat on Gampy's bench and tried to figure out what he would say. We thought about it privately. We went to bed without making a decision. We slept on it. We woke up in the morning and had waffles. We finally decided to send back a single sentence. "We're thinking it over."

Six hours later, the reply came back. "We'll pay for the meeting. A thousand liters of sea-level oxygen. A thousand liters of sea-level nitrogen. Two thousand liters of water. Five thousand seed packets. A thousand protein cultures."

"They're rich," I said.

"They're desperate," Ganny replied.

"They're afraid we'll launch without them."

"I wish I had their faith in our abilities. We're still a month away from lighting up the new IRMA."

"It's only a meeting," I said.

She shook her head. "I'm not sure I want to trust a stranger on the gig, not this close to launch."

"One person. Bring him or her in through the security lock, deep-scan down to the bone, and surround him with armed-bots?"

"Maybe."

"We could use the seeds. And the water. And especially the gas." I added, "It's enough to get us to Saturn."

"They did their math. They're smart."

"We have something they need. Maybe they have something we need...? I think we should listen."

So Ganny wrote back. "And ten gallons of Double Double Chocolate Fudge Swirl ice cream."

They replied. "You drive a hard bargain, lady!"

"Hmp," said Ganny to me, not to them. "I'm no lady."

"They'll find that out soon enough."

Six hours later: "Our agent is on the way."

Ganny turned to me abruptly. "All right, that's settled. Now tell me what you're so mopey about."

"Does it show?"

"It shows."

"Jimmy Sawyer."

"I thought you didn't like him."

"I don't. But I owe him an apology."

"So write him."

"I did. But he's gone."

"You searched?"

"I can't find him anywhere. He's disappeared. It's like he doesn't exist anymore." I finally said it aloud. "I think he went and got wiped. And it's my fault."

"It's not your fault, sweetheart. Everybody is responsible for their own decisions. If he did, then he did what he did because *he* chose to do it. You're halfway across the solar system. All you did was send him an email."

"But it was a bad email!"

"It's not your fault."

"But it still feels like it."

"Yes, that's the part that hurts."

Ganny hugged me and I cried into her shoulder. And that helped a little. But not as much as I'd hoped. This was something I was going to be ashamed of forever. Gampy used to say, "Being stupid is no disgrace. Staying stupid is. Clean up your messes and move on." But how do you clean up a mess that can't be cleaned up? Jimmy was the only dirtsider I ever really liked.

Ganny whispered in my ear. "The pain doesn't go away, Starling. You just learn how to live with it. And that's the hardest part of growing up. Walking around with all that pain that just won't go away." I guessed that was what I saw in grownup eyes, the part I didn't like. I didn't want to look like that, but now I knew I did. There wasn't enough frack in the universe to express how I felt. So I cried into Ganny's shoulder until I couldn't cry anymore. And then I went to my cabin and crawled into bed and wrapped myself up in my favorite soft blanket and just felt bad about everything until I finally fell asleep.

When I woke up, everything was in uproar. Ganny had asked IRMA if we had to, how soon could we launch. IRMA said 23 days. That's how soon the engines could be brought on line and tested. Almost all the rest of the construction could be finished in transit. And the stuff that had to be done now, so we could launch—IRMA compiled a list. So Ganny activated every bot and put them to work. Even the new cat. She activated every processor in the local cloud and commandeered everything with a clock cycle. IRMA coordinated schedules and there was an e-page and a sandwich stuck to my door. All I had to do was take things in order and check them off as fast as I could get to them.

A lot of it was simple manual labor. Grab this, carry it here, install it there, bring it online, let IRMA test it, certify it and sign off. Some of it was supervisorial. Double-check the certification of all the sub-units. Eyeball the pod-load. Send in a probe, walk it by remote, look through its eyes, listen through its ears. When you're satisfied, put on a starsuit and walk both wheels, all five levels—the three habitat levels and the two storage spaces, five different gravities. This time, *feel* the environment. Motion sensors will tell you it doesn't wobble, doesn't tremble, the pseudo-gravity is stable. Walk it anyway. Feel it. I didn't see Ganny until dinner time and she looked as frazzled as I felt. But I didn't have to ask why.

If one somebody had figured out what we were up to, then it was possible—almost inevitable—that someone else had figured it out too. And if it was someone who didn't want us to launch, we could have bad news on a collision trajectory. Oops, I'm sorry. Your spaceship accidentally got in the way of our missile test.

After dinner, Ganny said, "Okay, here's the part I did without checking with you. You can get mad at me later." She opened a schematic on the big display. She didn't say anything. She just let me study it.

"Hm," I said. I pointed. "Rail-guns. Needlers. Laser-cannons. Missile launchers. Particle beams. Silent screams. Pain projectors. Funny-foam. Tanglefoot fields. Spider-nets. Stunners. Disruptors. Isn't this a little overkill for pirates? Are we going to topple a government? Or are we just going to war against the Klingons?"

"Yes," she said.

I wasn't kidding about the Klingons. There's a whole colony of them on Luna—fanatics who've gone from cosplay to full-sim to body-mods and the more extreme are even going for genetic modification. Most of them don't have much to do with humans anymore and the feeling is apparently likewise. Dirtside intelligence engines have already projected open hostilities when the third generation hits maturity, sometime in the next twenty years—with the Klingons losing badly and having to go into psychometric rehabilitation. But that's another discussion. Personally, I find the wannabe Vulcans a lot more annoying. Kind of like objectivists, but passive-aggressive. I don't understand any of that stuff. Why pretend you're from a fictitious planet when there are real planets just a few mega-klicks away?

Ganny said, "We've had a pretty large arsenal for a long time, pun-kin. We've only needed it once, but that once was justified. We've kept most of the defensive gear hidden in the core of the junkyard, the rest is very well disguised and scattered in the most unlikely places. Spinward doesn't know about this stuff, at least I don't think they do, and I'm not leaving it behind for them. So as long as we're schlepping it, we're going to make it cost-effective."

"Ganny, *this* is a warship. Just pulling into orbit will look like a threat to some folks."

"As long as we don't look like a warship. As long as we don't make noises like a warship. As long as we pretend we're not, they'll pretend too. Because it's convenient not to have large crowds of people running around in a panic. You know your history. Remember? The big dog sent its ships sailing into ports all over the marble with nuclear weapons in their bellies, but nobody talked about it, nobody got publicly upset, but everybody knew, at least the ones who most needed to know. And the big dog stayed the big dog until it got so flea-ridden it bled to death. The little dogs feasted on its bones and the ones who got too big inherited the biggest fleas. That's life on the marble. And they're trying to export it starside."

"But—if we install all these weapons, aren't we behaving the same way? Just as paranoid as they?"

"Absa-tootley," she agreed. "There's the paradox. You want to leave any of this stuff behind?"

"Hell, no. But I think you might want to mount the heavier weapons closer to the center of gravity to take some of the stress off the keel."

"Already considered that. It reduces our coverage. And the gear isn't mounted to the keel, it's mounted to a framework that clamps around the keel. It actually adds to the longitudinal strength. Oh, and I'll want you in the fire-control simulator at least an hour a day from now until launch."

That was a lot to think about. I knew Ganny didn't want to be the big dog. Hell, she didn't even want to be in the same pack with most of the other mutts. But maybe, like everything else, there was a lot more to this. My first thought was that Ganny wanted us armed against—against whoever it was coming to meet us. The "fast ship" they were sending might very well be a cruiser.

But the unknown guys in black hats who might be a bigger threat, the ones who might not want us freelancing—maybe that's who the heavy armaments were for.

But there was a third possibility too. It didn't seem likely, but there was a lot that didn't seem likely before that looked absolutely inevitable afterward. I had a lot to think about. And not a lot of time for thinking. I goggled what I could and skimmed it whenever I could grab a spare half-minute—in the toilet, on an enforced rest-break, or even while shoving a sandwich into my face.

Two hours before the fast ship was scheduled to arrive, I finally spoke up. "Ganny? Whatever he offers…we can't accept it."

"Eh?"

"If he knows we've built a ship, then he's gotta be smart enough to know we've armed it."

"Yep."

"So he wants to hire us as muscle."

"That is a possibility, yes."

"Ganny, he's bringing a Corporate Letter of Marque. It's the only thing that makes sense. Hiring us as independent agents to do somebody else's dirty work. We'd be privateers—pirates!"

"Arrrgh," said Ganny. "And it isn't even the nineteenth of Septemberrr yet." [1]

"Ganny!"

"Starling, what do you think they're going to call us when we start taking back our cargo pods?"

"We have the Martian court's judgment."

"The Earth courts didn't recognize it." She put her hand on mine. "We haven't said yes. We only promised to listen."

"I wish we'd never built the damn ship."

"You don't mean that."

"Yes, I do. No, I don't. I just didn't realize—"

"You didn't realize, did you, that when you bring a really nice toy to the playground, you end up surrounded by a lot of other kids who want

---

1   Look it up yourself, I'm not doing all the work. Arrgh.

to play with it too. And if you won't share it, some of them will try to take it away."

"Ganny, I didn't grow up dirtside. I've never seen a playground, remember?"

"Yes, and I'm sorry about that. There are a lot of lessons you've missed."

"Foof!" I made one of those noises that I make when only a noise will express what I'm feeling.

She put her hands flat on the table. "Don't be too quick to make judgments. Sometimes, the pirates are the heroes."

"I'm sorry, I don't understand that."

"That's my fault. I neglected that part of your education. Look, the Martians might applaud our audacity at stealing back our own pods, but now we're talking about delivering cheap ice to Martian farmers. The farmers might call us heroes, yes. But what do you think the Martian ice-cracking companies are going to call us? Not heroes. Carpetbaggers. Wildcatters. Poachers. Privateers. Probably even pirates—because we're stealing their market. So who's the good guy? Who's the bad guy?"

"We are. We're the good guys."

"That's not what they'll say."

"Well, then they're wrong—"

Ganny patted my hand again. She did that a lot these days. "Sweetheart, it depends on where you stand. Not all pirates are…bad guys."

The way she said it, her tone of voice, the look in her eyes—I suddenly got it. All those things she'd never explained. All that history. "You and Gampy—?"

"Uh-huh. Me and Gampy. All over the backside of Luna."

"Oh." It took a moment to sink in. "Oh!"

"That's right. We started at Turtledome and—never mind. There'll be plenty of time later on to tell you the rest. You'll be surprised."

I looked at her as if I'd never seen her before. Cap'n Ganny, scourge of the spaceways. Amazing.

"You never told me."

"You didn't need to know. You weren't ready to know."

"I guess not." My head was spinning as fast as the gig. I was having trouble wrapping my mind around this. This was going to take some time to get used to. Maybe it was all a matter of definitions. Words. Attitude.

Context. Where you were standing. I finally stammered, "So you think piracy might be a good career move?" It must have sounded stupid.

But Ganny answered matter-of-factly. "If we like the targets. If there's enough money in it. *And* if we're on the right side of the argument."

I thought about it. Yeah. This was what we'd been planning all along. We just hadn't called it what it was. No, I hadn't. I exhaled loudly. I nodded. "Okay. But only as long as we're on the *right* side of the argument."

"Agreed."

"Hey! Can we wear space-pirate costumes?"

"You can. I doubt I'd look good in a titanium bra."

"Ganny!" I gave her the look, at least as well as I could manage it. "You've been living in micro-gee since you were 18. You are a long way from Cooper's Droop."

"It's not the perkiness of the puppies I'm concerned with, sweetheart. You'll still look better in pirate drag."

"Arrrgh," I said. "You'rrre the Cap'n. Can I wearrr an eyepatch? Can I have a parrrot?"

"And a wooden peg-leg, if you want. But you'll have to be a boy. There aren't any girl pirates."

"I'll be the farrrst."

"You sure? You might like being a boy."

"Uh-uh. I don't want one of those dangly things. I don't even want to *think* like someone with a dangly thing. Yick." Ganny and Gampy had always said that even a short time as a boy would be good for me, but I never could see the point in it. And I didn't want to have the "try it, you might like it," conversation again. Time to change the subject. "So, um, what are we going to name our ship? We need something dramatic. Something to strike fear in the hearts of robber-barons everywhere. The Crimson Dagger? The Banshee? The Screaming Yellow Harpy?"

"Nothing."

"Huh?" I was confused. "But I have a whole list—"

Ganny shook her head adamantly. "Put your list away. A spaceship names herself. When you get intimate with her, when she trusts you, when it's time, she whispers her name to you. Even a ship with a brave heart won't even know her true name until she's earned it. We'll have to wait to find out who she is."

"I never heard that before. It's not on any of the sites I've visited—"

"There are a lot of traditions we don't write down. You'll learn." The clock chimed the hour. Ganny glanced at it, looked back to me. "There it is. It's time. Get to your fire-control station. Remember how we trained. You stay locked on target until I give you the all-clear, nobody else. Even if the ship is docked. I'd rather blow away half the gig than surrender all of it. You understand?"

"Aye, aye, Cap'n." I even saluted.

"Good girl. Now, go."

I bounced.

I was right about the "fast ship" being a cruiser. Like all traction drive ships it had an oversized array of "feathers" sticking out the back. Not as big as what we would eventually have, but big enough to push this little dumpling around the system at a steady one-gee acceleration. We'd been watching it long-range for several days, but we couldn't get a good visual. It was painted black. With Sol a few degrees off its stern, we couldn't see much more than its silhouette in front of the coronal cloud. But IRMA enhanced the view, so we had a pretty good idea what kind of armament it carried. This thing was coming in fast. Maybe furious. We wouldn't know until it was too late.

She wasn't decelerating. That was ominous. If she were on an attack run, she'd want to drop her fish as fast as possible to minimize her own vulnerability. But if she were going to fire missiles or a beam, she wouldn't need to come in close. She could have launched them an hour away. But if someone were going to attack us, they wouldn't have to send a cruiser, they could have launched from Luna or Mars. Unless they wanted to launch away from witnesses. But even if they did that, the trajectory of the missile or the path of the beam could be traced, and it wouldn't be too hard for a skilled data-miner to determine what ships could have been passing through the locus of possible launch spaces.

There weren't so many ships in the system that the ship watchers couldn't keep track of them. They knew the orbit of every man-made object in the system, they knew what it was and where it was. The only objects they couldn't identify or locate—were dark objects, things built and launched in secret. But if you dug into the databases, apparently they knew where most of those were too. But possibly not all. This was not reassuring.

Then the signal came in and I relaxed. A little. She wasn't decelerating. She was aiming to catch a hook on one of the whirligig's rotating cables. That was a sign of…I guess, trust. If we changed our minds, if we didn't want them docking here, we didn't have to catch them. But Ganny approved the connection and I watched my scopes as they began adjusting their trajectory to make the linkup. They had to match the speed of the line. They would have only a three-second window to catch the hook on the end as it came swinging up. If they missed it, or if the hook failed to latch, they'd keep on heading past while the cable swung away.

But they caught. Their hook caught our loop. Our hook caught theirs. The ship was already oriented nose in, so it showed only the slightest lurch when it was caught by the line and the centripetal force yanked it into opposition. Almost immediately, the gig began adjusting its balance, retracting several of the opposing ballast pods, reeling out the complementary ones. The service-bots were already attaching docking cables, what some people call the retractors, but they're just another set of lines. Even before they were secured, IRMA was scanning the vessel. Top-to-bottom, a full-spectrum deep scan.

The layers of the schematic began appearing immediately on my displays. I had a pretty good idea what to look for, I didn't see anything alarming, but I wasn't an expert. IRMA labeled everything she could identify and extrapolated what she couldn't. Nothing unexpected. More important, all weapon systems were inactive and cold. But that didn't mean anything. A military-class weapons-package could be brought online in seconds.

Eventually, Ganny signaled green, and the retractor cables began spooling up, reeling the ship in toward the center of the gig like a giant black fish. My job was to stay in place, a backup for Ganny. Watch and wait. The visitor's ship, curiously unnamed, connected to a docking pod opposite Level 2. Martian gravity. The two airlocks connected and equalized pressure, temperature, and gas mix. Neither they nor we were too far off standard, the process completed in 90 seconds. I readied my finger on the button. Whoever or whatever was coming through, there was still a chance he could come through armed. I didn't expect it, it wouldn't make sense, but that was precisely the reason for caution—that it didn't make sense.

The airlock hatch slid open. IRMA began scanning immediately. There was no one there. Only a refrigeration unit. Ten gallons of Double Double Chocolate Fudge Swirl. Nice. Ganny gestured and a cargo-bot rolled up, secured the unit, and wheeled it off to the galley. Very nice.

"Okay," said Ganny. "That's a good start. Where's the rest?"

The airlock door slid shut.

Just beneath the Martian deck, there was a cargo lock. Ganny and I both watched our screens. They opened their hatch, we sent a team of cargo-bots in. The seed packets were in a dozen cold-boxes, not big, I could have carried one under each arm. The protein cultures were a lot heavier. When the cruiser docked, IRMA had balanced its mass by rearranging cargo-pods, pulling some in, letting some out. But this was a balancing problem on a much more delicate scale. Now she had to pump water around the 'fuge to compensate for the shifting mass of cargo we were bringing aboard. The hibernation boxes with the protein cultures were heavy enough to warrant the concern. Plus, we had to scan them. We routinely scanned everything that came aboard the gig, but this time we deep-scanned each container from three angles and IRMA constructed an interior schematic of each for intrinsic analysis. There were no problems, but we didn't expect any. If these people, whoever they were, wanted to hurt us, they wouldn't do it this way. And if they wanted us to trust them, they wouldn't play games with the payment.

The gas and water we simply pumped aboard, but that took time too. IRMA had to balance all of it to separate ballast tanks. Ultimately, she'd move most of it down to the new wheels. But she wouldn't do that while the strange ship was docked, she wouldn't risk having the visitors monitor our operations any more than necessary.

It took over an hour to complete the transfer of cargo. When Ganny was satisfied that payment was complete, she went back to the lounge to meet our guest.

This time, when the airlock hatch slid open, there was a man inside. I couldn't see his face. He raised his hands and turned around slowly while IRMA scanned him. I was too busy studying the body-schematics to care what he looked like. He was lean. He was young. He was unarmed.

Ganny stood off to one side, where she was out of his field of vision. "Take off your jacket, please. Leave it in the lock. Your collar buttons are microphones. Your pocket buttons are cameras. And that look doesn't work for you anyway. You can keep your pants on, but remove your shoes please."

The stranger dropped his coat to the deck and pulled off the lightweight moccasins he wore. He waited until Ganny gave him the okay, then stepped out of the airlock. The hatch slid shut behind him. I resumed breathing and snapped the safety cover back onto the fire-button. By the time I finished securing, the stranger had already moved into the lounge. He had his back to the camera, he was silhouetted by the light, but the look on Ganny's face suggested something awful had just happened. I reached for the 8-second replay, but before I could hit it, Ganny said, in a very flat voice, "Starling, please come down to the lounge."

My heart sank. Ganny wouldn't have called me down like that unless—unless something happened we were both totally unprepared for. Had Ganny just surrendered?

"Starling?"

"On my way," I replied. I bounced out of my seat, swam down the access tube to the fuge, oriented myself appropriately and floated down to Level 1. Hit the stairs to Level 2 where real Martian gravity started to kick in and slowed down. Straightened my shirt. Ganny didn't know about the needle-beam strapped to my forearm—

I stopped at the bottom step. Standing next to Ganny was a tall, broad-shouldered man. He had a folder in his hands and he was smiling at me. He had ruddy skin, freckles, buck teeth, big nose, bright red hair, and he looked an awful lot like—

"Jimmy?!"

"Starling!"

"You're not dead—?"

"Neither are you." He grinned. He was older. Two years older than the last picture I had of him. He had filled out. He had shoulders, a chest, a haircut. He looked like a man now.

I took a half-step toward him, my body wanted to leap across the intervening space and hug him forever, but I stopped myself, hesitant, confused, still distrusting. The questions poured out of me. "I thought you were—I tried to find you, I couldn't. How did you get here? What the hell is going on? Ganny, did you know about this?" And finally, "Jimmy—" And that's when I stopped. My knees buckled and I sank to the deck. Slowly. In 0.38 gee.

Ganny crossed to me and grabbed me under the arms before I finished settling. She pulled me back up to my feet and whispered softly to me, so Jimmy couldn't hear. "Starling, sweetheart. First get rid of the needler strapped to your arm. I don't think you're going to need it and it's pulling your bra sideways. I'll teach you later how to conceal a weapon. Here, give it to me." She stood between us, keeping him out my view and me out of his; she reached efficiently up my sleeve, peeled away the gun and made it disappear into the folds of her jacket. She straightened me up, held me until she was sure I wouldn't fall down again, then walked me over to a couch. Like the majority of our furniture it was mostly foam sprayed on a plastic-wrapped frame, with a nice knit cover.

She pointed Jimmy to the couch opposite. "I think you have a lot of explaining to do, young man." She sat down next to me.

"It's not that hard to explain," Jimmy said, settling himself. He put his folder on the table. A bot rolled up with a pitcher of water and three glasses. "We were going to lose the rest of my college allotment anyway, so I sold it on the futures market. I mean, I know it was silly, but the money was going to disappear anyway, what else could I do with it? It's against the law to harvest future dollars, you have to reinvest them. So I bought a probe. Ordered it through a proxy. Sent it out from a Martian company with your Red Team. I didn't mean any harm. I just wanted to take a photo of Starling waving at me, and I'd transmit back a photo of me waving back."

He paused. "Okay, that's not entirely true. All those long conversations we had—" He looked across at me. "It wasn't a hypothetical. You were designing something real."

"What gave it away?"

"You kept insisting it was a thought experiment. I believed you the first time. But the more you said it, the more I wondered why you needed to keep saying it."

"Oh," I said.

Ganny poked me. "Remind me to teach you how to lie. You're not very good at it."

"I guess not."

Jimmy spoke up. "I told you I wanted to come out to the gig. When I saw you were building a spaceship, I was all the more determined. When I got your message, the angry one, I knew I had to get out here, somehow. To apologize. To make it right, somehow."

"Apologize? But you didn't—"

"Hush, child." Ganny patted my knee. "If a man wants to apologize, let him. It doesn't happen very often."

"Look—" He spread his hands wide. "When we first started trading messages, I thought you were a fake, just another online joker pretending to be a starsider. There are a lot of those. I didn't even think you were a girl, just some old fat guy trolling for attention. Because you were too smart, too literate, too everything. I'm not the only one who thought that either. Nobody else on the forums knew if you were real. We had a whole private discussion group. I mean, we liked you, you seemed honest enough, nobody ever caught you in a lie, but why would a starsider want to pay any attention to us? We heard starsiders were all self-righteous and arrogant and elitist snobs who wouldn't talk to groundlings, so it didn't make sense that you were really who you claimed to be. So I just led you along for a long time, asking you questions, drawing you out, trying to trip you up. But then you started sharing stuff you couldn't possibly have known unless you were real. I mean, see, anybody who wants to know about the Big Gig or Spinward Station or Anderson Base or any other station can goggle or wiki them. You can search for blueprints, crew rosters, supply schedules, virtual tours, economic analyses, annual reports, news articles—and of course, all the conspiracy sites too. But you knew stuff that wasn't on any of the sites. You knew the Red Team and the Blue Team. You knew everybody's nicknames. You knew personal histories. You knew everything. And the way you wrote about—it wasn't like you were making stuff up or reporting from a distance, you were writing it as if you were living it, so if you were a phony, then you were the best ever. *Or you were real.* But no sock puppy would ever go to that much trouble to fool a skinny geeky nerd-boy like me. I looked you up, but there was hardly anything about you. Just your age, who your parents were, how they died—I felt real bad reading that part—but not a lot else. Some school records. And a picture or two of you with the Blue Team, when you were small. You had the biggest eyes. You still do. But, I mean, your messages could have come from anybody pretending to be you. Except... there was that other thing. I researched the tracking records on your messages. When they were sent, when they arrived, how they were routed. A phony might have proxied his messages, bouncing them off Mars with appropriate time-lags, but your messages bounced in from everywhere, whatever was the shortest path, but...I mean, after a while, I just had to believe in you. I just had to. And then when I got your message...I realized you thought I was the phony. I am sooo sorry." He looked across at me with an expression of such desperate hope I had to put my hands over my mouth to keep from laughing. It wasn't funny, but it was. Like one of those old screwball comedies Gampy used to love so much where everybody thinks everybody is somebody else, not who they really are, and everyone is running around in circles like a big game of crazy-bot, because they're all tripped up in their own wrong assumptions.

Jimmy must have thought I was angry. With my eyes wide, with my hands covering the bottom half of my face, I must have looked appalled. "Starling? Please? I came all this way just for you."

I didn't know what to say. It was too much. Ganny spoke for me. "But, James—Jimmy—how did you get here? Who is this mysterious company that sent you?"

"Um." He stopped. He looked embarrassed. "Promise you won't get angry?"

Ganny looked at him sternly. "Y'know, when someone says that to me, I just know that what comes next is going to be very very bad news." She took a long deep breath. "I'll tell you what I will promise. I promise I won't kill you."

She squeezed my hand. Hard. Until I said, "Okay. I promise I won't kill you either. At least, not quickly. And certainly not painlessly."

"Um." Jimmy swallowed hard. I could hear the gulping sound. It would have been funny, if what he said next wasn't so…so *wrong*.

"Okay. Um. I was approached. My company was approached—"

"You have a company—?"

"Um, yeah. Kind of. It doesn't do anything really. It's only a dummy. But everybody has dummies. It's how they move their money around. I started a whole bunch when I was thirteen. Because I figured someday I'd be rich and I wanted to be ready."

"So you're rich now?"

"I wish." He looked embarrassed. "But, see, I did all my inquiries and everything through one of the dummies. See, whatever you do, if you do it through a dummy company, then you're kinda protected because if somebody tries to sue you, they can't—they can only sue the dummy, and it doesn't matter if they win or not, because it's only a dummy, there's nothing there to collect."

"Yes," said Ganny, absolutely deadpan. "We know how that works." She gave me a sideways look. *Gampy and I mastered that trick seventy years ago.*

"Um. Yes. Anyway, my company was approached. They asked me if I did research, I said yes, they asked what kind, I said data-mining. Shipping. How cargo moved. Stuff like that. They asked me if I'd take on a special project. I said why me? They said that their data-mining division reported that I was doing the data-mining that they needed. That didn't make sense to me. But after we all finished dancing politely around the subject for a few cycles, they said that I was in a unique position to do the kind of research they wanted done. Um. They said they wanted to know what you were *really* doing out here."

He held up a hand quickly. "I didn't tell them what I suspected. I didn't say anything at all. Because I didn't know who they were. I mean, not at first. But I figured it out later."

Ganny wanted to interrupt, wanted him to get to the point. So did I. But neither of us spoke. Watching Jimmy fumble his way through his narrative was like watching a ballet dancer being both elegant and clumsy at the same time. I perched on the edge of the couch, leaning forward, elbows on knees, chin parked firmly between my hands, eyes wide, fascinated, astonished, enchanted. Ganny confined herself to an impatient get-on-with-it wave.

"They said they were studying the belters. Even tracking email. But they said it was a matter of global security. They said they were looking for comet-tossers who might throw something at a planet. The intelligence engines would flag any messages that had certain keywords. I mean, that was how they located you. And then me. And after they argued with themselves for a bit, that's what they said, they contacted me because they thought I might be useful to them. Because you and I, we had a—a relationship. Sort of. A friendship. A long-distance thing. They said that it wasn't just useful, it might even be profitable. They said all the right things. They were really very good. But, um, oh, see here's the thing. I never met any of them in person. It was all email, but I got the feeling that they were—well, it wasn't that they were hostile, but they weren't respectful. Not toward you. I mean, not like I thought they should be. So I began to, y'know, think that they might not be friendlies. And that whatever I might say to them, they would want to use it against you. That's when I started to think what could I do to help you? Because I just didn't want you to be hurt. I just couldn't stand it if something I did ended up hurting you. And then they said they'd pay my way out here, so I could look around, take pictures—" He waved his hand vaguely in the direction of the airlock. "They wanted me to spy on you!" His voice cracked nervously. "I couldn't do that—I just couldn't. But it was the only way I could get here. Honest."

"Who?" demanded Ganny quietly. Coldly.

His voice dropped to almost a whisper. *"They never said, but I figured it out anyway.... Martian Electric."* He fumbled with his hands as if trying to mold the words into shape. "It was the time-lags of their messages. I figured it out the same way I figured out yours. And because of a lot of our messages to each other—about your thought experiment—were relayed through the Martian links, that was kind of obvious. To me, anyway. I mean, I only look stupid. People underestimate me sometimes."

"You don't look stupid—" I blurted, but Ganny put her hand on top of mine and I shut up.

"The Martians...." Ganny shook her head. She made a face. She said a word. "It's *always* the Martians. The goddamn Martians. What is it with those people? Do they have to own everything?" She sighed, more in exhaustion than exasperation. "It wasn't a very big secret, Jimmy. We already knew it was the goddamn Martians. But—" She leaned forward intensely. "The whole point of this interrogation was to find out if we could trust *you*."

"Please," he said intensely. "You *can*. I thought I just proved that."

"Actually, you proved just the opposite," Ganny said, all the time squeezing my hand tight to keep me from speaking. "You just told me you're willing to betray your employer—that you'll accept money under false pretenses just to get what you want. If Martian Electric can't trust you, how can I?"

His face went ashen. He deflated. He looked like someone had suddenly sucked two liters of air out of his lungs. He sagged where he sat.

"What I mean is..." Ganny raised one legendary eyebrow. "Why shouldn't we just stuff you out the airlock and then go eat your ice cream?"

Poor Jimmy. For half an instant, he looked like he wanted to cry. But instead, he gathered himself up, he stuck out his jaw, he put on his game face. "Because," he said. *"You need me."*

"We do? Why?"

"Because. I know what the Martians are planning. You don't."

Ganny scratched her head.

"It better be good."

He cleared his throat, he looked around both ways, he lowered his voice. "Don't eat the ice cream."

"Really?"

"Really." He nodded grimly.

"Those bastards," I said. "Ten gallons of Double Double Chocolate Fudge Swirl. *Those bastards.*"

"Don't worry, honey. They'll pay."

Jimmy said, "I'm very angry at them." After a beat he added, "Because I paid for that ice cream."

"You did?" That was me.

"Uh-huh." He nodded eagerly. "And all the other stuff too. The gas, the water, the seeds, the ice cream. The Martians wouldn't pay for it. They said they'd pay for ticket, but they refused to pay for the cargo. I told them you wouldn't talk to anyone unless there was an advantage in it for you. They said if I wanted to buy my way in, I'd have to do it on my money, not theirs. So...I used the last of my credit, all my dummies. Everything. I spent ten years building it up, lending the same three hundred real dollars back and forth from one company to another, back and forth, back and forth, until they looked like half a million plastic dollars. On paper anyway. And I spent it all on you. Hoping you wouldn't make me walk home."

"Jimmy—" I interrupted. "I know how much that cargo is worth. That's more than a half million dollars. The gas, that's nothing. But the seeds and the protein cultures—"

"I did the math too. You didn't have enough air and water to fill your ship. But you only need enough gas to get to Saturn to pick up some ice. After that, it's not an issue. But if you're going out on the long ride, then you need the seeds and the protein cultures—"

Ganny and I looked at each other. Startled. Ganny nodded an acknowledgment. "Yep. He definitely is not as stupid as he looks."

"But...how did you pay for it?"

He hung his head for a moment, swallowed hard, looked up again. "I had to indenture myself to buy it. I'm contracted for the next seven years."

"You didn't! Jimmy—" I dropped my hands to my lap. "You did that for me?"

"Yeah, I did. I guess I'm what you would call a big stupid hopeless romantic jerk. Because I didn't even know if you felt the same way, I could only do what I thought you would want a boy friend to do for you."

Ganny leaned over and whispered in my ear. "He is definitely a keeper. If you're not going to take him, I will."

"Ganny!"

"I'm just letting you know—"

"Um, excuse me?"

We both turned back to Jimmy.

"There's more," he said. "I do have…a business proposition. I mean, I knew you were building a spaceship. You did a pretty good job of hiding it, but I had one advantage nobody else did. I knew Starling. I know how she thinks. A little bit anyway. I mean, all those conversations have to count for something."

He leaned forward intensely. "Starling, remember how you said a spaceship is just a big can of gas. It only has to hold air and move, the rest is details. So if you've already got a life-support system, all you need is an engine. When they added engines to it, they turned the first International Space Station into an interplanetary craft. They sent it back and forth to Luna, then to Mars and back, even to Jupiter once, and what's left of it is still shuttling cargo to the L4 point. And after the Martians cancelled your order and you announced a hotel in the middle of nowhere that nobody would ever want to come to, it wasn't too hard to figure out what you were really planning. You've got all those drive engines you use for pushing asteroids around. I didn't see them when we came in. The Captain scanned you, of course. You've already got them installed, haven't you? I was afraid I wouldn't get here in time, that you'd launch without me. Without hearing me out."

He reached for a glass of water, but before he could drink, Ganny reached across and took it from him. "Not that one." To the bot, she said, "Klaatu barada nikto." The bot rolled away and another one came back with a fresh pitcher and three new glasses. Jimmy looked from the water to Ganny and back to the water.

"It's all right, go ahead."

He took a careful sip. "Um, okay. There are some people. Not the Martians. *Other* people. They're looking for a ship. A big ship. A fast ship."

"And you told them you had one."

"No." He shook his head. "Of course not."

"You told them you knew someone who had a ship."

"No." He took another drink, bigger this time. "I told them I wanted to get out to the belt."

"That's it?"

"I told them I might know some people who knew how to build ships. Who could build them a ship. A big ship. A fast ship. Away from prying eyes. That got their attention. I told them I was probably one of the few people who could even get in the door. They said they were willing to listen."

"Arrrgh," I said, quietly. Ganny poked me in the rrribs. Harrrd.

Jimmy shook his head. "I don't think so."

"Tell me it's not Klingons."

"It's not Klingons," he said.

"Who?"

"So, you're interested?"

Ganny and I looked at each other. Ganny spoke first. "If they have enough money to send us *twenty* gallons of Double Double Chocolate Fudge Swirl, they might have enough money to rent our attention."

"Invisible Luna," he said.

Ganny snorted. "Invisible Luna doesn't exist anymore."

"Yes, that's what they want you to believe." The joke wasn't funny. He spread his hands. "I mean, that's how invisible they really are."

Ganny rolled her eyes. "Listen to me, sonny boy. Gampy and I were part of Invisible Luna. Seventy years ago. The *real* Invisible Luna."

"Yes, I know. That's why these people will trust you. They don't like the Martians any more than you do."

"Hmpf," said Ganny.

I said, "We have some obligations we want to take care of first."

"I assumed that would be the case." He put the glass of water back down on the tray. "The people I represent—sort of represent—the other entity I want to put you in touch with, they want to see a sample of your work. So that's what I came to ask. Could we arrange a flyby? Or a visit to a neutral port?"

Ganny and I looked at each other again. *We?*

"Um, yeah. That's the other part of my...um, plan. I want to join your crew." He looked embarrassed. "If you'll have me. If you'll buy my indenture."

"Hooo...." I said. A noise, not a word. Totally involuntary. I meant it one way, he probably heard it the other.

Ganny put her hand on my leg—to stop me from making any more noises. "We'll talk it over."

Jimmy nodded nervously. "My ride leaves in six hours. Whether I'm on it or not."

Ganny said, "We'll talk it over *quickly*."

"How much is the indenture?" I asked.

He picked up his folder off the table and passed it across to me. "It's all in here."

"Who owns the indenture?" Ganny asked.

"The Martians," he admitted, embarrassed. "They've already put it up for auction. There are bidders."

Ganny's smile had a cold edge to it. "So if we don't buy it--?"

"—I'm screwed. And you're a lot richer."

Ganny took the folder from me. "Jimmy, the fact that you've made a series of impetuous and foolish decisions, all based on a hopelessly romantic assumption—perhaps even a delusion—does not obligate us in any way to rescue you. This is a business for us. And our lives."

"I know," he gulped apologetically. "But…." He looked at me, hopeful. Then he shrugged and surrendered to his fate.

"All right," said Ganny. "We'll talk it over." Something in her tone of voice. The conversation was closed. She stood up. So did I.

Jimmy realized he was being dismissed, so he stood up too. "May I wait here for your answer?"

Ganny nodded, an "if you wish" kind of nod, then led me spinward to an unused cabin. She opened the folder, studied at the terms of his indenture contract. "Not too stupid," she said. "Y'know…we could purchase this indenture through six levels of dummy companies. One of our Lunar shells could do it. Put a small down payment against a larger payout on the back end. And then…after reselling the indenture to another dummy, it goes bankrupt and defaults, dissolves without assets. It'd be another nice way to screw the Martians. And we end up with an already paid-for hired hand." She pulled a keyboard over, started tapping, losing herself in the process for a moment. "Yeah, we could do it. We've got a couple shells that we've been deliberately taking losses on, just for a possibility like this. And I do like the part about screwing the goddamn Martians. Okay, the mechanics are doable." She typed a moment longer, setting up the channels, then turned to me. "What do *you* want, munchkin?"

"I don't know—"

"Kiddo, you're the one who's going to have to live with him. He's a love-struck puppy. So was Gampy. He chased me till I caught him. So that's the question here. Do you want to catch this one? Or are you throwing him back?"

"He's awfully presumptuous."

"So are you."

"I am?"

"Yes, you are. But I love you anyway." Her voice became softer and more serious at the same time. "Just tell me what you want and I'll make it happen." She rattled the folder. "This indenture is expensive, but he's already paid for it in cargo, so it evens out. Or it would, if we were going to buy it with real dollars. Screwing the Martians is a bonus. But I expect they're expecting it. And if they are, then we're going to have to dodge another pod, real soon. Or something. But—" She put a hand on my shoulder. "—it looks like Jimmy's loyalty is unquestionable, sweetheart. And he's smart, awfully smart. He didn't get out here by accident. He can pull his weight. And we do need crew. So we can make this work. *If you want it.* But you'll have to decide fast. I have a lot of juggling to do here."

I thought about how I would feel if Jimmy got back on the black ship and we whirled it back to Earth or wherever, what it would be like, how I would feel. It wouldn't be like the past fourteen months of me being angry at him and then another few months of being angry at myself. And then even more months of feeling bad because I couldn't make it up to him. This would be worse. This would be knowing I'd maybe had a chance and thrown it away. I'd end up wondering about all the might-have-beens.

So I knew all the reasons I wanted to say yes. I missed talking to him. I missed sharing things with him. I missed wondering what he would look like without any clothes on. Well, no, I could still do that. I'd been doing that for a long time.

But I also knew all of the reasons why this could be a colossal mistake. I didn't really know Jimmy as a *meatspace* person, had never spent any one-to-one time with him, didn't know if we really matched at all. I'd never even held his hand! What if this was a lot more wishful thinking than practicality? What if five weeks from now I realized how much I really hated him, his mannerisms, his quirks, his idiosyncrasies, his bad habits, that funny little hair that stuck out of his left ear, and just wanted to shove him out the nearest airlock? What then? I'd still be stuck with him, wouldn't I?

How was I supposed to make a decision about the rest of my life with no time at all to think about it? My belly hurt. Other parts of me tingled. Not all of it was unpleasant.

"Ganny, I don't know. What should I do?"

"What does your heart tell you?"

"It's not my heart. It's my gut."

"Starling. Darling Starling. You know what's right. You do."

I lowered my eyes. I studied my feet. I shook my head. I didn't know if my heart could tell me anything anymore. I swallowed hard. I caught my breath. This was going to be hard. Very hard. Maybe the hardest thing I ever had to do in my whole life. But it had to be done. *Now.* "Okay," I said. "I'll tell him."

Ganny followed me back to the lounge. Jimmy stood up as we walked in. I crossed directly to him, wrapped myself around him and planted a great big kiss on his face. For a first kiss, it was pretty clumsy. So was the second. But we got it right the third time.

SPIDERWEB

All right, let's talk about the Oort Cloud. It's big. It's not flat. It's round. It's a sphere. It's 7500 trillion kilometers thick and it starts about 7500 trillion kilometers away. The denser, inner part of the Oort is called the Hills Cloud. That's a little closer in. Only 750 million kilometers; but it extends nearly 10 billion klicks out, give or take a cosmic smidge. The Hills Cloud is nearly 100 times denser than the rest of the Oort. So that's where the prospectors go.

You start at Luna, and you boost at 1.3 gee for 2-3 months, flipover, and decelerate for almost as long, leaving enough delta-vee to coast. When you get there, wherever you are, you will be as far from home as any human being has ever gotten. At least until the Long Voyage boosts, if it ever does.

Some people think space is a poetic adventure. Cold. Dark. Silent. Those are the people who have never been in space.

Out here, it is *not* cold, dark and silent.

Inside a ship, inside a suit, it's hot and bright and loud. Especially loud. Every little creak, clank, or clunk, the vibration rattles its way down the hull, across the decks, even into the carbon-fiber bolts that hold the whole damn ship together. There's no place else for the sound to go. Every ventilator fan whirrs, every pump throbs, every valve bumps, every pipe whistles, every moving part makes a sound. Hatches open and close, panels unfold, sensors uncover themselves, cameras swivel. It's a torrent of noises, a cacophony of chirps and buzzes, whooshes and bumps. Space might be silent, but the machineries that keep you alive are loud and incessant. And no, it doesn't matter what kind of ceramics and polymers and fibers and insulation you use for building the ship, there will always be sound. Even safe inside a suit, the noise never ends; your blood throbs in your veins, your heart thumps in your chest and your breath roars in your ears.

Yes, I know there are some people who say they can tell the health of a ship simply by listening to the sound of it. I say they're deluding themselves. There are just too many sounds, too much to hear, assimilate, impossible to know. The point is, it's not silent.

And it's not cold either. Just like the sound, the heat has nowhere to go. A spaceship is an oven. You can shield it, you can rotate it, you can insulate it with reflectors. You can add radiator fins and heat sinks. You can paint the ship with micro-dots and nano-demons. But the heat still builds up. You have to hide behind a wall of shielding. Two walls. One wall in front, facing the direction you're going, and the other facing the sun. It works. Well enough.

The shield in front is called the cow-catcher. Back in the days of railroads, the cow-catcher was an iron apron at the front of the locomotive, designed to knock unwitting cows or deer or moose or buffalo off the tracks. The cow-catcher on a spaceship is there to protect the ship against micro-dust. Figure it out. Constant acceleration means a steadily increasing velocity. Space isn't empty. That's another one. It only looks empty. Actually, it's full of stuff, mostly little stuff, all different size pieces. You can stop looking for dark matter, there isn't any. What there is, is dust. All the leftover flakes of cosmic dandruff. The faster you go, the faster they hit you. One particle per cubic kilometer isn't a problem—until you're traveling through a couple hundred million kilometers or more, like getting to Mars when it's coming around the far side of the sun. Then it's like driving through very fine sandpaper. It adds up. So you put a shield in front. And every so often, you replace the camera mirrors that are peeking out from behind it.

Now about the dark. Space isn't dark. It only looks dark because the human eye doesn't gather enough light to see how full of radiation space really is. All kinds of radiation. A lot of radio, yes, but all up and down the spectrum there are blares and flares and glares of heat and color. Space is really dazzling. We just can't see it.

So, if space isn't dark and it isn't cold and it isn't empty and it isn't silent, what is it?

It's boring.

There's nothing for kilometers in any direction except kilometers. And micro-dust—and not much of that, just enough to be an expensive nuisance. And even at 1.3 gees, 5 giga-klicks is still a month-long ride. Except there aren't many who want to take that ride. Most ships are bot-driven. There's not a lot of need for a human aboard. Take the human out of the ship and you can carry a lot more payload. It's not the weight of the human, it's the weight of all the oxygen and water and food and life support gear and additional fuel to push that weight. Do the math. But sometimes, you need a human onboard anyway. Because there are some decisions bots can't make, and it isn't always practical for a ship to phone home for advice, when that advice won't come back for a year or more. So that's when you load up the meatware and send it out.

Given that the bots drive the ship, crawl around the outside monitoring and repairing, handle most of the chores inside as well, there's not a lot for a human to do. Except inhale and exhale. And answer the mail. There's always the mail. So you're not even alone. So you can't even say that space is lonely. It's hot and loud and bright and busy.

But you can turn off the mail, you can put on the isolation-hearmuffs, and you can run around naked as long as you want. If you don't mind your tits or your balls flopping around, whichever you have at the time, either or neither or both. This trip, neither. Myself, I prefer wearing micro-fiber skivvies, if for no other reason than they catch skinflakes, the little crud that turns into dust and eventually clogs up things like filters and fans. If I need to, I'll wear a bra or a jock while pounding around the centrifuge, an hour a day while I listen to music, but most of the time I prefer to let things float instead of pulling at the musculature.

What I do like about space is that it gives me long uninterrupted hours to work on my book. Every so often, something beeps politely; a double-tone with a half-step up; then I'll look up at the status board to see if everything is still green, it is, and then I'll go back to work constructing the webs of connections and matrices, all the specific velocities and dynamic interrelationships, and how they carve their separate channels into the non-linear environment, and which collisions will produce transformations and which will result in emotional implosions. It isn't easy being a writer. Most people think you just sit and type. That's only what it looks like. The real job is sitting and thinking, which is something most people don't like to do. That's why they buy books—so they don't have to be alone inside their own heads.

Except this time, the beep was a triple-tone, with a half-step down and a half-step up. A question mark. Boss, you wanna take a look at this?

The status screen showed a yellow question mark.

The Baked Bean—that's my ship—was supposed to spiral outward for a long while, then spiral back inward for an equally long while. I didn't know what I was looking for, but I'd know when I found it. And it looked like I'd just found it. According to the IRMA, we were experiencing a slight—but measurable—course and velocity deviation. A tenth of a tenth of a tenth of a tenth. Not small enough to be an artifact of the hash at the bottom. When we dithered the noise and weighted the curves and sharpened the data-points and correlated and corrected the neural assessments, it was still there.

It wasn't unexpected. This was what I'd come looking for. Low-level delta-perturbation. We had more theories than answers. Some of the questions dated all the way back to the first Voyager missions. Those two spacecraft experienced just enough slowdown to have folks at Mission Control scratching their heads about Newton's second law for a long time. But the V'gers weren't the only ships to hit the solar shelf. After a century or two, it was a predictable phenomenon. One theory, easily discounted, was that the buildup of dust on the surface of the probe added just enough mass to affect the efficiency of the engines; but any grade-schooler with a calculator could easily demonstrate that the amount of dust collected, even on a thirty year voyage, would be statistically insignificant.

Nevertheless, according to the instruments, *The Baked Bean* was no longer moving as fast as she had been a week ago. The drives were off and the ship had been coasting for ten days. I had lasers pointed at two dozen different retro-reflector sites: positioning satellites stationed all over the system, and another thirty satellites we had dropped on the way out. Based on the time-corrected, correlated bounce-back, I could locate this ship within 15 meters, anywhere out to a light year. According to IRMA, *The Baked Bean* was a few kilometers short of a happy meal—26.4 kilometers, to be exact, plus or minus 7.5 meters.

Either the *Bean* had gained mass or space was a lot thicker here.

Interesting problem.

The first thing to do was triple-check all the readings, then re-calibrate all the instruments and triple-check the readings again. 48 hours and three sleep shifts later, the numbers came up the same. Almost the same. We were now 27.2 klicks short of where the software said we should be.

Hmm. Hardware glitch? Highly unlikely. The IRMA unit had nine separate cores, three each of three different architectures. A glitch on one architecture would not be repeated on the other two. Software error? Equally unlikely. IRMA ran multiple instances of seven different astrogation programs. 7 different programming teams would not all make the same coding error. The astrogation systems were triple-linked with Mission Control Ganymede. They were parallel processing everything. 15 months from now, I would receive their confirmation that all systems were green and confidence remained high.

So, it wasn't the equipment.

Next up, test the mass of the ship.

There were several ways to do this. The easiest was to bang it with a hammer and measure the vibrations. Of course, you needed a very special hammer, and a very good ear, but the *Bean* had both of those. Additional tests could be performed by applying an incredibly precise thrust in a specific direction and measuring the shift in velocity. We could also shut down the centrifuge and rotate the ship on her gyros and measure how long that took. There were other tests as well, some as esoteric as comparing the ship's stress points by comparing her current holographic interference patterns with the patterns recorded on previous tests. All these separate measurements had been performed routinely before launch, and at least half-a dozen times during the journey, including three times during flipover. Nine days later, the ship's mass had been sliced and diced 37 different ways. Allowing for the expenditure of fuel, allowing for the expected accretion of a half-gram of micro-dust, *The Baked Bean* massed essentially the same as it had ninety minutes prior to first boost.

So, if the ship hadn't gained mass, then either space had gotten thicker, or time ran slower out here. Or something else we hadn't imagined, and we just weren't thinking far enough outside the box. This is why a human being had to make the journey.

I don't know how long I sat there, staring out the window and picking my nose. I suppose I could look it up on the monitors. But it was a long time. First, I had to assume that the answer was knowable, that there was a physically measurable and testable phenomenon at work here. Starting from that assumption, what tests could I run?

There aren't a lot of ways to measure the speed of time without also measuring the speed of light. And the nasty thing about the speed of light is that it always measures the same, no matter where you are, or how fast you're going. You can only measure your location and your speed and your time-rate by comparing it with the location and speed and vector of another object. Out here, those measurements would take a long while. But in the meantime, I had to assume that the laws of physics did not metamorphose with distance from Sol. Why? Because the low-level perturbation was not a constant. 293 robot-vehicles had left the Sol system in the past century. 17 of them had ceased functioning by the time they crossed Neptune's orbit. 187 of them had experienced perturbation, most of them along the forward edge of Sol's movement in the galactic spin-cycle. Therefore, the phenomenon could be localized.

Gravity. Maybe we had miscalculated the gravitational pull of local objects. Maybe we had miscalculated the combined gravitational weight of multiple objects. Maybe the solar shelf was a gravitational ripple from Sol. But no. The gravitometers hadn't shown anything unexpected for 5 giga-klicks, and they weren't showing anything weird now. It wasn't that.

Solar winds? Maybe this far out, the effect of the solar wind dropped off precipitously? Nope. Nothing. No evidence of that. The solar winds were behaving exactly as they had behaved ever since we started measuring solar winds.

Solar wind. Wind. There was a thought. What if we'd run through a cosmic dust storm? Something with a lot of micro-particles—a zillion little high-speed collisions. Not a lot of mass, but a significant exchange of velocity. What if the low-level perturbation phenomenon was just a dense, fast-moving, cloud of micro-particles that had impacted on the cow-catcher and transferred some of their momentum to the *Bean*?

But the sensors would have detected that, wouldn't they? Or would they?

I ran it through IRMA. Given the mass and velocity of the *Bean*, how much mass traveling at what velocity, would have to strike us head on to produce the drag we were experiencing?

The answer was simple. Enough to vaporize the *Bean*. Force equals mass times acceleration. No matter how you juggled the mass and momentum, the amount of force necessary to slow the *Bean* was more than enough to shred the cow-catcher and the ship. You could do it slowly or instantly, the result was the same.

What if—? No, that didn't make sense either. If we had overtaken a patch of dust heading in the same general direction, it wouldn't have slowed us—not this much.

Hm. What about the external bots? And all the other moving parts outside? The rotating panels? The remote arms? The sensors and antennae? Were they still fully operational? Several hours of tests later—yes, they were all still optimal. Maybe a smidge off, maybe not. If there were any measurable differences, they were so small as to be lost in the hash.

Everything was working just the way it was supposed to. I was almost disappointed.

What else? What was I missing?

Back in school, my graduate thesis required several thousand hours of coding. I intended to prove that software ecologies would inevitably stop evolving when they hit their Skotak radius, the limits of the hardware. The underlying algorithms would generate new ecological entities at random, then evolve them until their inevitable collapse. While long-term stability was achievable, permanent stability was impossible in an evolutionary environment. The stats on the project were impressive. Over thirty thousand mutable objects, agents, and bots, four hundred billion generations of parallel evolution per run. Sixteen hundred hours of high-impact debugging and deconstruction. Three weeks before the submission deadline, I thought I was done. Except—there was something gnawing at the woodwork of my brain. Something didn't feel *right*. I spent the better part of a week, studying columns of numbers until I found the one column that didn't balance. A point and a half of something—one of the minor elements of the ecology—was simply evaporating. It wasn't a rounding error, that was a beginner's mistake. It was something else.

Logically, I knew that no one would ever notice this discrepancy— but I would know it was there. I spent most of a week tracing the hundred different processes that accessed element AXO-1011. I could have taken the element out of the ecology, but it had become an obsession. I was going to be right about this. Eventually, I did find the source of the discrepancy—I'd made an assumption about a relationship instead of testing it. That tiny uncorrected assertion was why the system was unstable and always collapsed. When I corrected it—I had to change the conclusion of my thesis. Software *can* evolve to a state of permanent stability, given a fixed evolutionary range.

Of course, I had to report this in my oral examination. Professor Whitlaw gave me the fabled Whitlaw frown and asked, "So what did you learn?"

"I learned that ... if God is in the details, so is the devil."

Whitlaw laughed. "Close enough."

Fifteen years and 5 giga-klicks later, I was looking for the devil again. The difference of 33.7 kilometers was statistically insignificant. But where were those kilometers going? And why? What fundamental conclusions about the nature of space-time were being challenged here? I wasn't thinking about awards or prizes or scientific immortality, I just wanted to solve the damn mystery.

I hauled down the hardcopy of the Mission Book and began paging through it idly. There were over three hundred pages of theories and ideas and suggestions for experiments. I wasn't sure what I was looking for, but maybe something would leap off the page at me.

But the only thing that leapt off the page was a little bit of dust. Several of the pages came up together, they had a cobweb on the edge— that annoyed me. I hate dirt. That's one of the reasons I go to space. I wondered if the authoring-spider had done its work before the book was loaded or if it had done its work enroute and starved to death for the lack of flies. Perhaps its curled-up corpse was nestled behind a panel somewhere, impossible to find.

As hard as human beings had worked to avoid bringing non-human volunteers into space, more than a few had found ship-life to their liking. Tales of star-faring mice, ants, flies, gnats, cockroaches, cats, snakes, and snails were not uncommon. Assorted spore and mold and fungal passengers had also found their way aboard spaceships. Some had escaped from their transport capsules; others had simply demonstrated that old truism that *life will find a way.*

Hm.

What if we were dealing with some kind of ... no, not life, but something that had some of the characteristics of life? Invisible glass spiders. Hundreds and thousands of tiny little mites, not alive, but crawling all over the outside of the ship as if they were? It was as likely as any other crackpot idea. Spinning webs to catch interstellar butterflies—

No, wait. There was something in the book. I flipped through the pages, almost frantically, until I found it again. Suggested by some late-night comedian. He thought he was being funny. Cosmic spiderwebs. The universe is so old, it should have cobwebs hanging from the rafters. Where are the cobwebs? Mission Control had thoughtfully tucked that into the book along with all the other crackpot ideas.

But ... what the hell? It almost made sense. What if *The Baked Bean* had flown through some kind of a ... something? And it was just enough to slow the ship down. Just a smidge.

Right. Giant space-spiders. When they do that episode, you know they've jumped the snark.

But ... I leaned back in my couch and thought about it anyway.

What if there were some kind of—I dunno—some kind of fuzzy stuff that floated through interstellar space in vast immeasurable clouds? It would have to be very light. It would have to be—

I sat up straight.

Aerogel.

The lightest material ever made. Light and strong. There were fifty or sixty different formulations, each one lighter and stronger than the last. Half a kilo would fill a football stadium. Something like that.

Some kind of nano-stuff, maybe. Interstellar cotton candy. You could move around inside it and never know you were caught. But if you moved through enough of it, and if you were caught in a large enough net—say, a thousand or a hundred thousand klicks across—it would have enough mass to function as a drag chute.

Hm.

It would have to be self-assembling.

Very slow growth.

But that's okay, there's nothing between the stars but time and dust. If it's possible, it's inevitable.

Hm.

Worth thinking about for a minute or two.

Okay, assume the possibility. Why hasn't anyone discovered this stuff yet?

Because no one has come out far enough? Only some bot-controlled probes.

Maybe the webs were strictly an interstellar phenomenon. Maybe they couldn't assemble themselves within a star system. Maybe too much light and heat worked against the process. Maybe the webs were so light the solar wind just pushed them out into the darkness. Maybe all the various rocks and meteors and asteroids and bits of dust that churned around the solar disk ripped the webs to pieces as fast as they formed.

But out in the Oort Cloud, in the Hills Cloud, there would be enough material for a web to assemble itself, but not so much as to shred it. Hmm. Maybe the deepest darkest spaces between the stars were filled with clouds of cosmic aerogel?

What a strange silly idea.

Too silly.

Much too silly.

Besides, how would you test it?

How do you grab a handful of nothing? Almost nothing.

I had a thought. I had IRMA list all 293 vehicles that had left the solar system and their relative speeds. 89 spacecraft had not experienced any detectable slowdown. Of those 89, 77 were long-life probes, *accelerating* toward distant stars. Gotcha. They were going too fast. They ripped right through, like a bullet through custard. But the others were slower-moving planetary probes, like the V'gers, which had finally drifted far enough out—or probes that were aimed specifically at the Oort and the Hills. Going slow enough to get caught. Aha. Okay. Maybe. There's a piece of useful evidence.

But unless I could grab some of the stuff and bring it back, it was all just theory. The Cosmic Cobwebs—right. Do that episode instead of the space spiders and you're still jumping the snark.

If this stuff was as light and as far-flung as I suspected, it was probably as undetectable as the rest of the space dust that hammered at the cow-catcher. We would only know if it had been there by the effects it left behind—did it score or scratch the shield? But there weren't any instruments designed for detecting threads so light they couldn't be measured. And if they were impossible to detect, then it would even more impossible to gather up a shiftload. I'd need a net as big as … as big as the webs I was trying to catch. And probably twice as strong.

My brain hurt. I checked the monitors one more time, then climbed down into the centrifuge for a sleep shift—

—came awake laughing. I'd been dreaming of fly fishing on the river. And then I'd dreamt about a taffy-pulling machine. And then I knew how to catch a starweb.

It took a couple weeks for the bots to cobble it together, a couple of giant paddlewheels, one on each side of the *Bean*—slowly, slowly rotating, winding up invisible threads like a fisherman pulling in his nets.

The paddlewheels dwarfed the ship. They were each third of a klick in diameter, and their paddles extended almost half a click out. They were spidery Tinker Toy constructions of carbon-fiber beams so thin, they were almost invisible; but they didn't need to be heavy, they only needed to be sturdy—and they were plenty of that. There were only six paddles to a wheel. Each carbon-fiber rod had a couple dozen meter-long teeth spaced out along its length to help snag any threads we encountered. I didn't know how big a starweb might be or how far it might extend. Its total mass might be so great that instead of the *Bean* reeling in a slice, we'd be reeling the *Bean* into the thickest part of it. We could end up getting caught in a mass so huge, there was no possible escape. But on the bright side, that would be evidence too.

It was all guesswork. There was no way to know how big a web could be. I didn't know how much of this one I'd ripped through, and how much of it I'd actually snagged. Assuming the *Bean* had simply snagged without ripping, then we were dragging enough mass to cost us a measurable percentage of delta-vee. Not quite a flying mountain, but considering our velocity when we hit the Hills Cloud, something at least as large as the *Bean*, and probably quite a bit larger. So the paddlewheels and their axes had to be sturdy enough to carry that weight and not break off.

But if we'd ripped a hole and were caught by a smaller piece of a much greater whole—something we'd find out the hard way—then the stress on the paddles would start rising, and keep rising until they snapped off.

Of course, if the paddles did break off, that would prove the existence of the starwebs. Most embarrassingly.

On the other hand, if they churned for a year and there was still nothing caught up and wound up on them, that would prove equally embarrassing.

But if I was right ... well, this might even solve the dark matter mystery. Where's all the missing matter in the universe? It's right here, where it's always been, floating between the stars. Occam's Chainsaw. Sometimes the simplest answer is right in front of you.

But as long as there was a measurable drag on the ship's velocity, the *Bean* was in the right neighborhood, so it was just a matter of time and patience. I watched the big wheels turning until I got bored, then

I watched a while longer, then I went to bed. I woke up, checked all the monitors, watched the big wheels turning for a while, checked the monitors again, saw that everything was optimal, yawned, ate something forgettable, read my mail, checked the big wheels, checked the monitors, went to the toilet, and then did it all again.

IRMA predicted that *if* the webs existed, it could take several months to reel in enough material to have anything visible to the naked eye. It depended on the tensile strength of the threads. Assuming they were strong enough to catch a spaceship, they were probably strong enough to wind around the paddles without breaking. Another assumption, but the only one that made sense. The difference in relative velocity—the *Bean* vs. the starweb—could be thousands, perhaps tens of thousands, klicks per hour. If we were simply ripping through and shredding the webs, then it was the same problem as with micro-particles. The amount of mass times acceleration needed to slow down *The Baked Bean* would also be enough to shred the cow-catcher. It didn't matter how you weighted the factors—the product was still deadly. No, we had to be catching something and dragging something. Something strong enough to wind. I'd know for sure in a month or six. I checked the monitors again, because I like looking at green lights, then printed up a sandwich.

The paddlewheels were a third of a klick in diameter. That meant, every three turns, they would roll up a kilometer of thread—if they were rolling up anything at all. The paddlewheels turned once every five minutes. If we caught thread, they'd wind up four kilometers of it per hour, 96 per day, 672 klicks per week, over 2700 kilometers of thread in a month. Assume a kilometer-long thread might weigh—oh, I dunno, let's say—a gram; then in 30 days, the *Bean* should have at least 3 kilos of cosmic starweb wound around its paddles. Depending on how many threads the paddles caught, how long they were, and how much they actually massed per klick.

I didn't have to wait even that long for evidence. After 21 days, the first glints of something were visible on the paddlewheels—like a hint of plastic-wrap stretched between the rods. I couldn't see it directly, but the IRMA-enhanced videos showed multiple instances of consecutive frames of what looked like *lines* stretching from one paddle-rod to the next. There was no maybe about it. I lit the wheels all up and down the entire spectrum, trying to catch a reading. There wasn't enough mass yet to get the reflected signal up above the hash, but every turn of the paddlewheel gave us more.

I began writing up my report.

Three months later, I had nearly 20 kilos of material; either it was heavier than I thought, or I'd gathered more than I'd expected. This stuff was going to be a bitch to analyze. But it was time to bring *The Baked Bean* home. That meant collapsing the paddles and storing the web-stuff in something. I couldn't risk having it be shredded by micro-dust on the way home, and I wasn't sure how sensitive it would be to the solar winds, let alone the heat and light of Sol. I suspected the web-threads weren't just made of some pretty tough stuff, but that they were also assembled in some ingenious ways. Just the same, I'd hate to come home with an empty framework and a terrific story about the fishing line that got away.

I was pretty sure I'd found the dark matter. Or at least a big chunk of it. That alone would guarantee me a shot at the Benford Prize. But I wasn't done yet. First I had to find out how the threads assembled themselves. I had one of the external bots crawl out onto one of the paddles and look at the threads close up. Yes, they were self-assembling nano-tubes. That part was obvious. The mechanics of it were not so obvious, but if it's possible, it's inevitable somewhere. There were molecular hooks, places on the strand where a molecule was desperate for an electron. Any stray atom—and there were plenty of those—would find itself caught. But now, it would be shy an electron or at least sharing one, so it would become the hook for the next stray bit to attach. And so on. That old truism—*life will find a way*—even when it's not life, it still finds a way.

But that wasn't the big surprise. I didn't find that one until I'd already crossed the orbit of Neptune. By then, I had forty kilos of web-stuff in various containers—you could cut it with a laser—but one of the containers had *something else* in it, something that had gotten caught in the web. Not much of something, but enough. A definite piece of ... well, not quite life, but something that could become life, given an opportunity to find the first rung of the evolutionary ladder.

See, here's the thing. Some folks talk about the possibility of life arriving on Earth from outer space. Okay, not impossible. But that fiery plunge through the atmosphere—? Most protein isn't going to survive. If not the journey down, then certainly the abrupt stop at the bottom.

But what would happen if there were a nice little seed of life caught in a cosmic spiderweb. After a couple of million years, a planet wanders through that web, ripping it apart, but also wrapping large chunks of it around itself. The threads drift in the upper atmosphere for years until maybe they get caught in a storm system and washed down to the ground, where they eventually dissolve or whatever. But if some of those threads are carrying proto-life, that stuff gets a nice safe ride down to the surface without a fiery bump at the bottom.

I don't know if this little piece of stuff I found was an ancestor, but it might well be a distant cousin. Very distant, of course.

But that still wasn't the big surprise.

I suspected it before I'd crossed the orbit of Neptune. I was sure of it by the time I crossed Saturn's orbit. *The Baked Bean* was traveling a lot slower than it should have. As if it was dragging a small mountain behind it. I'd be 18 months late for dinner. But I was bringing home one hell of a big surprise.

I'd have to avoid Earth orbit though. I'd hate to think what would happen if all 100 million klicks of this stuff wrapped itself around a single planet. Global cooling? Another great extinction? I don't want to find out the hard way.

The good news is that the ship is a lot quieter now. The stuff is great for dissipating vibrations. 40 thousand cubic kilometers of silencing material will do that.

ABOUT THE AUTHOR

David Gerrold is the author of more than fifty books and hundreds of short stories, essays, articles, and columns.

He has written scripts for over a dozen hit television series, including *Star Trek, Twilight Zone, Star Trek Animated, Sliders, Babylon 5, Land Of The Lost,* and *Tales From The Dark Side*. His most famous script is "The Trouble With Tribbles" episode of the original *Star Trek* series.

His most popular novels are *When HARLIE Was One, The Man Who Folded Himself, The Voyage Of The Star Wolf, Jumping Off The Planet,* and *The War Against The Chtorr* series.

In 1995, David Gerrold won the Hugo, Nebula, and Locus awards for *The Martian Child,* the autobiographical tale of his son's adoption. That story was also the basis for the 2007 movie *Martian Child,* starring John Cusack and Amanda Peet.

FOR MORE BOOKS AND STORIES BY DAVID GERROLD, PLEASE VISIT

HTTP://WWW.GERROLD.COM.

www.ingramcontent.com/pod-product-compliance
Lightning Source LLC
Chambersburg PA
CBHW051129030726
47504CB00004B/775